the dissection and reassembly of COHEN HOARD

Other Books in the Splinterverse

Splinter's Edge by Boydell Bown
Mere Mortal by A.J. Stevens

the dissection and reassembly of COHEN HOARD

BY

ELESA HAGBERG

SPLINTER PRESS

The Dissection and Reassembly of Cohen Hoard

A Splinterverse Book
by Elesa Hagberg

Typesetting by Faralee Pozo

Cover art by Midjourney

Cover design by Elesa Hagberg

Published by:

Splinter Press,
Spanish Fork, Utah

splinterpress.com

ISBN: 978-1-960108-00-5

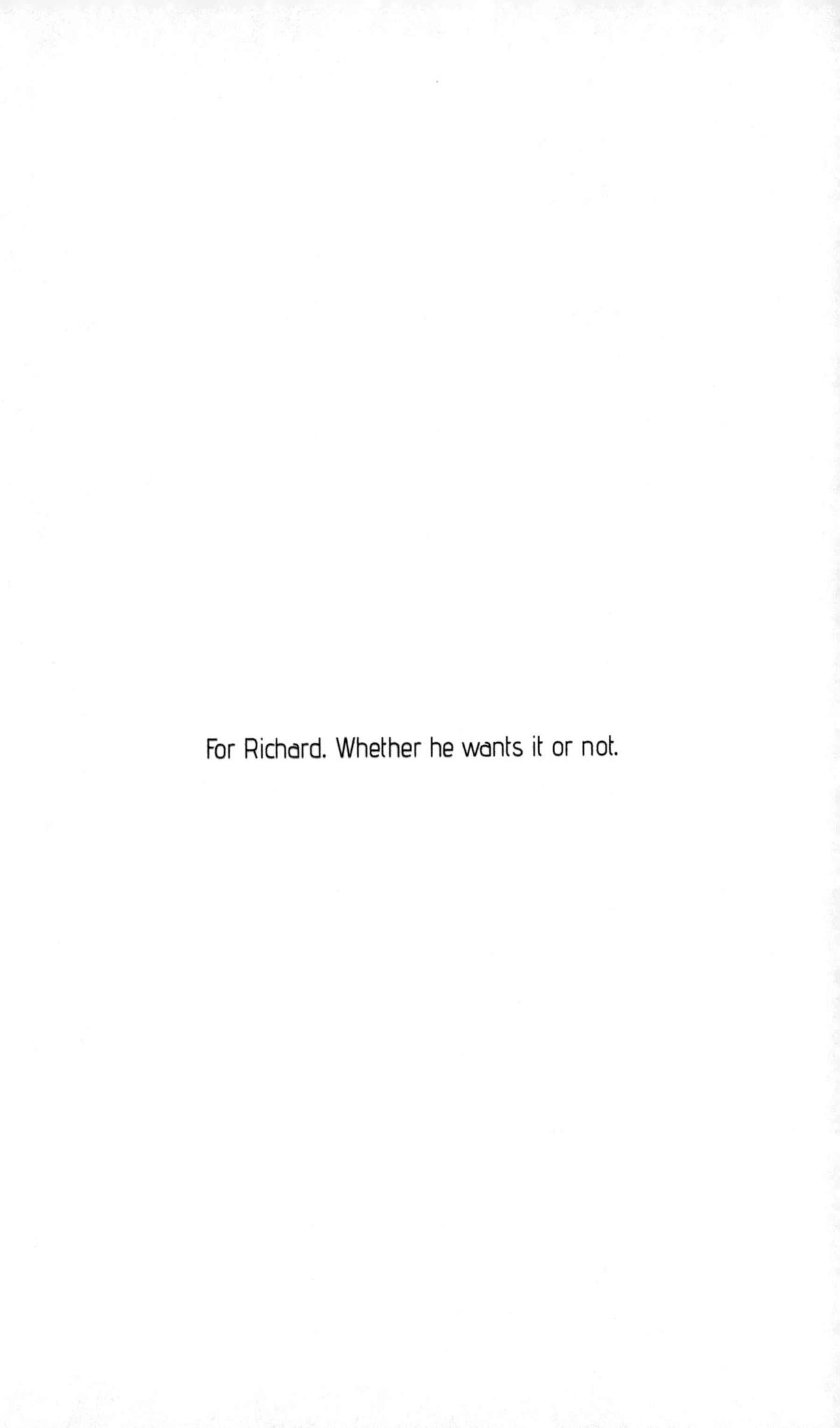

For Richard. Whether he wants it or not.

1

The hammering on my door startled me so much I dripped raspberry jam all over the table. It splatted, red and globby, like my kitchen table was the scene of a very small murder. I grumbled, running my hands through my hair and grabbing my robe off the back of the couch since I was still in boxers, and shuffled toward the door. It was too early for guests, but a tiny part of me wondered if it was Jocelyn.

She'd smiled when I said hello to her yesterday, so it wasn't completely impossible.

I opened the door as the retreating form of the SMax rider jogged down the steps. A flat, SwiftMax Extreme cardboard envelope lay on the doormat, big black "Urgent" stamp in the corner. I glanced toward Jocelyn's door, then bent over to pick it up, noticing as I did so that the name on the address label was wrong.

I rushed over to the stairwell. "Hey!" I called, though there was no sign of the SMax rider. "This isn't for me! My name is Cohen! This is addressed to a Calla!" I checked the shipping label again. Calla *Human*? What kind of a name was that? But the address was definitely mine.

Boy, somebody really screwed up.

A door opened behind me, and I turned as Jocelyn peeked out, her red hair mussed in a bright halo around her head, makeup blurry around her blue eyes. She held a giant cup in one hand, phone pressed to her ear with the other, eyebrows raised in question.

"Oh, hey Jocelyn." I tightened my robe and ran my hand over my hair a few times, knowing it was sticking up all over the place. "Sorry about the noise. Just got delivered something by mistake. Do you know a . . ." I looked down at the cardboard envelope in my hand to reread the name. "Calla Human?"

She frowned in confusion, then looked away nodding. "I know," she said into her phone. "I said the same thing so many times, but she never listens to me." She noticed me still standing there and shook her head, waved her fingers at me, and shut the door.

I stepped back into my own apartment, pushing the door closed behind me, and dropped the envelope on the table just before remembering the jam splatter. I grabbed a rag and wiped the package off the best I could, but there was a definite pink splotch in one corner.

I really didn't have time for any of this. I'd been up till one last night working on my code for the DarkWave Demo, and I still couldn't figure out what the problem was. It was driving me nuts. And now I was going to have to deal with correcting some schmoe's shipping error. Well, it would have to wait. I had to get to work.

When I left a half hour later, I took my usual path through the park to get to work. The sun shone down like it owned the sky, but water from last night's storm still dripped from the trees that arched above the sidewalk. As usual, I was the only person carrying an umbrella. I shook my head wryly. Birds chirped at me from nests attached to the underside of the broad tree leaves, ready to face the world again now that the rain had stopped for the day. A bright red bill poked out of a nest ahead of me, then the bird jumped out and set to work tidying its home, reweaving the twigs and branches that the storm had pulled apart. Saluting him, I stepped around a puddle on the path in front of me. Several joggers ran toward me, their wet running gear splashed with water, and I scooted over, my brief-case with the inconvenient envelope held out to the side.

I felt the whoosh of air before I heard it and looked back as a hydrocyclist rode straight toward me like she was in a race. Before I had time to react, she swerved past, wheels slicing through the puddle in the path without even slowing down. Water splashed across my pants, destroying the crease I had ironed in them and cascading onto my shoes.

"Thanks a lot!" I called after her as she turned and headed toward a river the rain had carved into the landscape. Without stopping, she jumped off the bike and ran straight through the thigh-high water, holding her bike over her head. *Hydrocyclists.* Sure, they could go some places cars couldn't, but they were just so annoying. I hurried toward the GridLox building, trying to ignore the squishy, sucking sound of my shoes on the sidewalk.

I had only just gotten settled at my desk when Mr. Steenrod came by.

"There he is," he said, patting my cubicle wall. "How's the weather out there, Mr. Hoard?"

"Dry and getting dryer, Mr. Steenrod!" I said with a smile. It was a silly question. Ever since they broke the weather twenty years ago, that question had been unnecessary. Daytime? Here in Portland it was sunny and warm. Nighttime? Rainy. Well, no, not just rainy. More like *torrential.* Like the earth was a marble sprayed off with a hose, rinsing away anything that wasn't holding on tight enough. People still asked about the weather though, an old habit that never seemed to rinse away.

"How's the demo coming?" Steenrod asked. "Got it finished yet?"

"Still working out that bug. But don't worry. It'll be ready for Friday. I promise."

It *had* to be. We were running out of time. Automated Safety features (affectionately called Auto Save) had revolutionized driving for a large part of the population, but there was still plenty of room for improvement. While we were still a few years away from truly driverless cars, the advanced collision avoidance technology of Auto Save had cut traffic accidents in half. DarkWave's purpose was to fill in the gaps by connecting all the vehicles, traffic lights, and other smart traffic signals into a sort of collective intelligence. DarkWave's AI functioned as the central brain, coordinating all the moving parts so that traffic ran fluidly, more safely, more coherently.

Testing for the DarkWave product had gone as planned. My job was simple: create a demo to show what the AI could do, something that would wow the investors and excite the dealers. It should have been so easy. But there was a bug in the demo code that kept rearing its head when I least expected it. Every so often, for no apparent reason, the whole thing would crash and reset the system. It made no sense, and it was driving me crazy. But I'd figure it out. I always did.

"You sure it'll be ready?" Steenrod brushed the cubicle wall fabric. "If we need to postpone again, we can, and I'd rather know it now than at the last possible second."

I held in a sigh. It was too late to postpone. It was Monday.

The launch was *this* Friday. But Mr. Steenrod had been tiptoeing around the whole thing for months. Besides the fact that DarkWave was a huge, powerful, lifesaving tool, it was also GridLox's first new product since Steenrod's wife passed away after a short battle with cancer two years ago. She'd been the publicity manager, and not only had *he* fallen apart when she died, but GridLox nearly had as well. DarkWave was a crucial step in keeping the company afloat, and we all knew it. My guess was that Steenrod had been dragging his feet because he just didn't want to move forward without her.

"No, no. It'll be fine," I insisted. "Even if I have to scrap the whole demo and start over, I can. We'll be ready." There wasn't time to start over, but it didn't matter because I was going to figure this out—before lunchtime today, if all went as planned—and then we could go on with our lives.

Steenrod smiled and shook his head doubtfully, then he took me by the shoulder and stared deeply into my eyes. Like he was looking for something. I gulped and tried to maintain eye contact, but the awkwardness made my eyes sting, and I started blinking like he was spitting in my eye, not staring into it. He finally let go and gave my shoulder a pat, then wandered off to pour his insecurities into someone else's cubicle.

I exhaled and dropped into my chair. Mr. Steenrod was a great boss. Definitely worth the idiosyncrasies. But they were multiplying, and I was getting worse at this new morning eye contact ritual, not better.

The map of the traffic lights downtown hung from my cubicle wall next to an actual traffic light I used for testing. My desk was tidy except for the stack of sticky notes, which Steve had obviously ransacked again. I took a deep breath, content in the predictability of my life, and opened my briefcase.

The SMax envelope lay on top, almost completely eclipsing all of the other essential items I carried with me everywhere I went. I exhaled and grabbed a pen, scribbling "not at this address" across the label.

Guilt poked at me. The contents must be important for someone to Extreme ship, and this was surely going to cause a delay, but I didn't have time to do more. I wove my way through the cubicles of the GridLox building, then slid the envelope into the SMax dropbox in the receptionist's office. They'd recently updated all of their dropboxes to the fancy model with the sensor, so that as soon as someone dropped in a package, a notification went out. The nearest rider should be there to pick it up in the next twenty minutes. It would have to do.

Sheila looked up, noticing me.

"Good morning, Cohen." Her smile flickered on and off, like she couldn't decide which expression to choose. She tucked her hair behind her ear. "Um . . . how was your weekend?"

"Same old, same old," I said without stopping. "Lots to do—have a great day." I buzzed past her desk on my way out, then rushed back to my cubicle. If I was going to find that bug, I had no time for chit chat. It was time for a stakeout.

I grabbed a big bag of pretzels and a large bottle of water from my mini fridge and parked myself in front of my monitor. Then I turned on the demo and just let it run. And I watched it. And waited. And watched some more. I was afraid if I looked away, I would miss it. So far, I hadn't been able to replicate the set of circumstances that shut everything down. It would run perfectly for hours, or even days, and then crash out of the blue.

But this time I would not miss it. I had diagnostics running in the background and a bag of pretzels in my hand: I was ready for whatever this code could throw at me.

I was still staring at the screen at six o'clock when most of my coworkers had gone home. My eyes burned and my back ached. I would pull an all-nighter if that's what it took, but first I needed a bathroom break, and there wasn't anyone left to sit watch in my place.

I pointed at all my monitors in the most commanding way I knew how. "Don't. Do. Anything." I tiptoed away, looking back at the screens every millisecond or so, but the demo kept plugging along, running just as it should. I rounded the corner toward Steve's cubicle and heard the whirring of a computer fan kick on behind me.

"No, no, no, no!" I darted back to my desk to find the demo display window frozen, completely unresponsive, the terminal window reading: *LookupError: Vehicle with id XRF000435 does not exist.*

"Ah HA! I caught you! You really *were* waiting until I wasn't looking, weren't you?"

I scanned the rest of the diagnostics for anything that stuck out, but nothing did. Still, now I had a lead, which meant I could go home and work from there. I saved everything and then sent it to print so I could review it at home even if the internet went out during the torrent tonight. Steve appeared while I waited for my reports to inch their way out of the printer and rolled his eyes. Everyone always made fun of me, but they simply didn't understand how helpful reviewing hard copies could be.

Half an hour later my footsteps echoed in the stairwell as I climbed toward my apartment on the fourth floor. I whistled tunelessly, listening to the sound bounce around the concrete and metal enclosure. I'd picked a flower on my way home and now I laid it on Jocelyn's doormat. As I did so, I noticed my own, and a shipping envelope lying on top of it. I marched over and as I neared, I noticed the pink splotch in the corner and my own scribbled note.

The envelope for Calla Human was back.

2

Had SMax even looked at it before they'd sent it back to me? The address was mine, and sure, Cohen Hoard and Calla Human started with the same letters, but that was no excuse for Ms. Human to have her packages delivered to my door. There were no previous tenants in my apartment by that name that I knew of. It made no sense.

The envelope was shipped from Muster Inc., but I'd never heard of it. Too annoyed to even go inside my apartment, I looked the business name up on my phone.

Their slogan flashed across the screen: "Looking for Something? Look No Further!"

What kind of crap slogan was that? It didn't tell me a single thing. Yes, I was looking for something: their contact number. But there wasn't one.

I grunted in frustration. Companies that didn't list their contact number drove me crazy. What if someone needed to talk to them immediately?

I squeezed the envelope a bit, the thin cardboard giving under my fingers. The envelope was mostly flat, except for a small bulge in the middle, square and hard. Dental floss maybe? Who would Extreme ship a box of dental floss?

I walked over and knocked on Jocelyn's door. A few loud heartbeats later, it opened, and Jocelyn stood in the door gap wearing tight cutoff shorts and a low-cut tank top with the words "Heart Attack" printed across the chest. My heart thudded painfully inside of me, like it was taking the words as a command. She seemed confused to see me standing there. But she always seemed confused to see me standing at her door, like it was strange for neighbors to stop and check in with each other from time to time.

"Oh, hi. Do you need something?" she asked, pulling on a pair of running shoes, shimmery earrings dangling from each ear. "I'm just heading to work."

Heart Attack was a sports bar downtown that specialized in beef hearts and hot employees. I'd been there a few times, but it was too loud and the sauce they put on the hearts was way too spicy.

"Sorry, I'm just trying to find the person this envelope is addressed to. They keep sending it to me by mistake." I held it up as evidence, proof that I wasn't inventing a reason to knock on her door.

"What's the address?" she asked, leaning toward me. She smelled amazing, her flowery perfume so overwhelming it made me a little dizzy.

"Well, it's *my* address, but the name is wrong. Do you know a Calla?"

"As in calla lily?"

"Yeah, but it's to Calla *Human*."

She took a step toward me to get a closer look at the enve-lope, then stepped back, the remains of the smunched flower lying on the doormat at her feet. She lowered her eyebrows at me, frowning. "Is that from you?"

"Um, well." I coughed, trying to dislodge whatever had wedged itself in my throat. "I . . ."

"Listen," Jocelyn cut me off. "I've never heard of that Human person. But I gotta go. If I don't leave now I'll be late again, and my boss will kill me. Good luck, okay?"

The door banged shut in front of me, leaving me standing with a ruined flower at my feet and a mystery envelope in my hand. The door on the opposite side of Jocelyn's opened and Mr. Suggs stuck his head out.

"You say you got a shipment there that ain't yours? Might belong to me. I been waiting for a delivery all day, but nobody come. I got better things to do, but do you think they care?"

Mr. Suggs had nothing else going on and he knew I knew it. He was nearly eighty years old, short, and round, with ears like the wings of an airplane. They must've given him superhuman hearing, because he always seemed to know what was going on out in the hallway.

"Let me see it, kid. It's probably mine." Mr. Suggs beckoned to me like there was a line of people rushing up the stairs to claim the envelope right out of my hands.

I headed toward him with a sigh. "Sorry, Mr. Suggs. Unless your name is Calla Human, this is definitely not for you."

He snatched it out of my hands and held it out, stretching his arms to get the small print far enough away from his face so he could read it. His outfit was surprisingly similar to Jocelyn's, though his tank top and shorts were grubby and faded, and he had a large amount of white hair poking jauntily out of his enormous ears. The cardboard envelope flapped against my chest when he shoved it back at me and I grabbed it to keep it from falling to the floor.

"That ain't no name," he said, like me and my shenanigans had seriously inconvenienced him. "You tell me if you see my shipment. I need those catheters tonight!"

I opened my mouth to respond, but the door banged shut before I had the chance.

It was possible that Calla Human was in this building, and the shipper had simply gotten the apartment number wrong. But if I knocked on every door, it would take forever, and I'd had my fill of doors in my face for one day. I spun and headed down the stairs to the building manager's apartment on the first floor and pounded on the door a few times.

Esteban answered with a grin when he saw me. His short hair was gelled and spiky, sitting like a black crown above his pencil thin eyebrows and his deep dimples. His standard black button-up shirt and khaki slacks were well pressed. I'd always thought it was a uniform until he'd told me he dressed that way so that people would take him seriously.

"Hey, Cohen. How's it going, man?"

He pulled the door open, so I followed him inside. "Hi, yeah, this envelope was delivered to me by mistake. I'm thinking maybe they got the apartment number wrong? Is there a Calla Human in the building? Or is that the name of a former resident?"

Esteban snorted. "A *who*?" He took the envelope when I handed it to him, looked it over, then sat down at his desk.

"I would think I'd remember if I ever heard that name before, but I'll double check for you." He clickety-clacked on his keyboard for a few seconds. "So," he said, glancing at me over his shoulder as he waited for the software to load. "You ask out that girl from work yet? Sheila, I think?"

"Oh yeah, uh, I decided we probably didn't have much of a future anyway, so . . ." I ran my hands through my hair, leaving it standing on end now that I'd loosened the gel.

"What do you mean? I thought she was super into you?"

I shrugged. "What's the point if it's not going to last?"

He raised an eyebrow at me. "There's a lotta point, and if you need me to explain it to you, you're more hopeless than I thought." He chuckled when I leveled a look at him. "Cohen, you gotta stop playing it safe all the time, man. She might've been good for you. How will you ever know if you never take a chance?"

I shook my head. "Ah, it's okay. I'm saving myself for Jocelyn." I said it with a grin, though I was only half joking.

Esteban laughed. "So, you asked *her* out yet?"

"I know this is something *you* won't understand, but I actually like to be friends with a woman before I date them."

"Aren't you two friends yet?"

"Well, yeah, I mean . . . we're neighbors, so . . ."

He snickered and typed some more.

I cleared my throat. "It's . . . It's a work in progress."

"Whatever you say, man." Esteban shook his head and spun to face me in his wheeled office chair. "There is not, nor has there ever been, a Calla Human on our list of residents. Now, if they're staying with someone else, I wouldn't know. I'm supposed to get notice of every person occupying the premises for more than two weeks, but you know nobody ever follows that rule. Pretty sure the Whitehursts on the second floor have at least eighteen people in their little two bedroom, but as long as they pay their rent and pass their cleaning checks, I'm not really going to worry about it. Sorry, man."

I tapped my thigh. "Eh, it's okay. It was kind of a long shot.

I think everything about this is one big typo, but I had to try. They sent it SwiftMax Extreme, so I figure it's important. Just wanted to do my due diligence."

Esteban nodded, a crooked smile on his face as he handed the envelope back to me. "I know. That's your thing, and I respect it."

"Say, I've got some of my grandmother's lasagna upstairs. You wanna come up for dinner?"

"Can't. I've got a job with Ranji. You should join us some-time. You need to get out. You could come tonight; I know Ranji wouldn't mind."

"No thanks. I've got a lot of work to do. You go ahead." I carried my mystery envelope toward the door. Even if I hadn't been too busy, I would have said no. Ranji was . . . a lot to han-dle. "But be careful out there, Esteban," I said on my way out. "Make sure you get home before the rain starts."

He laughed his easy, infectious laugh. "Always, man. Always."

I went upstairs and called SwiftMax, explaining the whole situation. Fifteen minutes later, a rider picked up the envelope, and it was officially no longer my responsibility. Whoever was waiting around for this mystery envelope wouldn't receive it any-time soon, but SwiftMax Extreme or not, I'd done all I could. Time to let SMax correct their own mistakes. Hopefully, they'd get it right this time.

I heated up Gran's lasagna and sat up in bed with my laptop and my printed sheets, searching through all the diagnos-tics, hoping to find an explanation for the crash, a clue that would tell me where to look next. The only problem was that I wasn't seeing anything. The "LookupError" had shown up out of nowhere, and the system had just shut down. I huffed in frustration, then logged in to the GridLox server and set up a diagnostics test to run twenty-four seven and the demo to automatically restart whenever it crashed. If I got lucky, it might crash a few more times tonight, and I'd have enough information to actually figure out what was going on.

Since I had run into another wall on the world's most infuriating bug, I forced myself to work on my latest mini diorama for a while to help myself unwind. I was almost ready to slip the minuscule building I'd constructed into the test tube. All it needed was some plants to finish it off. More tiny test tube dioramas that I'd painstakingly created over the last several years lined the shelf in the corner, but this was one of my favorites.

I'd been hoping that working with my hands would let my subconscious relax and magically figure out the bug on its own, but instead of finding answers, I found myself nodding off. Even so, I was still awake when the lightning started, and before long the rain ran down the windowpane of my bedroom like I'd driven my apartment through a car wash.

I woke up to a pounding at my door again, the last of the rain dripping down the window, the sun up and burning away the last of the heavy clouds. I pulled on a robe while I jogged toward the door.

No one was there.

But on my doormat, lying there like it couldn't bear to be apart from me, was my old friend, the SwiftMax Extreme envelope, white sticker slapped over my "not at this address" note. Even from my height I could see the addressee name:

Calla Human.

Growling, I stooped and picked it up, then slammed the door behind me.

I poured myself a giant bowl of cereal, glaring at the address on the shipping label. It seemed like the universe, or at least

SwiftMax Delivery, really wanted me to have this envelope. Maybe it *was* meant for me. And only the name was wrong. The first initials of the name were right, so perhaps someone had had a small seizure after starting *Cohen* and *Hoard* and no one had ever caught the error.

Plus, hadn't I done all I could? Curiosity got the better of me. The only way I would know if it was for me or not was to see what was inside.

I pushed my bowl out of the way and held the envelope in front of me, pulling gently at the tear-open tab, trying to keep the cardboard intact as much as possible. I lifted the flap and peeked inside.

The envelope held only a small plastic case, white and smooth and hinged in the back. There was a sticker across the opening at the front that read "Medical Specimen." My curiosity shot through the roof. I peeled back the sticker with a fingernail and lifted the top.

Inside the plastic case was a human tongue.

3

"**A**aaagghh!"

The little box clattered softly to the table as I shoved my chair back and jumped up, breathing deeply through my nose a few times. A tongue? Why would someone send me a *tongue?* Why would someone send *anyone* a tongue? I stepped to the sink, downing a large glass of water before I turned back to the table again. The pale pink appendage lay in its open case, mocking me, like it was blowing a long, soundless raspberry.

I blinked, not sure whether I felt more confused or unnerved. Was this how medical specimens were always transported? Body parts just biked around the city?

So what now? Should I take it to the police? This Calla person was probably sitting somewhere, waiting for their tongue transplant, but while the police could probably find out exactly where this tongue needed to go, it would likely be tied up in bureaucracy until it was far too late. The image of Grandpa popped into my mind, hooked up to a machine, waiting for a kidney that never came.

I paced the length of my tiny kitchen, banging my knee on the chair I'd left in the middle of the floor, and cursing as pain shot up my leg. I wasn't sure why this specimen came to be in my possession, but it didn't really matter. What mattered was that I had it. And since SMax was unable or unwilling to deliver it to the right location, the responsibility fell to me.

I closed the lid on the white plastic box, looking at the contents as little as possible, and pressed the Medical Specimen sticker back in place as smoothly as I could. Then I slipped it back into the envelope and carefully taped it shut. It was time to take matters into my own hands.

—o

I hated to pay for a cab, but I didn't have time for the bus. The car picked me up outside my apartment building, tires sloshing through the puddles from last night's rain like a boat through a river. I was expecting it though, standing as far back from the road as I could to keep my shoes dry, an umbrella over my head to protect me from the rain runoff of the buildings and trees.

The cab driver looked like she had just survived an explosion. Her clothes were tattered and frayed, and her hair stood on end. Grunge had come back with a vengeance the last few years, and apparently, she was a huge fan.

"Good morning," I said, sliding into the backseat. "You got the address?"

She nodded. "Yeah, we're good. S'all good. Don't forget to buckle up."

I sent a quick text to Mr. Steenrod.

Dealing with a minor emergency. Will be a bit late. I'll tell you the crazy story as soon as I get there.

The driver peeled out into the street and we were off, water from the puddles we splashed through cascading over us like waves in the ocean. I secured my seat belt and held on, peering around her head to try to see the road in front of us through the water and wipers.

My phone dinged. A response from Mr. Steenrod.

Not a day for emergencies. Can you take care of it after work? I need you here!

Great. Sounded like Mr. Steenrod was in full stress mode. If I didn't get to work soon, he would erupt like a geyser. I typed in a reply, promising to get there as quickly as I could. I'd have a lot of apologizing to do, if I survived this car trip.

"My name's Cohen," I shouted. I didn't need to shout. But the speed and the splashing of the water against the windows made everything feel louder than it was. "What's yours?"

"Uh . . . Ruby, I guess." She swerved around a car in front of us and I closed my eyes to avoid seeing my death bearing down on me.

"Pleased to meet you," I shouted back. I knew some people preferred not to talk to their drivers, but how was I supposed to ride around in a car with someone if I didn't even know their name? It was just basic human courtesy. And we were still alive, so I kept talking. "How long have you been a cab driver?"

She scratched her matted hair and swerved needlessly back and forth across the street. "Um, a while. Listen, do you mind if I turn on the radio? I gotta focus on the road, you know?" She turned on the radio, which screamed at the both of us.

I texted my grandmother, to give myself something else to focus on besides my impending doom.

Morning, Gran! Is your car still leaking oil? Do you need me to come check it out?

Thanks, sweetie, but Lenore's nephew is a mechanic. He took care of it for me.

Oh. Okay. Great. I didn't have time to go over there anyway. But, I mean, her neighbor's *nephew*? Was she fine with just anyone working on her car these days?

Sounds good! Let me know if it gives you any more problems.

I will. Gotta go. Tae Kwon Do class is starting. Love you!

I pulled out a copy of my diagnostic report, but trying to read it during Ruby's driving nauseated me. I gave up and shoved it into my pocket, then pressed my face against the window, watching the trees as they flew past, their branches heavy with the water from the rain.

We pulled over on a quiet side street in the industrial side of town, an area I'd never been in before. The car stopped so suddenly, only the seatbelt saved me from ejecting straight through the windshield and gliding through the puddles like a speedboat. I wanted to thank her but worried that if I opened my mouth to speak, what little breakfast I'd eaten would end up all over the upholstery. Almost before I'd shut the door, she was gone.

The Muster Inc. building was small and gray and indistinguishable from any number of similar small, gray buildings scattered across Portland. There were no signs posted out front, but the street number stamped on the door matched the one on the envelope, so the tongue must have been sent from here. Everything on this side of town was concrete and gravel, with barely enough soil to support the ever-determined plant life. Compared to the rest of the foliage in the city, this area seemed almost dead. A few buildings over, a woman in coveralls wacked down the vines, weeds, and tropical flowers that had the audacity to grow.

From Muster Inc.'s website it was impossible to tell what the company actually did. I didn't know if they provided a service or a product. The website looked like somebody's brother-in-law had designed it twenty years ago as a favor. Maybe while I was here I could convince them to hire me for a website redesign. I hadn't done a website in a while, but a little side income never hurt, and these poor people needed it *badly*.

I pulled open the glass door and walked into the reception area. There was no one at the reception desk, just a yellow note in the middle reading "Be Right Back" with a smiley face on one side. I dinged the bell on the counter, then sat in one of the green plastic chairs. An idea struck me, and I pulled a black marker out of my briefcase and scribbled out my address on the envelope. I went over and over it with the pen so that nothing but black remained, and no oversight or laziness on the part of the delivery rider could cause this envelope to come back into my life.

And then I waited.

And waited.

I considered leaving the envelope on the desk and being done with it, but if whatever error that had sent it to me in the first place was in their system somewhere, and they just turned around and sent it to me again, I'd be right back where I started.

My phone dinged.

How's it going, Mr. Hoard? Everything all right? How soon can we expect you in the office?

Steenrod was getting antsy. So was I, come to think of it. How could you run a business like this? With no receptionist on duty at all? I silenced my phone, walked back up to the receptionist's desk, and rang the bell again.

"Hello? Is anybody there? You've got a potential customer out here!" I *could* be a customer, if I had any idea what they did here. The only clue I had so far implied that they either cut out people's tongues or collected tongues that had been cut out by other people. I wrinkled my nose. It didn't seem like the tongue belonged here any more than it belonged to me. This was just a boring office.

A guy with a black afro, possibly just out of high school, peeked around the wall behind the receptionist's desk. He must have heard me yelling, but he still seemed shocked to actually find someone standing there. He stepped hesitantly around the wall, checking once behind him, and then came around to the receptionist's desk.

"Can I help you?" His voice was unexpectedly deep for someone wearing pants that tight.

"Yes, this was sent to me by mistake." I set the envelope down on the counter between us, spinning it so the address label faced him, trying not to think about the thing that lay inside. "It shipped from this company, I believe."

The boy looked at the envelope and up at me. He looked back over his shoulder, at me, down at the envelope and up at me again, his afro bouncing back and forth. "Where did you get this?"

"It was delivered to my apartment. It was my address on the label, but that's not my name."

He looked at me as though to say "duh" then looked back over his shoulder again.

"So, can you take care of it for me? I want to make sure it isn't sent to my address again. Maybe you can pull up the shipping label in your system?" I gestured toward the computer on the desk, and he glanced at it like someone might look at a porcupine they'd just found in their bed.

"You say this came to your apartment?"

He seemed so confused I started to feel bad. Perhaps I needed to handle this differently.

"Yes. It came to my apartment." It was the tone I used when I talked to Mr. Suggs's dog. "My name's Cohen. What's yours?"

"Jimmy Lewis Jr." He said it all in one breath, like he was glad I finally asked him something easy.

"Nice to meet you, Jimmy Lewis Jr. Listen, I really need to make sure that this shipment is handled correctly. Can I talk to someone who *can* help me?"

He shuffled on the spot, like the question was way above his pay grade, then spun and walked back around the wall behind the desk. I drummed my fingers on the desk a few times and checked my watch. It was nearly 9:00. If I didn't make it to GridLox soon, Mr. Steenrod's head might literally explode.

Jimmy Lewis Jr. poked his head back around the wall and beckoned me to follow him. I groaned. They weren't going to make this easy on me, were they? Couldn't the shipping manager just pop out and take this problem off my hands?

I followed Jimmy down a hall as sparsely decorated as the front office, passing a few closed doors on the way. We stopped beside one, no different from the rest. Cheap wood slab set into dingy white walls. He knocked, then walked away, disappearing behind another door identical to this one.

"Come in."

I opened the door, envelope in hand, and stepped inside. A woman sitting behind a gray metal desk smiled at me. She must have been close to my age, probably early twenties, but the way she sat, even the way she smiled, somehow conveyed confidence and authority in a way that was undeniable. She wore a navy-blue blazer and her shiny black hair just brushed across her shoulders. She was pretty in a subtle way that somehow made it clear that she couldn't care less whether I thought so or not.

"How can I help you?" She motioned toward one of the chairs, and I tried not to sigh visibly. This was a simple problem, one that we could manage without anyone having to sit down at all.

I sat and passed the envelope across the desk to her, wondering if she knew what it contained, and if the thought of it made her as queasy as it made me. "This envelope was shipped to my address by mistake. That's my address under the black marks." I pointed at the black scribbles beneath the name Calla Human, suddenly embarrassed, like I'd scribbled all over the couch. "I've tried returning it through the shipping company, but they keep sending it back. So, I figured, being SwiftMax Extreme, it was urgent that it get where it needs to go as soon as possible."

She smiled, her eyes softening. "That's very thoughtful. Someone else in your shoes might have just thrown it away."

"Oh, I don't know," I said, unnecessarily shy at her compliment. "Most people try to do the right thing, most of the time."

She raised her eyebrows.

I cleared my throat. "I guess maybe I shouldn't have crossed out my address now that I think about it. Now you don't know where *not* to send it next time." I scratched my neck. I was supremely curious as to why this little, out of the way, nothing company was sending a tongue to anyone, but that was beside the point right now. "Should I give you my address, or, uh, do you happen to know where it needs to go? Is Calla Human a person? Do you know?"

She pulled the envelope toward herself, reading the label as she did so and looked up with that same smile.

"You're in luck. The envelope is addressed to me."

"*You're* Calla Human?" I asked, confused and derailed. She clearly *had* a tongue of her own. And she didn't seem like the kind of person I pictured dealing in black market tongues. Nothing about this made a lick of sense. I smiled at my unspoken pun.

She held out a hand. "Nice to meet you."

"Cohen Hoard. Nice to meet you too." Her hand was soft, her handshake strong, and I wondered suddenly what it would be like to arm wrestle her. "No offense, but your name sounds like something a robot or alien would use to try to fit in."

She lifted her shoulder. "One does what one can."

I grinned and she grinned, and time stood still for one long heartbeat.

I cleared my throat. "Why did you send it to yourself?" I knew it wasn't any of my business, but this envelope begged so many questions, and I felt like I deserved at least an answer or two.

"I didn't," she said with a small shake of her head, tapping the envelope against the desk. "It came from our corporate office. They must have somehow entered your address into the shipping label by mistake. I'm sorry you had to come all the way down here, but I really appreciate you taking the time." Her smile was so genuine it almost made me forget what a huge hurry I was in. If I'd had the time, I would've liked to stay and find out more. But not today.

"Happy I could help," I said. "But if you'll excuse me, I really must be going."

"Of course," she said, standing and walking around the desk toward the door. "We don't want to keep you." She held the door open for me. "Thanks again."

I stopped in front of her, not quite ready to walk away. "Just out of curiosity, why is your corporate office sending you . . . *that?*"

Calla's face fell, and she pushed the door closed, leaning against it. "You opened it?" Her voice was small and tight.

Oh cripes. Why was I such a buffoon? It may not have been technically illegal for me to look inside the envelope since it was sent to me, but it was definitely idiotic for me to tell her I had. "Uh, no." I was a horrific liar.

"You *did.*" Her composure shattered, and she clung to the doorknob like it was the only thing keeping her upright. "Why? Why would you do that? What in the world were you thinking?"

"I was thinking it was for me! They sent it to me three times!" I shouldn't be yelling at her, but she was making me extremely nervous.

She ran her free hand over her face, then her gaze flicked around the room like the empty paneled walls could fix whatever conundrum I'd caused.

I held up my hands in supplication. "Listen. I'm sorry. I really am. I know I screwed up. But if I don't get to work in the next thirty minutes I'm going to lose my job. So, I gotta go."

I pointed at the door, the one she was blocking with her body, to remind her that she was the only thing standing in my way.

Her lips turned up, but her eyes were sad, and she suddenly looked like a little girl.

"I'm sorry, Cohen. I can't let you do that."

4

I laughed, but it wasn't remotely funny. She had to be joking. But she just stood there, watching me. I pushed more laughter sounds out of my mouth. "You can't just keep me here."

She couldn't have been a whole lot more than five feet tall, so I towered around a foot above her. It would have been easy to push her aside or pick her up and physically move her, yet she stared me down, daring me to try to go through her, until I felt small and insignificant in front of her.

"You *can't* just keep me here!" I croaked. "I'm pretty sure this is kidnapping. Or unlawful restraint, or, or . . . you can't just keep me here!" My voice cracked through the small office, absorbed by the popcorn ceiling.

She nodded, as though to herself, and her mouth tipped in a tiny smile. "Calm down. We're not staying here. I need you to come with me."

"What?" My voice was still high and squeaky, and I didn't know how to make it stop. "I'm not going anywhere with you. I'm getting the cripes out of here before I lose my job."

"Wake up, Hoard," Calla said, pinning me with a powerful

stare. "This was sent to *your* address. You opened the envelope. You're a part of this now, whether you like it or not."

"But I . . . but you . . ." Coherent speech seemed to have abandoned me. What did she mean, I was part of it now? A part of *what*? What in the Sam Hill was going on? I'd just been trying to do the right thing. I didn't have time to get sucked into some severed-tongue soap opera.

Calla walked around her desk and picked up a faded blue duffle bag with a badge sewn onto the strap. I sat back down and pulled out my phone, but didn't have a clue what to do with it. Should I call the police? Would they believe I was being held hostage by an attractive woman with a tongue in an envelope? My notifications were filled with several frantic messages from my boss asking where I was and why I was abandoning him. I started typing a reply, hoping to talk him down from his ledge.

Calla stepped in front of me and snatched the phone out of my hands.

"Whoa." I tried to grab it back, but she stayed just out of reach. I drew myself up to my full height. "Now you've gone too far. Return my phone. This instant."

She shoved it down her shirt, then tucked the shipping envelope under her arm. "Let's go."

She grabbed my arm with vice-like fingers, dragged me out of the room and toward the back of the building.

"What is wrong with you?" I asked, yanking my arm out of her death grip. "Did you learn your social skills in prison? This isn't how you treat people! Or phones!"

She rolled her eyes and kept walking. "I'll give your phone back as soon as we've had a chance to talk. Until then, I can't let you call anyone. Just come with me. Okay? Everything will be fine."

It absolutely was *not* okay. But I wasn't leaving without my phone, and I couldn't see how to get it from her without digging it out of her shirt by force. The very idea made me cough uncomfortably.

We approached the back door and walked out to a parking lot dotted with a few cars, rusted and tireless and grown over with vines. Calla led me across the parking lot and toward a narrow alley where vines assailed the walls, then she pushed aside a curtain of greenery, revealing a door. She opened it and ushered me through. I stepped out of the bright midmorning light and into the darkness inside.

Fluorescent tube lights hung from the ceiling and cardboard boxes lined the walls. My first thought was that the warehouse was full of people, but then my eyes adjusted to the dim light.

"Nope." I spun back to the door, reaching for the knob, but Calla grabbed me and turned me back around, pulling me into the warehouse stuffed with nightmares.

They were mannequins. White and red and beige mannequins with their faces cracked and broken, leaning all over each other in carts; chipped wooden mannequins stood in rows like soldiers preparing for battle; mannequins with missing limbs and extremities lay on top of each other in a pile right next to a shelf full of legs. Calla towed me deeper into the room.

"What is this place? Why are you here? How can you stand it?"

She ignored me and dragged me further away from the safety of the sunlight and the fresh air and the mannequin-free outside world.

"We've got a problem," Calla called out.

Who was she talking to? Me? The mannequins? If these mannequins responded, I was going to be very unhappy.

"What?" a voice called back in response. A short kid with round cheeks and big black eyes popped around a cluster of mannequins that were all missing their heads. I did a double take. It was like the past had jumped out and punched me in the face. He looked just like Peter. Of course, it *wasn't* Peter. I knew that. But seeing him so suddenly shook me all the way down to my freshly polished shoes.

Calla towed me around the headless horde and pushed me out in front of her. "This." She held her hands wide, gesturing from my feet to my head, like every inch of me was the problem.

The Peter look-alike grinned and waved. Behind him, Jimmy Lewis Jr. stood at a work bench that ran the length of the wall, next to a tall woman with waist-length blond hair facing away from us and typing on a laptop.

The blond woman glanced at me over her shoulder and scowled, her eyebrows so pale they blended right into her face. "What is *this?*"

"I don't know."

"My name is Cohen Hoard," I interjected. "I'm a software engineer, and I really need to leave now."

Calla threw her duffle bag onto a couch tucked between the workbench and a shelf full of boxes and handed the envelope to the blond woman. "This got sent to his address. So I wanna know if we screwed up, or if it was the Client."

The blond woman nodded, taking the envelope in one hand while typing furiously with the other.

Calla looked at me and gestured toward an empty spot on the couch.

I glowered at her. "I'm ready for some answers," I said instead of sitting. I folded my arms across my chest, hoping that all the push-ups I'd been doing lately showed in my shoulders.

"I brought the tongue here assuming it was on its way to some poor tongueless soul, but now I don't have a clue *what's* going on. Who are you? What is this company you work for? And what under the cloud-filled sky does any of it have to do with me?"

I cleared my throat. I hoped that had come out as authoritatively as I'd intended it to.

Calla lowered her eyebrows. "A tongue?" She directed this toward the blond woman instead of me, but the woman held up her hand in a "hang-on" gesture. "We haven't had a tongue yet," Calla said. "Was this sent by someone else? Does he have more than one team?"

"Does *who* have more than one team? Are you CIA or something?" I glanced toward the two younger boys taping up boxes, racing to prove who was more skilled with the tape gun. "Or . . . something else? And what do you mean you haven't had a tongue yet? Are you cannibals?"

I'd meant it as a joke, but as I said it, I realized it could very well be true. This place was *weird*. Anything was possible. And I had to get out of here. For one brief second, I considered running for it, but they *did* have my address. And Jocelyn lived so innocently and deliciously next door. I had to keep them away from her.

"You're not, are you?" I laughed awkwardly. "What do you want with me? If you plan to eat me, I swear, I will not make it easy on you."

"Wow." Calla smiled, almost to herself. "Cannibals. I like it. But you're not really our type. We like 'em young. Babies, if possible. I will not eat anyone who is a day over five."

"That's horrible," Jimmy Lewis Jr. said.

"I will!" the Peter look-alike said. "Put some sriracha on it, and I'll eat anything!"

The tall blond woman shook her head. "You guys are disgusting."

I stared at the four of them, trying to figure them out. "You know what? I don't even care. I just need to leave. I have to get to work. I won't tell a soul what I've seen here. Honestly, I don't know *what* I've seen here, so I couldn't tell anyone if I tried. If you give me back my phone, I'll call a cab, and disappear, and we can all pretend that none of this ever happened." I finished by putting my hands on my hips. Doesn't get much more authoritative than that.

Calla looked unimpressed. "You aren't going anywhere until we figure out what's going on. So you may as well make yourself comfortable." She gestured toward the couch again, more forcefully this time.

"You dragged me here by force," I barked, staying on my feet. "If you want me to be comfortable, you should give my phone back. And I've already told you everything I know, so there is zero reason to keep me here. You can get to the bottom of this without me."

The tall blond woman walked up during my speech and handed me a water bottle.

"Thank you," I said, twisting off the cap and taking a swig. I sat on the couch before remembering that I had no intention of sitting down. *Drat.* I couldn't stand back up now. I took another drink and smiled in what I hoped was a somewhat threatening way. The water tasted off, like maybe the plastic was leaching into it.

Calla looked at me like she was trying to see inside of me. It made me lightheaded. Like the world was spinning faster than it ought to. The room began to spin as well, and the mannequin behind her blurred and dripped toward the floor.

My head hit the cushion and melded into it until the couch and I became one. Calla walked forward and knelt on the floor in front of me, her face waving in the breeze. She placed her hand on my forehead then took the water bottle out of my hands which were slowly turning to sand.

"Really?" she asked, looking toward the grinning face of her tall blond friend. "Again?"

And then the light was sucked out of the universe and all life was extinguished with one confused beat of my heart.

5

I came to slowly, realizing that, though I felt like roadkill, I was still technically alive. My tongue tasted like I had *eaten* roadkill. Roadkill that had been wearing a diaper made of cactuses.

I tried to force my eyelids open, but a rough pillow smothered me. It smelled musty and damp and I wondered if maybe a couch had swallowed me whole.

A hand on my back shocked me upright, pulling my face out of the couch cushion. I sucked in a breath and turned toward the person who'd touched me, but though they were an arm's length away, I couldn't make out their features.

"You drugged me?" I asked, but all the consonants rearranged themselves on their way out of my mouth. It sounded like Greek. Could I speak Greek now?

The featureless person-shape rose and floated away. I grabbed my head and leaned over till I hit the armrest as a wave of nausea rolled over me. At least I still had my tongue, as evidenced by the flavor of cactus diaper still lingering there. I patted myself down to make sure I wasn't missing any internal organs, but I couldn't tell through all the skin and clothes I wore.

Someone blurry pushed a glass of water into my hands. The water was cool and clear, and I desperately wanted to wash the roadkill taste off my tongue, but I wasn't ready to be fooled again so quickly.

"If you think I'm going to drink something else from you, you've got another think coming!" No, *German*. I was speaking German. Did they understand German? "How am I supposed to know whether this is water or some evil potion?" Oh, the last half of that sentence actually sounded like real words, in English.

The figure in front of me curved its mouth into a smile, and I met the eyes of Jimmy Lewis Jr.

"I'm glad you're awake. You were out for a really long time. I was getting worried." He seemed genuinely pleased, but the more I woke up, the angrier I became.

"Awake? You make it sound like I came down with a sudden case of narcolepsy. Calla *drugged* me, I'll have you know. With full malice aforethought. Just knocked me right out for who knows what reason, so yeah, I'm awake, but it was *her* fault I was sleeping in the first place!"

"Who?" Jimmy asked.

"Who what?" I said, but then something else he'd said sunk in. "Wait? How long was I out? What time is it?" Butcher paper and plywood covered most of the windows set high in the walls along the ceiling, but one still gave me a view of the darkening sky outside. A sinking dread collected in my gut.

Jimmy checked his watch. "8:45 . . . *p.m.*"

"What!" I jumped to my feet, then swayed, my head no longer comfortable with heights. "The rain will start soon, and I'll be stuck here. I can't stay here all night! Give me a phone. I'm calling a cab."

He shrugged and offered an embarrassed smile, like I'd just

discovered that his mom still tied his shoes. "Cars won't come out here this time of night."

"I'll walk, then!" It was a lie. I wouldn't walk anywhere if it was raining. Not as long as I wanted to keep being alive.

Jimmy stood too, rubbing his neck and smile-frowning at me. "Where do you live?"

"Dayspring," I said, throwing back the glass of water without thinking. I grimaced, waiting to pass out again, but nothing happened. The water wasn't cold, but it washed the furry feeling off my tongue, and I instantly wished for another.

"It'll take at least a couple of hours to get to Dayspring on foot. But don't worry. Everything will be fine, I promise. That water I gave you was only water, right?"

Lightning flashed, leaking around the edges of the covered windows. Thunder crashed into the side of the building. All of the mannequins shook as the room rattled, clacking and knocking into each other.

The lightning had arrived.

The door banged open, and Calla marched in, followed by the tall blond woman. "Time to go."

This woman made no sense. She absolutely did not fit into any definable areas of my life. She was confusing and powerful and if she dragged me out of one more building, I was going to lose it. "I'm not going anywhere with you, Calla Human. I want some answers!"

The pale blond woman looked at Calla, eyebrows raised, the faintest smile on her lips.

Calla pursed hers, then leaned toward the other woman, softly saying, "See if the boys need any help." She came toward me, arms folded across her chest in a perfect imitation of the authoritative stance I had used earlier.

I pulled myself up to my full height, all six foot three of me, and glowered at her, determined not to be intimidated, and annoyed that I still was.

"Okay. Sure. Answers," Calla said. "Me first. Why are you here? Who do you work for?"

"I work for GridLox. I'm here because you brought me here. I *tried* to leave, remember? But you stole my phone. Now it's nighttime, and I missed work completely!" The enormity of that crashed on my shoulders. I *never* missed work. I was never sick; I never went on vacation; I'd only been gone a few days when I'd had surgery. My boss loved me for it, and I hated that I was messing up an amazing streak right before the DarkWave launch. "Steenrod's going to kill me. I was supposed to have the demo done weeks ago, but there's a bug I've got to fix, and I don't have time for this!"

Calla narrowed her eyes. "I don't know what you're talking about."

"This is the reason nobody trusts anybody, you know. It always comes back to bite them in the bum. You help one little old lady cross the street and the next thing you know you're arrested for treason!"

She stared at me for a second then shook her head. "Who sent the tongue to you? Why bring it to us? Did you hack into SMax? What were you hoping to gain? Were you just trying to get me to bring you here?"

"Why would I want you to bring me *here*?" I fisted my hands in frustration. "I hate it here. It smells like burnt hair, and I'm fairly sure *that* mannequin just moved." I pointed violently at a faded gray mannequin staring at me with its soulless eyes.

Calla studied me for a long time, her eyes narrowed, as though trying to figure me out. It was unnerving, like having a doctor expect me to diagnose myself. Maybe I was still speaking German? What was it going to take to get some answers out of this woman?

"Listen," I said, trying to calm down. "Everything I told you back in your office was true. That envelope was shipped to my address. I don't know why. I tried to return it, but they kept sending it back. So I opened it. I shouldn't have; I can see that now, and I'm really sorry. I want to fix it. I'll do what I can to fix this. But I can't fix anything until I understand what's going on."

"Told you," a voice said from somewhere behind us.

I looked around. "Told you what?"

Calla rolled her eyes. "Oh, she looked you up while you were sleeping and found out everything about you. She insisted you don't know anything."

Calla laid her hand on my arm and warmth shot through me in a way that made no sense under the circumstances. She smiled, baring her teeth, a challenge in her eyes. "But I don't trust you. I figure we can either take you with us, or drug you enough to wipe your memory, but Jimmy says that your heart might also forget how to beat, so lucky me, I'm stuck with you for now."

I growled in frustration. I was a fairly reasonable guy, as a general rule, but Calla was pushing my patience beyond every previous limit.

Raising her voice, she called out to the room, "I want wheels on the ground as soon as the lightning stops. That gives you twenty minutes."

"Can't we just stay here tonight?" the Peter look-alike said, appearing out of nowhere and sliding his feet into a pair of sneakers. "I like it here."

"Not tonight," Calla said. "It's time to head back to base.

Go gather your stuff, okay?" She tousled his hair and strode away, leaving me alone with the Peter look-alike.

"How can you like it here?" I asked him as he picked up a backpack with *Lt. Commander Storm* pins all over it.

"The mannequins are cool! Don't you think they're cool?"

A row of silver heads faced us on a shelf above the workbench, each being eternally suffocated in a transparent plastic bag.

"I feel like they're watching me," I said, giving them a sidelong glance.

"But they don't have any eyes," he said, like I was being silly.

"Yeah, well, you can see why that would kind of creep me out."

The kid snorted and hitched up his pants, then scooted off, pushing his feet the rest of the way into his shoes. His face was rounder than Peter's had been. The eyes wider. He was probably only twelve, and looked even more innocent, if that was possible. But there was something about his enthusiasm that was like staring straight into a past I'd rather have forgotten.

I rubbed my hands through my hair, and it fell into my eyes. I didn't even care. Thunder shook the building again, and I realized the fatal error in Calla's plan. The storm was here. How in the hemisphere did she think we were going anywhere? We might as well try to walk across the ocean floor.

I followed in the direction Calla and the Peter look-alike had gone, finding them gathering supplies. They reminded me of a tiny hive of worker bees, bustling about, oblivious to the boot about to smash their hive to smithereens.

"What is your plan here?" I said to the group of them, hoping at least one of them would see reason. "Even if you have a functioning car hidden somewhere, the Automated Safety features won't allow it to run after dark." Assuming they hadn't overridden them, which was not only stupidly dangerous, but illegal. The military and law enforcement had amphibious vehicles for nighttime use, but those weren't allowed for civilians. "What are we going to do, swim through the sewers?"

They shared a glance, then looked at me, a smile on every single face.

—o

Standing under the covered parking, we watched the lightning fade and travel out of sight, the rumble of thunder trailing behind it like a grumpy child. For a moment we were submerged in total silence, like the sky held its breath.

The first raindrop fell, splattering against the cement. It was followed by another, and then by several billion more, until huge raindrops pelted the ground in front of us, splashing up like small explosions.

A row of hydrocycles stood behind us, ready and waiting to carry us through the storm.

"This is worse than the sewer," I said.

In all fairness, I had never ridden a hydrocycle. They were designed for the water with two big knobby tires in the front, and an extra set of disc brakes. But even so, I wasn't really in the mood to be fair.

"Calla," I yelled, grabbing her arm as she rushed past. "We should stay here. Even that creepy mannequin horror show in there would be better than this. We can go in the morning when the rain stops."

"We're leaving now. Better get your bike legs under you."

"I can't ride one of those." I wiggled my pointer finger

toward the hydrocycles. "And I definitely can't ride in that." I wiggled my finger at the cacophony of rainfall over our heads.

She looked up at me, one eyebrow raised. "They're still bicycles. Basically. You *are* from Portland, aren't you?"

"Yes, but I don't ride! Not anymore!"

"Why not?"

"Because I'm an adult!" I yelled, throwing my hands into the air. "Because it's not safe. Because this town is too darn wet!" I couldn't believe that I had to explain this, but she smiled at me like I was telling her I had a secret fear of bunny rabbits.

The Peter look-alike jumped up, yelling over the racket of the rain, "I can do it! Can I take the electrocycle? And he can ride on the back?!"

"Absolutely not," my voice boomed out.

Calla met my eyes. Then she turned to the Peter look-alike. "Next time, okay? Who knows what this guy is going to do once we get him out in the rain."

He looked crestfallen, but nodded.

Jimmy cleared his throat. "*I* can do it."

Calla raised her eyebrows at him. "Are you sure? Even on the electrocycle he's still going to be as heavy as sin."

Jimmy sized me up then nodded, giving me a conspiratorial smile. He was skinny, but tall, and seemed strong enough. And at least he was an adult. Hopefully.

Everyone else donned full water gear. High-intensity raincoats with vyprene pants tucked into knee-high rubber biking boots that fastened onto the pedals. They pulled ponchos over their heads, followed by full biking helmets with large round bills and hefty goggles.

This was all insanity. People didn't go out in the rain unless they were actively trying to drown themselves. Why didn't these lunatics know that?

The blond woman appeared in front of me, standing nearly as tall as I was, and dumped a bundle into my arms. I looked down at it, lost.

The Peter look-alike ran up to me, calling, "I got you!" He took the box of garbage bags from my hands, shook out a black plastic bag, then knelt in front of me, bag open. "My name's Saifi," he said. "And you gotta put your foot in here! Hurry!"

So, I did. And then I put my other foot in another plastic bag. He duct-taped the bags closed around my thighs. He sliced the end off another bag, then made me step inside and wrapped it around my middle, taping it off along the top and bottom. He cut a hole at the end of the fourth bag and pulled it over my head like a poncho, taping this along the bottom as well. After stepping back to look at me, he laughed to himself and then quickly cut a hole for each of my arms. He slipped a small yellow life jacket around my neck. The kind that used to be used for emergencies on airplanes back when those still worked.

"Just in case," Saifi said, smiling and wrinkling his nose.

He was so fast the whole process only took a couple of minutes, but even so, everyone else was straddling their cycles and looking back at us.

Jimmy beckoned me toward him and his electric hydrocycle, ready and waiting.

"Calla . . ." I said, my voice pleading, raw, vulnerable. This was a colossally bad idea. I didn't care how well decked out we were. I didn't care how fancy their bikes were. No one survived in the rain. No one *went out* in the rain. At all. Because it was moronic. Because it was suicide. We really, really needed to stay right where we were.

Calla must have heard the terror in my voice because she got off her cycle and walked toward me, the duffel bag beneath her poncho making her look like a ninja turtle. She put her arm around my back, taking one of my hands in her free one. She pulled me forward, keeping eye contact until we reached Jimmy, then she placed my hands on his shoulders, closing my fingers around the straps sewn into his raincoat. She squatted down and guided my feet one at a time onto the pegs on the back of his cycle, then pushed me down to sit on the rack. Jimmy and Saifi started giving me basic advice about how to balance and stay safe in the rain, but their words blurred and blended and I didn't catch most of it.

"Calla, I don't think . . ."

"Cohen," she said, her voice firm, and she turned my head toward her. "I forgot to tell you the most important thing of all."

I held my breath, ready for the words that would make everything suddenly okay.

She looked deep into my eyes and said, "My name isn't Calla." Then she swatted me on the backside like I was a horse, and Jimmy and I took off into the night for what would surely be the last rainstorm of my life.

6

*T*his *is how I die,* I thought. *This is how we all die.*

I perched on the rack that I didn't really trust to bear my weight, hunching behind Jimmy and trying not to screw up his balance. Water splashed constantly in my face, making it hard to catch my breath. But with the hydrophobic goggles and the bright yellow headlight that cut straight through the rain, I could see over Jimmy's shoulder no matter how much water sprayed at me. I wasn't sure I wanted to, but I could.

The power was out, which was no surprise on this side of town. The rain always played havoc with the power grid, and this area was extra neglected in the utilities department. It was pretty neglected in most departments, actually. The buildings on one street we rode down were completely overgrown with vines and lichen. This whole part of town reeked of abandon and decay and was as creepy as all get-out.

Even the electric hydrocycle struggled under my extra weight, and Calla and her cronies zipped past us, sloshing through the torrent that fell from the sky and pooled around us in the night.

Or rather, *not* Calla, since that wasn't her name. I didn't have time for the rage that came with that little betrayal at the moment, but I added it to the list. The water splashing off them as they passed made them look like dark spirits, wet auras moving and throbbing around them.

In some parts of the world, the nightly storms were violent hurricanes, but in Portland, the biggest danger was the sheer amount of water falling out of the sky. It was like riding through a waterfall. Portland had solved their drainage problems by reconstructing their roads in a large V shape, each side of the road slanting down toward grates that ran down the center. At the moment, the channel in the middle of the road was half full of water that barreled past us like a herd of charging bulls. That left a narrow strip of asphalt on either side of the street just wide enough for a bike to ride on. Not dry, but not under water either.

Finally, *finally*, we started slowing down. We pulled under the corrugated fiberglass roof of a carport and skidded to a stop. I let go of Jimmy and collapsed onto the carport floor, breathing heavily. We were *alive*. I couldn't quite believe it. We had ridden through the rain and lived to tell the tale. I hugged the wet concrete beneath me, breathing in the smell of motor oil and cement.

The rain kept falling, banging against the roof, taunting me, indifferent to the miracle we'd just pulled off. I wasn't sure whether to laugh in triumph or curl up in a ball and cry. I was *never* doing that again.

Jimmy bent over, hands on his knees, breathing deeply. The floor moved beneath us, and I jumped up, ready for a fight, without a clue what I was fighting against.

"We're on the water," Jimmy said, still breathless, but talking loud enough for me to hear him over the din of the rain on the roof.

I tried to wipe some of the rain off my face, but my hands were wetter than my face was. "We *are* the water," I said.

"Ooh, I like that," Jimmy said between gasps. "That's deep."

Saifi appeared next to us, stripping off his wet gear, steam rising off him. I reached out a hand, tempted to poke him in the face to be certain he was really alive and unharmed. He grinned at me and shouted, "He means here. The house. It's on the water."

My brain was foggy, and I was both freezing and overheated at the same time. The floor rocked again, and Saifi's words finally made sense. We were in the carport of a floating house. They'd been all the rage years ago, but after the weather broke down, most of the civilized city had pulled out of the waterfront properties and headed toward higher, dryer ground. Staying here was not a good idea, but that seemed to be the only kind of idea these people had. At least we were out of the rain.

The one who wasn't Calla appeared next to us, pulling off her poncho and helmet, and wiping water off her face. She patted Jimmy on the back. "You okay?"

Jimmy gave her a thumbs up and started pulling off his wet gear, moving toward the house as he did so, his chest still heaving in and out. Saifi, however, stripped down to boxers and jumped out from under the awning singing "Hallelujah!" The rain pummeled him as he quickly scrubbed his armpits and back of his neck as though he were taking a shower. I ran toward him, ready to pull him back to safety, but he jumped back under the awning and out of the rain, soaked and sputtering.

He caught my worried stare and shrugged, blowing away

the water that ran down his face into his mouth. "You gotta take what you can get, you know?"

Ready to be free of my plastic prison, I tried to pull off the duct tape, but couldn't find the end. I fumbled with numb fingers around the taped-up joints and tried to poke a hole straight through the plastic to let some air in, but the plastic was too thick, my fingers too cold.

The person formerly known as Calla turned to me, brushing wet hair from her eyes. She pulled out a knife, flipped out the blade, and came for me like she intended to cut me open. I pulled back as she grabbed the plastic at my throat, but she stabbed the knife deftly through the garbage bag and ran the blade from my neck to my navel. She slit the tape around my waist and bent down to cut through the tape on each thigh. Then she stood and met my eye, tapping the flat of the blade against my chest. My pulse hammered through my veins like thunder, but I couldn't tell if it was from the threat or simply the nearness of her. I tried to breathe normally, but I no longer knew how.

"That's a nice knife," I murmured. "Is it a Holtzman, or . . ."

"Give me one reason why I shouldn't slit your throat and shove you into the Willamette right now." Contrary to her words, her tone was genial. Like it was a perfectly reasonable question for one person to ask another. Drops of water still clung to her eyelashes, making her eyes look shiny and vulnerable as she waited for my answer.

"Because it wouldn't be very nice, for one. Not to mention Jimmy just wore himself out dragging me all the way here. If you were going to kill me, it would have made more sense to kill me back at the warehouse. Also," I swallowed and lowered my voice, "I don't really think you're the killing type." She was standing so close I could see the tiny green flecks in her dark brown eyes. They didn't look like the eyes of a murderer, but what did I know?

She shrugged. "I might be, if the occasion calls for it. This is the first time we've had a stranger show up unexpectedly claiming he got a tongue in the mail, so there's no telling what I might do."

I threw up my hands in frustration. "So what do you want from me? You won't let me leave, but you also don't trust me enough to let me stay. You can't have it both ways."

She pulled the knife away, fingering the blade. "You're right." She gazed at the knife for a long time, though she didn't seem to see it. "I don't trust you," she said at last. "But I trust Celeste. And Celeste thinks you're okay. She also says we have to keep you here, so as much as I don't like it, that's what we're going to do. But understand this—" she leaned in close so that I could feel her breath against my cheek, "these people are my family. You hurt them in any way, and I will rain down destruction on your head the likes of which you have never imagined." She flipped the knife closed with one hand and turned away.

"Wait," I said before she could disappear.

She gazed up at me, dark eyes shining in the pale light.

"I still don't know what your actual name is."

She narrowed her eyes and twisted her mouth to the side. "Lei."

"Lay??"

"Yes. Lei. It's Chinese. I'm Chinese. *Lei.*"

"I'm still Cohen. Nice to meet you." Was it? I mean, she *had* drugged me and abducted me, and threatened me and nearly drowned me. But still, that was no excuse for bad manners.

She cocked an eyebrow then tipped me an unexpected smile

and slipped away, leaving me alone in the carport. I exhaled and the rain beat against the roof and the world was suddenly noisier and emptier than it had been a moment before.

My garbage bag suit came off easily and I ripped it away, so refreshed to feel air through my clothes again as steam rose off my body. I spied a large green recycling can against the back wall and threw my wad of plastic and tape away. Then I followed everyone inside the house, shutting the door, the storm, and the cacophony outside.

The interior of the house looked like it had been decorated by someone with a deeply personal love for paint. I turned slowly, trying to take it all in. The walls were peacock blue; the floor bright red; the ceiling striped with yellow and white. It was a little jarring to the eyeballs. It had probably been well cared for at one time, but now the paint sagged, peeling from all the moisture.

I waited wetly in the living room as people flitted past, knowing where to go and what to do. I was still lost and confused, but I wasn't the same man who'd walked out of that mannequin factory. I'd survived a rainstorm. I hadn't even thought that was possible. It all made it a little hard to get my bearings.

The room gently bounced upon the water as Jimmy came up and handed me a towel. He tipped his head toward the kitchen. "Come on. Meeting time."

Everyone crowded around a dinette table painted with little white birdies. I slid into the spot Saifi made next to him on the bench, and Jimmy set a bowl of chicken noodle soup from a can in front of me. I hadn't eaten since breakfast, and I dug into it without even considering if it was safe to do so or not. Nothing had ever tasted so delicious. A stack of canned biscuits sat on a plate in the center of the table, and I followed Jimmy and

Saifi's lead, slathering one with butter and dipping it in the hot broth.

The blond woman, Celeste, sat at the head of the table, laptop open in front of her, hunched over, reading and typing while she nibbled on her biscuit. All of the bowls we were eating out of were crusted with jewels in every color. They shone in the light, making the kitchen table look like the floor of a disco.

I smiled in spite of myself. "Wow. These bowls are fancy."

Jimmy laughed softly, nodding. "They're left over from a job. Client decided not to pay, so now we get to use the world's sparkliest dishes."

"A job?" I asked.

Lei set a small blue insulated box in the center of the table, cutting off the conversation. I stopped eating and sat up, wiping my face on my sleeve.

"Okay. Here's the deal," Lei said. "We have two . . . *situations* that need to be dealt with. This tongue," she pointed at the repackaged tongue as though it were a reasonable thing for a group of people to have on the dining table, "and this man." She pointed at me so no one would have to check the vicinity for other strange men.

The two boys smiled, but Lei and Celeste had a silent conversation across the table. Celeste nodded slowly at Lei until Lei finally sighed in defeat, shaking her head at the ceiling as though praying for strength.

Lei gestured toward me in frustration. "I'd like you all to meet Cohen Hoard. Hoard, this is Jimmy, Saifi, and Celeste." She waved her hands dismissively as though that was all the niceties the occasion called for. "The tongue was sent to him—"

"Three times," I interjected, holding up three fingers. I had to make sure they knew that part. I hadn't just opened it for no reason.

She eyed me and nodded. "Right. Three times. It went to his address, but whose name was on the label?"

"Calla Human. Which you said was *you*." Everyone looked at each other and not at me. Saifi covered his mouth with his hand, his eyes wide. Lei nodded at Celeste, who tapped a few keys, then spun the laptop around so I could see the screen. It showed a website, a white screen with orange text.

Call-A-Human.com.

"Wha . . . ?" I couldn't even finish my word. That's how lost I was. Was this supposed to be some kind of explanation?

Saifi smothered a laugh.

"This is how it started," Lei said. "I was emailed a link to this website. Only it doesn't actually do anything. There aren't any clickable links or tabs or menus. It's just text on this page. Celeste is the one that realized it's a phone number."

I counted the letters, converting them to numbers in my mind. So simple. Stupid even. But it explained nothing. Except that I'd sounded like an idiot calling her *Calla* all day.

"So we called. And he hired us on the spot."

"Who did?"

She pointed to the website.

"But it's not a person. You just said—"

"It's a company name, maybe? We don't really know. We really don't know anything." She huffed slightly in frustration, though it looked like she was trying to hide it.

Without looking up, Celeste raised her biscuit like a fist of triumph. "We're collectors."

I shook my head. "You mean like figurines and comic books and stuff?"

"I collect comic books!" Saifi piped in.

"No one would call your stack of ratty comic books a collection," Celeste said.

"He's got a *Lieutenant Commander Storm* issue forty-three. It's pretty rare," Jimmy said.

Saifi held one finger in the air. "And it's in mint condition."

"No," Lei cut in before they could get too far on their tangent. "Not that kind of collectors. It's a job." She nodded like that was all the explanation a person should need.

It was not.

"People hire us to find and collect things for them," Jimmy offered helpfully. "Things that the average person can't really find on their own."

"Ohhkay. Sure. Alright." Esteban did that with Ranji sometimes, on the side. He talked about it like it was some kind of dream gig or something. "And whoever owns this website hired you to get some stuff for him."

Everyone nodded.

I looked at the tongue on the table. I looked at Lei. She said nothing. No one else spoke. Saifi broke the silence by taking the last biscuit, and shoving it into his mouth, chewing loudly.

"You're collecting *body parts*?" I swallowed again. "For someone you don't even know?" My mouth hung open in shock and disgust for a moment. "Are the people . . . still alive?"

"No! We're not insane," Saifi laughed. "We're just body snatchers."

Lei whacked him on the arm. "We are not!"

"But you *are* stealing body parts," I pointed out.

Celeste rolled her eyes like I was being ridiculously uptight. "Not really stealing. More like rescuing and repurposing."

"Yeah," Saifi said around his food. "It's like that old game Operation."

"This isn't Operation." I clasped my hands together. "Operation was all puns. A wishbone and a charley horse. This is nothing like that. This is the scavenger hunt of a psychopath."

Jimmy shook his head. "Not really. Our Client is putting the body parts to use before they get thrown away. And we get to help with that."

I rubbed my eyebrow, trying to make sense of all this. "So he's running some kind of charity? Finding parts for those people who can't find them for themselves?"

Jimmy shrugged, looking at the table. "Maybe."

There were several charities that did that very thing, but I had never thought to wonder *how* the charities came upon the parts they needed. Surely any legitimate ones ran them through the hospitals.

"But what you're doing *is* illegal," I insisted.

Lei lifted her chin defensively. "It's the job. We don't ask questions. We just find what people ask for."

Yep. Super illegal. I sighed, annoyed.

I looked again at the tongue box on the table. "So, what am *I* doing here? Did you send the tongue to my address by mistake?"

Celeste shook her head. "We've never been assigned a tongue."

"And if the Client doesn't assign it, we don't collect it." Lei sniffed, like only a monster would run around pilfering body parts they *hadn't* been asked to collect.

"But then . . . how . . . why . . ." I wasn't even sure what my question was.

"The Client must have sent it to you," Celeste said.

"For some reason, he wants you here, so, consider yourself recruited."

A derisive laugh blew through my nose. "But I don't want to be recruited. Don't I get a say in this? Don't you?"

"Not usually," Lei said. "We do what he says and he pays us, end of story."

"Well, that's swell and all, but I'm going to have to respectfully decline. Give your client my apologies."

"Unfortunately, your opportunity to *decline* flew out the window when you opened that envelope." She eyed me as though to say I should have known better. "Until we know what the Client wants with you, you have to stay."

I ground my teeth. Reasoning with this woman was nearly impossible. I mentally compiled several excellent arguments and opened my mouth to tell her what was what.

Lei's phone played a little song, and she stood and held up a hand. I threw out my arms in frustration as she tapped the screen a few times then waited for it to load. The rain hammered and beat against the walls and roof, and a steady drip, drip, drip sounded from somewhere behind me. Lei leaned her hip against the yellow laminate countertop, arms crossed. Finally she exhaled, like everything made sense with the world once again, and looked up with a smile. "We have our next assignment."

7

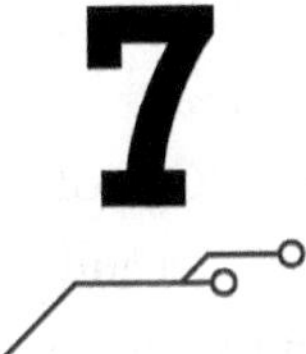

"**W**hat is it this time?"

"A toe."

"Which one?"

"Big toe. Right foot."

"Ooh, that's a good one."

Oh, great grundy, would this never end? "You took some guy's tongue, and now you're taking his big toe?"

"We didn't do the tongue," Lei said.

Saifi chuckled. "Not the same guy. Everything comes from a different person. And it's not like they need the parts anymore."

"You don't need your big toe when you're alive either, technically," Celeste said.

"I thought you needed your big toes for balance?" Jimmy said. "Like without them you might fall over?"

Celeste shook her head. "I knew someone that lost all his toes in a lawnmower accident. He could walk fine."

"And you have no idea why this client wants them? What he does with them?" I asked.

"Not our business." Lei's voice was curt.

"He's Frankensteining," Saifi said, waving his hand like that settled it.

"Stop it," Celeste moaned. "You can't just turn words into verbs like that."

"Of course I can!" Saifi leaned toward me conspiratorially. "It means he's building a *person*."

I leveled a look at him. "Out of a tongue and a toe?"

"*We didn't do the tongue!*" Lei and Celeste said together.

I held up my hands in surrender. I was listening, honestly, but my brain seemed to be rejecting ninety percent of what I heard.

Saifi shook his head, eyes wide with possibility. "We've done more parts than this. Next time we might get an arm!"

"But that's—you can't—mismatched body parts are never going to turn into a person!"

"You don't know," Saifi said under his breath, like I was taking all the fun out of things.

I folded my arms. "So . . . so . . . what, you're going to sneak into a hospital and cut off a corpse's toe?"

Lei gave me a funny look. "You've never lost anyone close to you, have you?"

I cleared my throat. "I was raised by my grandparents after my parents died when I was a baby. And my grandfather passed away when I was eight . . ." I trailed off under the weight of everyone's eyes. I coughed. "Why do you ask?"

Lei met my eyes and part of me felt like I was falling into a very deep hole. "Because as soon as someone is declared dead and their body found to be disease free, they're taken apart."

I knew that, of course, but she acted like it was the only way things were done. "But what if they aren't a donor?" I asked.

"*Everyone* is a donor," Celeste said.

"I'm not."

Jimmy's eyebrows shot up. "Really? How is that possible? I thought it was mandatory."

"You can opt out," Lei said. "But it's a lot of paperwork."

I nodded. "Absurd amounts of paperwork, along with fees and several blood tests, but if you're willing to cut through all the red tape, it *is* possible." I hadn't given it a lot of thought, but they were looking at me like my ears had detached and were flapping around my head.

"Blood tests? What would they want blood tests for?" Lei asked, incredulous.

"Why aren't you a donor?" Saifi asked.

I chewed on my cheek. "Not that it's any of your business, but I have a genetic disorder. Best to keep all my organs and body parts to myself."

Saifi looked like he was about to ask some follow up questions, but Lei silenced him with a wave.

"*Anyway*," she pushed on, "everyone *else* is a donor, and they don't waste time. If the death isn't part of an open investigation, and the deceased didn't have some kind of communicable disease, they harvest all usable parts and put the rest of the body in the queue for cremation."

"And that includes toes?"

"That includes *everything*. Anything that can be transplanted or reattached."

"My friend's dad has toes instead of thumbs," Saifi piped in. "He lost his thumbs in a table-saw accident. Two different table-saw accidents. They couldn't save his thumbs, so they gave him somebody's big toes instead. They must have been from donors."

I looked at him. "Why didn't they use *his* toes?"

Saifi shrugged.

I scratched my head. "I'm sure you all are the Robin Hood of Transplants, but what if this client of yours is *not* running a charity? What if you are taking these parts away from people that desperately need them?"

"We're not." Lei was emphatic. "The donation banks have plenty of parts, and a limited time that they're viable. Even with all the advancements they've made with storage, in a week these parts'll be disposed of. Dozens of organs and body parts are going to waste every day. Maybe hundreds."

Going to waste. A tepid rage flared inside of me. My grandfather had waited for a kidney for months, never finding a match. That was right before the laws had been changed making donation obligatory and then cremation had become the norm. The rain saturated the ground so much that only those graveyards at the highest elevations had survived the weather breaking down. Burial plots in graveyards were extremely hard to come by. I'd read about people burying deceased family members in their backyards to avoid cremation, only to have those same deceased family members wash up onto the back porch a few months later.

And now they were just throwing body parts away?

"That's horrible." There was more venom in my voice than I'd intended. Why hadn't anyone fixed this? "But you're still *thieves.*"

No one spoke. Because I was right, and they knew it.

Lei heaved a massive sigh and spread her arms. "You said it yourself. We're like Robin Hood. And the current regulations and bureaucracy are the Sheriff of Nottingham. Something has to be done. If not us, then who?"

We stared at each other for an endless moment.

Celeste flicked an annoyed glance my way. "Can we move on now?" She turned the laptop so it was facing us, an obituary on the screen.

Lei slapped the screen closed. "Are you *positive* you want to do this with him here? We could just lock him up somewhere until the Client tells us otherwise." She spoke softly, like I wouldn't be able to hear from three feet away.

Celeste snorted. "He's completely harmless," she said dismissively, like I was a cute little kitten. "Honestly, we're probably in more danger from Saifi than we are from this guy."

"Hey!" Saifi said. "*I'm* dangerous!"

I wanted to side with Saifi. I *was* harmless, but somehow when Celeste said it, it sounded like an insult.

"Seriously," Celeste pressed on. "He's a good employee, he doesn't break any laws. He doesn't really do anything at all. I watched video footage of him for the last month. He goes to work and then he goes home. That's it."

"Hey, you can't form a complete picture of someone's character by watching them on traffic cams. There is a lot more to me than that." I shouldn't be arguing with her. I wanted them to trust me so I could go home and this nightmare would end. But she made me sound so boring. My life was not as empty as she made it out to be. I was pretty active on several discussion boards she probably didn't know anything about.

Celeste pointed a thumb at me with a smile as though to say I was proving her point. "See? But if you don't want to chance it, I'm happy to drug him again."

Saifi waved a dismissive hand my way. "Nah, Cohen's good. I can tell."

Lei growled, then glared at me, reasserting her previous threat with her eyes. "Fine, whatever, let's just get this over with."

Celeste nodded, and tilted the screen back up so that we could all read it.

Grecia Suttles, of Vancouver, passed away today after a car accident involving several vehicles on Fremont Street. She was born April 9, 1976, to the late Harvey and Yolanda (Smith) Suttles. Grecia served in the US Army and then worked in Hotel Administration, pouring her heart and soul into everything she did. Her greatest pride was competing in the Olympics in Barcelona, where she ran hurdles. Her second greatest pride was her dog, Apollo. She is survived by her brother, Stan Suttles, and her nephew Marshall Suttles. Donations will be accepted in her behalf at—

Saifi looked mildly heartbroken. "That is so sad. What do you think happened to her dog?"

Everyone waited in sober silence for a few seconds, then Celeste flipped the laptop back around and started typing again.

"She died at OHSU Hospital. That was nice of her," she said.

I gave her a weird look. Jimmy saw my face and explained, "Because it's so close."

"Wait," I said. "Which one?"

Celeste sighed but didn't even look up. "The close one."

"The one they just built at the bottom of the hill," Jimmy added, checking his watch. "We can get there in twenty minutes, even with the rain."

"Yeah!" Saifi piped in proudly. "And Cesar works there!"

"No." Lei held up a finger at him. "We aren't going to see Cesar."

"Who's Cesar?" I asked.

Saifi waggled his eyebrows. "Lei's boyfriend."

"Ex," Lei said, glaring at Saifi. "And we're not going to see him. He cannot know about this job."

Saifi *hmphed* and Celeste gave Lei a patient look. "And how do you propose we get inside?"

"We'll figure something out."

"Like what? Check in at the front desk? 'Cuz those are your options: strolling through the front doors where we will have to sign in, or biometric scanners at the back."

"I'm aware of that," Lei spat. "Is there any way *my* finger-prints would still get us in?"

"Nope, and I will show you why." Celeste typed a few words and spun her laptop around so we could all see her screen again. "They upgraded to these handprint scanners six months ago, so unless we've got the hand from one of the current employees in a box somewhere, there's no way we're getting past it."

A picture of a wide flat handprint scanner with an orange case and the IDS Corp logo stamped in the corner filled the screen.

"Actually," I said, pointing at it, "those handprint scanners have a flaw. If you switch a couple of the wires around, you can press just about anything with a pulse against it, and it will let you through."

Everyone turned to me.

"We used to have those at GridLox. They short out all the time, so I found a workaround. Apparently, IDS Corp doesn't care about providing a quality product to their clients."

Celeste smiled.

"No," Lei said. "No way."

"We have to take him."

"Me?" I asked, alarmed. "No, thank you."

"See?" Lei said, gesturing toward me. "He's already told us what to do. Jimmy can do it."

Jimmy shrugged, wrinkling his nose and shaking his head

noncommittally. "Maybe, but it would take longer, and something might go wrong. This could be exactly why the Client sent him."

"I'm not going to help you break into a hospital," I said.

Celeste ignored me. "It would be stupid to go out into the field without all of the tools we have at our disposal. He's a tool. We should take him."

I raised my eyebrows. "Thanks, so much, for that."

"I really don't think we can do this without him," Jimmy said.

Lei swallowed, eyes hard. "And what if he won't come?"

"Maybe we just need to ask him nicely," Jimmy said.

The two women looked at him as though that would never have occurred to them, and then turned to me. They both stared at me but didn't speak. Celeste opened and closed her mouth a few times but didn't seem to know how to begin. She'd probably never asked for anything nicely before and wasn't sure how to do it.

Jimmy smiled and clasped his hands in front of him. "Cohen, we need your help. This is important. And your expertise could be a huge asset. Will you help us? Please?"

I groaned. "I'm sorry. But you're *still* criminals. I can't get involved. I have a life to get back to. A job with a deadline looming. Milk in the fridge. A plant that needs to be watered." It sounded so boring listed like that. Ugh, maybe Celeste was right about me. "I don't belong here. I'm a law-abiding citizen. I only have four—no *three* days to fix my demo code. I *can't* get involved."

Lei smiled in a devastated way, shrugging. "I told you so." She swallowed, the exaggerated movement of her throat looking almost painful. "We'll have to figure out something else."

"There *is* nothing else!" Celeste shouted, slamming her fist on the table.

Lei threw up her hands and stalked out of the room and up the stairs. Celeste glared at me. Was this supposed to be *my* fault?

I sighed, then pushed back from the table and followed her. Maybe now she'd return my phone. She'd made it clear she didn't want me here, and I'd made it clear that I wouldn't help. Seemed like the perfect time to part ways.

They called this floating house their base, but they seemed to live here, so I figured Lei probably had a room of her own upstairs. I wasn't sure which room was hers, but soft sounds came through the door standing ajar at the end of the hall. I made my way down and raised a fist to knock on the door, but a sound from inside stopped me.

Sniffling?

I peeked inside without meaning to. Lei sat on the floor, back pressed against the wall with her knees pulled up to her chest, staring sightlessly ahead of her. Not crying, but breathing shakily, swallowing with effort, face white. She looked . . . *terrified*. This strong, angry, suspicious woman was *terrified*? She flexed and curled her fingers several times then clasped them, as though holding on for dear life.

I stepped back, shaken. If she was that scared, how much trouble were they in?

Exhaling, I knocked softly on the door and waited. Shuffling sounds came from inside and then Lei appeared in front of me, yanking the door wide.

"What do you want?" she demanded, all signs of fear and vulnerability almost completely gone.

"What is your arrangement with him? This client of yours?" I asked, voice gentle.

She lowered her eyebrows, confused, like that wasn't the question she'd expected. "I'm not at liberty to say."

I leaned closer, lowering my voice. "Are you in trouble?"

"No." Her voice was adamant. Too adamant. "We're not in trouble. It's just a job. A very high-paying job and it is essential that we finish it, no matter what."

"Is there a contract? Can you walk away if you decide it's too dangerous?" I'd only been there half an hour and I could already tell it was *way* too dangerous.

"Yes, there's a contract. A legally binding one. So the Client may call the shots, but as long as we stick to the contract, he will pay us. Nothing can get in the way of that."

Unless he'd written a loophole that screwed them over in the end. Which meant they probably *were* in trouble. And Lei seemed very determined not to admit it, especially to herself.

I exhaled slowly, rubbing my face.

I was going to regret this.

"I will help you with this *one* assignment," I said, already wishing I hadn't. "But then you are returning my phone and I'm leaving. You and your client and his *repurposing project* be hanged. I won't cause any trouble for you, but I cannot stay here."

Lei glared at me. "I don't want or need your charity."

"Yes, you do. Both Celeste and Jimmy said you can't do this without me. And now I'm offering. And then I'll leave, and you'll finally be rid of me."

She stared at me, mouth knotted up in deliberation. "Okay. Just this one job. We will, of course, cut you in for your fair share, you have my word."

"I don't want the money."

"Too bad. Cuz I'm not the thief that you think I am. You help, you get paid. Period."

She squared her shoulders and pushed past me into the hall, all hints of distress left behind in her bedroom. I followed her back downstairs to where the others still sat at the kitchen table, Saifi trying to balance a stack of plastic cups on Jimmy's head.

"Good news," Lei said. "Cohen has deigned to help us get into the hospital. We're leaving in fifteen minutes."

Jimmy grinned at me, and Saifi gave me a thumbs up. Celeste pointed at me with a smile, as though once again I'd done exactly as she expected.

What Lei had said sank in. "What, now? You're kidding." Surely they were talking about going in the morning, after everyone had rested and the rain was over. We'd *just* gotten back. We were still wet. Right now was stupid.

"I'm really not."

"But it's eleven o'clock at night."

"Are you tired?"

"Well, no, but . . ."

"See? Aren't you glad you had a nap?"

"You drugged me!"

Celeste laughed softly and waved her hand dismissively. "*Pfft.* It was only a mild sedative. You should feel lucky. That one is really hard to come by." She narrowed her eyes at me. "And I always keep some on hand. Just in case."

"But what about Saifi? You aren't taking him back out into the rain, are you?"

"I'm not staying behind!"

"This is crazy. Why not just go in the morning?"

"We can't be seen. The rain is the perfect cover," Lei said unequivocally. "Any other questions?"

I growled in frustration. I had a billion questions. But one seemed more important than the rest. "What is the plan?"

Lei looked at me like she didn't understand the word.

"The plan. The course of action. You can't just run out into the rain without a plan."

She half smiled at me. "Celeste already said. We're going to OHSU Hospital. Easy peasy."

"That isn't a plan."

"Then what would *you* call it?" She actually seemed amused. How she could be amused when I was being so logical was a complete mystery.

"It's more of a suggestion. A goal."

She smiled. "Good enough for me."

"But if you would listen—"

"I appreciate that you care, Mr. Smarty Pants, but we know what we're doing. We got by just fine before you showed up, and we'll get by just fine long after you're gone."

I sighed.

"Alright, everybody," Lei grabbed her stuff and waved us out of the room, "get your wet gear on. We're going back out."

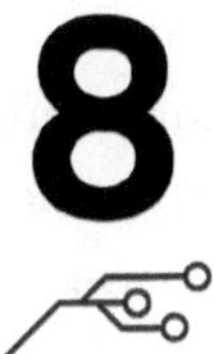

8

At least this time I wasn't wearing garbage bags and duct tape. Lei and her crew had a decent store of wet-weather gear and I'd sorted through it until I found what I needed. The boots I'd chosen were a bit tight in the toes, but they stretched and fit to my legs so that I could walk easily enough. I cinched the rain-coat tight around my face and wrists and pulled the zipper all the way up to my chin. It was a step up from garbage bags, but I still felt like a hand-me-down Navy SEAL.

When I went to grab the first aid kit out of my briefcase, my heart sank right to the bottom of the river. I'd left my briefcase in the mannequin warehouse. I kept *everything* in there; I'd sooner have left my arm behind. I patted myself down to see what I had on me, but found only my small flashlight, my multi-tool, and the diagnostic report I'd shoved in my pocket in the cab. That was something at least. As soon as I had a free minute, I could go over it and hopefully make some progress on the demo bug and get some actual work done.

After a long debate, Lei and Celeste agreed that OHSU Hospital was close enough to get to on foot. We still wore our helmets so our heads and necks wouldn't have to take the brunt of the water pressure alone, but the downpour seemed even more violent on foot. My tall rubber boots gripped the wet sidewalks and kept my legs dry as we ran through puddles that went up to my knees. We splashed from house to house, taking refuge under porches to give ourselves respite. We didn't bother being quiet. Even if anyone inside the homes did hear us, they would never be able to distinguish our sounds from the beating of the rain on their roofs.

My morning workout suddenly seemed woefully inadequate. We were running in short, desperate dashes in rain that pounded us so hard it was like jogging through a boxing ring. Just keeping on the move was exhausting, and I was finding it difficult to keep up. We stood on a saggy porch lined with drip-tip plants, water cascading down them like a fountain. I leaned on my knees to catch my breath. Jimmy fell into the porch swing, but Celeste and Lei stood, winded, but holding together far better than I was. The surrounding trees were like swamp monsters in the wet dark, waving and writhing in the downpour.

"How close are we to OHSU again?" I asked as loud as I could, each word sandwiched in a gasp.

"We just have to cross the bridge," Lei yelled back to me.

"Over the Willamette?" My voice rose in dismay.

"Do you have another river you'd like to cross tonight?"

She turned away, not waiting for an answer, which was just as well because I didn't have one. There was no cover on Ross Island Bridge. It would be almost three-quarters of a mile of us running in the wide open, pummeled and beat by the rain. We would never be able to make it that far.

"There has to be another way!" I yelled.

The rain seemed to pick up at that moment, and the noise of it drowned out my voice. Lei turned again and took off into the rain.

We ran after her. The darkness and the blindness of the water falling from the sky coalesced into the frames and beams of Ross Island Bridge. I slowed, trying to get a handle on the size of it and how long it would take to cross, and almost missed the others turning off and running down the hill.

I followed, afraid that they were all going to slip straight into the Willamette, but then they dodged under the bridge and out of sight.

The muted sound of the rain beneath the bridge felt like I'd shoved cotton in my ears. Bulkhead lights along the underside of the bridge cast everything in a dim orange glow. A walkway ran between the support beams, and we followed Celeste across it in single file. I clutched the cables set up as handrails, wanting to be sure I kept my feet beneath me.

Lei ushered Jimmy and Saifi ahead of her and I scrambled to catch up to her.

"Crossing the river *under* the bridge, huh?" I gasped. "Clever."

"Hard to believe, I know. I'm glad we could surprise you."

"No, you didn't surprise me, I just . . ." I didn't know how to finish that sentence. I didn't really know what to say at all, I just wanted to keep talking to drown out the sound of the churning water of the Willamette as it rushed and thrashed beneath us.

I heard a voice to my left and turned. In the shadows I could just make out several groups of people perched up in the beams, a few extra boards tucked beneath them for support: eating, talking, sleeping. Lei raised a hand in a silent salute, and one of the figures saluted back.

Our steps echoed against the solid surface above us, like we were being followed by an endless army of ourselves. Lei's eyes were on the path in front of her, alternating her gaze between the walkway at her feet, and Jimmy, Saifi, and Celeste, ensuring that they too kept their footing. She seemed to see everything. She walked with so much confidence and command: as though she were in her element here. The reverberating sound of our footsteps seemed to crescendo and I spun, sure that what I heard was more than just echoes—

There was nothing there but shadows that stretched and danced, creeping along behind us.

"Hey, Lei!" Saifi turned to face us, walking backward along the catwalk. "There's an entrance to the Shanghai Tunnels not too far from here. We should explore it on our way back."

I snorted. He was joking, right? The Shanghai Tunnels were a network of tunnels and catacombs that ran beneath the oldest parts of Portland, steeped in legends and myths. People said hobos and tramps were abducted and taken through the tunnels to ships waiting at port, to spend the rest of their lives serving as sailors.

Lei rolled her eyes. "You're never going to let that go, are you? They're flooded, just like everything else."

"Even before they flooded, most of it collapsed or was filled in," I added.

Saifi smiled persuasively. "Maybe, but how will we know for sure if we don't check it out?"

Lei sighed. "Someday," she said at last. "*Possibly*. When we aren't on a job."

Saifi grinned, satisfied for the time being, and ran to join Jimmy. Yep. He was just like Peter. Willing to take risks, confident in his own immortality. Reckless.

We were nearing the other side. The transition from the bridge to the sidewalk that led back up to the road looked like it might be tricky. Not wanting to leave anything to chance, I pushed carefully past everyone so that I could help them off the struts and beams and down onto the very wet concrete.

I reached for Celeste, but she didn't even look at me, instead stretching her long legs across the gap with more ease than I had. Jimmy, on the other hand, grinned. He grabbed my hand and jumped, landing with both feet on the pavement beside me. He clapped me on the back good-naturedly and moved beside me, then took Saifi's other hand as the both of us helped him cross safely.

When I held out my hand to Lei, she shook her head, but it was more in disbelief than refusal. She took my hand, and I pulled her across, where she landed right in front of me, momentum carrying her forward until we collided. She looked up at me, dark eyes shining in the orange light.

I cleared my throat. "After you." I stepped back to let her pass.

As I stepped, the corner of concrete beneath my feet gave way and took me with it. I slipped, landing on my back in the mud and sliding down the steep riverbank with the rain. I threw my arms out to slow myself down, to drag on anything that I could, but the wet runoff was thick with mud, and only the fact that we were still beneath the cover of the bridge kept me from washing straight into the river like a drip down a drain.

I yelled, scrambling, scraping at the ground, grabbing at cattails, but they slipped under my fingers. The raging river waited beneath me, ready to swallow me whole as I thrashed, flopping like a fish, spinning in the mud until I thudded bum first into a bridge support beam. It hurt like the devil. I grabbed it and hugged it with all my might. "Thank you. Thank you, thank you."

Lei, Celeste, Saifi, and Jimmy stood at the top of the bank, yelling, and pointing, hustling back and forth. Lei pulled a rope out of her duffle and tossed one end to Jimmy, who wrapped it around a beam and tied it off with impressive speed. A loop at the end of a rope landed next to me, and I managed to pull it over my head and arms so that it wrapped around my chest. Then I gripped the rope tightly while they pulled me up and up and up, water and mud sliding past me as they dragged me up through the muck. I finally reached the concrete and heaved myself onto it.

"Did you have to be so heavy?" Saifi panted.

Gasping for air, I held up an apologetic hand. "Sorry. Thanks for saving me. All of you. Thank you. Sorry." I hugged the concrete beneath me, finally sure that I wasn't going to end up in the river, still whispering thanks and apologies.

Jimmy pulled me to my feet—he really was stronger than he looked—and grinned. "No problem. But this is the last time I'm carrying your butt anywhere tonight, got it?"

I nodded. I wanted to stop right then. To stay there and catch my breath. I was more mud than man. But as soon as it was clear that I wasn't about to go toppling down the riverbank again, everyone took off running, and the only option I had was to pick up my feet and limp after them.

—o

The hospital loomed out of the rain like a massive ocean liner pulling into port. Lei led us through the covered parking structure and around to the employee entrance in the back. We paused by a raised flower bed overflowing with daylilies that had closed up for the night, and Saifi reached inside it and grabbed a couple of rocks. He pitched them one after another toward the lights on either side of the door. Both rocks found their mark, and we were plunged into darkness.

"Whoa," I said, impressed. The destruction of hospital property was scandalous, but I was impressed nonetheless. I doubted I could take out a light with a rock in the rain in *ten* shots, let alone one.

We ran up to the entrance and out of the rain where we were finally able to remove our helmets. I tried to catch my breath, but it was like trying to breathe deeply while drowning. And somehow, though it felt like the entire contents of the ocean had been dropped on us, I was still half covered with mud. After a moment I realized someone was standing in front of me.

"Are you okay?" Lei asked, looking genuinely concerned.

I held up my hand. "I'm fine." My breath was still coming in gasps. "But I can't believe you brought Saifi out into this. He could have died."

"He did better than you," Celeste muttered as she walked past.

Lei took my helmet and shoved it into her bag. "Come on. You're up."

Jimmy was shaking out his afro and it poufed in a dark halo around his head. Celeste's white braid fell in a heavy rope down her back, and it seemed in that moment that, had she wanted to, she could have used her hair like a weapon.

I limped up to the door, my backside sore after its run-in with the bridge beam. The handprint scanner attached to the wall was the exact model we had used at GridLox before we'd discovered that it was complete garbage. I pulled out the screwdriver on my multi-tool and popped the cover off, then switched the wires around like I'd done a hundred times before. My fingers were clumsy fiddling through the gloves, but I managed it in the end. I turned back to Lei.

"That's it?" she asked.

"Yep, just about any skin will work now, but it might not be wise to leave your fingerprints all over it."

Jimmy grinned. "I have an idea." He took Saifi by the head and pressed his cheek against the scanner. The door popped open with a clunk.

Saifi tipped his head modestly and patted his cheeks. "I always knew that this face could open doors."

The hum of the generators through the empty hallways was the only sound to greet us as we filed inside. The ceiling lights had a greenish tint and seemed to cast more shadows than other lights did. Lei led us down a hall to our left, and we followed her as it branched and bent. We kept our hoods up and our chins down and avoided all cameras as much as possible.

We passed administration offices and artwork of large abstract flowers. A man in scrubs and a lab coat turned a corner and headed our way. My heart started pounding, but no one else paused. Lei nodded at him as he passed. He nodded back, barely glancing our way.

I tried to focus on the route we took as we walked down some stairs, through another hall and down to the very end where we stopped in front of a hefty, metal door.

"Where are we?"

Celeste pointed lazily toward the sign helpfully hung on the wall next to the door reading "Morgue," then opened the door and gestured us inside.

Metal cabinets and drawers lined the walls, and a row of

stainless-steel tables ran down the middle, which I had to assume were used for autopsy and body part harvesting. A desk with a couple of computers on it was tucked inside a wood-paneled nook.

Celeste sat down at the desk, the office chair backward, and rested her arms on the chair back. She typed and clicked for a minute while we waited. It was freezing in there. All of my wet places were becoming frozen places. My hair felt like a dripping crown of ice.

"Do you mind?" Celeste snapped, not turning around. "This is hard enough without the whistling."

The rest of us looked at each other confused. But then I heard it too. Whistling. From the hallway outside the door. Someone was headed this way.

9

$\mathbf{L}$ei drew herself up, like a bear making itself appear bigger, and stepped forward, putting herself between the door and the rest of us. Everyone else jumped into a fighting stance, and my heart surprised me by twisting up into an affectionate knot at the sight of that scrappy gang of body snatchers.

The door flew open and a doctor with dark silky hair and darker eyes strolled through, whistling and looking at his phone.

"Cesar!" Saifi yelled.

The man, who I could only assume was Cesar, lifted his head in surprise. No one moved for half a breath and then Cesar grabbed Lei by the shoulders and hugged her, resting his head against hers and closing his eyes. Lei chewed her lip, not meeting anyone's eyes as we stood and waited for the longest hug in the history of hospitals. Saifi dove in part way through, wrapping his arms around both of them, smiling contentedly.

"Okay, Cesar, geez." Lei pushed him away. He grinned unabashedly at her, then nodded at Celeste.

He held a hand toward Jimmy. "Hey, Jimmy man. How's it going?"

Jimmy jumped over and the two men performed a complicated handshake. Jimmy grinned. Then Saifi dove in for another hug and we waited again.

Cesar patted Saifi's back. "So, what brings you all here?" he asked, like he'd run into us at the grocery store.

Lei still had that deer-in-the-headlights look. She finally opened her mouth. "Uh . . ."

"Are you on a job?" He sounded excited. "You *are*, aren't you? What is it this time? More medical records?"

Saifi was grinning happily, looking between the two of them. His expression seemed impatient for Lei to spill the beans.

Lei exhaled loudly and pursed her lips. "Would you accept it if I said I couldn't tell you?"

Cesar *tsked*, waving dismissively. "*Venga*, you know you can tell me. I'm your guy on the inside. Whatever you're looking for, I can get it."

Lei shook her head. "Not this time, I'm sorry. Our Client is . . . particular. And weird. We're in trouble just for talking to you."

"Ah, clients don't bother me." He shook his head, smirking like this was all a big joke. "Let me talk to him, I'm sure I can change his mind."

I watched this exchange with growing annoyance. Celeste, Jimmy, and Saifi, however, all acted like this was a conversation they'd heard many times before.

Lei clenched her jaw and took Cesar by the hands, squeezing them like it could make him listen. "Cesar, I'm serious. I *can't*," she said slowly, though I doubted it was slow enough to get through his shiny hair. "If you really want to help, just . . . make sure no one else comes in this room for the next half hour, okay?"

Cesar seemed to be on the verge of arguing further, then nodded. He looked crestfallen but shook it off and looked around at the rest of us again. "How did you get so muddy?"

Lei exhaled, tipping her head toward me. "*Smarty Pants* over here tried to jump into the Willamette, and we had a hard time talking him out of it."

Cesar turned toward me, hand out. "Cesar Maldonado, at your service."

"Smarty Pants," I said, grabbing his hand. I was gratified that he had to look up to meet my eye, and I shook his hand a little more firmly than necessary.

He smiled. It was so charming I wanted to punch him. "Nice to meet you, Mr. Pants. Jumping in the river is a bad idea, you know. That's a lot of water right there." He smacked me on the shoulder, then looked around. "Well, carry on. I only came for this." He picked up a water bottle from the desk and wiggled it back and forth. "I gotta tell you, it is so good to see a friendly face. Mind if I hang out while you work?"

"Cesar," Lei snarled, looking vaguely murderous.

Cesar held up his hands in defeat. "*Me rindo*. It's just so good to see you again, you know? I will go and leave you with your secrets. I can take a hint."

I snorted, but the sound came out much louder than I'd intended. I covered it with a cough that turned real and went on far too long.

Cesar slapped me on the back, then sauntered out of the room, bidding us goodbye with a small salute. Saifi ran after him, grabbing him for one last hug.

When Cesar had gone, Celeste turned back to the monitor, then scrawled something on a sticky note and passed it to Lei. "Here's the serial number we're looking for. *Aaand*, there is a memo in here saying they are having generator problems at the storage facility in Vancouver, so they sent their entire stock of donation items here yesterday."

"Of course they did," Lei moaned.

Lei walked over to the wall and, after looking it over for a second, opened a stainless-steel door and slid out a drawer. Plexiglass dividers separated the drawer into a grid of compartments. About half of them contained what I had to assume were toes in small plastic bags, each carefully labeled with a barcode and serial number and placed in their own compartment. But next to those sat a pile of bagged and labeled toes in a haphazard heap, like someone had decided halfway through that organization was pointless. Philistine.

Jimmy groaned, "It's never easy, is it?"

With Jimmy and Saifi's help, the two of them withdrew the drawer completely and set it on the table in the center of the room. Everyone gathered around the table. Except me: it was covered with toes.

"Come on, Hoard," Lei said, glancing at me. "We've got to find the right toe, and the quicker we do it, the better."

I took a few steps nearer the table. "Why are they all separate like this? What if someone loses their whole foot? All these toes aren't going to help them all that much."

"There are feet too," Lei said absently. "They're stored in a different drawer."

The idea of a drawer full of feet bothered me even more than the toes. "Does it really matter which toe we take?" I tried to see them as parts, and not think about where they'd come from, like chicken wings. "Would your Client even know if you sent him the wrong one? Aren't all toes pretty much the same?"

"Actually, they're quite distinctive," Lei said, holding up two toes and comparing them. "Just like the people they came from; all the little things add up to something unique. But even if they weren't," Lei said, looking at me pointedly, "we need the right toe."

A shiver ran through me, though I couldn't tell if it was from the job or how wet and cold I was.

I pulled up a stool and forced myself to sit, the rubber of my pants squeaking against the metal surface. I jumped back up with a small cry of pain, smiling wanly at everyone's alarmed faces and rubbed my sore backside. That metal beam might have saved me from the river, but it had come at a cost. Sitting down was going to be painful for a while.

Lei pulled out a section of dividers and passed the tray to me, along with a copy of the serial number. She picked up another toe, checked the serial number and set it aside.

"Can't we use this barcode?" I asked. "Scan them all instead of checking the number manually."

"No," Celeste said. "It doesn't include that kind of information. They only use them for tracking purposes as they travel from place to place."

"Well, that's useless."

"Suck it up," Lei said. "It's time to toe the line."

My eyes snapped to hers. She gazed innocently back at me. Jimmy snorted.

I picked up a bag, forcing myself to forget what was inside and focus on the label instead. "I don't know how you are so cool right now. This whole thing makes my toes curl."

Celeste groaned. "Are we really gonna do this?"

"Yes," Lei said, "we are. Because we've gotta stay sharp. This is a tough line of work. And puns help keep me on my toes."

"You're telling me!" Jimmy said. "You jump down my throat

if I even put one toe out of line." He smiled apologetically at her, but she was laughing.

"I can't think of anything!" Saifi said. "Something about going toe to toe?"

We continued to sort through the pile of bags, and Lei was right; toes *were* distinctive. Some were small and narrow, some large and bulbous. Some had long gnarly toenails, some were ingrown, and others looked like their toenails had been chewed down to the quick. It was like a *Goldilocks and the Three Bears* situation for a cannibal. I was both disgusted and fascinated. And then I spotted the numbers I was looking for.

"I don't want to step on anyone's toes, but I think I found it!" I said, raising the toe aloft, then passed it to Lei.

She double-checked the number and stood up. "This is it!"

Lei and Jimmy packed the toe carefully in an insulated medical specimen donor case filled with a blue, viscous substance.

"What's that?" I asked, curious.

"Freezing body parts damages them, causing ice crystals to form that rupture the cell," Jimmy said. "They store them here just above freezing, but we use this preservative antifreeze for transportation. It allows the parts to be ultra-cold, but prevents the formation of ice crystals."

I nodded, impressed. "So why wasn't the tongue sent in a gel like that?"

Lei pasted a placid smile on her face and spoke in a sugary sweet voice. "It's hard to say, because—and I cannot emphasize this enough—*we didn't do the tongue!*"

I cleared my throat uncomfortably as Lei turned away. She took the SMax label Celeste handed her and stuck it on the shipping box. Then we headed out toward the receiving bay. The rain was still falling, steady and sure, hammering on the roof and echoing off the walls around us.

Out on the loading dock, Lei carried the small package over to the SMax drop box where a bright orange Out-of-Service sign covered the front. "No!" Lei cried.

"It's all right," I said, my voice consoling. "They'll still check it when they come by for their deliveries in the morning."

"We can't wait till then. It has to ship *now.*"

"SMax doesn't do deliveries in the rain."

"Oh, Hoard. Are you really this clueless?"

Apparently, I was. But the weather was *broken.* It had been devastating when it happened, but we'd adapted, after a fashion. Auto Save features were required for vehicle registration, which prevented cars from driving at night, and as far as I'd ever known, when the sun went down and the clouds rolled in, the whole world went inside and stayed there until morning. I was still trying to wrap my brain around the idea that that wasn't so, that people rode through the rain for fun, and . . . that SMax did deliveries all night long? It was like finding out that I'd been wearing my pants backward my entire life.

Jimmy had his phone out, typing and swiping, and then he held it up. "There's another SMax drop off on Gaines Street. It's only a few blocks from here." He showed his phone to Lei, who traced the route with her finger.

"Okay. That's probably our best option."

Everyone started replacing gloves and pulling on helmets. I tried to take plenty of deep breaths, but I knew it wouldn't make any difference. I surveyed the rainy world we were about to run into, and my eyes caught on a shadow. A discoloration, really. Something in my line of sight that didn't seem like it should be there.

It was probably a tree. A very tall shrub, perhaps. Except that it didn't move like a tree. It didn't wave or sway but stood tall and straight. And as I watched, I could swear that it shifted, one step to the left.

"Hoard!"

I spun, startled.

Lei was staring at me impatiently. "Wake up. We gotta go."

I turned back, but I couldn't find the shadow anywhere. In all that rain, I wasn't sure where it had been before, and couldn't find anything out of place in the blur of the scenery.

I checked on Saifi to be sure that his helmet was tight under his chin, then I made sure the collar of his jacket was tucked up inside it to keep rain from running down his neck. When I was satisfied that he was as protected as he could be, I patted his helmet.

Saifi smiled patiently at me, like I was a child figuring out how to tie my own shoes. "You know how to do yours now? You need any help?"

"No, I . . ." I smiled. "Uh, no. I think I'm good."

Luckily, this stretch wasn't as far as the last one, but I was still exhausted by the time we arrived. McClaren Boulevard was completely flooded, and we'd decided to go an extra block out of our way rather than swim it. Now we huddled next to the SMax drop box under the covered porch of the Less U Than B4 Weight Loss Clinic. Lei slid the box inside and the sign flipped from "Ready" to "Waiting." The clock on it showing the time was almost three in the morning. I thought we might leave then, but Lei didn't want to go anywhere until the package was in the hands of the SMax guy.

I tried to dry my face, but every part of me was too wet, so I gave up. We stood in silence, resting against the brick wall behind us and trying to catch our breath.

As I stared, exhausted, out into the night, shapes started to form in the rain again, like static on an old screen. I watched them without really seeing, my eyes unfocused, my mind wandering. My brain seemed determined to reconcile this new world I found myself in with the sanity and monotony of my regular life. Nothing about any of this made sense, least of all Lei. She was part mercenary, part incompetent babysitter, and part mob boss. Her complexity was shorting out my brain.

I started to doze off, so I didn't register what was happening as Saifi peeled himself off the brick wall we rested against and tore straight out into the street.

At the same moment, a hydrocyclist careened around the corner and straight toward us. He saw Saifi in front of him in time to brake and swerve, his wheels skidding along the pavement, shooting an arc of water through the air. Saifi turned and dodged, but the cyclist's helmet connected with Saifi's arm with a clunk I heard even over the thrum of the rain. His arm bent and flopped in slow motion, as though it had suddenly developed several new joints. Saifi spun in a full circle and then dropped, slapping onto the pavement with a splash.

10

I was stunned into stillness. My chest felt like it was caving in on itself as Saifi lay motionless on the pavement, battered with rain. The worst had happened, just like it always did. Just like I'd known it would.

Lei and Jimmy ran to Saifi. The cyclist stopped, aimed his hydrocycle toward the landing where we stood, and in one swift movement, rode up the stairs and jumped off. He had a SMax logo stamped across his helmet and wore a full hydrophobic face mask. I braced myself and followed Lei and Jimmy, with Celeste and the SMax rider on my heels.

Saifi stirred and shifted, trying to raise his head. I was so relieved my legs nearly gave out. I wanted to hug him, but the others reached him first.

"Saifi, you idiot, what do you think you're doing?" Celeste cried, but Lei silenced her with a wave.

"We've got to get him out of the rain!" she shouted.

"Dude," the SMax cyclist yelled, flipping up his face mask, "He came out of nowhere. You saw that, right? He jumped right in front of me."

Saifi tried to sit up but couldn't quite manage it. "It's my arm," he moaned, soft enough I wasn't sure I heard him, his face contorted in pain.

"Is that all?" Lei insisted. "Are you sure?"

Saifi nodded, and we slowly helped him to his feet.

The SMax rider sidled along next to us as we walked Saifi onto the porch and out of the pouring rain. The raindrops didn't even seem to touch him, like his whole suit was water repellent. "Is he all right then? I can't have any more marks on my record or I'm gonna lose my job. Do you think he'll be okay? He really came out of nowhere. I only came for a pickup."

Lei waved him away. "It's fine. We got this. The package is in the drop box. You can go."

Without hesitating, the SMax rider crossed to the drop box and retrieved the toe. "Are you sure? You guys really gonna be all right?" He walked while he spoke, slipping the box into the waterproof bag slung across his shoulder. I memorized the ID number stamped across his helmet, just in case, but made no move to stop him as he climbed on his hydrocycle, deftly maneuvered it into a three-point turn, then rode down the stairs and back into the rain.

Lei focused on Saifi, carefully prodding his shoulder and arm. When she reached his elbow, he drew in a sharp breath.

"*Argh*," she growled. "It might be broken, but I can't tell anything through this rain suit. You're going to have to take it off."

Jimmy worked to help him get the jacket off, but it was slow and looked painful. I hovered nearby, trying to help, but mostly being in the way. Sometimes I hated being right. Saifi should not have been there. He was only a kid. This rain and this nighttime excursion were no place for him. At least it was only his arm; it could have been so much worse. Next time it might be. These people were just a fatality waiting to happen.

Lei watched Saifi, features sculpted in concern, then yanked me away from them and shoved me with both hands.

I stumbled back against the door behind me. "Hey!"

"This is all your fault." She kept one sharp finger pointed into my chest, channeling all her anger into it.

"*My* fault? How could this be *my* fault?"

"We've never had an accident before. Never. Then you show up and Saifi gets hit? Are you telling me that's a coincidence? I should have just let Celeste drug you!"

I drew myself up and wiped some water uselessly out of my face. "You were the one that begged me to come along, remember? If you had listened to me, none of this would have happened. We could have waited until tomorrow and we'd all be safe in bed right now. You can't run headlong into every danger-ous situation that presents itself. If you would take a little time to plan and prepare and stop taking chances, you could make it through this with a modicum of injury."

Lei looked angry enough to strangle me and I swear a little steam came shooting out of her ears.

"*Ahem*," Celeste said, in a slow exaggerated tone.

Saifi had finally managed to slip his arm out of his jacket, and he stood flanked by Celeste and Jimmy. Lei stalked over to Saifi and pulled up the sleeve of his shirt to get a better look at his elbow in the dim, damp light. His arm looked deformed, an odd twist at the elbow.

She swallowed visibly, her mouth tight with worry. "I think it's dislocated."

"Good," Celeste exhaled, looking relieved. "Fix it so we can go."

Saifi gasped in pain as Lei inspected it one more time.

"I've never done an elbow before. What if it's broken? I can't be sure without an x-ray." She looked up at us, eyes wide. "But the angle of the joint feels all wrong. I hope it's only dislocated, but I don't really know." She seemed so scared and unsure that I wanted to hug her, though it probably would have gotten me punched.

I walked over. "You want me to look at it?"

Celeste laughed right out loud, but Lei raised her arms in a huge, helpless shrug. "By all means." She sounded frustrated and annoyed, but she moved back so that I could get closer.

I felt Saifi's elbow as gingerly as I could, though he flinched away. It was dislocated, all right. It had been years since I'd done an elbow reduction, but I was confident I still remembered how.

"Let's get him over to the bench." The low stone bench against the wall was close enough to the edge of the porch that it got a fair amount of spray, but I needed him prone if I was going to do this right.

Saifi whimpered and shivered, but limped toward the bench with the help of Jimmy and me.

"Did you hurt your leg too?" I asked.

A pause. "No."

"Why are you limping?"

"Because I hurt my arm really bad."

"I know, but you're going to be fine, I promise. Just lay here, face down, with your arm hanging over the edge. Slide over a little more so your shoulder is up on the bench too."

He moaned with every movement, but soon he was where I needed him.

"Okay, Lei, you come here and hold his wrist, and Celeste and Jimmy come over and hold on to him. He's going to need support. Hug him if he needs it." I looked them both in the eye pointedly. Jimmy grimaced and Celeste closed her eyes, but they both nodded. They were going to have to hold him down if he tried to pull away, and he *would* try to pull away. They gathered around him, hands on his arms and back.

"Are you sure you know what you're doing?" Lei asked.

I pointed at Saifi's arm. "Lei, just pull his arm straight down here, and I'll guide the bone back into place. Keep pulling until we've got it in. You'll be able to tell." Her face was pale and tight with worry, but after a moment she nodded.

"Saifi, buddy, this is going to hurt. But just for a second or two and then it'll be over, and you'll feel a hundred times better. Okay? Are you ready?"

Saifi nodded, breathing in short, quick gasps.

I tipped my head to Lei, and she pulled. Saifi screamed and tried to pull away, but Celeste and Jimmy held him as still as they could. I pushed firmly on the ulna until it shifted back into place with a slightly sickening clunk. Saifi passed out, his eyes fluttering closed.

Everyone sat back, breathing hard. My insides were writhing like water in the Willamette, but I'd done it. Just like the old days. Feelings I'd buried deep inside tried to crawl back up for air, but I shoved them away.

"So," Jimmy said, hesitantly, "is he okay?"

I sucked in through my teeth. "He probably needs an x-ray to be sure there isn't a fracture, but for the moment, yes, he should be fine. We'll need to wrap the arm to keep him from using it for now, and he'll need a sling, eventually. I assume you have one back at base?"

Celeste stood, breathing hard, facing away from us while Jimmy patted Saifi's back. Lei stared at me. I nodded simply, but she continued to stare until I had to look away. I stood, putting some distance between us, walking to the edge of the covered porch where there was a bit more oxygen.

She followed and stood right in front of me, her eyes trained on mine. "How did you know how to do that?" She stood so close I could see faint freckles sprinkled across her cheeks.

I couldn't read this woman. Well, I couldn't read any woman, but this one seemed to be written in especially invisible ink. Was she grateful, or was she about to punch me?

I shrugged, trying to be casual. "I do know basic first aid."

She pursed her lips. "That was hardly basic."

I blew out a breath. "I have some . . . experience with injuries of that sort. It was only logical for me to learn how to deal with them." I turned away, hoping that answer would satisfy her, but she turned with me.

"What sort of experience?"

I finally looked at her again. She seemed like she was ready to wait until the rain went home if that was how long it took for me to answer. It was warm in her presence, like the heat radiated off her in spite of the rain. It drew me in, made me want to stand even closer.

I exhaled, trying to clear my ridiculous mind. "I used to ride," I said. "Race, actually. Mountain bikes. A lifetime ago. Sometimes there were accidents, and we had to be prepared." I swallowed so loudly you could hear it over the rain and went on before she got any ideas. "One accident was bad. Really bad. So . . . I had to stop."

She kept looking at me. Like I had the whole story written out in small print across my face and she was reading it, one painful word at a time. She narrowed her eyes. "And you haven't ridden since?"

I shook my head.

"But maybe you could. You'll never know if you don't try. Think how much faster our trip here could have been if we'd been on our bikes instead of on foot."

I was really going to regret telling her. Everyone always wanted me to get back on the horse. And it was always the same argument. *You'll never know if you don't try.* Except I did know. I knew more than I wanted to. "Weren't you listening? I was a kid! It's been *years*. I'm not sure I even remember how to ride anymore."

Her mouth tipped into the tiniest smile. "I'm pretty sure bicycle riding is one of those things you always remember. It is literally the example they use of things people never forget."

Her tone had turned playful, and I smiled slightly and turned away, glad we were done talking about it, hoping she'd focus on someone else now and let me think.

Rain poured off the eaves of the building like a giant bucket had been upturned in the sky. I'd never spent this much time in the rain. Sure, there was the occasional night when I'd worked late and the rain had begun without me realizing it, forcing me into a mad dash home before the downpour got too strong. Every day there was another story about some drunk, drug addict, kid on a dare who stayed out in the rain too long and drowned.

Yet here I was. Out in the rain. Not drowned. I'd been in it most of the night. The idea would have been unthinkable to me yesterday. Everything that I'd done tonight seemed impossible. Unimaginable. But I'd done it. We'd done it. We were out in the rain and we were alive. Saifi had been hurt, but he was going to be fine. Frankly, this was more alive than I'd felt in years. I tried to remind myself that the feeling was an illusion, a result of adrenaline and endorphins. Experience had taught me that feeling alive was often a precursor to injury and suffering. Yet in spite of how reasonably I talked to myself, a thrill of triumph still ran through me.

I looked through the rush of water flowing down around us, and an unusual movement caught my eye. I squinted, like it could clear up the rain obscuring my vision. The tall shrub was back. The shrub that seemed to have legs. Legs that carried it a step closer—

Saifi moaned, and I turned at the sound. He opened his eyes and tried to push himself up, but he hissed when he put pressure on his left arm.

Lei knelt beside him, helping him to a sitting position. "You okay?"

"I think so. It feels a lot better. But I still can't really use it, though."

I walked over and ruffled his wet hair. "It's going to be tender. You'll have to take it easy, but you're going to be fine."

If only I'd had my briefcase with me; I had enough gauze in there to make a rudimentary sling. As it was, Lei zipped up his jacket with his arm bent against his chest and hoped that it would provide a little support until we could get him something better.

She looked him over, face pinched with worry. "Saifi, what were you doing? Why did you run out into the rain like that?"

He wiped his chin against his shoulder, eyes on the pavement. "I thought I saw something."

"What?" Lei and I asked at the same time.

"I don't know." He kept his eyes down, like not knowing was shameful. "Something didn't look right, and I wanted to find out what it was."

Lei met my eye. Saifi had seen it too. Had she? Saifi was such a sweet kid. So earnest and devoted. But still too young to be mixed up in this. Where had Lei found him? Had she done her recruiting at the junior high school?

I shook my head at him. "That was brave. But next time you see something strange, let's investigate together, okay?"

He nodded, eyes down again, and Lei squeezed his shoulder.

—o

Dawn approached as we headed back to the floating house. It was still dark, but the sky held the promise of more light to come. The rain had petered out to a drizzle, and we marched through it at a pace that bordered on leisurely.

Jimmy and Lei flanked Saifi as they walked ahead of us. Saifi gestured emphatically with his good arm as he talked, Lei and Jimmy laughing. Celeste walked in front of me, head held high, striding around puddles without even looking at them.

I quickened my pace to catch up to her. "Are you all right?" I asked, stepping over a thick green vine growing out of a crack in the sidewalk.

Celeste glanced at me, appraising, but didn't answer.

I tried again. "I wanted to thank you. For vouching for me tonight. I'm glad that at least one of you trusts me."

Celeste laughed, a short, mirthless sound. "It's not that I trust you. I just don't think you pose a threat. You're like stepping into a boxing ring with an old man taking a nap: nothing to worry about. And you did end up being useful tonight, so it was good I made Lei bring you along."

"Okaaay. *Less* thank you, I guess." I could not figure out where her opinion of me had come from. Did I really come off as that much of a weakling? Even after everything I'd done tonight?

"Look," I said. "Lei is clearly a strong leader and has earned her team's respect. It's obvious you would all follow her anywhere, even if death waited on the other side. But Lei also listens to you. She trusts you. You could convince her to make some changes that would keep you all safer."

Celeste eyed me without slowing down. "We're not just a team."

"I can see that. You obviously care about each other. You may even feel like family. But that just further illustrates my point. Just because Lei says to jump doesn't mean it's safe to follow her."

Celeste shook her head. "We *are* family." She stopped, grabbing my arm to make sure I was looking at her. "Literally."

"I think you mean metaphorically."

"No, I mean in the way that we were all adopted by Carl and Lorraine Lewis."

I opened my mouth to respond, but her declaration took me so much by surprise that words abandoned me completely.

"We are all any of us have, now." She drew in a deep breath. "We've gotten pretty good at taking care of each other." Celeste turned and continued to walk. "That's not going to change just because the Client decided to have us babysit some bossy accountant." She went on without looking at me. "So yeah. You're stuck with us for now, whether you like it or not. Keep being useful. Don't cause trouble. Don't get in the way. And everything will be just fine."

Her tone was friendly, her face placid. But a chill ran through me, and I stepped back, leaving her to walk ahead of me the rest of the way back to the floating house.

11

Thunder rumbled in the mountains as the storm slowly rolled off, tied to the dark, flowing away with the night like it was attached to the sky. We approached the floating house, its faded, peeling paint turquoise in the near morning light. One of the giant concrete floats it rested on had lost some buoyancy over time, and the far side of the carport dipped dangerously close to the water's surface.

I copied everyone as they stripped off their water gear and hung it on hooks on the carport wall. I was somewhat dry, but wet in the oddest places, like my elbows, knees, and belly. I followed the others inside, trying to formulate a plan to get myself home as quickly as possible, but on the verge of falling asleep where I stood. Jimmy paused on his way past and put his hand on my arm. "Hey, you need a shower?"

I snorted. "Do I have to jump into the storm like Saifi did?"

Jimmy shook his head. "You can if you want. But there's a hot water tank here. If you're quick, you can take a shower right now."

The idea of being in those same clothes for one more

minute was unbearable, and I readily agreed. The warm water felt wonderful, easing the aches in my sore muscles and tender behind. I finally managed to force myself to turn the water off, and was drying off when a soft knock sounded at the door. I wrapped myself in a towel and peered around the door, expecting Jimmy, so was surprised to see Lei looking up at me through tired eyes.

She handed a fold of clothes to me. "Here. I don't know if they'll fit you, but they'll probably be okay for now. I can throw your clothes in the laundry if you'll give them to me."

"No, I've got to head out as soon as possible. I will have these clothes cleaned and returned to you," I said, holding up the pajamas she'd given me. "And hey, I'm sorry about what happened to Saifi and any part I might have played in it." I wasn't sure what I was apologizing for, but it seemed like the right move.

Lei narrowed her eyes at me, as though she couldn't quite believe that my apology was sincere. "I appreciate that." Her tone was hesitant, like she was waiting for a *but*.

"You have far more experience in all this than I do. I'm sure you know best."

Her mouth twisted into an unsatisfied frown. "Okay."

I cleared my throat, and tapped the door frame, "I mean, *you* already know how dangerous this job is. But with some planning, you could eliminate a lot of the risks."

She shook her head, rolling her eyes. "Are you a risk assessor or something?"

"No, but eliminating risk and the chance of danger is at the heart of what I do. I program traffic sensors."

She grimaced. "Wow. That sounds really boring."

I gave her a flat look. "I'm sure *you* think so, but

it's actually quite rewarding. Keeping people safe is my job."

"Oh, come on, Hoard," Lei groaned. "There are no guarantees. There is risk, and there is chance, and you have to take both if you want to get anywhere."

"On the contrary, with careful planning and preparation, you can eliminate almost all risk from nearly every situation. For example, is hiking Mount Everest dangerous? Yes. But tell me the difference in the survival chances between Joe Schmoe, who just woke up one morning and went hiking out of the blue, versus Robert Responsible, who has planned and prepared carefully for the last year, making sure he has everything he needs."

She clicked her tongue. "Robert Responsible? What were his parents thinking? The kids at school must've teased him like crazy."

I ignored her, soldiering on with my analogy, even as it fell apart. "Okay, well, I don't even know the survival statistics, because no one in their right mind would try to hike Mount Everest without the proper preparation. See what I mean?"

Lei waited to make sure I was done. I cleared my throat and nodded.

"Thank you," she said. "My response to that is 'Duh.' Also, people who have prepared for every eventuality still get injured or killed hiking Everest because the activity is inherently risky, and you cannot possibly prepare for everything. But all that aside, we're not climbing the world's highest mountain. We're going outside in the rain. Risk is necessary. It's not like I'm taking everyone's lives in my hands. We've been doing this for years. We know how to handle the rain. We're experienced riders. I appreciate your concern, but we're fine. We're going to be fine. Now, if you're done apologizing, I'd like to go to bed."

Boy, I was really bad at this. "Uh, I'll probably be gone when you wake up," I said.

She considered me, chewing on her lip as damp hair fell across her face. My fingers itched to brush the hair away, so instead I opened the door wide and leaned out to offer her my hand instead. She looked at it like it might hold a scorpion, but then took it, her handshake warm and firm, skin soft as flower petals.

She cleared her throat. "Thank you, for what you did for Saifi. We got him in a sling and got him to sleep. He seems like he's going to be okay." She smiled while she said it, but her eyes traveled downward to my very unclothed upper body.

My heartbeat sped up and I laughed awkwardly to ease the tension. "Are you staring at my chest?"

Her eyes snapped up to mine and she bit her lip. "Yep. Sorry about that." She coughed but looked at my chest again. "Sorry. Really. You . . . are just way more jacked than I expected you to be. I mean, I knew you were broad, I just didn't expect . . ." She waved her hand at me as though at a loss for words.

I took my hand back from her and hugged the clothes she'd given me, trying to cover myself as best I could. "If I said something like that to you, the entire female population would flay me alive."

"I know, right? So . . . do you work out?" She asked it like it made no sense. Like I couldn't possibly be the sort of person who worked out, but she could come up with no other explanation.

"Why are we still having this conversation? I do calisthenics, okay?"

"Calisthenics?" She looked up at me, eyes filled with laughter. "What are you, eighty? Do you also do Tai Chi in the park?"

"This is harassment."

She lifted her shoulder in a little half shrug. "Take it up with HR. You can file a complaint on your way out." She turned to go once again.

"Lei," I called after her. She looked back, eyes full of expectation. "My phone."

She nodded. "Right. Your phone. I'll bring it down to you before you leave. Don't worry." Lei waved lazily as she walked off into the room at the end of the hall, closing the door behind her.

The pajamas she'd given me had been stolen from a hobbit. They were roomy around the middle but ended somewhere in the area of my calves. At least if the house filled with water—which was a distinct possibility—my pants would stay dry.

Jimmy was the only one still up when I made my way into the kitchen. I had him order a cab for me, though he didn't seem all that happy about it. I sat on the couch to wait for the ride and for Lei to deliver my phone. I fidgeted to keep myself awake, jiggling my knee and rearranging my damp, folded clothes across my lap. Something in the pocket of my pants made a crinkling sound, and I fished out the paper to see what it was.

The diagnostic report.

Oh, right.

I was a computer programmer. Not the king of nighttime adventures. I had a demo to fix, and I was running out of time. My real life came crashing back into existence, pushing out the unexpected euphoria of the last several hours. If I was going to find this bug, I couldn't waste any more time. I rubbed my hair, trying to focus. I could do this. I still had time. I looked over the report, my eyes wide to keep them open, but the text soothed my brain like a mother singing to her child. The letters and numbers marched back and forth across the page, then morphed and bled into rain drops, sliding down the paper and puddling on my chest as my eyes slid shut.

12

I woke up to the most salivatingly delicious smell. I sat up, trying to rub the sleep out of my eyes and the kinks out of my neck. The couch was too short for me, leaving my legs poking out at odd angles, yet I'd slept deeply, dreaming of sailing on the ocean, the captain of a great ship. I checked my watch. It was past noon. I jumped up, smacking my head on the chandelier, and stumbled painfully into the kitchen. Saifi was dancing as he set the table, a radio playing staticky music on top of the fridge, the house rocking gently in time with his moves.

"Why am I still here?" I groaned. "What happened to my cab?"

"I'm so sorry," Jimmy said, looking over his shoulder at me from where he stood scrambling eggs at the stove. "I tried and tried to wake you up, but you were sound asleep. I finally sent the cab away. He was not too happy about that."

I fell into a chair at the table, holding my head. "It's Wednesday, isn't it? DarkWave launches in two days! I can't believe I'm missing work again. I've got to get that demo working before my boss gives himself a heart attack."

"Yeah, but now you can eat with us," Saifi said happily, swinging his good arm and bobbing his head so his hat nearly bounced right off, the floor of the kitchen rocking like we were jumping on a waterbed.

At the stove, Jimmy threw a few more things into the pan of scrambled eggs; mushrooms, cherry tomatoes, and green onions. My stomach sat up and roared like a lion.

"Where did all this food come from?"

"We got paid!" Saifi sang.

Lei appeared in the doorway, a small smirk on her face. "A stipend for groceries and supplies. Just enough to keep us afloat, if you know what I mean." She winked. Getting paid seemed to have put her in a good mood.

Jimmy slid the eggs into a heap on a plate and pointed at me with his spoon. "You wanna make some toast? Butter's on the table."

The toaster only held two slices at once, and seemed determined to either burn the bread, or only sort of warm it up, but nothing in between. Even so, I took my assignment seriously, manually popping the bread up when the timing was right in an attempt at optimum toastedness.

While I manned the toaster, Lei checked Saifi over with a tenderness I hadn't realized she was capable of. When she decided he was all right, she gave him a hug and kissed him on the forehead. I quickly turned back to my toast post before she could catch me witnessing her sweetness.

When Celeste appeared, everyone gathered around the table. I ate in silence, watching them interact, bicker, and tease each other, so at ease in each other's company. It now seemed so obvious they were siblings that I was surprised I hadn't figured it out on my own, despite the difference in skin color. I'd never had companionship like that. I hadn't been exactly lonely as a child, but I'd always wished for a brother or sister. Even with friends, I'd never had this. This ease of self. This trust and realness. I realized with a gulp of toast that I was painfully jealous.

"That is *not* why they broke the weather," Lei insisted, laughing.

"Yes it is," Saifi said. "Kevin Costner was trying to recreate *Water World* in real life."

"That is the dumbest thing I've ever heard," Lei laughed.

Jimmy tapped the table. "I'm pretty sure it was an accident. Like they were trying to fix the drought problem, and things didn't quite go as planned."

Celeste shook her head. "No. No way. This was no accident. This was intentional. Just another way to control us, to make us subject to them."

Lei nodded in agreement, but Jimmy raised a skeptical eyebrow.

"Subject to *who?*" he asked. "Subject *how?*"

I frowned in thought. I'd honestly never really thought about why the weather was like this. It just *was*. I was six when the weather broke down, so I sort of remembered a time when it didn't rain every night. But I didn't remember it being better; it was just different.

"So, Cohen," Jimmy said, turning my way as though he could sense the distance between them and me. "Tell us about yourself. Lei said your work has something to do with traffic? That sounds interesting."

Pride at the work we were doing at GridLox collided with the terror of all the work I'd missed, but I smiled at him. "It *is*. We're getting ready to launch a new AI that will interact directly with Auto Save, so that the road and all the vehicles are virtually communicating with each other."

Jimmy swallowed a mouthful of egg. "Like, how?"

I grabbed the salt and pepper so I could use them for a demonstration. "See, the real benefit of Auto Save is how safe it is. Cars with Auto Save are designed not to crash, and in most situations they perform their function very well. But essentially, each car is out there on the road all alone, operating independently, doing the best it can. The problem is, all the car knows is what it can see and sense in its immediate vicinity." I drove the salt around in endless little circles. "Our software is designed to fill in the gaps. By coordinating all the cars and signals with each other, each car is finally working with complete information, and can therefore function in the safest way possible." The salt and pepper drove straight toward the plate of eggs, but turned as one, avoiding a collision at the last moment.

"Good thing," Saifi said. "Those eggs are too salty already. Sorry Jimmy."

Lei lowered her eyebrows at me. "So, when you say, 'interacting' with the cars, what you mean is 'controlling' the cars."

I shook my head. "Not controlling them. *Coordinating* them. The AI's only purpose is to keep traffic moving safely and smoothly, like gears in an elaborate clock."

She shook her head. "Sounds like the same thing to me. And I'm not a gear, I'm a person. What if I know something the AI doesn't? And what if the AI decides that all these humans are too much trouble and decides to crash all of the cars instead?"

"But why would it do that? It's not sentient. It's not going to gain sentience. It's just an AI like the ones you can use to write articles or design rocket engines. Besides, even if it *was* sentient, I don't see why it would start killing us. People always think an AI is going to rise up and lash out, but that's based on the assumption that an AI would think and feel like we do. We assign it human emotions, human reactions, but in actuality, it would be far more logical than any of us, and I can't see any reason that would lead to violence." I shuffled the salt and pepper around on the bird-painted tabletop. "That being said, some programmers are paranoid, so there are fail-safes in place, just in case. The AI system requires a certain amount of human input to make sure that a bunch of ones and zeros can't take anyone's life. But the fact is, the only car accidents we've seen so far have been due to human interference. Believe it or not, we'll be safest once we put ourselves completely in the AI's hands."

Lei raised an eyebrow like I was being ridiculously naive, but didn't argue. Probably because she knew I was right but didn't want to admit it.

Saifi, on the other hand, looked impressed. "That's awesome. I hope AIs do come to life and take over, so I don't have to go to school anymore."

Jimmy laughed. "You don't think our new robot overlords would make you go to school?"

"No. They'd want us dumb so that they could stay in control. They'd probably let us watch videos online all day."

"As magical as that sounds," Lei said, pointing at Saifi, "I will make you go to school even while the world is ending. So enjoy your summer break while it lasts." She smiled sweetly and batted her eyes. Saifi studied her for a moment and then his shoulders sank, all his hopes for the freedom of a robot apocalypse dashed.

Jimmy turned back to me. "How about in your free time?"

I shrugged modestly, though I was glad he'd asked. "When

I'm not at work I like to build tiny models in glass test tubes," I said.

"Really?" Jimmy asked. "But test tubes are so small. How do you get anything in there?"

"Tweezers. I build the little models on the end of the cork and then slip everything inside the test tube."

Saifi raised an eyebrow. "Models of what?"

I shrugged. "Anything. Scenes and buildings mostly, with a few tiny little plants. They're like a mix of miniature dioramas and terrariums. I call them diorariums." I'd never called them that before. The name had just come to me like a stroke of genius.

Celeste snorted.

"That is horrible," Lei said with a grin. "It sounds like a big, fancy bathroom."

"I think it sounds like a butt museum," Saifi said.

Jimmy shook his head. "That would be a derrierium."

"That sounds like a butt *disease*," Saifi said. "You should call them 'Itty Bitty Cities' instead."

Hmm, that wasn't bad.

"It sounds really cool," Jimmy said to me, giving Saifi a meaningful look. "I hope we'll get to see them sometime."

"Sure. Anytime." I bobbed my head awkwardly and checked my watch. "But now I've got to go. Thank you so much for breakfast, or lunch, or whatever meal this was. Give me my phone and I'll order another cab."

"I thought he had to stay," Saifi huffed.

Lei shook her head. "We can't keep him here if he's deter-mined to leave. I'm not going to let Celeste drug him again. Especially after how he helped us last night." She kept her eyes on Saifi, as though I was already miles away.

"Ah, come on," Saifi whined. "Why not?"

"The Client hasn't said anything, so I'm assuming he just sent him to help us get into the hospital. And Cohen's promised to be discrete, so . . ." It didn't seem like she thought my word alone was enough, but acted like she had no other options.

Celeste folded her arms and cocked her head to one side. "And when the Client finds out we sent him away?"

Lei scratched her arm, chewing on her lip. "We'll deal with it. Just like always. It might require some . . . creativity to cover for him, but we'll figure it out."

Oh, flip, what kind of a pickle was I leaving them in? This Client of theirs was probably about as ethical as a school of piranhas. What would he do to them after I left?

Craaap.

Lei's phone dinged. "Speak of the devil," she said, reading it over. Her eyes widened. It was the message she'd been waiting for, but she didn't seem happy. Not at all.

13

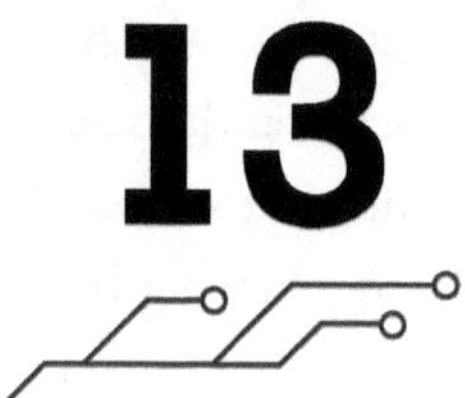

"**T**wo parts? We've never gotten two parts before."

"Do you think that means we're doing a good job?"

"Or are we doing a bad job, so we've got to catch up?"

"What are they?"

"Are they from the same person?"

Lei waved her phone in the air. "Will you all shut up for five seconds so I can tell you?"

Everyone fell silent, but Saifi stopped talking with his mouth open, like he was preparing to start talking again the second he got the go ahead.

"If Cone's leaving, the less he knows about this the better," Celeste said.

"It's *Cohen*," I said.

Lei studied me, chewing her lip. She pointed toward the living room. "I washed your clothes while you were asleep, so you're good to go." She turned back to her phone, staring at it fiercely, like my whereabouts didn't concern her in the least. But she hadn't returned my phone yet. Her words said I could go, but she clearly didn't want me to.

The diorama I was working on suddenly popped into my head, the tiny building with its tiny chimney, and perfectly crafted windows. My skill set involved focusing in on a problem down to the most minute detail. I could plan things out to perfection. And there was no one who took safety more seriously than I did.

I sighed.

I didn't know how I was going to help Lei *and* fix my demo code, but somehow I had to make it work. I inhaled slowly, hoping beyond hope that I was doing the right thing. Morally, anyway. "Maybe just one more job."

Lei rolled her eyes, but she looked like she was holding back a smile. "Whatever floats your boat, Smarty Pants." She slid her finger up the screen, scrolling through the info there. "Looks like it is an ear, and . . . a hand. And no, they aren't from the same person."

Celeste shook her head, looking thoughtful. "It's weird that he's never assigned us any internal organs, don't you think?"

"Maybe he's already got those parts," Saifi suggested.

"Maybe he was horribly disfigured by fire, or by falling into a vat of acid, and he's using these body parts to replace his own, hideous body parts," Jimmy said, stretching his face into an exaggerated grimace.

Saifi's eyes widened. "Ooh."

But I couldn't help pointing out, "If that was the case, he could go to the hospital and get transplants like everyone else."

"Oh, yeah."

"You haven't done any internal organs at all?" I asked.

Celeste shook her head.

It *was* strange. It wasn't like organs and body parts were hard to get. There were several legitimate organizations that provided transplants free of cost to those in need, since gangrene and trench foot were so common in some areas. Maybe he was a madman building a cyborg, and he was using these parts to make it look as human as possible?

"We've done a few bones," Lei said with a shrug. "The jaw and a hip, a couple ribs. Everything else has been composite tissue: like appendages. I'm not complaining, cuz internal organs would be so much more complicated to secure and transport, but Celeste is right. It's weird. Just one more weird detail on this whole, weird job."

I shivered, the morbidity slapping me in the face. Like the disembodied hand we were supposed to collect never would. "What are you scrolling through?" I asked, curious why four lines of info should take so long to read.

"The Client likes to hide the info in a bunch of gibberish, so that if it's intercepted it just looks like nonsense. Okay. The hand belongs to Bob Cobb. The ear to Helen Beaumont."

"Should we divide and conquer?" Celeste asked. "Knock them both out at the same time?"

Lei's mouth pulled into an O, like she loved the idea, and I blanched. That was a terrible idea. I bit my knuckle to keep myself from shouting out that it was a terrible idea.

I hesitantly raised my hand. "Don't you think it would be better if we stayed together?"

"Come on," Celeste pleaded. "Lei, you can take Saifi and Smarty Pants, and I'll take Jimmy. Imagine if we could finish two parts at once!"

I tried to stay cool, but my stomach knotted up. Who knew what might happen to them? None of us had any idea what we were running into. Lei nodded slowly, like it was almost too tempting to pass up, even with the risks.

I caught Lei's attention and shook my head, trying to use

my eyes to make her understand how much more dangerous it would be.

Lei groaned, frustrated. "Argh, I think Cohen is right."

I exhaled, relieved.

On seeing Celeste's face, Lei went on as if hearing my thoughts. "Collecting two parts at once would be awesome, but what if something happens? What if we need you? What if Cohen tries to jump into another river?"

Okay, not quite my thoughts, but it was probably a much better tack than mine had been anyway. I bobbed my chin in agreement. "Seriously. It could happen again at almost any moment."

Celeste rolled her eyes but nodded. "Fine. Which one do you want to do first?"

After several rather useless suggestions about how we should decide, we agreed to go after whichever one was closest. While the rest of us cleaned up the table, Celeste researched them both, face close to the screen, typing away at a speed I was truly envious of.

"Well," she said at last, "I can't find Bob Cobb or his hand anywhere. I mean, I could probably find him if I spent more time, but maybe we should just get the ear first."

"Sounds good to me. Agreed?"

Everyone agreed.

"Where is it?" Jimmy asked.

"Heritage Funerals and Cremations. It's up in the Heights."

Saifi ran to the large map on the wall and traced the route with his finger. "Yes! Yes! Yes! Ow!" He pumped his uninjured fist excitedly again and again so that it shook his whole body and the floor swayed beneath us. "Ow! Hurts my other elbow, but it's totally worth it! Ow! Woohoo!"

Saifi's excitement felt like a bad omen. I walked over to the map to see what he was so fired up about. Jimmy took pity on me and came to my aid.

"There's a canal that leads almost directly from here up to the Heights."

I shook my head in confusion. "There are canals all over the city. What's so special about this one?"

"To get up there, we're going to have to take a jet boat."

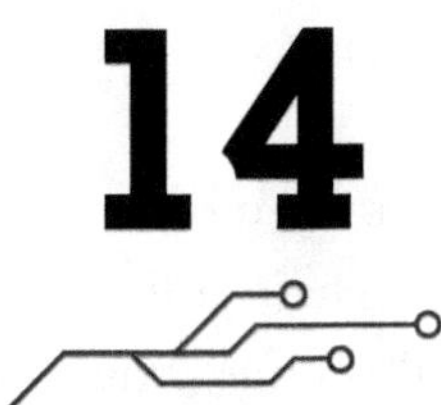

14

Before I could devote any energy to worrying about the jet boat, I had a more pressing problem. I really hadn't had a chance to properly freak out about the work I was missing and the looming DarkWave launch, but if I was going to stay here any longer, I had to do something about it or I would lose my mind. Steenrod was probably losing *his* this very moment. I had worked at GridLox since I was in college. Steenrod had mentored me. I'd never bailed on him like this. After the mysterious way I left things yesterday, and my not showing up this morning, Steenrod probably thought I was dead.

"Lei," I said, "May I please have my phone back? I need to contact my boss."

She shook her head. "No time. We have too much to do to get ready for tonight."

I held in a sigh. "That's fine, I can help. But returning my phone should only take a minute."

Lei stared at me but didn't answer. Good grief. What was it going to take to get this woman to trust me?

"Lei, please. I just—"

"I don't have it," she cut in.

"Baloney."

She looked intently at her shoes. "It fell out of my pocket on our ride here from the warehouse. By the time I realized I dropped it, it was too late." She met my eye again, chin held high. "I'm sorry."

I tried to speak, but my mouth just hung open, distressed gasps falling out of it. "What?" I finally managed. "You've been stringing me along all this time, promising to return my phone, and it's *gone*?" I pictured it hitting the asphalt in the pouring rain, cracks spiderwebbing across the screen. How was I supposed to function without my phone?

She didn't respond, just watched me with something like a challenge in her eyes. I gritted my teeth. It was just a phone. It could be replaced. Theoretically. At the moment though, it felt like losing my dearest friend.

"Uh. Okay." I swallowed with effort. "But I still have to talk to my boss. I disappeared on him yesterday, and I didn't show up for work today, *without sending notice*." I paused so that the weight of that could sink in. "He's going to call the police, if he hasn't already. I *have* to contact him."

Celeste walked into the room and shared a look with Lei. The two of them somehow communicated more with their eyes than I'd ever communicated with anyone using words.

Nodding at Lei, Celeste turned to me. "Okay, Cone. Let's send a note to your teacher."

I followed her as she walked into the living room and sat on the floor, back against the fireplace, with her laptop on her crossed legs. She insisted she didn't want me *messing with her stuff*, so I gave her Mr. Steenrod's email address so she could send the message on my behalf.

The room gently rocked as I paced, trying to find the right words to put my boss at ease. "Okay. Just say: *I'm so sorry about yesterday. There's been an emergency. Something serious has come up and I won't make it into the office today either.*" I squinted, trying not to think about what a disaster this was. "*Sorry I didn't contact you sooner. But don't worry, I'm sure I'll be back in before the Launch Party, and will definitely have the demo done before then. Sorry again. Thanks for your patience,* signed Cohen Hoard, etc."

I looked down at Celeste staring flatly at me.

"Are you sure you included enough apologies?"

I lowered my eyebrows, thinking. "I don't know. Read it back to me."

She rolled her eyes. "Good grief, Cone. Is this letter to your boss or your grandma?"

"He's not just my boss, he's my friend. More like a father. He lost his wife to cancer a couple years ago and this company and the people in it are the only things he has left. I *hate* that I'm leaving him in the lurch like this. I'm in charge of the demo for the launch on Friday, but it keeps crashing, and I can't understand it because my code is *perfect*."

Celeste raised an eyebrow at me.

"Okay, fine. There is no such thing as perfect code, but it's pretty darn close. As close as it can be. As close as anyone could ask for under the circumstances."

She gave me an indulgent smile. "Good for you."

"You know, if I could use your laptop for just half an hour, I could get the demo fixed and it would take a huge load off my mind." The diagnostic test I'd set up on Monday night had been running for almost forty-eight hours. I probably had enough info to solve this thing once and for all if I could just get online.

"As much as I would like *not* having to listen to you whine about your demo anymore, I'm not letting you anywhere near my computer." She hit send, closed her laptop, and tucked it under her arm as she carried it away, checking on me over her shoulder as though I might try to rip it out of her hands.

I grunted, irritated. Promising Steenrod that I would fix the demo code was pushing it, but if I could get access to a computer, I knew I could do it. Steenrod had probably already put someone else on it as a contingency anyway. The idea made my skin crawl. I hated other people messing with my code. They would never be as thorough as me, and Steenrod would end up with some slapdash demo on the night of the launch. I couldn't let that happen. This email wouldn't fix everything, but hopefully it would help. Especially as it was the best I could do under the circumstances.

—o

The house was a hive of activity as everyone prepared once again to take their lives in their hands and go outside in the rain. I stood in the living room, listening to the rain beating against the house like it had a vendetta. In a corner of one of the windows, a dribble of water ran down the paneled wall to a bulge in the floor. That would have to be dealt with, and soon, or the damage would get much, much worse.

I turned and headed for the stairs, taking them two at a time. I found Lei in the back bedroom, shoving things into her trusty old duffle bag. She started in surprise when I barged in.

"Cloud Busters," I said, pointing at the badge on her duffle bag strap, finally getting a good look at it. "I had all their albums in high school."

She rubbed her thumb over the stitching of the electric

guitar made of clouds and looked at me like she didn't believe a word I said. I considered singing a few lines to prove it, but sighed instead. So much for small talk.

"Lei. I'd like to help more than this. If I could do some research, I could figure out who this Client of yours is, what he's up to. If I had some more information, I know I could—"

"No," she cut me off. At the sight of my face, her voice softened. "I can't, Cohen. Even if I knew I could trust you, Celeste doesn't let anyone touch her computer. Besides, you act like we need to be rescued, but all I want is to finish the job."

I exhaled loudly. "Fine. Fine. I get it. But what can I do? I'm trying, Lei, but you've got to help me help you. Can we please revisit the time of day you go out?"

She exhaled even more loudly than I had. "No. We can't. We cannot be seen. It's in the terms of the contract. So, unless you have some kind of cloaking technology on that multi-tool of yours, nighttime is the only option."

"But Cesar saw us. The SMax rider saw us."

She wiggled her head back and forth. "We can only be seen where unavoidable. A person here and there is bound to see us. But if we start marching around in the middle of the day, the Client is going to cut us off without a penny."

I grunted, annoyed. "Fine, but we have to leave Saifi and Jimmy here."

She scoffed. "Why?"

"Because it isn't safe."

She shoved something else into her bag. "Sorry, but you don't get to make the decisions around here."

"Well, maybe I should."

She let go of the duffle bag and straightened, one hand on her hip. "Do you have a problem with the way I'm running things?"

"I have a *huge* problem with it!" I marched up to her so that I towered over her, her dark eyes shining up into mine. "You're dragging kids out well past their bedtime, into the rain, where people have *died* by the way, without giving any thought to their safety!"

"Past their bedtime?" Lei asked, laughter returning to her eyes.

"Argh!" I growled, and let myself fall onto the bed, burying my face in my hands. She was so aggravating. How were you supposed to make someone see reason when they turned everything you said into a joke? I wanted to help her. I wanted to keep them all safe. But they were throwing danger around like confetti, and it was more than I could handle.

I felt Lei's hand on my shoulder. "Cohen," she said softly.

My eyes flew open.

"Get off my bed."

I swallowed and stood up, suddenly hyper aware of where I was, and how alone we were, how inappropriate it might seem, and how cute she looked with her goggles on her head.

She stepped back, thankfully putting some distance between us in the small room. "Jimmy is invaluable to have in the field. And Saifi—"

"Is what? Twelve?"

She scoffed. "He's fourteen, and old enough to make his own decisions."

"Saifi worships you and would do anything you asked him to!" I shoved my hands deep into my pockets and tried to get my breath to slow down. "He's injured. That's going to make him slower and more likely to get injured again. And it will take him even longer to heal with two injuries instead of one. Taking him out in his present condition is reckless."

Lei twisted her mouth into a frown, chewing on her cheek.

I cleared my throat, talking as calmly as I could. "Please ask him to stay here this time."

She stared at me for a long, long time. My face got very hot. If this came down to a staring contest, I wasn't sure that I could beat her.

"Look," I pressed, "I just . . . I want to contribute. I want to help. Keeping Saifi here is the best way I can think of to keep him safe."

Lei heaved a gargantuan sigh and finally said, "Okay," but there was a hardness to her tone, like a knife at the edge of her words. "But I don't like it. How do I know he'll be safe here all alone?"

"Leave Jimmy here."

"I need Jimmy in the field. How about *you* stay here?"

"You need *me* in the field."

Her mouth fell open, but she seemed to be at a loss for words. Finally, the corners of her mouth tipped up ever so slightly. "What makes you think you know what I need?"

I didn't have an answer for that. If she hadn't looked like she wanted to hurt me thirty seconds ago, I could have sworn she was flirting with me.

—o

Part of Portland's plan to deal with the rain had been to construct several canals and aqueducts, replacing some roadways completely to help contain the excess water. Various companies used them for shipping things around the city, but as a mode of transportation, they had never really caught on. However, *we* were about to travel by jet boat straight up one of those canals, on purpose. Careening through millions of gallons of water gushing at deathly speeds through narrow, manufactured waterways. What could go wrong?

Saifi was, to say the least, crestfallen. Jet boats were his favorite thing in the universe, according to him, and he didn't need two arms to ride in one and making him stay behind was the worst thing that ever happened to him.

"Do you want me to drug him?" Celeste asked Lei out of the side of her mouth.

"You need to cool it with the sedative," I said without even lowering my voice. "You're going to do some serious damage."

She snorted and walked away. Jimmy appeared next to Saifi, holding a sandwich and a glass of ice water. Saifi pouted, but took the food and trudged upstairs, waving dejectedly at us.

So, there we stood under the small pavilion where the canal fed into the river, a boat moored near the mouth, bouncing and jousting with the waves caused by the runoff. We'd been waiting for over ten minutes, and I was just about ready to jump into the boat and try driving it myself.

And then I saw it. A shadow in the rain. Around fifteen paces from where we huddled on the dock. Watching us. Waiting. I couldn't see a face. Couldn't even tell for sure if it was a person. It was really just a shape that didn't quite belong. A density in the night. But why did it keep showing up in all the same places that we did?

I turned back to the group as a bearded man in a yellow raincoat stomped out of a shed and over to the docked jet boat. He motioned us violently toward him. We ran through the downfall and onto the jet boat where he ushered us into the tiny cabin encased in plexiglass. It reeked of pitch and neoprene. I tried not to take up too much room, but I still ended up with

Lei's back pressed against my chest. My heartbeat sped up and I couldn't figure out where to put my hands.

Beardy McGee started up both engines, signaled, and a figure materialized out of the rain and untied us from the dock. Our captain steered us toward the canal. The flow of water into the Willamette pushed us back again and again, but he continued to steer and force his way in until his nose sat between the two constructed walls of the canal. And then he powered up the jets.

We flew up the canal with such a jerk that everyone in the cabin lurched backward. It only took a few moments acclimating to realize why Saifi loved jet boating. It was like riding a roller coaster while standing. The boat bounded up the river, tilting and swaying in the current, bouncing us around the cabin like popcorn. I threw out an arm to steady myself and whacked Jimmy in the head. Lei lost her footing, and I grabbed her to keep her from slipping, but both of us ended up colliding with Celeste. Lei burst out laughing and Jimmy and I joined in, clinging to each other to keep from ending up on the floor. Celeste wedged herself in the corner and looked for all the world like she didn't even realize the rest of us were there.

Rain continued to pour out of the sky and beat on the plexiglass cabin walls, but our captain didn't seem to need to see. He ignored our laughter and navigated the canal as if by memory. And if a wave of water proved powerful enough to slow us down, he pushed on and on until he finally fought his way through it.

All too soon, the captain started pointing at me and shouting. "I'll pull into the notch so you can jump onto the dock and tie us off. She's gonna jerk you around, so you better keep track of your feet."

He steered the jet boat into a small turnout with a dock on

the port side. The boat leaped and swayed as he fought the current, then he turned and glared at me. "Well?"

Finally understanding what he wanted me to do, I grabbed a coil of rope off the floor and stepped out into the rain. I wasn't very familiar with boating knots, but I tied the rope to a cleat using a couple simple overhand loop knots. I stood near the side with rope in hand, watching the water roil and churn, then I inhaled, stepped up on the gunwale and leaped with all my might.

My feet nearly slipped right out from underneath me, but I grabbed a piling and forced my sliding shoes into submission. The captain cut the engines and I pulled on the rope, propping myself against the piling for support. He maneuvered the boat alongside the dock, and I tied it off on another cleat, hoping my wet knots would hold.

I looked up to see Lei grinning at me through the rain. She, Celeste and Jimmy stepped from the boat onto the dock, where Jimmy immediately undid my knots, threw the rope back onto the boat and gave the captain a salute. I guessed that meant he wasn't going to wait for us.

The four of us looked at each other for a moment, then Lei nodded, and we took off into the rain.

15

We arrived exhausted and dripping at Heritage Funerals and Cremations, a huge midcentury house that had been converted into a funeral home.

I hated that once again I found myself in an absurd situation where I didn't know the plan. Didn't know if there even *was* a plan. We were going to rob a *funeral* home? I wished for one fleeting moment to be back in my bed, curled up with my laptop, wondering where Jocelyn was. It may not have been much of a life, but before this I had never once tried to rob a funeral home, and it was kind of a point of pride for me.

A heavy metal door swung open, yellow light spilling out onto the wet asphalt, and I waited for a security guard with a big stick to chase us off. Instead, a heavy-set, middle-aged man with no hair on his head whatsoever beckoned us inside.

We dripped all over the tiled entry, and I grabbed a brochure as we followed him, leaving a river behind us on the lush carpeting.

Heritage Funerals and Cremations specialized in providing the full funeral and viewing service to all of their customers, even if there was no body to bury. To that end, before being dissected and parsed out for donation or incineration, each body was lovingly dressed, made up, and immortalized in a work of art. These were most often used in shrines, memorials, or personal galleries.

Oversized postmortem portraits lined the hallway we walked down, each in thick gilt frames, showcasing the talent of the mortician and photographers. Instead of attempting to make them seem alive, the portraits enhanced the waxy corpseness of the dead, like a viewing that went on forever. A photograph of a woman with an intricate gray beehive hairdo and gray skin to match was posed in front of a sky-blue backdrop, large glasses perched on her nose. Beside that hung an oil painting of a dead man in a Hawaiian shirt and sunglasses, his lips pulled into a wide smile, both thumbs up. At the end of the hall, a nearly life-sized 3D-rendered statue of a man in a black suit looked blankly off into the middle distance, an enormous plastic python wrapped around his hand and draped across his shoulders. According to the brochure, poses were optional (and cost extra), but were very popular. Their loved ones wanted a pose that perfectly captured the personality of their aunt, father, or grandmother, and no one did that better than Heritage Funerals and Cremations.

"Umm . . ." Jimmy said, inspecting each piece of art with macabre fascination as we walked down the hall. "These are . . ." He didn't finish, like he couldn't find the word.

I couldn't find it either but was unable to look away.

"Tacky?" Celeste asked. "Vulgar?"

Well, yeah. She kind of had a point. But if most people didn't even end up with a grave to visit, they needed something, didn't they?

"How was your trip here?" the bald mortician asked Lei.

She shrugged. "Wet. But we got through all right."

"I'm glad." His voice was soft. Halting. "It's been a long time."

"It has." She nodded. "How's business?"

"Booming. I'm on photography now."

She gave the photo we passed a cursory glance. "You are? That's amazing. Are any of these yours? They're beautiful."

"Not yet. But I took a few photos last week that turned out well, so they might make it to the wall soon. I still harvest from time to time, but mostly the interns do it. You know the drill."

"Yeah. Only too well."

He smoothed the front of his lab coat. "New guy was finishing up Helen Beaumont when I got your message. I had him set the ear aside for you. Gotta admit, it was a weird message to get. Don't get me wrong, it was great to hear from you. Just never had a request like that before. Not that I mind. All these parts are going to end up in the incinerator next week anyway. We don't have the capacity to store anything longer than that."

"You guys do harvesting here too?" I cut in to ask.

"Well, yeah. Can't expect hospitals to do them all, can you? They're backed up as it is. We take a decent lump. Saves our clients a step."

He led us down to the basement into what must have originally been a second kitchen they had converted into a preparation room. The walls were covered with flowered wallpaper and olive-green cabinets, and two tables with stone countertops lay in the center of the room. Lei's friend opened the fridge and pulled out a small, white plastic case, identical to the one I'd gotten the tongue in.

I pulled Lei aside while he packed it in the blue gel and carefully boxed it up. "Lei."

"Hmm?" She kept her eyes on her bald friend and the box in his hand, as though afraid to let it out of her sight.

"Lei, listen. This is important." She looked at me then, and her dark eyes nearly swallowed me whole. "I saw someone. When we were waiting for the jet boat."

She grabbed my arm and pulled me over to the wall. "What do you mean?" Her gaze flicked around the room to see if anyone had overheard. Jimmy and Celeste were fiddling with a skeleton propped up on a stand, posing him with one finger in his nasal cavity. "Who did you see?"

"I don't know. It was just a figure. I think. Standing there. Watching us. I saw them last night too, right before Saifi was hurt."

"Are you sure? The rain can play all kinds of tricks on your eyes."

"I know, believe me, I know. But I'm . . . seventy-seven percent sure there was someone there."

She chewed her lip, her mouth twisting into a charming knot, and nodded. "Don't say anything to anyone else. And let me know if you see them again. But be cool. Give me a sign or something. The others will freak."

The bald man, whose name I still had not caught, cleared his throat, rocking back and forth on the balls of his feet while he waited for us to finish talking. Lei took the box he handed her.

"If you ever need any extra work, let me know. You had a gift. I know they'd take you back on." His face was so red when he said it, you'd have thought he'd knelt down right there and proposed. He gulped, his throat moving jerkily.

Lei smiled at him with genuine affection, but it was the face she used when she talked to Saifi or Jimmy. "Thanks, Fred. I'll keep that in mind. And thank you so much for letting us crash your party here. You're a lifesaver."

They both threw back their heads and laughed at that, like it was an old joke they'd told each other many times before.

He let us show ourselves back out the way we'd come in, and we filed down the hall, watched over by the pictures of the dead.

"You used to work here," I said to Lei.

She gripped the box in her gloved hands like she was afraid it would try to escape. "I was an intern here, yes. I interned all over, actually, before I got the job at the harvesting department at OHSU. The pay is not as good as you think it is going to be, and the job is somehow worse."

I smiled ruefully. "So that's how you have all these contacts."

She nodded.

"It's almost like you are uniquely suited to this collection job."

She eyed me in silence for a minute. "It does seem to be that way, yes."

We stared at each other, each waiting for what else the other would say, but neither of us seemed to have the words.

We pulled open the heavy door and headed back out into the dark and stormy night.

We paused under a covered drive big enough for three hearses and I turned slowly, squinting through the inky rain. I couldn't see anything. I wasn't certain I ever had seen anything, but as far as I could tell there were no shrubs in the vicinity that didn't appear to be shrubs.

"So," Lei said to me while everyone made sure that their

gear was secure. "Everything . . . cool?" She stood close, her voice raised just enough for me to hear her over the pounding rain.

I looked again, but nothing seemed wrong. "I think so." I stepped back from the others. "But perhaps I should take the package, just in case."

Lei's lips were red in the blue light, and she twisted them into a knot. Was that a new thing, or had she always been doing it? It was adorable.

I pulled my eyes away from her mouth. "I'm the biggest and the strongest. If anything happens, I'll probably be able to hold on to it the best."

She rolled her eyes but nodded. "Okay fine. But you better be right."

I unzipped the front pocket on my jacket and slipped the box inside. The jacket bulged out around the square lump, like a geometric alien was trying to force its way out of my chest. Then we turned together to face the storm, bracing ourselves for the run we had ahead of us. The nearest SMax drop box was three blocks away.

"Hey," Celeste called. "Can we go now? Are you guys done telling secrets?"

Lei sniffed and walked to Celeste and Jimmy, the three of them highlighted in the light of the covered drive. "Yes. Let's go. Everybody ready?"

"Lei?"

The voice seemed to come from the night itself and we turned in unison to find the source. Saifi stepped out of the darkness into the light of the covered drive, gaze darting around like he wasn't sure where he was.

"Saifi? Where did you come from? How did you get here?"

Lei sounded as confused as I felt, walking toward him to make sure he was all right. How *had* he gotten here?

"No!" Saifi yelled, holding up his hands to keep her away. They were zip tied together, his injured arm still in its sling. He wasn't wearing any wet-weather gear, and he looked like he was soaked through to his skin. "He's still here, somewhere, and I don't know what he's going to do!"

The fear in his voice unnerved me almost more than his words. I spun, senses on high alert, searching the darkness for anything amiss, but all I could see was rain and black no matter where I looked.

Lei crossed the space to Saifi's side. "Who is? What are you talking about?" She grabbed him and hugged him, her arms wrapped protectively around him though he was nearly as tall as she was.

Footsteps beat the wet asphalt behind me, and I spun just as a tall figure in a wet suit and diving mask jumped toward me, fist aimed for my face. Dodging, I threw my forearm up, blocking his punch. I swung with my other fist, connecting with his ribs, and then pain exploded through my skull as he bashed his other giant fist into my head.

I tried to grab him or hit him while he pulled at my jacket, but my eyes wouldn't focus, and my arms felt like noodles. Before I could stop him, he pulled the package free and ran away.

"No!" Celeste screamed as the sound of footsteps faded off into the night.

My eyes slid closed and I hit the ground.

"Cohen!" Lei's voice dug in through the pain and then she was beside me, raising me up so that my head rested on her lap. The pain pulsed through my head again and again until it finally eased up enough that I could breathe.

"Who *was* that?" I moaned. "What was his hand made of?"

"He hit you with a rock. Luckily you have a very thick skull. Now shut up and let me look at you." Lei ran her fingers through my hair, checking for visible wounds, and I drew in a sharp breath when they brushed the point of contact. Another hand took my arm, and I cracked open an eye. Saifi knelt next to me, looking like he was on the verge of tears.

"I'm fine," I groaned.

"Shut up," Lei said again. "You are not."

I wrenched my eyes open and pulled her hand away, clinging to it. "Lei. He got the ear. It's gone."

"I know. Celeste and Jimmy ran after him. They're both fast. They might catch him."

"But what if they don't?"

She didn't answer, instead gently turning my head to check the other side for wounds. She brushed something off my cheek, pads of her fingers soft against my skin. "Do you think you can sit up?"

I wanted to jump up and shake it off, but my head felt like it had doubled in size. I nodded, and with their help pulled myself to a sitting position. My head throbbed with the rhythm of the rain. I was going to have a lump the size of the Pacific and a headache to match. Lei cut Saifi free, and they helped me to my feet and led me to the steps. I didn't want to sit. I wanted to be strong and capable so that Lei would know she was safe with me, but the world tilted, and I ended up on my backside on the stairs. I let my head fall into my hands, willing the pain away. Lei disappeared into the funeral home, and Saifi patted me on the shoulder. It made the pounding in my head worse, but I didn't have the heart to tell him so.

Lei came back out holding a freezer brick and bandages. She

gently bandaged my head, gave me a couple of painkillers, then handed me the freezer brick. I wanted to lean over into her lap again, but took the cold block from her instead, and she moved over to Saifi's side. "Are you okay? What happened? Did he hurt you? How did you get here?"

"Same as you, on a jet boat, I think. He showed up back at base and I wasn't ready for him. I didn't want to come with him, but he had a gun, and my arm's still not great . . ."

She pulled him into another hug, wiping the wet hair out of his face. "No, no, no, you did good. I'm glad you brought him here. Who knows what he might have done if you hadn't."

Saifi swallowed and shook his head. "I didn't *bring* him here. I didn't even know where we were going until we got here. It's like he already knew exactly where you guys were. I think he just brought me as a distraction. He kept me blindfolded the whole time. I didn't even get to see anything on the jet boat ride."

Lei's gaze snapped to mine, her eyes full of questions, eyebrows lowered in doubt and worry.

I shook my head in confusion, instantly regretting it as pain flashed through my skull. "How did he know where we were?" I grunted.

Lei stood up and paced around the carport, but didn't answer.

"Has he been following us all this time?" I pressed. "Who is he? What does *he* want with the ear?"

"I don't know!" Lei snapped. "I know exactly as much as you do right now." She turned away, and I could see her shoulders rise and fall as she tried to calm herself.

"I'm sorry," I said at length.

She didn't respond.

"I mean, I should have been able to stop him," I pushed

on. "I shouldn't have . . ." Failure coated my tongue and made it impossible to speak.

Lei started pacing again. She'd been so tender and caring for those few moments when she'd checked my head, but now anxiety poured off her like water off the roof. The longer Celeste and Jimmy were gone, the more agitated she became. She took out her phone and tried to call them both over and over but couldn't get through. We were going to have to go find them. I pulled myself up, a bit dizzy, but the pain had settled down to a deep and annoying ache and was nothing I couldn't handle. I needed to fix this.

"I'll go find them."

Lei shot me an annoyed look. "Sit down and rest."

"I'm fine. This is my fault. I was supposed to be guarding the ear, but instead I practically handed it right to him. I should have prepared for something like this."

"Stop it. I made a choice. If I hadn't handed the package to you, that guy would have attacked me. Stuff happens. This is the job."

She looked away again, the tone of her voice communicating so much more than her words had. This was only a job. Not a casual outing among friends. Not her soft fingers brushing against my cheek. It was a job. That's all.

The rain continued to beat on the driveway roof above us, rivers running toward the drain in the parking lot. The water swirled and rushed around our feet, heading undeterred to wherever it intended to go. Lei paced, chewing her thumbnails, eyes searching the dark in the direction Celeste and Jimmy had run.

I peered at Saifi cradling his arm next to me on the steps. "Are you all right?"

He shook his head, just once. "That guy is bad news. And with this stupid arm, I couldn't . . ."

"Did he hurt you?" I asked.

Saifi shook his head. "No, but I shoulda been able to stop him—"

"Hey," I said. "Hey. It's okay sometimes to not be strong enough." I tried to make myself believe the words, but my own incompetence ate at my insides like acid. "I'm just glad you're all right."

"Yeah, but Celeste and Jimmy ran after him. I hope they don't catch him. I'm afraid of what he'll do."

I didn't respond. I'd been thinking the same thing.

Lei gasped. I looked up as Celeste and Jimmy walked back under the covered drive, breathing heavily and dripping, like they'd just climbed out of a lake. Lei and Saifi ran to them, each grabbing whoever was nearest, and Saifi drew them into a group hug. He looked around until he found me and beckoned me over. I watched them, but held back, knowing that was not a circle I was allowed to join.

Celeste pulled away and leaned over, hands against her knees, still breathing heavily.

Jimmy shook his head at Lei. "We followed him for ages, but could never catch up, and then he vanished. I wanted to come back then, but Celeste wouldn't give up. You say I'm the runner, but Celeste left me in the dust."

Lei looked at her, but Celeste's face was guarded. Finally she swallowed, her throat moving with effort. "He's too fast."

"Okay, it's okay," Lei said.

When Celeste shook her head in frustration, Lei grabbed her arm. "It's gone, okay? We tried. But I have an idea for how to get it back."

Celeste turned to her, annoyed, pale eyebrows low.

"Who do you call when you need something that you can't get anywhere else?"

"Ghostbusters?" Saifi asked. "James Bond?"

"Us," Jimmy said. "You call us."

"Yeah. I think it's time to call a collection crew of our own."

16

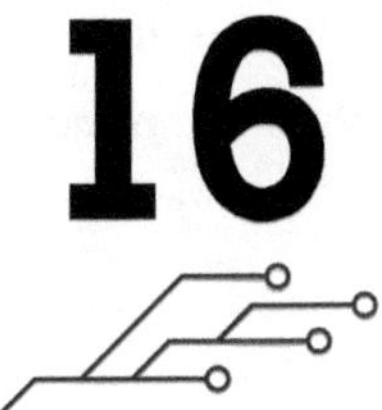

One text message and nearly a mile later, we approached a building with the word Vigil tacked to the front in bright pink lights. The light glinted off the falling rain drops, giving the whole building a pink haze. We'd passed several other groups of people on our way here, and it struck me again how oblivious I had been. People hadn't let the rain stop them. They didn't hide in their houses each night waiting until morning. They made do. And judging by the squeals of laughter I heard around me, they were having a good time.

We ran inside the bar, leaving the pounding rain outside. True, I didn't get out all that much, but I knew a bar when I saw one. No one checked IDs at the door. No one even blinked when Jimmy and Saifi walked in. Celeste assured us that there were no cameras, and we stripped off all unnecessary rain gear and hung it on rows of crowded hooks along the walls. Lei found someone in charge, and in a few minutes, they handed Saifi some clothes from the lost and found, and he gladly ran off to change.

The clientele ran the gamut. There were rain worshippers

in their Tal-Azra masks, and people who had kept their gear on, hanging out in waders and raincoats. There was a group in the corner wearing only swimming suits and laughing so loudly it felt like a show. It was like walking into the Mos Eisley Cantina. I kept expecting some ugly alien to tell me that he didn't like me, and Lei would have to come to my rescue.

I touched Lei's arm, leaning in to whisper, "What happened to not being seen?"

"Yeah, well, we crossed over into absolutely unavoidable territory, so we're just going to have to take our chances."

Some of my least favorite words. Nothing good ever came of *just taking chances*. "What about them?" I pointed over at Jimmy and Saifi who were now in the corner in front of an ancient arcade machine, its lights still happily blinking. "Is it okay for them to be in here? What if someone offers them a drink?"

Lei raised her eyebrows at me. "This isn't an after-school special, Hoard. And none of us is drinking. That includes you. No better way to get yourself killed in the rain than to go out in it with your judgment and reaction time impaired. I'd actually guess that most people here aren't drinking, and the ones who do will probably have to stay here until morning."

Celeste pushed past us, knocking into my shoulder with her own, and melted into the crowd. I tried to give her the benefit of the doubt. She was probably angry about losing the ear, angry about losing the thief, angry about being here. And apparently had decided to take it out on me. So be it. I stuck behind Lei, not sure where to be or how to walk. After I stepped on her shoes a few times, she turned and glared at me.

"Sorry," I mumbled.

She sighed. "Let's dance, okay?"

When I hesitated, she pulled me toward a gap in the tables in the center of the room where several other couples were swaying to the music. She grabbed my hands and put them on her hips, slipping her hands up around my neck. My heartbeat sped up.

"This way we can keep an eye on the room without looking like we're looking for someone."

"What's wrong with looking like we're looking for someone?"

"It'll make us stand out. It would help if you were shorter by the way."

I tried to force myself to relax, but it was difficult with her standing so close to me, hips moving beneath my hands. "I could kneel down if you like. I'm here to serve."

The corner of her mouth ticked up. "So I've noticed." She narrowed her eyes, contemplating me. "I can't get a bead on your endgame. You play the good guy perfectly, but I can't figure out what it's for. What are you trying to accomplish?"

"It's not an act. I'm just trying to help."

She raised an eyebrow. "No one can be this *nice* all the time." She put nice in air quotes with her fingers.

I guffawed, somewhere between flattered and annoyed. "That's not true. There are genuinely nice people all over. I meet them all the time."

"I've never met one."

"What about Jimmy?"

She grinned. "Jimmy's an exception. It's a choice he makes, every day. He has to work at it."

"So does everyone else. I meant what I said when I first met you. I think most people try to do the right thing most of the time."

She cocked an eyebrow at me and shook her head. "You are so naive it's adorable."

I scoffed playfully and threaded my fingers through her belt loops, itching to pull her closer. "It's not naivety. It's called 'good will toward men.'"

"Never heard of it."

"You might even call it 'optimism.' Or 'a sunny disposition.'" I bent my head down until my forehead was touching hers and looked deeply into her eyes with all of the mock seriousness that I could muster. "You should give it a try sometime."

She bit back a smile. "Nah. Being grumpy is working out just fine so far. No reason to mess with a good thing."

I grinned. She let herself smile and her eyes crinkled up. She held my gaze as the world slowed down until we were left in our own private pocket of time. Her thumb skimmed along the skin at my collar, zinging electricity down my spine. She licked her lips and my hands slid around her back of their own accord.

Another dancing couple crashed into us, knocking us out of our bubble. They apologized profusely, and Lei waved them off, but she pulled back and rested her hands on my shoulders instead of around my neck, leaving enough room for a history book between us.

Lei cleared her throat. "You're better at this than I expected you to be," she said.

"Better at what?"

"Dancing."

I tried not to feel offended. "Why did you think I'd be a bad dancer?"

Lei shrugged. "I don't know. You just don't seem like the type. I picture you volunteering at rest homes, standing in line at the DMV, that sort of thing."

"Really? Like that's my entire life?"

"That and your soul-sucking job, which I assume involves sitting all day in front of a computer in a tiny cubicle."

I sniffed. "It's not that tiny."

She smiled.

"Besides," I said, "just because *you* choose not to work in an office doesn't mean there's anything wrong with it. I happen to like my job." If I still had a job. If the stress hadn't unhinged my boss so he called off the DarkWave launch and the company went under.

"So, what else?" Lei asked casually. "Who do you have at home that you're so anxious to get back to?"

My cheeks grew hot. I swallowed. Then I opened my mouth and the name fell out. "Jocelyn."

"Wow. Blushing. I'm guessing that is *not* your sister's name. Cat, perhaps? Parakeet?" Her fingers tapped my shoulder in time with the song. "Girlfriend?"

"It's . . ." I coughed. "Well, it's a work in progress."

She nodded knowingly. "What's she like?"

I exhaled, unsure where to begin. "She's beautiful."

Lei gave me a flat look. "Aw, come on, Hoard. You do realize that's not enough to base a relationship on."

"I know." My tone was unnecessarily defensive. "She's also wonderful. And lovely."

She raised an eyebrow. "You sound like you're describing someone you've never met."

"*Pfft.*"

"Alright." She was laughing at me. "Whatever you say, big guy. She's a very lucky lady."

I was *still* blushing, but Lei tensed, the muscles in her back going taut.

"That's him."

I spun.

Esteban and Ranji were walking through the door.

17

I hunched, scrunching down and using Lei as a shield. Having my real life collide with Lei's world felt like I was breaking an unspoken rule. What were they doing here? Esteban should be home, in bed, resting up for another day of building management. And his buddy Ranji needed to rest up for . . . however it was he spent his time. Being an obnoxious lady's man, as far as I could tell.

"What are you doing?" she hissed. "Knock it off. Those are the people we came here to meet. Will you cut it out?"

Really? We were here to meet Esteban and Ranji? Esteban alone would have been fine, I'd trust him with just about anything, but *Ranji? Really?*

Lei walked toward them, and I gave in and followed her, trying to act like I belonged there. They hung up their helmets and ponchos and Esteban looked my way. His gaze slid straight past me at first, but then snapped back in surprise.

"Cohen, man! What are *you* doing here?" He smacked me genially on the back. "I didn't think you went out after dark.

Like, ever." He seemed so happy to see me, yet not totally convinced that I was real.

"I, uh, made some new friends." I gestured toward Lei, who was looking just as surprised as Esteban.

Lei looked back and forth between us, then narrowed her eyes as though trying to figure out what other secrets I'd been keeping from her. She turned to Esteban and Ranji and held out her hand. "Lei. I'm the one that contacted you."

Esteban pointed at us with both hands, unsure who to point at with which finger as he tried to piece it together. "Wow. We have really got some catching up to do." He cleared his throat. "You remember Ranji. Ranji, this is my buddy Cohen."

"Delighted." Ranji had a narrow goatee of ringlets with curly cues shaved into the hair on his cheeks. His fancy beard dipped in a nod toward me and then he turned to Lei. "More than delighted." He grabbed her hand and caressed it while I considered ripping his ringlets out, then he gestured toward a booth that had just been vacated. "Come. Let's sit and talk and you can tell me what you know."

Celeste reappeared as we were sitting down. I offered her my seat, but she refused. Instead, she stood and glowered at Esteban and Ranji. It was so scary I was suddenly glad she'd decided I could be trusted after all.

Ranji smiled deeply at Celeste, then spoke to Lei. "You were lucky to catch me today. Very, very lucky. This is a busy time for me. What can I say? Business is good. My record is impeccable. You will not be disappointed. So, please, tell me, what are you looking for today?"

We'd already agreed that telling him about the ear was out of the question. The Client had made it clear that total secrecy was of the utmost importance. Celeste had argued that by contacting them at all we were in breach of contract, that we didn't have enough info to give them for it to do any good anyway, and that dragging someone else into this was asking for trouble. But Lei had insisted that we would never be able to find the ear on our own. So here we were. Sitting in a bar in the middle of the night, sharing a booth with Ranji. My life had never felt more upside down than it did at that moment.

"I'm looking for a person." Lei splayed her fingers on the table.

"Ah, superb, yes. Wonderful. People are my specialty. I always get my man. Do you have a name, or a photograph?"

"No. Nothing. We can't even tell you what he looks like. I'm not even positive it *was* a man."

"He was a man," I said with certainty. "Forgive me for the generalization, but I've never met a woman who could hit like that."

Lei raised an eyebrow at me. "Get hit by a lot of women, do you?"

Celeste snorted softly. "Have you met him? Of course he does!"

Ranji narrowed his eyes thoughtfully, writing in a small notebook he'd pulled out of his pocket. "Okay. What else? Please, tell me everything you know."

"He was tall. About as tall as this one," Lei said, pointing her thumb at me. "But thinner. He was wearing a wet suit and diving mask if that helps anything. And at 2:25 a.m. he showed up at Heritage Funerals and Cremations and he took something from us. The item is unimportant," Lei added quickly when it looked like he was about to ask. "We just need to find *him*. He ran off heading east." She glanced at Celeste. "Where did you lose him?"

Celeste made a noise like a peach pit stuck in a garbage

disposal. "Burnside. Near the 405." She said each word like she hated herself for speaking them.

Ranji whistled, smiling. "That is not much to go on."

"But can you do it?" Lei asked.

We'd questioned Saifi for as many details as he could give us, but the diver had kept him at gunpoint and never spoken, so he knew barely more than we did. The fact that Saifi was now standing in the corner playing Pac Man and laughing with Jimmy was a testament to his resilience.

Ranji smiled. "Never have I worked with so little information to go on. But never have I failed in my pursuit."

"We don't have to pay unless you find him, right?" I asked.

"Only the deposit. But it is fair, it is very fair. I sent you the contract, so all that's left is for you to sign."

Lei nodded and pulled out her phone.

Celeste leaned over and put her hands flat on the table, glaring at Esteban and Ranji. "Can you give us a moment, please?"

Ranji nodded magnanimously. "Of course, of course. Please, discuss." He waved his hands over the tabletop and he and Esteban slid out of the booth and moseyed over to the bar.

Celeste fell into their seat and leaned her arms on the table, staring at Lei. "*Now* you decide to trust somebody? Will you just step back and think about how reckless this is for two seconds? We don't need them. We can find him ourselves. This is what we *do*."

I looked between them, trying to gauge Lei's response. I hated for her to have to spend her hard earned money, but letting someone else deal with the diver would make things a lot safer and easier for the five of us.

Lei's face was flushed, her eyes almost wild. "We don't have time to step back. We don't have time to find him ourselves.

Every passing second he slips further away, and I am smart enough to know when I'm beat!"

"What are you talking about?" Celeste asked. "Why are we suddenly so short on time?"

Lei closed her eyes and took a deep breath, then flipped through a few screens on her phone and handed it to Celeste.

Celeste read the screen and leveled a look at Lei. "When were you going to tell me?"

"I wasn't. We were going to finish in time, and it wasn't going to matter."

Celeste rolled her eyes in frustration. "Will you stop treating me like a child? You act like you are the only one who can handle this, but all you're doing is crippling us by keeping us in the dark like this."

"What?" I asked. "In the dark about what?"

"The message. From the Client. The one he sent this afternoon," Celeste said, shoving the phone at me. "He says we're almost done. Only four more parts to go."

"Well, that's great, right?" I scanned the screen, trying to find the information that had upset Celeste so much.

She nodded and shook her head in turns, as though too frustrated to decide which head movement worked best. "Oh, it's great. We just have to be done by Friday."

"This Friday?"

Lei's jaw was tight as she swallowed with effort. "Yes. This Friday. The day after tomorrow. Or the deal is off."

I set down the phone. "This is ridiculous. Who is this guy? Who conducts business this way?" I realized how ludicrous that sounded given the job we were doing for him, but even so. Couldn't he at least be professional?

Lei ignored me, focused on Celeste, her eyes pleading.

"We are so close. With help, I know we can make it. We have to try."

Celeste exhaled like it hurt her to do so. "Or maybe we cut our losses."

Lei goggled at her. "You cannot be serious."

"I'm dead serious. It wasn't supposed to be like this, Lei. Things have taken a bad turn. It's just a job. We can get another one. We can figure out something else."

Lei looked like she'd swallowed a spider and was doing everything in her power to stay calm. She opened her mouth to speak several times but kept snapping it shut again. She finally seemed to get a hold of herself and raised her chin. "Thank you for your input. I hope you know that I'm only doing what I think is best."

She picked up the phone and flipped back to the contract.

"Lei!" Celeste pleaded. "Don't—"

Lei clicked the electronic signature button before Celeste could stop her. She tucked her phone away and waved at Ranji, giving him a thumbs up. Celeste threw up her hands in frustration and stormed off.

Ranji smiled and walked back over, sliding into the seat across from us. He picked up Lei's hand and caressed it some more. She raised an eyebrow at him.

His voice was deep and buttery as he spoke only to her. "Even if we find your mystery man, the item that he stole from you might be long gone. If it's the item you're after, let me find that for you as well. Then you would have your thief, *and* your missing property. You could relax and let me take care of everything. Wouldn't that be wonderful?"

Irritation coursed through me like it had been injected directly into my bloodstream. I really wanted to strangle him. At least a little bit. No one would blame me, would they? Esteban met my eye and shrugged slightly, a tolerant smirk on his face. I leaned over and stage-whispered to Lei out the side of my mouth, "Would you like me to punch him for you?"

She tipped her head toward mine, whispering out the side of her mouth like I had. "No thanks. I've seen you try to punch someone."

I imagined how I must have looked trying to stop the diver, flailing wildly with my equilibrium knocked off center. I swallowed with effort, smiling wanly.

Ranji let go of her hand. "Are the two of you . . . involved?" he asked, waving a finger between us.

I glanced at Lei in surprise, expecting her to laugh, but saw color rise in her neck.

"Of course not," Lei said, voice a little higher than usual. "Cohen here has a . . . work in progress."

Esteban grinned and shook his head. I avoided his gaze.

Ranji nodded. "Good for you. No one should be alone, you know? What's her name?"

I turned away. I was *not* having this conversation with Ranji.

Lei bumped me with her hip. "Don't be all private now. What was her name? Jessica? Joshua?"

"*Jocelyn.*" And there she was. In the very same room as us. Radiant as she set down a tray of drinks. She had traded her Heart Attack shirt for a Rolling Stones shirt that draped off one shoulder and a short apron tied around her waist. She smiled at the guy in front of her like he was the only person in the room. He would fall in love with her. Just like everyone else did. It was inevitable.

Lei followed my line of sight. "That's Jocelyn?" Lei asked. "Wow, you weren't kidding. She *is* beautiful. Are you going to talk to her?"

"No, she's working."

"Perfect! Let's go. I'll come with you. Thank you, Ranji. Contact me as soon as you have anything."

She shoved me out of the booth, and we walked toward the bar where Jocelyn was talking to the guy behind the counter. I dragged my feet, but we still made it. I swallowed loudly. Lei nudged me with an elbow.

"Hello there." I waved, then couldn't think of what to do with my hands so shoved them into my pockets so deep I nearly ripped through the bottoms.

Jocelyn smiled, no sign of recognition on her face. "Hi. Do you need a table?"

I was very aware of Lei standing next to me wearing an expectant grin. "Uh, no. Just wanted to say, 'Howdy Neighbor.'" I waved again, then let my hand drop. It dangled limply at my side.

Jocelyn stared at me for an eternity before her eyes flew wide. "Oh! It's you! I didn't even recognize you for a minute. I couldn't place you out of context, you know what I mean?" She laughed, her hand on my arm.

I laughed too, and the sound was loud in my ears. "Yeah," I said. "It's like running into your doctor at the grocery store." I cleared my throat. "I, uh, didn't know that you worked here."

She shrugged. "Yeah, sometimes. When I need the extra hours."

She smiled and I smiled and there didn't seem to be a single other thing in the world to say. "Well,"—I cleared my throat again—"It's great to see you, Jocelyn."

"You too," she said, grabbing a tray off the bar behind her. "And remind me what your name is?"

My heart stopped beating. Gave up pumping blood and left

me slowly dying as all the blood in my body pooled in my feet, leaving me all alone there in that crowded bar with Lei standing behind me. *She didn't know my name?* We'd been neighbors for three years. I'd helped her move in. I'd set up her network for her. I'd fed her cat when she went out of town. How could she not know my name?

"Cohen." Was that my voice? My face ached as it pulled into a smile. No sane person would believe it was a smile. No one that had ever seen me smile before would think that what I had smeared across my face was a smile.

Jocelyn smiled back and nodded, walking off to deliver the food. Taking all the oxygen in the room with her. Lei squeezed my arm. Without a backward glance I walked away from her and out the front door.

It was dry enough here under the awning, comparatively, but to my right where the roof gable ended, the water fell in a solid wall. I jumped out into it.

The rain pummeled me, and I welcomed it, willing it to wear me down to nothingness. I *was* nothing. The rain would be able to make short work of me.

Something yanked me from behind and pulled me back under the awning. I spluttered, wiping the water from my eyes to find Lei staring me down with all of her five-foot-four fury.

"What is wrong with you? Are you trying to drown yourself?"

I met her eyes, too humiliated and angry to even bother arguing with her.

"Oh, *pfft.*" She stepped close so that the heat of her fury warmed my face, but she still had to yell to be heard over the thunder of water. "Be as angry at her as you want, but please don't get yourself killed. I *need* you."

She was so close. There was so much fire in her dark eyes. She'd soaked herself just reaching into the water to rescue me, and her wet clothes clung to her.

All in one move I closed the distance between us, pushing against her until the wall at her back stopped us. Before she had a chance to protest, I lowered my mouth to hers, pressing her lips beneath my own.

She didn't stop me.

A klaxon went off in my brain, in case any parts of me weren't paying attention, letting me know that she was *kissing me back*. I slipped my hands to her waist, grabbing her hips and pulling her tight against me. She tasted amazing. I felt her fingers on my abs, warm through the wet of my shirt and they slid to my chest. I could kiss her forever. This was all I wanted to do from now on.

Her hands on my chest were hard and she shoved me away.

I stumbled, trying to catch my breath.

Her breath was short too, her chest rising and falling as she held me at arm's length.

That had been stupid. Incredibly stupid. But if her arm hadn't been holding us apart, I would have kissed her again right then. I tried to read her face, but her eyes were on the ground. Wet hair stuck to her cheek, and I reached out to brush it aside. She slapped my hand away so fast I didn't see it coming.

"I'm gonna let that go, cuz I think you just had your heart broken in there. And it meant nothing. Obviously."

She looked up at me then, but her expression was unreadable, her eyes totally closed off. "I don't have time to be angry at you. But pull yourself together, Hoard. You're better than this. Don't be an idiot." She gave me a little shove, then spun and slipped back inside the bar.

I leaned against the wall. What in the water world was I *doing?* I barely knew this woman. And I had way too much respect for her to treat her this way. Not that I treated anyone this way. Normally. *Oh rains,* what was *wrong* with me? I felt slightly sick with myself, but the memory of her lips against mine raised a heat in my face that the rain should have washed away. I let myself fall, sliding down the wall to sit in a soggy heap on the pavement.

Don't be an idiot, she'd said.

I wasn't entirely sure that was possible.

18

I don't know how long I sat outside on the pavement. A few groups went in and some out, some laughing at the rain, others barreling through it like the ranks of an enemy army, but all of them ignored me, like I was just another part of the building. When I finally sucked it up and went back inside, Lei, Jimmy, and Saifi were sitting in a booth in the back corner, hovering over a massive pile of poutine fries. As I approached, clothes still dripping, both boys smiled at me. Exaggerated, encouraging smiles. Saifi slid over, squishing Jimmy into the pink wall and patted the seat next to him. I sat half off the seat to keep from soaking him but kept my eyes on the fries.

Lei's fingers drummed the table. "So, are you guys doing all right?" The question was directed at Jimmy and Saifi. "Do you need to sleep?" Her voice sounded extra casual, like she really hoped they would say no, but felt compelled to ask. Maybe after ignoring the advice from Celeste and I earlier, it was something like an olive branch.

Saifi laughed, waving her off. "No. I love the night life. The middle of the night is when I'm at my best! Let's get the hand right now."

"We only have a few more hours till dawn. We won't have time," Jimmy said.

So, she hadn't told them about the Friday deadline. It was probably just as well. They seemed to have complete faith in her, positive that she had the whole situation under control. I tried to catch Lei's eyes to see what she was thinking, but her gaze never quite traveled my direction.

"I know," she said. "But if we wait until it's dark again to send something to the Client, he's going to blow a gasket. He expects us to deliver soon. I think Saifi's right. We need to find the hand now. Even if that means we end up still working during the day."

"Woohoo! I'm right!" Saifi cheered.

Jimmy raised his eyebrows at him as though in shock, but nodded at Lei.

"Okay. Good. Now we just have to convince Celeste. Because we can't find the hand without her."

Lei dropped her head into her hands, exhaling loudly. Saifi did the same. The pink wall behind Lei was splashed with neon signs of every possible color, shining and reflecting off her straight black hair.

Jimmy reached out and patted her on the hand. "She'll come around. She always does. We just have to wait her out."

Lei sighed then looked up, sniffing and brushing a hand under her eyes. "We're leaving in five minutes. You guys think you can be ready to go that fast?"

They agreed, and Lei slid out of her seat to find Celeste. The three of us were left alone, smooshed on one side of the booth, and I had the sensation that it was about to tip over.

"So," Saifi said, surveying the room. "Which one is your ex-girlfriend?"

I coughed, choking on a fry. "Excuse me?"

"Lei said your girlfriend dumped you, so we needed to be extra nice to you. But if you tell me who it is, I could go call her a bad name or something. Nobody messes with Cohen!"

"You will do no such thing." My voice was stern, but I realized I was on the verge of laughter, hysterical though it might be. "She didn't do anything wrong. We just . . . didn't have a future." I hadn't even meant to say that, but as I did, I realized it was true. I rubbed my eyes, refusing to let myself think about it now.

Jimmy nodded wisely. "Sorry to hear that, Cohen."

Saifi frowned. "She didn't slap you or anything?"

"No. Why would she?"

"Did she throw a drink in your face?"

"No."

"Did *you* hit *her*?"

"Of course not!"

Jimmy started laughing, burying his face in his arms.

Saifi scoffed, disgusted. "Did guys even get in a fight?"

"Nope."

"*Ugh*, adults are so boring."

Lei and Celeste were walking toward us. They were tense, but Lei forced a smile. Celeste gave us a sarcastic thumbs up. Apparently, we were back in business.

Sort of.

"I can't find him." Celeste sat hunched over her phone like a starving hobo over a meal. She typed some more. And then some more. Grumbled a bit, scrolled through a few screens, and typed some more. "I can't find Bob Cobb."

"How can that be? We've never had a problem finding any-one before."

"I don't know. As far as I can tell, he wasn't taken to a hos-pital. No mortuary has a record of him. He must have opted out of donation, because he seems to have bypassed harvesting. I might have more luck if I had my laptop, but as it is, I'm coming up empty."

"Then where *is* he?"

"What if he's already been buried?" Jimmy asked.

Saifi sat up straight. "Yea! Maybe we'll have to go dig him up!"

"No, there would be a record of a burial too, but I can't find anything. The only thing I can tell for sure is that he died the day before yesterday."

Lei chewed on her lip.

"We could go to his house," I said. Everyone looked at me. "I mean, if you think we should," I said to Lei. "His house has got to have a clue or two. Let's see what we can find out. If you want. Whatever." I held my hands very still, looking anywhere but at Lei.

"Where does he live?" Jimmy asked.

"An apartment in Vancouver." Celeste tapped on her phone, then set it on the table so we could all see. I did a double take. Was that really where he lived?

Lei nodded. "I like it. But it's not going to be easy to get into that building. We might have to get creative."

I grinned, shaking my head, and finally met her eye. "No, we won't."

19

It took a little over an hour to get to Vancouver on the train. The train was the one system of public transportation that ran twenty-four hours a day, but it provided a limited range of destinations. The tracks ran high above the ground to avoid any possibility of flooding, traveling at slower speeds during the rain. I'd always known the train went through the night, but I had wrongly assumed they would be running practically empty.

Lei had received exactly four messages from Ranji since we'd boarded. She'd been ecstatic at first, but her excitement had waned, as each message was encouraging, but mostly pointless. *We are making excellent progress. I assure you we will have our success very soon. You will not be disappointed.*

Jimmy and Saifi sat next to each other, playing a trivia game on Saifi's phone. Lei sat next to the window, staring at the water streaming down the plexiglass, with Celeste next to her, typing manically into her phone. I felt like a fifth wheel. My wet clothes beneath my rain gear still hadn't dried, and I embraced it. Being wet and wrinkly was my penance. Penance for trying to be something I clearly wasn't. I was a computer programmer with a job to do. Time to face it.

With my damp diagnostic printout in hand, I scrooched down in my seat, glad to finally have a real chance to go over it. The purpose of the demo was, obviously, to demonstrate what DarkWave could do. I'd created virtual cars that people could pretend to drive while the AI watched over everything and kept them all safe. I went over all the diagnostics and verified that the connection with the DarkWave network was working. The executing functions all showed the proper success messages, the ID numbers for my virtual vehicles getting passed around just like they should. As far as the diagnostics were concerned, the demo was behaving normally. There was no reason for it to crash. But it had, with the following error: *LookupError: Vehicle with id XRF000435 does not exist.*

Where the cripes did that vehicle ID number come from? I'd stuck my initials, CRH, at the front of all my vehicle ID numbers specifically so I could easily keep track of them. But even without the initials, this wasn't an ID number I recognized at all. Was there a bug in there somewhere that was randomly generating these weird ID's? And if so, why?

I stared out the window, frustrated. Huge drops of water flew past us in the dark, glistening in the pale light from the train. I took a deep breath and leaned across the seat to speak to Celeste in a low voice. "Switch seats with me for a second, will you?"

Celeste looked up at me then down at her seat and over at Lei. She shook her head, focusing on her phone again. She acted like I was to blame for everything that had gone wrong so far and was making sure I knew it.

"Oh, come on, please. There's no one sitting next to me. You could spread out. Stretch those long legs."

She glared at me, which I probably deserved.

"I'd like a word with Lei. Please."

She glared at me some more, then finally rolled her eyes and stood, moving out of the way so that I could slide into her seat. Lei looked over when I sat, surprised to see me there instead of Celeste, then turned back to the window without a word.

"Hi," I said.

She didn't respond, the reflection of her face pensive in the dim blue light overhead.

"You said you weren't going to be mad at me," I said.

"Did I?" She spoke straight into the window, her words bouncing off the glass.

"Yes. But you still seem . . . mad."

The wobbly light of the city glinted off her face as she kept her eyes on the world outside. "It's possible that my mood has nothing to do with you."

Oh. Okay. Sure. There was a lot going on, and frankly I still didn't understand most of it. I breathed in, then out. "Well, I—I'm sorry anyway. I wasn't thinking, and it was a selfish thing to do. It was stupid. I am stupid."

She turned to me then and raised an eyebrow, one side of her mouth tipped in an almost smile. "Yes, you are. Sometimes."

My eyes lingered on her mouth, remembering it against mine and I cleared my throat, shifting in my seat.

She watched me squirm for a minute, chewing on her lip. "So how do you know Jocelyn?"

She didn't seem to be mocking me. Just all earnest curiosity. "She's my next-door neighbor. For three years. But I really barely know her. We didn't hang out or anything." Not once. Not in all that time. How had I thought there was something there? I felt ridiculous. What other lies had I been telling myself?

"This is no fault of Jocelyn's," I said softly. "I was the one that built a courtship out of smiles and favors."

"I don't know," Lei said, considering. "She's lived next door to you for three years and she doesn't even know your name? I think she's a *little* bit to blame." She flashed her half smile at me.

I wanted to keep her talking, so I brought up the safest topic I could think of.

"Celeste told me you all are family."

"*I* told you that when I introduced you to them."

"I know, but I thought you were being sentimental."

Lei shook her head, raising her eyes toward the heavens.

"How old were you when you were adopted?"

Lei slid down in her seat and rested her knees on the seat in front of her. "I was a baby. Less than a year. They adopted me from foster care." She spoke the last line as I opened my mouth to ask for details, so I asked the next question queueing up in my mind.

"Do you have any contact with your birth parents?"

Lei shook her head. "It was a closed adoption. As far as I know, my birth mom just didn't want to be a mother. She wasn't interested in reunification or further contact. Dropped me off somewhere and never looked back."

"I'm so sorry." It felt very lame, but I couldn't think of anything else to say.

She shrugged. "I really don't think about it. I love my family. My parents—my *adopted* parents—are good people." She shifted in her seat. "And I'm glad I'm alive. Glad she gave birth to me instead of having an abortion. So now I can be here sitting next to the biggest dork I've ever met in my life."

"Hey—"

She bumped me with her hip and grinned. Maybe she could call me whatever she wanted.

"So, what about the rest? Are their stories the same?"

"Jimmy was three and Saifi was five. But Celeste was twelve." She lowered her voice but went on. "She grew up bouncing between her birth family and foster homes. I'm only a year older than her, but she's been in the family the shortest. I know it bothers her sometimes. Like she still feels like an outsider or something."

We glanced over at Celeste, but her eyes were glued to her phone.

"And . . . what about your parents? Where do they live?"

"In prison." Lei's tone was light and airy and sounded like she couldn't quite breathe.

"What? Really? Both of them? Why?"

Lei raised her eyebrows at me.

"Sorry. Sorry. But . . . *really*? Both of them? Why?" That was the same question as before. I opened my mouth to try again, and then gave up, knowing those same words were set to ask themselves once more if I tried.

She sighed, and I got the impression again that she couldn't quite catch her breath all the way. "It was the orphanage in India where they got Saifi. I've never been able to get all the details, but I guess the people who ran it were doing some sketchy stuff. My parents tried to alert the authorities, and then tried to adopt some more kids to get them out of there, and I think they cut some corners they shouldn't have cut. But they definitely pissed off someone with some very powerful friends."

My stomach clenched in knots, my sense of injustice flaring up inside of me like a torch. "Are they together?" I asked after a time.

"You mean like at a couple's prison? Where they can eat dinner and take art classes together?" Her tone was a bit nasty, and I realized this wasn't the safe topic I thought it was. She looked back out the window. "Sorry. This is hard for me to talk about. I just have to get them out."

I nodded. "How? What can you do?"

"We've got a lawyer. He says we have a really good shot. But we've got to be able to pay him, and this was the best way to get the most money the fastest." She paused, fiddling with the Velcro on her sleeve. "I hope I can trust the lawyer. I just . . . don't have a choice."

I held in a groan. Hopefully they'd found a real lawyer, and not some charlatan who was going to rip them off. I phrased my next words carefully, so she wouldn't think I was telling her what to do. "If he doesn't feel right, you could always find a different attorney. This is a big deal, and not a relationship you should jump into lightly."

Lei turned to me, a deadness in her eyes. "Thanks for the tip. If only you'd been here a year ago. I'm sure you could have saved us from the crooked lawyer who took all our money and let my parents go to jail."

I tried to swallow but couldn't. She turned away, staring at the scenery again, and swiped a hand across her eyes. She held her chin high, but her shoulders drooped, as though no matter how strong she tried to be, the weight of all her responsibilities was proving to be too much for her.

Against my will, my hand reached out and touched hers, then gently picked it up and intertwined our fingers. I waited for her to slug me, but she didn't.

"How can I help?" I asked.

She closed her eyes and let her head fall back against the seat. I couldn't tell if she was grateful for the offer, or annoyed, but she didn't pull her hand away. And I didn't let go. I didn't want her to carry the weight of all this alone anymore.

Finally she spoke, voice thick. "Just help me finish the job. I know the Client is off his rocker, but he's kept his word so far. If we can finish in time, he'll pay us what we need. And this lawyer is a good one. He *has* been working on our case. A lot. And he's going to get it reopened and he's going to win, which means I've got to be able to pay him."

"Okay. I'm glad. Sorry." How many times was I going to have to apologize to her? I brushed my thumb along the back of her hand.

She stared at our hands and took a breath. "Platonic," she said, as though it were a complete sentence. She cleared her throat and sighed. "I'm sorry about Jocelyn. But I'm not a good back up plan. Taking care of my family, finishing the job, that's all I have time for."

"That's not what this is," I stammered. "I—"

I what? I liked her? Wanted to take care of her? Just wanted to hold her hand? So far, my plan to not be an idiot wasn't going very well. This new world I found myself in tied me up inside like an old set of wired headphones.

Lei didn't move, just watched our clasped hands as though waiting to see what they would do. I'd told my hand not to hold hers, but do you think it listened?

I sat up and untwined my fingers from hers, my face flushing with heat. She was right. Here I was, messing things up once again. Not what she needed at all. I scooted over so that there was a gap between us, and the heat of her body could no longer transfer to mine.

It didn't work. I deeply respected her desire to focus on her family, but the more I told myself to stop thinking about her, the more aware of her I was. I twiddled my thumbs and jiggled my foot until finally the train slowed, brakes squealing loudly.

So that Lei could get out of the seat without any undue physical contact, I jumped up and moved out of the way. Celeste narrowed her eyes at us but passed by without a word.

It was seven blocks from the train station to our destination. We had a couple hours before sunrise, and the rain now fell in a light but steady shower. Just enough to keep us wet. Saifi's arm appeared to be bothering him, but he raised his chin and soldiered on like he was determined to be brave and strong. I wanted to help him, but I couldn't think of how. Finish the job, I supposed, like Lei said. So we could get them out of this. So he could be a kid again.

The apartment building was currently undergoing renovations, an attempt to restore and refresh the original art deco style interior and the water damaged exterior. There was scaffolding along the south foyer wall surrounded by buckets of tile, the mosaic pattern beneath the crown molding still unfinished. I led them to the elevators and the security guard/elevator operator waved.

"Cohen! What are you doing here in the middle of the night? Is everything all right?"

"Hey, Reggie. Yes, everything's okay. We've got a little emergency, and I've got to see my grandmother. No, no. We're fine, but it can't wait. Am I okay to go up?"

"Of course, of course. Middle of the night might be the best time to see her anyway. That woman is never at home."

Reggie colored ever so slightly, and I smacked his arm

good-naturedly. He'd had a crush on Gran for as long as I could remember but was far too professional to do anything about it. He pushed the button for the eleventh floor, his gigantic gray mustache vibrating under his nose.

We rode up in silence, serenaded by the elevator music, until I finally realized it was a Cloud Busters song. I hummed along softly, bobbing my head. Lei was doing the same, and when I caught her eye, she dipped her head, hiding a smile.

We got off on the eleventh floor, said our thank-yous and goodbyes to Reggie, and started off down the hall, footsteps soft against the faded red carpet. As soon as the elevator closed, I steered the group around and down a different hall. This one had its carpeting removed in preparation for new flooring, and our shoes clomped against the bare wood. I pulled the door to the stairwell open, checking our surroundings to make sure no one was watching us, then ushered everyone inside.

"We *aren't* going to visit your grandma?" Saifi asked, his voice echoing around the small space.

"I don't think we have time." Especially not time to explain my new friends or explain what we had come to Vancouver to do. I hated lying to Reggie and was going to have to come up with another lie on top of the first to keep him from asking her about our visit later.

"But I *want* to meet your grandma."

"She is pretty awesome. But not if you wake her up in the middle of the night. Then she's just scary."

He nodded. "How many more flights do we have to go?"

"This is the eleventh floor."

"And where do we have to go?"

"All the way to the top. Penthouse on the fourteenth floor."

Saifi sighed loudly. Celeste sighed too and stretched her legs, passing the rest of us as she took the stairs two at a time, like she couldn't bear to walk beside us any longer.

"Hey Saifi," I said. "Wanna race?"

"No, I got these short legs. You'll beat me for sure."

"Yeah, but you're young and energetic. I'm a tired old man."

"But I hurt my arm!"

"What if I go backward?"

Saifi grinned mischievously then darted up the stairs at a run.

Jimmy dashed up behind him. "I'll wait for you guys at the finish line. So we can tell who the winner is."

I turned and tried walking up the stairs backward but tripped and landed on my behind. Lei watched me, amused.

"I didn't realize this would be so hard," I said.

"I didn't realize you would be so slow." She sped past me, leaving me alone.

I turned my head enough so I could see the steps and started backward at a trot. I got better after a flight, and I thought I might catch him, but heard Jimmy say, "We have a winner!"

At the top of the stairs Saifi lay face down on the floor, panting loudly. "I wasn't built for stairs!"

"You guys feel like we should be quiet?" Celeste asked. "Or is this just a big party?"

Jimmy and I folded our arms in contrition and Saifi covered his mouth with his hand.

Celeste turned to open the door, then paused and pressed her ear against it. Her eyes widened and she stepped back. "There *is* a party. In there. Right now."

Jimmy stepped back with Celeste, and Saifi raised his head halfheartedly off the floor. Lei and I stepped forward, pressing our ears against the thick wooden door, facing each other. It was muffled and muted but there were definitely sounds coming from inside.

Someone was in the dead man's apartment.

20

"**W**hy are there people there? It's the middle of the night."

"What now? What do we do?"

"Can I pull the fire alarm?" Saifi asked, excited. "Everyone would leave then."

"Yes, but they would all leave *this* way, since this is the fire escape."

"Oh."

"Shh!" Lei hushed us all loudly, ear still flattened against the door like it could somehow help her know what to do.

"Lei, I don't think—" I started.

She swatted at me with another, "Shh." Then she pulled back from the door, confusion all over her face. She tried the knob, while we all protested as quietly as we could. Fortunately, it was locked.

"We're going to have to leave and try again later," I said.

Celeste groaned and pulled out her phone, like she could mobile her way through the problem.

Lei shook her head, determined. "Jimmy, come and pick this lock."

"What if it's his wake? We can't break into his apartment during his wake. That would be disrespectful."

"No one has a wake at four thirty in the morning," she said as Jimmy worked, and with a click, the door popped open.

"I'm going to," Saifi said. "My wake is going to be a party that lasts all night long."

"It could be a cleaning crew," Jimmy said. "Maybe we could hide out here until they leave."

"It's not a cleaning crew," Lei said.

"How do you know?" I whispered anxiously.

"I just do." She pushed the door open.

We stood, staring down a narrow hallway lined with dark wood paneling. I waited for a gaggle of janitors to run down the hall, brandishing mops and spray bottles, but instead what ran into us was the smell, like cat litter on steroids. It was so strong I could feel it, thick in the air. The sounds were far louder now, and Lei was right. This didn't sound like a cleaning crew. But what it did sound like seemed impossible.

Lei crept forward and the rest of us followed. The paneled hallway opened into a kitchen decked out in mahogany cabinets and marble countertops. The space was expansive, with an open floor plan. The windows ran from floor to ceiling, and everything else was covered in dark wood paneling, maroon velvet, and leather.

Everything screamed bachelor pad, except for the monkeys, which were just screaming.

A giant enclosure filled the far wall, running the width of the room. Inside it, two golden monkeys swung and screeched, like they were angry we were there. An immense blue macaw flew around the vaulted ceiling, swooping from window to window and landing in the rafters. A group of tiny yellow and black frogs jumped around in an aquarium pressed against the back of a green leather couch. A red panda sat on a boulder behind a plexiglass wall, eating an apple and watching us.

Everyone else seemed to be as stunned as I was. We stood in a row, trying to take it in, and trying very hard not to breathe through our noses. Every corner of the room was packed with cages and aquariums full of reptiles and fish and birds. It was like walking through an exotic pet store that had been invaded by a zoo. The macaw flew into her cage and started flinging her food at us, picking it up in her beak and tossing it our way, one piece at a time.

"How is this possible?" Lei asked in an awed voice. "How could he keep all these animals up here?"

Celeste gently tapped against the plexiglass in front of her. "Well, clearly he was loaded. Money makes all manner of things possible."

"What's going to happen to them?" Saifi demanded. "To the animals? They can't stay here all alone. Somebody has to help them."

"Not our problem," Lei said.

He glared at her. "It is *too* our problem. We're the ones that broke in here and that makes it our problem."

"Ugh, fine. We'll figure something out. But first, clues. We need to figure out where this guy is. Everyone, fan out. Take pictures of anything that seems even mildly like a clue to his whereabouts and call the rest of us over if you think you have something. We can't stay here all day."

We obeyed and fanned out. The pantry was enormous, holding mostly animal food of one sort or another. I took a mental note since I had no camera, but doubted it was helpful.

"Awesome!" Saifi yelled and I stuck my head back out of the

pantry. He stood in front of a cage, jumping up and down and pointing. "It's a boa! It's a boa! Can we keep him? Please?"

"Saifi. Stop trying to adopt these animals. I can barely feed *you*. There is no way I can feed a boa. Now would everyone focus on the job, please?"

"Oh, it's probably starving. Should we find its food?"

"Boas can go a few weeks without eating after a large meal," Jimmy said.

"What about monkeys?"

"The monkeys have food," Celeste said. "They're throwing it at each other, along with their poop."

I found my way to the one and only bedroom. The room was large, but the oversized dark furniture and the maroon curtain pulled around the four-poster bed made it feel smaller. On the wall just inside the door hung an enormous painting of a slight man, with poufy, pale brown hair, wearing a white tux, sitting in a couple's pose with a chimpanzee. They were both staring off into the distance like they shared the same dream, the same vision of the future.

The nightstand appeared to be a filing cabinet, but it wouldn't open. Locked filing cabinet kept in the bedroom seemed like the ideal place for a person to keep all the info about where they wanted their body to end up postmortem. I stuck my head back out into the hall and called to Jimmy so he could break into it with his handy lock picking skills.

Jimmy was followed by Saifi, Lei, and Celeste, who must have expected something more exciting than a locked nightstand. Saifi started circling the room, knocking on all of the wall panels looking for hidden compartments.

"Is this where he died?" Jimmy whispered loudly.

"Probably. It's also where he's dead." Celeste pointed through the maroon curtains around the bed at the body lying inside.

They all screamed.

"Oh, come on. You collect body parts for a living," I said. "We were in a mortuary a few hours ago."

"Will you guys pull yourselves together?" Lei snapped. "Saifi, you go stand watch. If anyone hears us, they're going to come investigate. They'll probably think it's the animals making all this noise, but I'd rather be safe than sorry. We'll hold down the fort here."

Saifi saluted and ran off. Celeste drew back the curtains and the three of us gathered around the bed. It was the man in the painting, the one with the chimpanzee. This had to be Bob Cobb. He was dead, alright, but he didn't look like a man who had simply died in his sleep. He was propped carefully and deliberately up on his pillows of navy-blue silk, quilt of gold brocade tucked conscientiously under his arms. His face was not the ashy gray of a corpse but was made up with rosy cheeks and a healthy glow. His sandy hair rested against the pillow around his head like a lion's mane.

This certainly complicated things. A click sounded behind me. Jimmy slid open the drawer on the filing cabinet and flipped through it. He selected a few folders and tossed them to us. One slid across Bob's legs and Celeste caught it. Then he ran out to keep Saifi company.

"I know he's right here in front of us, but *this*," Lei waved her folder in the dead man's direction, "is not quite what I was expecting. I need answers. Find something for me, fast."

Lei flipped through her folder, Celeste sat on the foot of the bed, and I tried to get comfortable leaning against the wall.

I'd never spent so much time around a dead body before. It grew increasingly unsettling the longer we were there. And my folder was useless. Several letters to someone named Eugene. Verbose sonnets of gratitude and grief. Promises of forgiveness. They were heartfelt, but for one reason or another he'd never sent them. I kept reading, looking for clues, but it seemed very pointless and very intrusive.

"I got something," Celeste said, pulling out a paper and dropping the folder on the bed. "I was right. He opted out of donation."

Lei groaned. "I really hoped we were just too early. What is he doing here? When are they going to bury him? What are they waiting for?"

I reached across the bed and from the folder Celeste had laid down I pulled a sheet of paper with an embossed seal at the top.

Lei growled, papers fanned out in her hands, her expression one of exasperation. "There's nothing here. Tell me one of you has something for me."

"I can tell you why he's here," I said, shaking my head in disbelief. "We are standing around what is now the final resting place of a Mr. Robert Cobb." So much for collecting his hand.

"Here? He's *buried* here? Can he do that?" Lei looked between me and the lifeless form of Bob Cobb in his bed.

"I cannot believe the building owners would ever agree to that. I don't care how rich he is," Celeste said.

I flipped through a few more pages. "Apparently he owns the building."

"How do you own a building when you're dead?" Celeste asked.

"I don't know, but according to his will, there's a clause stating the top floor is to remain untouched."

"Nice. I'd love to be there when the rest of the tenants find out."

Lei tapped her folder against her leg. "Someone is going to find a way around that eventually. No one is going to let this prime real estate go as a mausoleum."

"What's with the monkey?" Celeste asked, pointing at the painting.

"The Chimpanzee's name is Eugene," Lei said, waving another piece of paper.

I did a double take. Those letters were written to the monkey? "What happened to him? I didn't see him with the rest of the zoo."

"Oh," Lei gasped. "He was put down. But it doesn't say why."

I looked again at the painting of Bob and Eugene the Chimpanzee. He held the chimpanzee gently. Lovingly. Like a child.

We all stood, staring at the prostrate form of Bob Cobb. Lei seemed to be searching his face, like his still features might hold the clues she needed to make sense of everything.

Celeste nodded slowly. "Well. Get the hand, and let's go."

Lei tipped her head back, staring at the ceiling in frustration. "What do you mean, get the hand? It's still attached."

"I know. So detach it, and let's get out of here. This place is creepier than the mortuary."

Lei stared at her. I watched the two of them in their silent battle of wills over how to steal a hand from a deceased animal lover. Never had I ever expected that these would be the kinds of problems I would be faced with.

"What's the matter?" Celeste's voice was impatient. "You used to do this at the mortuary. Why is now any different?"

"I'll tell you why it's different." I jumped to Lei's aid, pointing at the paper Celeste still held in her hands. "He was a non-donor. He wanted his body in one piece after he died just like it was when he was alive, and it is not our place to ignore his wishes. Not to mention that this is his final resting place. You'd be desecrating his grave *and* his body, which I'm pretty sure is a felony."

Lei nodded enthusiastically, gesturing toward me, as though glad I had mentioned it. "Yes. Yes. Exactly. Every time before we were taking things no one wanted. It was like stealing garbage from the dump. But *this*. This is . . . it's . . . I don't know what it is. A whole new level of wrong."

Celeste threw her hands up. "So, what do you wanna do?"

Lei closed her eyes and screwed up her face, like she was considering whether now was an okay time to cry or not. I wanted to comfort her but wasn't at all sure how to platonically comfort someone who was in the process of deciding whether they should remove a corpse's hand or not.

Celeste watched me do my indecisive dance and shook her head. Like she couldn't believe I was for real. "You know we don't have a choice," she said to Lei, her voice softer now. "Just like you told me at Vigil. We finish this job, and we can get out of the game, and you can go to nursing school, and Mom and Dad will come home, and we'll be a happy family again and everything will be right with the world." She stared at the window while she said it, voice almost wistful.

Lei turned around and faced the painting of Bob and his chimpanzee. I didn't see any more answers there than there were in Bob's dead face, but she seemed to be searching the artwork for a solution.

"Well?" Celeste prodded.

"Get out and let me think."

Celeste shrugged and glanced my way. I shook my head help-lessly. She rolled her eyes, exhaling loudly, and walked out.

"Do you want me to go too, or . . ."

Lei looked over at me like she wasn't sure who was talking. "Oh. Not you. Stay. Please."

I tapped my hands against my thighs while she contem-plated the painting, gazed at it, scrutinized it, making a clicking sound with her tongue. I shuffled from foot to foot trying not to rush her, but more than ready to be out of there.

I coughed. Cleared my throat. "Surely, your Client doesn't expect you to remove the hand yourself. Can't you just explain the situation to him?"

Lei inhaled deeply then let all the air out with a *whoosh*. "Celeste's right. We don't have a choice. He doesn't accept any mitigating circumstances. It's in the contract." A tear slid down her cheek. "I should never have accepted this job. This Client is bad news. He says he has more evidence against my parents, enough to keep them in jail for years. It's supposed to be an 'extra incentive' to fulfill the contract."

My eyes widened at that shocking bit of info, but I held my tongue.

She rubbed her face, then wrapped her arms tightly around herself. "I could tell he was trouble as soon as he hired us, but I was so sure we could pull this off that I agreed to it anyway." She pointed a shaky finger toward the kitchen area where everyone was. "No matter what I do I put them in more danger."

I wanted to hug her, but instead I ran a hand through my hair that had somehow found the means to stand on end once again. This was bad. Everything about this whole situation was bad, and we didn't have time to work up something to make it better. Sometimes the only plan that made any sense was the one that was laying right in front of you, staring you in the face, as it were.

I walked around to the other side of the bed, opposite Lei. "Which hand are we supposed to get?"

She swallowed loudly. "The left." She gestured at the hand lying in front of her on the bed. She inspected it. "He's got rather delicate fingers, doesn't he?"

I looked down at the hand in front of me. It didn't look especially delicate, but this wasn't the time to argue. I caught Lei's eye across the death bed. "I think Bob will understand."

She raised an eyebrow at me.

"I mean it. If he understood the circumstances, I think he'd be happy to give you a hand."

Lei rolled her eyes and turned away. "Are you kidding me right now?" The hint of a smirk tugged at her lips.

"Anyone who loved a monkey the way this man did would understand how important family is."

Lei rested her hand lightly on Bob's and slid up the sleeve of his paisley pajamas. She gently lifted his arm, her eyebrows knit in confusion as she inspected it. "He had some kind of surgery. It almost looks like . . ." She turned the arm slowly so she could view it from all angles, then shook her head. "I don't know." She laid his arm gently down again, suddenly all business. "But I don't have the right tools."

"Would a scalpel work?"

"Sure, but like I said, I don't have one. He's probably got a meat cleaver in the kitchen that I could use and yes, I do know how to do this with a meat cleaver. It was mandatory training. I was never sure what situations would necessitate harvest by cleaver, but we all had to do it. I think the harvest director had been a psychopathic killer in his past."

Wrinkling my nose, I tried not to picture a room full of mortuary interns chopping up dead bodies like beef at the butcher's. I pulled out my multi-tool and flipped out the scalpel, passing it to her handle first.

She looked at the knife and up at me in surprise. "Why do you have a scalpel?"

I gave her a funny look. "For when I need a really sharp knife."

She raised one eyebrow in question.

I stared back. "You have no idea how useful scalpels can be. I also have a saw blade that attaches to this system that I think is sharp enough to cut through bone, but unfortunately, I left it at home."

She took the multi-tool from me, shaking her head. "You are just full of weird surprises."

"What else do you need? How can I help?"

"I don't know. A cutting board, I guess, and maybe some plastic bags."

I ran out into the apartment proper. Celeste stood with her face pressed against the wall of a gigantic aquarium of sorts, cooing and gently tapping on the glass. She gasped, laughing, as the otter inside twisted and spun in the water in front of her. I found a cutting board next to the stove and grabbed a handful of plastic bags out of the pantry, then went back into the bed-room where Lei waited, tenderly running her fingers across the dead man's wrist.

She glanced up quickly when I entered, as though caught doing something she shouldn't be.

"Sorry. Just familiarizing myself with the specimen."

I handed her the items I'd brought in with me. "Anything else?"

"Just stay here with me, okay?"

Desecrating bodies. That was my life now. What next? Stealing Wi-Fi? Jaywalking?

I nodded. "Of course."

She smiled then, a smile that felt totally out of place for the moment, a warm, genuine, affectionate smile, and for a breath I forgot that we were standing next to a dead man holding the tools we intended to use to relieve him of his hand.

Lei took one of the shopping bags I'd brought in and wrapped it around the cutting board then turned to Bob and slid it under his hand. I stepped as far away as I dared. She slid her free hand into the dead one and balanced the scalpel between her fingers. "I'm sorry Bob. And thank you."

21

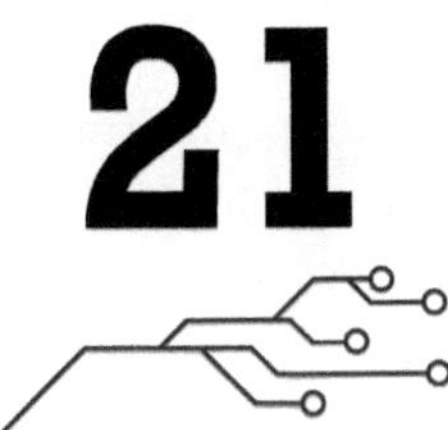

It took longer than I expected it to. Lei deftly slid the knife in at the wrist joint, and I turned away to study the wallpaper, trying not to think about the sounds I was hearing. I peeked over my shoulder when I heard her exhale. I'd been bracing myself for blood, but there was none, just some extra moisture. My stomach turned. Bob Cobb was embalmed and perfectly preserved. And it was still gross.

She picked up the hand, looked it over again, murmuring to herself. "I really don't understand . . ."

"What?"

She lifted her head. "Hmm? Oh, nothing. Will you grab a specimen case out of my duffle?"

I unzipped the faded blue bag and found a specimen case and a smallish SMax box and she wrapped and boxed the hand up before my nausea even wore off.

"Okay. I'll label it on the way. Let's move."

I followed Lei back out to the kitchen, nearly running into her when she stopped short and let out a strangled cry.

The tall thin figure in diving gear stood in the kitchen with

Celeste captive, the blade of a wicked-looking knife at her throat.

For a moment, shock usurped all my other emotions. "Wha—where did you come from? I was out here just a second ago."

"Is that really the most important question right now?" Celeste asked, tone cold. She looked angry enough to spontaneously combust.

The diver still wore the black diving gear: fitted hood, zippered boots, gloves, and a diving mask. He wore no tank or flippers, but every inch of him was covered except his washed-out eyes. "Hand first," he said, his voice was high and soft, muffled by the mask over his face.

"Why?" Celeste demanded. "What is your plan here?" She seemed annoyed more than anything else, and I was extremely impressed by her ability to stay cool under pressure.

Lei's eyes were wide with fear. "Who are you?" she asked, her voice soft. "What could you possibly want with these things?"

While she talked, I scooted over in what I hoped was a casual manner, sidling close to the cage on my left.

The diver cocked his head to the side in a way that seemed almost familiar. "Reasons don't matter. I'm taking the hand. You need to decide what you are willing to lose for it. *I* have *nothing* to lose."

"Everyone has something to lose!" I lifted the latch on the boa cage and threw the door open, then backed away as quickly as I could. Everyone looked over at the movement. The pandemonium I'd anticipated didn't come. The boa didn't move. I wasn't even sure it was alive.

The diver's shoulders started shaking as he laughed. Silently.

At me. The monkeys started screeching and throwing themselves at the cage door, like the diver was laughing at a frequency only they could hear. With one swift motion Lei undid the lock on the tamarin cage and one of them launched itself at the door, throwing it open. The diver wheeled around, startled, and the knife pulled away from Celeste's neck. Celeste threw back her head and smashed it into the stranger's face.

He stumbled, grabbing his face and growling, and Celeste hesitated, her arms reaching toward him like she wasn't sure if she should punch him or hug him. I ran straight at him and rammed my shoulder into his gut, pulling his legs out from under him. We hit the ground so hard the air whooshed out of his lungs.

Jimmy and Saifi ran into the room from where they'd dutifully stood watch in the hallway.

"Someone's coming up on the elevator!" Saifi shouted.

I'd planned to hit the diver as many times as it took to incapacitate him, but at Saifi's words, everyone froze. We needed to get out. Now. And I didn't know how to do that with a prisoner in tow. I met his eyes, and I had that familiar feeling again, like I'd met him somewhere before. I jumped to my feet, fists pulled up to protect my face. He wouldn't catch me with my guard down again.

The diver only hesitated for a moment, then jumped up and ran down the hallway leading to the fire escape stairs we'd used on our way here. The door slammed behind him and there was a thud and a crunch. Celeste, Jimmy, and I ran after him, reaching the door in a cluster. Celeste yanked on it, but it didn't budge.

"No. No! He's blocked it somehow!"

Jimmy and I both tried it, unwilling to believe it until we'd tested it ourselves.

"See?" Celeste yelled at us, annoyed, and we followed her back into the kitchen. She shook her head at Lei, whose face was white, chest rising and falling as she tried to stay calm.

The five of us looked at each other, each of us no doubt trying to come up with some magical solution for how to get out. The elevator dinged.

"Oh, I know!" Saifi said. "This way. Hurry."

We ran after him, stepping all over each other as he led us back into the bedroom containing Bob Cobb's now one-handed corpse. Saifi opened what I'd thought was a closet, revealing a small elevator.

"It must have been an old dumbwaiter or something that they converted for passenger use," Jimmy said, amazed.

Voices floated down the hall, something about transporting snakes. I'd been afraid Mr. Cobb intended to have his animals 'buried' with him, but I suppose I should have known better.

"In, in, in!" Lei ordered, shoving everyone inside, pushing at their feet with the toe of her boots. The elevator was about the size of a smallish phone booth and was absolutely not going to fit five people inside of it. I made Lei go ahead of me, then she grabbed me and pulled me in with them, smooshing back into the elevator until everyone moaned. I elbowed the button for the ground floor and the door slid shut.

We started to fall. Slowly. The way a balloon falls when it begins to run out of helium.

"Are we there yet?" Saifi's muffled voice came from somewhere I couldn't see. "I can't breathe! And my face is in Jimmy's armpit!"

Lei's nose was pressed against my chest, like she was intentionally keeping things as awkward as possible. And I realized all at once that I didn't feel awkward at all. I was more comfortable crammed into an elevator with her and her family than I had ever been at any after-work socializing function. My heart was racing, and I thought I could feel hers racing too. Was that because of the situation? Or possibly because of me? Her hair smelled like lavender, and I tried to breathe evenly so that she wouldn't know I was smelling her. It helped that we were packed so tightly inside the little elevator that there was no room for my lungs to expand.

"Are we there *now*?" Saifi mumbled again. Celeste growled and the elevator lowered a few more inches, only the faint squealing from above telling us that it was moving at all.

"Hey guys," Jimmy grunted from the vicinity of my shoulder, voice squeezed through a pinched pipe. "How much . . . do you think we weigh . . . all together?"

I followed his gaze. On a small plaque was a sign in lovely orange letters, "Weight Limit: 250 pounds."

"Oh, great," Celeste panted.

Lei tried to look over but couldn't turn her face far enough.

"It'll be fine," I wheezed, surprised how difficult it was to speak. This elevator had no doubt been perfect for Bob Cobb and his monkey, but we were definitely pushing it. "They always make those warnings lower . . . than they need to be, because they know . . . that people will . . . ignore it. They're just . . . covering . . . their behinds."

We drifted down a few more inches and the elevator lurched. We grunted in unison, as our squished bodies were jerked around. Another slight lurch, a nauseating grating sound, and then we dropped.

Everyone screamed as we fell for what felt like forever. We jerked to a stop again, and the elevator groaned, shifting and shaking. We groaned along with it but seemed to be okay. We were packed in so tightly it had kept us from ending up in a heap on the floor.

Everyone started talking. Or moaning rather, since speaking was no longer really possible.

"We have to get out." Lei managed to make herself heard over the rest of us. I tried to turn around to pull the door open, but there wasn't enough space. Lei forced her arms around me to squeeze her fingers between the doors but wasn't in a position to get them to go anywhere.

My brain took *that* moment to think about how much I liked being in her arms. I liked it a lot. Even in the face of certain death.

Jimmy and Celeste's arms reached past my head. They leaned forward to get into a better position and what breath I had left was forced out of me like my chest was a bellows. They pushed and pulled, and the door resisted. I finagled my arms up over my head, shoved my fingers between the doors, then reached down to some pit of caveman power deep in my belly and roared, forcing the doors open with all my might. The combined strength of all of us finally pried the doors apart. They separated an inch, then two inches, and then the elevator dinged, and the narrow doors slid open all the way. I popped out, like a refrigerated roll out of a can, falling backward and landing butt-first in a big yellow mop bucket.

The door had opened into some kind of cleaning closet on the seventh floor—so the sign said—but the elevator was a good foot below the opening, and I wasn't sure how much longer that would be the case. The elevator continued to bounce slightly like someone was yanking on it from below.

We were out of time.

"Move! *Now!*" I urged, lifting myself up and climbing out

of the bucket. I grabbed whoever was closest, which happened to be Saifi, as Lei pushed him out before her. I dragged him up and into the closet then reached for Jimmy. He slipped through the opening like a fish. I shoved him behind me and reached forward again as the elevator continued to heave and pitch. Celeste and Lei seemed to be having a private argument about who should go first.

"Hurry!" I yelled, frantic. Lei shoved Celeste out the doorway. I grabbed her and pulled as she scrambled up and out.

The elevator fell a couple more feet and tilted dangerously, like it was sad that everyone was leaving. Lei stumbled, landing in the low corner. I leaned in, very aware that the elevator could guillotine me at any moment, while she tried futilely to get to her feet. I pushed farther in to grab her, but she acted like a drowning person, pushing away help.

"Come on! Take my hand. I'll get you out. Please!"

The elevator wouldn't hold still, but she roared, braced her arms behind her and shoved herself up. Her hand slipped into mine and I pulled, hand over hand, until my arms were around her and I yanked her out, throwing both of us backward into the storage closet where she landed directly on top of me.

We looked back at the elevator. I held my breath, waiting for it to fall, wondering how close she'd come to having her legs ripped off. The elevator dangled, canted slightly, but held steady now, only a quiver as evidence that Lei had just climbed out of it.

I exhaled, gripping Lei around the waist, knowing I should let her go, but not ready to do so. She stared at me with her earnest searching stare, her face inches from mine, breathing heavily.

I cleared my throat. "I'm sorry I let him go. We could

have made him give us back the ear, or followed him or something, but there was no time. I'm sorry. I couldn't see any other way."

She nodded slightly but her eyebrows drew together forming a crease, her expression clouded.

That's when the fire alarm went off.

22

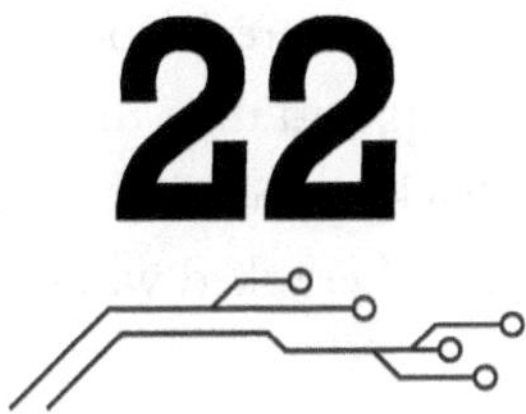

"**O**h, come on!" Jimmy shouted at the ceiling and shook his fist in the air. "Can we not catch a break? For once? One little, tiny break?" He caught us staring and defended himself by saying "It's just . . . arghh!"

"Can't argue with that," Celeste said. "Will you two get up?"

I stood up and held out a hand to Lei. "Do you think it's a real fire, or did some kid pull the fire alarm?"

"It wasn't me," Saifi said.

Behind me there was a sharp twang and a screech and a painful grinding sound. We turned in unison as something snapped and the elevator dropped out of sight. A moment later it smashed against the ground below, shaking the building.

We ran as a group to look into the elevator shaft at the destruction below.

"Holy—" Saifi said, his voice awed as the very real possibility of our deaths stared up at us from the bottom of its deep and narrow grave.

Then heat rained down on us from above. I looked up just as a ball of roiling fire chased the elevator down the shaft, heading straight for us. I spun and spread my arms, pushing everyone away from the doorway and blocking them with my body.

The heat blazed over me as flames rushed into the room, looking for the path of least resistance and most oxygen. We huddled down in a group, and then the fire was gone as fast as it had come, flowing back up the shaft to where it came from.

"Is everyone okay?" Lei asked without taking her eyes off me.

"Gran," I said, jumping to my feet.

"I think Cohen's brain got burned," Saifi said.

"This building is on fire. I've got to get Gran out of here."

Lei paused only for a moment. "Alright, people. Time to go. We've got a grandma to save. Move!"

"But what if that guy is out there waiting for us?" Jimmy said, standing in front of the door we were all trying to exit through.

"I hope he is," I said angrily. "So we can get back what belongs to us. Or rather, what doesn't belong to us, and needs to be retrieved from someone else it doesn't belong to, to be sent to *another* person that it also doesn't belong to."

"Well put," Lei said, straight faced.

I yanked the door open, peeked into the hallway and found it empty, then wildly gestured everyone through.

The remodeling hadn't reached this floor, and it was still resplendent in its ancient wallpaper. The baseboards and wain-scoting were nicked and dented from a century of luggage, feet, and shopping bags knocking against it. We rushed down the hall, and on turning the corner, joined with the elderly tenants shuffling their way toward the fire escape. How in the world were they going to get all these senior citizens out of the building?

Everyone seemed mobile enough, but stairs were the only option and we had seven flights of stairs to go.

I stood, unmoving, paralyzed by indecision. To get to Gran, we'd have to shove our way through four flights of stairs filled with old people in their pajamas. Frightened people. Who needed our help.

"Your grandma will make it out," Lei whispered to me, the hand package tucked under her arm. "Just like all of these people are going to. She's going to be fine. I'm sure of it." Several more elderly tenants brushed past us as I blocked the flow in my uncertainty. "Come on, Cohen," she said, "there are people right here who need us."

I nodded because I had no choice but to believe her, and we flowed with everyone else into the stairwell.

I held out my arm to a tiny woman with curly pink hair who was struggling down the stairs, breath labored as her hand ran along the railing. The others found tenants to help as well. Several of the more able-bodied tenants had stationed themselves throughout the stairwell, helping the others to move downward as quickly as possible.

"Don't know if it does much good to rush," said the tiny pink woman in a monotone voice. "My kids will put me in a home either way. They been waiting for an excuse."

I patted her hand distractedly. "We'll get you out of here. Even if I have to carry you on my back."

She looked up at me in shock, pulling away slightly like I was threatening to toss her over my shoulder that instant. She shook her head and picked up the pace, saying in her matter-of-fact monotone, "Better get a move on then. Not sure my heart can handle a piggyback ride."

While the fire alarm continued to blare, we filed down the

stairs, and at the bottom, stopped to make sure all of the people behind us got out as well. We exited on the ground floor, pouring out into the dim light before dawn. It was still raining, but lazily now, the sky no longer determined to rinse us off the face of the planet. The building was surrounded with fire trucks, police cars and ambulances waiting to check the health of everyone who came out.

We mingled with the crowd outside as I scanned the anxiety-filled faces. The smell of smoke clung to people's clothes and drifted through the air, settling like fog in the courtyard. Emergency personnel erected giant umbrellas and popup canopies to shield as many people as possible from the water that still drizzled from the sky.

Celeste scrunched up her shoulders, "We should probably slip out in all the commotion, and no one ever has to know we were here."

I ignored her. I wasn't going anywhere until I knew Gran was all right. If only I could find her. But she didn't seem to be here. She didn't seem to be anywhere. I turned back to the fire escape, where the firefighters had taken over the evacuation. One way or another I was going back up there to get her.

"Cohen Riley Hoard. What on this wet earth are *you* doing here?"

I turned, relief filling me up from the tips of my toes. Gran. She was okay. She'd gotten out without my help. I didn't need to fight my way through the firefighters and old people to drag her lifeless body out of a burning building. All I had to do now was answer her perfectly reasonable question.

My mind was empty, washed clear by the adrenaline of the last thirty minutes. I was going to have to tell her something. I'd never been a great liar, to my grandmother or anyone else. But it wasn't like I could very well tell her what we were doing there. Or who Lei and her family were. Or anything at all.

I darted to Gran and hugged her, my brain catching up slowly, like a boulder dragged through a river. "I'm so glad we found you." The umbrella in her hand jabbed me in the chest as I cast around weakly for any excuse I could think of.

"Cohen wanted to come check on you," Lei chimed in, coming to my rescue. "He had a bad feeling. He wanted to make sure you were okay."

I glanced back at her over my shoulder. I was psychic now?

Lei shrugged helplessly and went on. "I thought he was crazy, but then we arrived to find this." She swirled her hands around at the elderly tenants and emergency personnel milling about the grounds. "We looked all over for you. Do you have any idea what happened?"

Gran smiled blankly at her, confused, and I cleared my throat. "Forgive me. It's been a harrowing night. Gran, this is Lei, Celeste, Jimmy, and Saifi. They're . . . friends of mine."

She held out her hand, still dazed. "Charmed, I'm sure. I'm always delighted to meet Cohen's friends." She didn't mention that they were the first friends of mine she'd met in years, which I thought was considerate of her. She turned to me, white eyebrows low with concern. "And harrowing, yes. You couldn't have picked a better word. It is a comfort to see your face after this little ordeal, but what did you do to your head?" She gently touched the bandage Lei had applied after the diver hit me with a rock. "And I still don't understand. You say you had a *feeling* something bad was going to happen?"

I shot an annoyed glare at Lei and took Gran's arm. "All that matters is that I'm here and you're safe. Is there somewhere we can sit?"

Gran snatched another umbrella from a passing EMT and led us around the building to the garden on the east side. We gathered on some benches beneath a gigantic rubber tree whose branches had been trimmed and twisted to form an arch overhead.

"Look at me. Sitting outside in my housecoat before the sun is even up. I might as well be in a nursing home. You'll have to forgive me. When I heard the fire alarm, I considered getting dressed, but I knew I'd end up pinned under a fallen beam in my unmentionables. It didn't seem like the time to stand on propriety."

Her 'housecoat' was a pale pink silk kimono covered in white peacock feathers. She sat, wrapping it across her knees like she was straightening a ball gown. Silvery hair was twisted into a knot atop her head, her face fresh and rosy. Gran looked more put together in her robe than some people did in their Sunday best, but I knew she hated being seen without being fully done up.

Several of the building's other occupants were in the garden too, standing around, gossiping, and I could see Gran trying to listen, hoping to pick up on any news. Everyone nodded or waved as they passed but left her alone to talk with her guests. She regarded the group of us for a moment, like she was working to make sense of us, then shook her head. "I'm not at all sure what happened. The general idea seems to be that a fire started in the penthouse, but a fire on top of everything else seems too tragic to consider."

We all shared a look. Was it some kind of electrical problem caused by the tiny elevator? Or had the diver come back in after we left and started it himself?

I kept my expression as smooth as possible, though I knew

she could read me like a book if she had a mind to. "Um. Why?"

She reached out a hand and smoothed down my hair more tenderly than usual. "I'm not even sure how a fire would have started up there. Though I suppose it could have been some sort of gas leak? It is an old building after all." She stared at her hands while she talked, as though speaking to herself, then met my eye again. "You see, Mr. Cobb lives in the penthouse. Lived in the penthouse. He passed away the day before yesterday. It's just . . ." Her voice caught and she rested a hand on her chest, eyes on the ground.

"I'm so sorry, Gran. Was he a friend of yours?"

Gran nodded gravely, then shook her head. "I didn't actually *know* him. He was incredibly private and reclusive. Rarely left his apartment. He even had a private elevator built so that on the rare occasion that he did leave, he wouldn't have to see anyone." She smiled like she was confessing something scandalous. "So of course, I was fascinated. We all were. Eccentric billionaire living alone with his pets in the penthouse apartment?"

Eccentric didn't even begin to cover that man.

Saifi gasped, his eyes shining. "Lei . . . his pets," he pleaded, as though she could help.

Lei shook her head at Saifi and squeezed his hand. Saifi seemed to shut down, cave in on himself. Gran watched Saifi, face full of concern, hand fluttering at her neck.

Jimmy coughed. "Did you ever *meet* Mr. Cobb?"

Gran started, then turned to Jimmy with a sad smile. "I only ever saw him a handful of times, from across the foyer. I never was able to talk to him." We all nodded as the conversation waned, each of us seeming to be wrapped up in our worry and uncertainty.

"Actually," Gran said suddenly, voice unnaturally breezy, "the only thing I *do* know about him is that a few years ago there was some kind of accident involving a monkey." If she was trying to distract us, it worked. We watched her, waiting. No one spoke.

She sat up and straightened her kimono again. "Animal control came to the building, along with an ambulance. The building manager was beside himself. This is only a rumor, so I probably shouldn't repeat it, but they say that the monkey . . ." She swallowed, like she couldn't think of a decent way to say what she had now committed herself to say. "Well, the monkey . . . *removed* one of Mr. Cobb's hands. By force."

Lei paled. Her face was gray, and she looked dangerously close to vomiting.

"You mean the monkey ripped his hand off?" Saifi yelled.

Gran nodded, lips pursed.

"A monkey wouldn't do that," he said with conviction.

"Hmm. Well, I couldn't swear to it in court, but my neighbor Edith has a grandson who works at the hospital, and he was there when Mr. Cobb was brought in. Unless something else . . . *unhanded* him, but if so, what? Oddest thing I've ever heard. Honestly, the ladies in my poker club spoke of nothing else for weeks."

Saifi withdrew again. Lei leaned over, head between her knees. Jimmy patted her on the back, but she waved him off.

"Oh, I'm so sorry," Gran said. "It *is* a rather lurid story, isn't it? I didn't mean to upset you."

Lei shook her head as though insisting she was fine, but she clearly wasn't. She stood up and paced between the benches, then walked off, disappearing behind the rubber tree.

I followed, finding her looking small and afraid in a patch

of humongous heart-shaped flowers, gentle raindrops splatting against the leaves making them quiver around her. I approached her slowly, the way I might approach a bear who had stolen my lunch. "Are you okay? You seem . . . not okay. Are you okay?"

"I stole his hand!" She threw her arms wildly in the air, her face pale, her eyes crazed. "Just like the monkey did! Do you think the monkey ate it? Oh, I think I'm going to be sick?" She hunched over again, bending at the waist, but when I stepped closer, she stood up, throwing her hands in the air again. "What do you think it means? 'Cuz I know it means something, but I'm too freaked to figure out what, and I'm so tired my brain isn't working. And what about the fire? Did *we* start that fire? *Somehow?* I don't know what to do anymore. I can't be in charge. I'm doing this all wrong. I came up with this insane plot to try to help my parents, but what if all of us end up in jail? Will they let us be in jail together, do you think? Do they have family prisons?"

I took her arms and folded her into a hug. "*Shh.* It's okay. Everything's going to be fine, I promise." She shook slightly and buried her face against my chest. I smoothed her wet hair, brushing at the strands which clung to her face and reminded myself that I was only comforting her, and shouldn't be thinking about how nicely she fit against me. Shuddering breaths left her body as the last few raindrops of the night drizzled down, splattering against my head and running down my cheeks. Gradually her breathing slowed, and her lungs stopped heaving.

"Listen," I murmured, running my hand over her hair again. "I will personally see to it that you go to a family prison. Where you can eat dinner and take art classes together."

She laughed, a short burst of air against my chest and I rubbed her back in a very platonic way. Her arms slid around my waist and the SMax box jabbed me in the back. I cleared my throat to cover the hitch in my breath. We stood there, platonically, for who knows how long.

After a while she finally relaxed and leaned into me, head resting against my chest as though forcing the stress and worry away. "I can't believe your grandma lives in the same building as one of our assignments," she said without looking up at me. "I don't know if it's only a coincidence or . . . something else."

I chuckled softly. "Like what? Cosmic design?"

On the other side of the shrubbery a snooty voice began speaking, loudly and clearly so that everyone in the vicinity could hear.

"The authorities have cleared the building. It is now safe for you all to return home. The elevators are in perfect working condition. Please be assured that there was no damage beyond the penthouse. You will find everything in order. You are all free to return home. At your leisure, of course."

Lei considered me again for a moment, eyebrows lowered, then she cracked her neck, and I followed her back along the path that led to Gran. Celeste and Gran were chatting genially, Jimmy was asleep, and Saifi slumped against him, his eyes still open, focused on the ground.

"Excuse me!" I chased after Mr. Paisley, the building manager, as he strode away carrying his enormous umbrella to go make another announcement. He turned, looking shocked at being addressed. Some basic recognition came into his eyes, and he nodded for me to go on.

"Do you have any information on Mr. Cobb's pets?" I spoke loudly, so that Saifi could hear.

He seemed confused by my question, like he'd been

expecting a different query altogether, and it took him several seconds to switch gears. "Oh, my. Well, yes, I believe they're fine. The fire didn't spread beyond the master bedroom, so I believe it is safe to assume that, besides some smoke inhalation, they are all as well as can be expected, under the circumstances."

I exhaled more air than I'd realized I was holding. "And does anyone know how the fire started?"

He looked insulted. "That is for the authorities to determine, and really not your concern! I am *extremely* busy, so if you don't mind . . ."

I thanked him and he bustled off. Saifi closed his eyes as I turned back. He sighed with his whole body and his mouth stretched into a tired smile.

"Are you all right, dear?" Gran was saying to Lei. "I truly am sorry. Sometimes I turn into a gossiping old busy body if I'm not paying enough attention. Come upstairs and let me get you some water. You do look pale."

Lei smiled but shook her head.

"Thanks, Gran, but we'd better go," I said. "We had no intention of intruding on your morning."

"Nonsense. I insist. None of you look very well, if you'll forgive my saying so, and you need to get inside and have something to eat."

I gestured toward Jimmy and Saifi. "I think a nap is all we need. It's been a long night."

"Perfect," she said, like it had all been decided. "I'll make up the spare bedroom for whoever needs to sleep, and you can help me throw together something for breakfast." She lifted her chin and pushed past us, confident that we would follow.

Lei turned to me, chewing on her cheek as her eyes considered it.

"No!" I whispered. "I don't want her dragged into this more than she already is. We should go."

Celeste shoved Jimmy, pushing him against Saifi who fell over against the arm of the bench. "Wake up dummies. There's food upstairs." She stood and followed Gran without looking at either of us. Jimmy roused himself and he and Saifi followed Celeste.

"There *is* a SMax drop box in the lobby," Lei said in an attempt to convince me. "I saw it on the way in. And until we get our next assignment, all we can do is wait."

I shook my head, but felt my resolve crumbling as I watched the others follow Gran into the building. "Fine!" I growled, waving Lei on, and stomping after her as I followed them all back inside.

I had to assume that the diver was still around here somewhere, watching us. And now we were leading him straight to Gran. If I hadn't been so darn tired, I was sure I could have come up with a better plan. But by golly, if he laid one finger on her, I swore to the rain god Tal-Azra that he would *rue the day*.

Lei slipped the package into the SMax drop box in the lobby, planning to park herself there and wait for the rider to pick it up, but I convinced her that we had to keep a lower profile than that. I asked Reggie to keep an eye on it and let us know as soon as it was picked up, and the two of us headed upstairs to my grandmother's apartment.

23

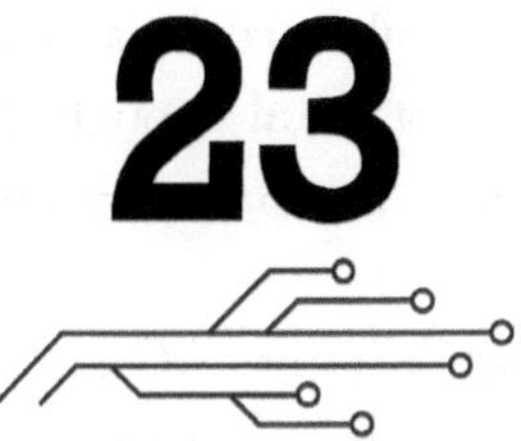

After I'd changed into some spare clothes I always kept at Gran's place, I got the guest room set up the way I knew she liked it: fresh sheets—though I was sure the previous ones hadn't been slept on; surfaces dusted—though I knew she dusted them herself each morning; and clean towels on the dresser. I came out to find Jimmy and Saifi asleep on the matching blue velvet love seats, and the three women standing in front of the stove. Giggling. I shoved my hands in my pockets and cleared my throat to get their attention. They looked back over their shoulders at me, and Celeste and Lei collapsed in laughter, hanging on to each other like they'd be on the floor without the other to keep them upright.

I cleared my throat again, though it didn't do any good, and strolled as coolly as possible over to the kitchen island. "Is there anything I can do to help?"

Gran had changed into slacks and a light sweater. She raised an eyebrow at me, a half smile on her lips. "Set the table, will you sweetheart? Nothing fancy. This is a simple meal."

That meant I didn't need a full table setting, only plates,

forks, and knives. I pulled out the dishes, arranging them on the round table the way I had every day at home for as long as I could remember. Gran said something in her deep voice that I couldn't catch, and Lei and Celeste threw back their heads and laughed, the move so similar that for a moment they looked like twins. Their laughter was loud enough that Jimmy's eyes slid open, one at a time, and he moaned, raising himself to a sitting position.

"Okay, let's eat while it's hot," Gran said, wiping her hands on a dishcloth and motioning us toward the table. "I hope you're hungry. It's been a while since I cooked for a crowd, and it seems like an awful lot of food. Everyone ready?"

I roused Saifi, who could only manage to get one eye open, but still pulled himself up and found his way to the table.

"I wish we had some biscuits, but under the circumstances these leftovers rolls will have to do." Gran laid a skillet of sausage, eggs, and potatoes on the table, which was flanked by a tray of sliced oranges from Lei and a plateful of reheated rolls by Celeste. Saifi's other eye flew open, and he dove into his food like he'd never eaten before.

It was delicious, as usual, but watching Saifi delightedly stuffing his face was by far the best part. He only stopped eating when the food was gone.

"That was really, really, really tasty." Saifi sighed happily. "You are kind of like the best cook I have ever met in real life. Sorry Jimmy."

Jimmy laughed. "Are you kidding? If we could eat like this all the time I would turn in my chef's hat. I don't even *have* a chef's hat. I would go buy a chef's hat and give it to you."

Gran beamed and her gaze floated over to me. "It's lovely to have some of your friends over, Cohen. It's been far too long since I had any visitors that weren't my own age, and I forgot how enjoyable it can be."

"Yeah," Celeste said, smiling innocently at me. "You should invite Gretchen to come over. She hasn't been here in forever."

I blinked at her, confused, then glared at Gran. "What did you tell them?"

Gran waved me off like I was being silly. "Oh, we were just telling stories."

Lei and Celeste were laughing again. Jimmy looked back and forth between us. "Come on, you gotta tell me now. I want to hear the story."

"No, you don't," I said. "It's long. And boring. Not worth repeating."

"Oh, I can tell the short version," Gran insisted. "It's about a little girl named Gretchen that Cohen had a crush on in seventh grade."

"Why? Why do we always have to dredge this up? Can't we pretend it never happened?"

"Because it's sweet," Lei said, casting a crooked smile at me.

"So, he was in the seventh grade," Gran began again.

"Eighth," I said. I should've been yelling or banging pots or creating some other distraction, but when had that ever done any good? At least if she was going to tell it, she could tell it right.

"Eighth, that's right," Gran said, and Lei and Celeste laughed more, like that somehow made it funnier. "And there never seemed to be the right time or place to talk to Gretchen about his feelings. So, he invited her to his birthday party. He invited *only* her to his birthday party."

Jimmy snickered quietly. Saifi lifted his eyebrows clear to his hairline as he grinned at me.

"And so, when Gretchen arrived, there was a sign—"

"A banner," I cut in, covering my face with my hands. "I made a banner."

"Yes, a banner, stretching clear across the room, saying 'Gretchen, you're the bee's knees. Will you be my girlfriend, please?'"

Celeste collapsed into her arms folded on the table in front of her, shoulders shaking with laughter. Jimmy choked on his water and Saifi smacked him on the back, smile so broad it looked painful.

"And Cohen was waiting there on one knee, holding flowers in one hand, and a jar of honey in the other."

They laughed even harder. I waited, staring at the chandelier over the dining table.

"What did she do?" Jimmy asked.

Gran shook her head in mock dismay. She had far too much fun telling people this story. "That poor girl took one look at Cohen and ran so fast she left flaming footprints on the floor."

Saifi was in tears. He kept wiping them away, and then bursting into a fresh bout of giggles which squirted all new tears out of his eyes. I let them laugh. Sure. Why not? It was just my heart. Might as well laugh about it now.

"What ever happened with Gretchen?" Lei asked when the laughter died down. "Did you become friends? Were you able to laugh about it later? Or was it always awkward?"

I rubbed my head and averted my eyes. I might as well tell them. No reason to hold anything back at this point. "That was the last time I ever saw her. I think she transferred to a new school. So she'd never have to talk to me again."

Everyone at the table lost it. I was glad they were having such a swell time at my expense. Lei caught my eye, laughing silently, shoulders shaking, eyes locked on mine. She held my gaze, grinning at me, eyes sparkling, and something deep inside of me clicked into place.

Jimmy slapped me on the back, snickering quietly to himself and shaking his head, and there was so much camaraderie in it I wondered what embarrassing things he'd done in the name of love.

"That was when you took up cycling," Gran said softly, an edge of sadness in her words.

Jimmy's and Saifi's heads snapped toward me, both of them looking at me like I'd betrayed them with my horrible secret.

This was not something I was going to talk about. I shook my head at Gran, my expression making it final. She could gab and tell her sordid stories all she wanted, but this one was off the table. She pursed her lips but kept them closed.

Saifi's mouth fell open as the depth of my betrayal sunk in. "Cohen, you said you *couldn't* ride a bike. Were you *lying* to us?"

Gran looked between Saifi and I, confused. It was past time to change the subject, but my throat seemed to have sealed shut.

Lei swallowed, looking like she was trying to figure out how to rescue this, and then her phone rang. She sobered. "I'm so sorry. But I have to take this. Is there somewhere private that I can . . ." She pointed with her phone in the general direction of *anywhere but here*, and Gran nodded and waved her away distractedly.

"I'll show her." I jumped to my feet and led Lei toward the guest bedroom.

She answered the phone while we walked. "Go."

I opened the guest bedroom door for her and hesitantly followed her in. "Do you want me to leave?" I whispered, pointing over my shoulder, and she shook her head, pulling me into the room and closing the door behind me. I sighed, grateful to not have to face the kitchen again yet.

She turned on the phone's speaker and held it between us so I could hear Ranji's effusive greeting. "—though I would expect nothing less. This job has been tricky, but I assure you, nothing is too tricky for me, oh no. We have *found* your thief."

Lei inhaled, raising her eyebrows in anticipation.

Ranji laughed, like he could see her face. "Yes, yes. We have found him. We are at his base of operations now. And all we must do is wait for him to return."

She deflated slightly. "But what if he doesn't come back? What if he knows you're there?"

"Ah, ah, ah, no. He cannot know. He will come back, I assure you. He has a pattern. He will be here soon. And then we will hold him until you arrive. I have done this many, many times. You will see. I cannot fail."

He did sound awfully sure of himself. It was kind of impossible not to trust him when he seemed to believe in himself so completely. This sounded like good news. Great news, in fact.

Lei bobbed her head. "Okay. Tell me where you are. We'll come to you now."

"Ah, no. That would not be advisable."

"I'm not going to sit around and wait while you guys do all the work."

"But that is what you hired us for, is it not?"

Lei snarled, like she knew he was right. "At least give us the location, so that if everything goes south, the information won't die with you. You know. In a manner of speaking."

Ranji laughed, his voice delighted. "I will not die. And if I give you my location, I give up my proprietary information and you will have no more need of me, yes? This call is a courtesy, that's all. We will contact you when we have success."

Lei screwed up her face, looking very much like she wanted to hurt him. I shared the sentiment. I wondered at the possibility of tracing his phone to find him, but I wasn't positive I had the skills.

"Fine," she said at last. "Keep me posted."

"Hey!" a voice yelled through the line before she could disconnect. "Is Cohen still with you?" It was Esteban.

I looked to Lei for approval, and she shrugged.

"Hey Esteban. What's up?" I said.

"Dude, man, we gotta talk. I've been calling and calling you, but your phone goes straight to voicemail. Do you have it turned off or something?"

Lei wrinkled her nose, smiling apologetically.

"Uh, yeah. Something." It would be great to talk to Esteban, but I wasn't sure how to tell him what was going on without telling him what was going on. "I can't talk now, but I'll tell you everything as soon as I get home."

Lei gave me a look that said *over my dead body*, and I shook my head placatingly, to assure her that of course I wouldn't tell anyone anything.

"At least tell me about the girl. The one who hired us. Where did you meet her? Cuz she is way cooler than you, no offense, man."

"You're still on speaker phone, Esteban. She's standing right here."

A pause. "Hi."

Lei shook her head but said nothing, a small smile on her lips.

"Hey, Esteban," I said softly, "are *you* on speaker phone?"

Another pause. "Yeah."

I sighed. "Okay, just . . . just, come through for us, okay?"

"Always, man. Always."

Lei hung up and slid the phone into her back pocket. "This is actually going to work. We're going to get the ear back. If the Client gives us the next two assignments today, we can totally do this." She grabbed my upper arms and shook me, excitement lighting her face. "We're so close to the end I can taste it!" Her hands slid down to mine and she grinned, squeezing my fingers in hers.

I smiled back, letting her enthusiasm wash over me. "What does it taste like?"

"Hot tamales," she said without hesitation.

". . . Really?"

"Yep. A whole mouthful. So many that my tongue is on fire and my teeth are red." She bounced her eyebrows up and down.

A guffaw burst out of me, and her eyes crinkled up in delight. Warmth blossomed in my belly, a heat that spread to my chest and filled me up. This really was almost over. Ranji and Esteban would catch the diver and we'd get the ear back, and maybe this insane job would wind down. By tomorrow night, I could be a regular, boring person who had a day job and slept when it was nighttime. And I could convince Lei to come with me to the DarkWave launch, and maybe a matinee on Saturday. And back here to Gran's for dinner on Sunday night. Because there was something here, crackling between us like lightning in the night sky. And she felt it too. I was sure of it. She could say platonic all she wanted but there was something here.

I tugged gently on Lei's hands, pulling her just a little closer. "Lei. Listen—"

"Hey," she cut in, "how do you know this Esteban?"

"He's the manager of my apartment building. He's a friend. But, Lei—"

She pulled her hands away. "What are the odds of that? You just happened to know one of the guys *we* hired when we needed help? Your grandma lives in the building we need to get into? The tongue being sent to your apartment three times?" The glee on her face had morphed into a pensive mask. "There are just too many coincidences."

I laughed, trying to get back the moment we'd just had, but didn't know how. "So, we're going with cosmic design then?"

She shook her head, not amused, then looked straight into my soul. "And what was that about, in there?"

"What?" I asked.

"That agonizing awkwardness when your grandma brought up cycling?"

I stepped back, running my hands over my face. This is not the heart to heart talk I wanted to have with her. Why did she always have to see everything?

"Is it because of the accident?" she asked. "Were you injured that badly? Because you seem fine to me. You know, as fine as can be expected."

I caught her smirk but couldn't react the way she wanted me to. I looked away, eyes sweeping sightlessly across the family photos on the far wall.

"I wasn't the one in the accident," I choked. I still couldn't quite bring myself to meet her eyes. That look she'd given me earlier, that was the one I wanted. Not the one she would give me after this. The pity or the judgment. "It was a boy named Peter."

She paused. Like she knew. "Is he . . . okay?"

I took a breath. In. Out. In. "He's dead." I looked up at

her then. Daring her, begging her to shower me with whatever emotion she wanted to so I could get it over with.

She didn't respond, just watched me, her eyes so big and bright, waiting for more.

I sighed, and gave in. "I raced mountain bikes. When I was younger. I actually got pretty good at it. Peter was only twelve. Just getting started. So earnest and dedicated. Saifi reminds me of him. All that energy and optimism. I kind of . . . took him under my wing." I swallowed with effort. "Like a mentor."

I never talked about this. Hadn't talked about it in ages. Didn't want to talk about it now. But I wanted her to trust me. Needed her to trust me. And if I shut down now, she never would. I started pacing as memories from the past flooded through the doorway I'd opened in my mind. "I felt like I was making a difference. The kids looked up to me. I was helping. I liked being the guy with all the answers." I chewed on my cheek, trying to get ahold of myself.

"And then the committee finally let me plan my own race. It was all sanctioned and sponsored and it was going to be amazing. But . . ." I sat down on the bed trying not to rumple the comforter. "There was an accident. And I know, I know. It's mountain biking. There are accidents all the time. It's part of the deal. But this one was really bad. Half of the kids ended up in the hospital. Peter didn't make it."

I cleared my throat, soldiering on. "I was only seventeen. I was too young. I didn't know enough to do the job properly. In my excitement, I rushed through it. I didn't sufficiently examine the soil quality on the route I had chosen. It was compromised. Unsafe to ride on." I swallowed, trying to hold it in, push it down, will it away. "If I had planned more thoroughly, considered every variable, taken my time and prepared as much as necessary, he would still be alive."

In a soft voice, like she knew she shouldn't, but couldn't help herself, Lei said, "You don't know that."

That's what everyone always said. It could have happened to anyone, even the most experienced of us. But it didn't. It happened to me. And I could have prevented it. I was certain. I could feel it in my bones. None of us should have been racing at all. What a pointless, dangerous way to spend our time. We were practically begging for trouble.

She sat down on the bed facing me, legs crisscrossed in front of her, then she slowly reached out and put both her hands on my chest, right over my heart, like she was holding it in place. "I'm so sorry."

I swallowed, placing one of my hands over hers. "Yeah. Well. I haven't ridden a bike since. It's just too dangerous. There are too many unknowns, too many unnecessary risks. Best to keep both feet on the ground. Literally and figuratively." I smiled in a way that didn't feel sincere and her dark eyes stared into mine. Not with pity, or shame, or judgment. But like she saw me, understood me.

Suddenly she leaned forward and planted her lips on mine. My brain lit up in surprise, and the rest of me lit up in a hundred other ways. Her lips were hot and salty from the food we'd just eaten, and she smelled like rain and lavender and 3-in-1 oil.

I reached to pull her closer but suddenly she was gone, and the kiss was over. It had barely even begun.

Lei blinked like she was getting her bearings and then smiled. A smile filled with so much sadness it nearly broke my heart. "Thank you for telling me," she whispered. Then she wrapped her arms around herself like a strait jacket and walked out, shutting the door behind her.

Oh, sweet morning sunshine, was that a *pity* kiss? It was good, as pity kisses went, but then, I didn't think I'd ever been kissed out of pity before. I flopped back onto the bed, exhaling loudly. I wasn't sure how she felt about me, but for my part, I was a total goner.

I expected Lei to be awkward or aloof, but when I ventured back out of the guest room, she was all smiles and warmth. I gave her space to talk to her family and fill them in on the conversation with Ranji, but my gaze was drawn toward her like a magnet. Each time my eyes found her she was already looking my way.

I scrubbed another plate and handed it to Gran to dry. She took it, watching me knowingly. I *hated* when she looked at me like that. I ignored her. But the expression on her face pushed at me, prodding, forcing me to reveal all my secrets.

"So," she finally said, taking the plate I handed her, voice unusually casual. "Lei seems lovely."

I looked at her in surprise. I'd thought she was going to demand an explanation for the psychic premonition that led us here. I laughed softly. "She *is*."

"Do you think I'm likely to see her again?"

I dipped the brush into the cup in my hand, swirling it around and around and around to remove any evidence of previous use. "I hope so, Gran."

She smiled, taking the cup. "I hope so, too. All of them, really. Though I can't help but wonder." She paused in that pregnant way of hers, the questions building up behind the silence until I was afraid they would pommel me. "What kind of trouble have you gotten yourself into?"

I didn't answer her. It wasn't my business to tell, and how could she even begin to understand?

She took a plate and wiped it off, then waved her towel in surrender. "Fine, fine. I know when to mind my own business. Just . . . you stay with them, okay?"

"I know. I will. They need me."

She laughed, surprised. "Oh no, honey. *You* need *them*."

—o

I went to the hall closet and collected the bag I kept there for emergencies, then met Lei, Saifi, and Jimmy near the front door.

"How did Celeste take it?" I murmured to Lei.

"Besides telling me seventeen times that we need to leave, she took it about how you'd expect," she whispered back in frustration. "She still thinks we shouldn't have hired anyone, thinks we can't trust them, and is positive this is all about to blow up in our faces. She doesn't have any other suggestions, but she is happy to shoot down mine. I really don't understand why she's giving me so much crap about this. Can't she just trust me?"

Gran walked up before I could respond. "The sun's been out for a while now, so you'll have a nice dry trip home." She looked each of us over, like she was checking the state of us before sending us off to school. "You just be careful out there, won't you?" Gran patted my arm then smiled at everyone else.

I kissed her on the cheek, and we took our leave.

Celeste waited in the hall, pacing feverishly. "Can we go then? Are you guys finally ready?"

"Where to?" Jimmy asked as we headed toward the elevator. "We can't go back to the floating house, right? If he snatched Saifi from there, who knows what else he did."

"He probably rigged the building to blow up as soon as we set foot inside it." Saifi sniffed. "That's what I would do."

I thought that seemed pretty unlikely, but Lei shrugged and her eyes flicked to Celeste, who exhaled in irritation.

"How about my place?" I offered. I knew there was risk there as well, but it seemed like the safest option, and at least I was familiar with the territory.

"Yeah!" Saifi yelled.

But Lei cut him off. "No. We have taken advantage of the Hoard family hospitality enough for one day."

"It's fine," I insisted. "I'll be able to keep us safe there."

Lei looked like she was considering it, but then shook her head. "No. We've got to keep our personal lives out of this as much as possible. Between the Client and the diver, it just seems like taking things too far. Better not."

It was hard to argue with her when she was being so cautious and reasonable, so I didn't press it further. "How about a motel?" I suggested. "One of those questionable types which don't require ID." I didn't like it, but they usually had very few cameras and we could come and go without any record of it.

Lei smiled crookedly at me. "As much as I love a good seedy motel, we'd still have to pay for it. A credit card would be too easy to track, and we don't have that kind of cash."

"I've got enough." I patted the satchel I always kept at Gran's house. It made me feel a bit like Indiana Jones, which, in turn, made me feel slightly invincible. That must have been why the seedy motel option didn't bother me as much as it should have.

Celeste lowered an eyebrow at me like I was being thick. "You have enough cash for all of us to stay in some crap motel?"

"Of course."

"How?" Celeste asked. "Did you steal it from your grandma?"

"Excuse me?" I asked, insulted.

"Who keeps that much cash handy?" Lei asked.

I thought the answer to that was rather obvious and spread my hands wide in response.

"Why, though?" Jimmy asked. "What if you lose your bag?"

"I never lose my bag. And the rule of thumb is, don't carry around more than you can stand to lose." At their incredulous looks, I said slowly, "*I like to be prepared.*"

Saifi reached for my bag. "Can I see it?"

Lei waved him off. "Stop it. Okay, yes, Cohen continues to surprise, but no, I don't think we should go to a motel."

"How about the warehouse?" Saifi asked.

I nodded. I'd left my briefcase there, anyway. The fact that I hadn't thought about it in so long was incredible to me. I was going to need that back eventually.

Jimmy scratched his forehead, considering. "Do you think the diver knows about the warehouse?"

"He does," Celeste said, and everyone looked at her in surprise. "Of course he does. He's known about everything else. We have to assume he knows about the warehouse too. Let's just go back to the floating house. I need my laptop. All our stuff is there. Going back there makes the most sense."

Lei considered, chewing on her cheek. "I don't know.

He could be there waiting for us. And what if he *did* booby trap it?"

Celeste tapped her foot impatiently. "There is just as much chance that he'll be waiting for us at the warehouse. He might even assume that we won't go back to the floating house specifically because that is where he took Saifi from."

Lei still looked unconvinced, but I grudgingly had to admit that Celeste was probably right.

I straightened my bag, shifting its weight on my shoulder. "Either way, we'll have to keep our guard up, but at least the floating house is small which will make it more defensible. It probably *is* the best option at this point, if you're sure you don't want to come to my place."

Lei eyed me then nodded, deciding. "Okay. Sounds good. Let's go."

"Great," Celeste snapped. "Thank goodness you'll listen to *Cone*." She turned and marched toward the elevator without a backward glance.

We trailed after her, Lei sighing and rubbing her temple.

"Well *I'm* glad we're going back to the floating house," Saifi said, "cuz I left my other shoes there. These ones keep falling off and they're really uncomfortable."

Just to be on the safe side, Jimmy led us on a route that avoided any cameras, and we kept our hoods up. We took the train back to Portland, and I tried to be alert and keep my eye out for the diver. Lei, on the other hand, seemed perfectly at ease: one knee propped up on the seat in front of us, the other flopped lazily against mine. I rested my hand on her knee as she talked sleepily about nursing school and her plans once her parents were out of prison. She grew quiet, and I worried that the topic had upset her again, but then her head fell against my shoulder. I looked down to find her eyes closed, her mouth opened slightly, breathing softly. I held as still as I could and tried to think comfortable thoughts so that she could get some rest.

25

"Are you paying rent on that mannequin warehouse?" I asked as we walked back to the floating house. They hadn't been back to the office once since I'd gotten there and the warehouse was way more space than they needed, so I hoped they weren't locked into any kind of long-term commitment.

Lei laughed. "No, we have an arrangement with the owner. He owns a bunch of buildings across the city. We find him all of the Holly Hobbie figurines we can, and he lets us use the office and warehouse whenever we need it. We had just found an estate sale full of them the day you got here, so we're paid up for a while. The office serves as a place to meet with clients who want privacy."

The minute we arrived at the floating house, Celeste parked herself in front of her laptop, typing away like mad. Saifi prepared several booby traps wherein any intruders would get kicked in the face with fiberglass feet he had pilfered from the warehouse. Jimmy set up a rotation for guard duty so we could all get a little rest, insisting on taking the first watch himself. I was sure that I was too wired to be able to sleep, but when I lay down on the cot Jimmy offered me, my eyes instantly started to droop.

It felt like only moments later when voices intruded on my nap, first as a murmur, then louder and louder, until my eyes slid back open of their own accord.

"I don't actually need your permission, you know." Celeste's voice from the kitchen was angry, and she sounded like it was all she could do to keep from screaming. "You're not my mom. You're not anyone's mom, in case you've forgotten."

"It's not like I *want* to be in charge," Lei hissed. "You are more than welcome to pitch in anytime, but it seems like you'd rather complain than help out."

I sat up, rubbing the sleep from my eyes. Jimmy sat on the floor rifling through a box of moldy fabric. He looked at me and raised his eyebrows in a way that felt significant. He looked exhausted. We were *all* exhausted. How long had they all been pushing themselves this way? Saifi shuffled down the stairs as the fighting continued, slumping glumly onto the couch next to me.

Celeste laughed bitterly. "Pitch in? *Really?* Like how? Sharing some of my brilliant ideas? That you'll ignore? I told you in the beginning that this job was a bad idea, but you're always keeping secrets, you're always thinking you know what's best for the rest of us."

"I listen to you all the time!" Lei barked. "I'm doing the best I can. Maybe if you offered a little more support instead of criticizing every decision I make."

"They're not your decisions to make!" Quiet followed, punctuated by the sounds of heavy breathing, and I could imagine Lei and Celeste glaring at each other. "It doesn't matter," Celeste said, finally. "I don't have time for this. And I don't have to explain anything to you. I'm leaving."

Lei protested, but was drowned out by the sound of a chair scraping across the linoleum. Lei's phone rang.

"It's Call-A-Human," she said incredulously.

"Whatever."

"But it's the Client. He's *calling*. He never calls."

Jimmy and I stood up at the same time, and the two of us walked hesitantly into the kitchen, Saifi trailing along behind us. Celeste glared at us, and I had to assume she knew we'd heard the whole argument.

Lei looked every bit as upset as Celeste, the emotion bringing a flush to her cheeks. She glanced at us in question, then answered the phone on speaker, and set it in the middle of the table.

"Where is the ear?" The voice sounded wrong somehow, artificial.

Lei's face went white. Everyone looked at each other, hoping someone else's face would know more than theirs did.

"Who is this?" Lei asked casually, sounding very much like she was stalling.

"The one who is paying you for it."

Lei turned to me for help. We should have thought up a plan for what to tell him the second we lost the ear. Of course he would want an explanation for the delay.

Lei's voice was forced. "You received the hand?"

"I received the hand. Where is the ear?"

Lei seemed to shrink, her authority evaporated, like a first grader in the principal's office. We had to tell him something, but to agree on a decent story we'd have to put him on hold, and I doubted he would stand for that. Everyone looked slightly paralyzed.

I grabbed Lei's hand and squeezed it, then cleared my

throat. "We know where the ear is," I said in my most authoritative voice. "But the family is having one of those old-fashioned open casket funerals like in the old days. We haven't been able to retrieve it yet." I watched Lei as I said it, asking for her approval with my eyes. She shrugged as though she'd come up with nothing better. He could probably find out if it was true or not, but perhaps this would buy us the time we needed.

There was silence. A long one. Had we been disconnected? I hoped so. Then we could put this conversation off for a little bit longer while we got our story straight.

Finally the phone crackled, like he was rubbing the receiver with a paper towel. "I don't believe we've been introduced."

I looked around, unsure how to proceed. Lei's eyebrows dropped in confusion. She looked at Jimmy and Celeste in question, but Celeste still looked every bit as angry as she had before. Jimmy shook his head helplessly.

"That's Cohen," Saifi said loudly, looking at Lei like she'd lost her mind. "The one you sent to help us."

More silence. This Client of theirs wasn't the chattiest lunatic in the world. "Of course," the voice on the other end of the line eventually said. "Cohen Hoard. Of course." The phone crackled again. "Get me the ear. Watch for my message. I will send your final two assignments now." The line went dead.

Lei exhaled, hands trembling. She was pale and faint, like she was one sudden move from vomiting all over the kitchen table. "I thought we were dead! I thought that was the end." She leaned back in her chair and closed her eyes. "But it's almost over. We're almost done."

As soon as she finished speaking, the ding of an arriving message sounded, but it wasn't Lei's phone.

"It's mine!" Saifi was looking at his phone. "He sent it to *me* this time!"

Celeste still stood near the door like she hadn't quite decided whether she was leaving or not.

"Well?" Lei said. "And?"

"Hang on. He put it in a picture this time. Looks like a bunny! I think. It's still uploading. Be patient."

"And?" Lei said, not sounding the least bit patient.

"It's a tongue!"

"Get *out*."

"Do you think we've got the right one?"

A smile spread across Lei's face. "Oh, wow, it *must* be. I don't understand it, but I *absolutely* accept it. Name. We need a name to verify it."

"Somebody named Farley. Just the one name, like they're a movie star or something."

"Good enough," Lei said. "Celeste, will you look up the serial number and see if we've got the right one?" She shifted back and forth from foot to foot, like she was raring to go. "Okay, lay it on us. What's the other one?"

Saifi scrolled some more. "It's an eyeball! The left eyeball."

"Ugh, of course it is," Jimmy said.

"Okay, but whose?" Lei asked. "We can't go find it until we know who it belongs to."

"Hang on, hang on." Saifi held up his hands, his fingers splayed like he was shushing a baby.

Lei tapped her toe. Jimmy tried to look over Saifi's shoulder, but Saifi kept pushing his face away.

"Seriously, Saifi. Has your data been throttled? How can it be taking this long?"

"It's up, it's up! Okay, the person's name is . . . Cohen Hoard."

"Ha ha," Jimmy said.

Lei rolled her eyes. "Hilarious." She yanked the phone out of his hands so she could read it herself.

Saifi's smile slowly fell, and he pointed at me. "Wait, isn't that *your* name?"

My eyes met Lei's as she looked up from the screen. Her eyes were so wide they looked unreal. Jimmy turned back and forth between us, waiting for the punchline that wasn't coming. Maybe it *was* a joke. Or some truly horrendous clerical error. Maybe we were all so tired that we were hallucinating or misreading or simply misunderstanding. What in the name of the broken weather would anyone want with my eyeball?

"Maybe it's a different Cohen Hoard." Saifi's voice was hopeful. "That's a pretty common name, right?"

"No," I said. I wanted to laugh, but everything about this felt very, very wrong.

"Yes, that's a good idea," Lei said, squeezing my arm as she stepped past me. "Somebody look it up. There must be a Cohen Hoard that's recently died. He's never given us the name of a living person before. It makes no sense for him to start now."

"Unless this explains why the Client sent him," Jimmy said softly.

Celeste still hadn't moved, so Jimmy pulled out his phone and started poking at it. Lei wouldn't look at me, but stood behind Jimmy, reading over his shoulder.

She finished reading, her tired eyes dark with concern. "This has got to be some kind of mistake. Possibly even the same mistake that sent the tongue to you in the first place. Why would he want your eye?"

"My left eye," I said.

"Who cares which eye? It makes no sense!"

"Actually," I said slowly, as a few pieces of this puzzle started to click into place in my brain, in spite of the sleep deprivation, "it might explain a lot. I had a cornea transplant two years ago."

The faces around the room all shared a "that isn't enough of an explanation" look.

"In my left eye." I pointed at it for emphasis, sure that someone else would start to understand.

"That's funny since you aren't a donor," Saifi said with a laugh.

"I know. But that's beside the point."

"Oh. Oh no." Lei shook her head, face slightly green.

"What?" Saifi and Jimmy demanded at the same time.

I held my hands up like a plea. "What if this isn't the only part that was donated? What if *all* the parts we are collecting were donated?"

Lei swallowed, looking small and frail. "The hand. Bob Cobb's hand. It was ripped off by a monkey, remember? Don't look at me like that, Saifi, you heard what she said. The hand I cut off was not his original hand. It was a transplant."

"But why?" Jimmy asked. "That doesn't explain anything. Why would anyone want a bunch of donated parts? When you can't even give these parts away?"

I shook my head. "I don't know. But at least it gives us a connection. Something that explains why *these* are the parts he wants."

"I have to go," Celeste said.

Lei ignored her, looking at me. "It's a good theory. But doesn't really help much. What are we supposed to do now? You're still using your eyes, I assume?"

"Frequently," I said.

"Cone should probably come with me," Celeste said.

"Can't we just call the Client and tell him he made a mistake?" Saifi asked. "He must have entered the wrong name by accident, since Cohen just talked to him on the phone. I've done that before: write the word I'm thinking of, instead of the one I'm supposed to write."

Jimmy shook his head. "We can't. He hasn't answered the Call-A-Human number since he hired us. We don't know how to reach him."

While Jimmy spoke, Celeste stood, grabbing a backpack from the floor near the table. She slid her laptop into it, pale eyes growing darker by the second.

She walked up to me and stood, face only inches from mine. "I need you to come with me. Now."

I met her eyes, startled. "Why?"

"You're still leaving?" Lei asked. "*Where are you going?*"

Celeste gripped her backpack, knuckles white. "I can't tell you. And I don't have time to explain."

Lei fisted her hands, shaking them angrily. "And Cohen should just go with you, even though you won't tell us why or where? And you accuse *me* of keeping secrets?"

"Can't you just trust me?" Celeste pleaded, voice desperate. "For once?"

Everyone started talking at once. Lei, voice full of emotion, couldn't believe that Celeste, of all people, would ask such a thing, while Jimmy jumped to Lei's defense, and Saifi insisted that he did trust Celeste, but that sometimes she was kind of scary. I watched her, trying to gauge what she would do, unsure how to proceed.

Celeste cocked her head to the side and threw up her hands

in defeat. "Fine. Go ahead and ignore me. But I won't be able to guarantee your safety."

She reached into her backpack and pulled out a gun, quickly ejected the magazine, checked the rounds, and slid it back into the gun.

"And now you're threatening us?" Lei's voice rose several more decibels.

"Come on!" Saifi yelled. "I just said I trusted you!"

I stepped back, trying to put some distance between us without startling her. "Whoa." I held up my hands so she could see where they were, my voice gentle. "Don't do anything rash. We're all running on no sleep. Just put down the gun and talk to us."

Celeste threw her hands wildly into the air, gun and all, causing everyone to duck. "I've tried talking to you. Apparently it takes a gun in my hand for anyone to listen to me. We're supposed to be a family, but you listen to *Cone* more than me." She waved the gun my direction then paused and looked at me, like she hadn't really noticed me before. "This might all be *your* fault." She pointed the gun at me intentionally then, all the anger in her eyes and stance directed at me. "I hadn't planned to shoot anyone, but shooting you *would* make me feel better."

Everyone else started shouting again. Trying to talk her down. Trying to make her see reason.

Celeste continued to stare at me, her cheeks flushed with more color than I'd ever seen them. "The Client wants Cone's eye," she said deliberately. "We give him Cone's eye."

Lei laughed, a hollow sound. "Cohen's right. We're all tired. You're acting insane."

The barrel of the gun was aimed at my chest. Such a small amount of metal and gunpowder, yet I could feel the power of it, the possibility, the potential for destruction. How had things escalated so quickly?

Celeste held the gun like she was completely comfortable with it, her hands steady and sure. "Come with me. We're leaving now."

I kept my face calm, my posture impassive. I had to talk her down before someone got hurt.

"Celeste," I said. "Come on. This isn't you."

Her eyes narrowed to slits, her mouth a line of wrath. "You don't know me."

"But *I* do," Lei said. "He's right. This isn't you. Put the gun down so we can come up with a plan." Her voice sounded calm, all things considered. It would work. Celeste would listen. She had to.

"New plan," Celeste whispered. She pulled the trigger.

26

I dodged, but Lei was already moving, diving in front of the gun. The bullet ripped through Lei's shoulder before I understood what was happening.

"No!" Celeste screamed, staring at Lei, eyes wide as the sun. "No no no no no!"

Lei stumbled back into me, and I caught her as she collapsed, Saifi and Jimmy yelling and rushing to her side.

I tried to stanch the blood flow, words bubbling out of my mouth without me really knowing what I was saying. "Lei? Lei? Please be okay. I really need you to be okay. Everyone needs you to be okay. Lei?"

Lei moaned as blood oozed all over the linoleum. Jimmy joined me, holding Lei's hand, telling her over and over again that she was fine. Her face was gray, and she seemed small and so fragile I was afraid she'd shatter.

"What do we do?" Saifi asked. "*What do we do?*"

"Call 911!" I ordered.

"Don't you dare," Lei gasped, her voice a ghost of what it was. "There's a med kit in the bathroom."

Saifi looked like he wanted to attack Celeste but snarled and took off for the bathroom at a run.

Celeste watched us, shaking her head, face paler than it had ever been, repeating the word "no" under her breath like it could rewrite the last few minutes.

Jimmy took out his phone, dialing with bloody fingers, his other hand still pressed to her shoulder.

"Jimmy, don't," Lei whispered, soft enough that I could barely hear her, and then her eyes fluttered closed.

"No!" Celeste cried again, pointing her gun at Lei this time.

"Will you put that gun away?" I yelled as I held my fingers to Lei's neck, checking for a pulse. "What are you going to do? Threaten the bullet back out of her body?" Lei's pulse was faint, but steady, and I looked up at Celeste. "She's going to be okay. I think this is more than a med kit can handle, but I'm sure the ambulance will be here soon."

Jimmy had been talking to the 911 operator through all this and he nodded in confirmation, still holding the phone to his ear. "I think they'll take her to OHSU Hospital since it's the closest."

Celeste's eyes widened further at the mention of the ambulance, then she aimed the gun at my head. "You have to come with me, right now!" She was shaking, and so pale she was nearly invisible, but the gun in her hand didn't move.

She grabbed the insulated box with the tongue in it from the fridge, then closed the distance between us, gray eyes shining, pale hair tangled around her face. She was slight and wispy, but the hand she clamped on my upper arm was like a vice.

"Get *up*, Cone," Celeste said, voice thick with emotion. "I *will* shoot her again. We have to go now!"

Saifi ran back in with the med kit and started pulling

everything out of it. I met Jimmy's gaze, and he nodded, though his eyes were wide with fright.

I spoke to him, my voice calm and confident. "Use the gauze from the med kit and apply steady, direct pressure. Press harder than you think you should. The quicker you can get her blood to clot, the less blood she'll lose."

He nodded again, and Saifi passed him the gauze. I moved my hands from Lei's shoulder and Jimmy took over, pressing the gauze against her shoulder, expression determined.

"She'll be okay," I assured him.

I didn't want to go. My fingers had left blood on Lei's neck, and I wiped it off with my sleeve. Celeste jammed the gun into the back of my head.

I stumbled to my feet as she dragged me outside and over to a car half-buried in vines. She pushed the vines aside with the gun, then she opened the driver's side door. For me. The kindness of the gesture while she still had the gun pointed at me almost made me laugh.

"I don't think this car runs."

"Well, you're wrong. As usual."

"What if I refuse to drive?"

"Then I'll shoot you in the leg, and make you drive anyway. I already shot my sister. Might as well shoot you too."

I growled, but climbed into the car, feeling impotent, weak, angry. Lei was bleeding out on the floor and I was driving off to who knew where. Celeste slid into the passenger seat next to me. The car smelled old and damp, left too long with no fresh air or butts across its upholstery. And there was no way it was equipped with Auto Save. Maybe the car wouldn't start. Maybe all of her evil plans would fall apart because this old car had been neglected and left to rot and Celeste could go screw herself.

The keys were in the ignition. She pressed the nose of the gun into my ribs. I turned the key and the engine turned over, sputtering and chugging like it couldn't quite remember how to be a car, but then roared to life, idling loudly.

"Drive. I'll tell you where to go."

Cursing this old reliable jalopy, I backed out over vines, weeds, and flowers. The siren of an approaching ambulance filled the space we left behind as we drove away.

Celeste led me deeper through the old, sad, neglected part of Portland. Trees grew straight up through the middle of some buildings, vines snaked down fire escapes, bright exotic flowers grew through cracks in the sidewalk.

"Where are we going?" I asked, forcing joviality into my words.

She jammed the gun a little harder into my ribs in case I'd forgotten that it was there. "Does it matter?"

"Just curious. Since I may be driving to my death and all. I tend to get curious when my life is on the line. Just a little quirk of mine."

She sniffed, relaxing a little. "Calm down. You're not going to die. Much. Now shut up, please. If I have to listen to you talk any more, I will shoot you just to have some quiet." She pulled out her phone.

"Is it the Client? Do you *know* the Client? Are you working directly for him? Are you his spy?" I doubted it but babbling seemed better than stewing silently in a pool of my own sweat.

The absurdity of my accusation wasn't lost on Celeste. "*Pfft*, no. I just happen to have . . . someone else that needs my help."

"Like *whom*? This is your family! Don't you care about them at all? What about your parents? Doesn't any of this matter to you? Is this about money? Are you so desperate that you would screw your family over?"

Celeste laughed, and for some reason it sounded like heartbreak. I felt the gun in my ribs give way a bit. She looked away from me as she focused on the phone in her other hand, typing with her thumb.

Without giving myself a chance to think it through, I stomped on the brakes. Celeste hit the dashboard, dropping the gun, and it clattered down to the floor at my feet. I grabbed it and aimed it at her. I really didn't want to fire, but I would if I had to.

Celeste glared at me, such a storm of emotion in her eyes that I couldn't read them at all. A small goose egg was growing on her forehead where she'd hit the dashboard. "Good job, Cone. You got me. Now you can shoot me and put us all out of our misery." She waited. Like she really expected me to shoot. Like she was ready for it.

"I don't want to shoot you," I huffed. "Just get out of the car."

She didn't move.

"Get out!" I waved the gun in her face. "Now!"

She still didn't move, face tight, breathing heavily. "I'm not actually the monster you think I am. I know you won't believe me, but I'm trying to protect them."

I snorted. I couldn't help myself. "You shot Lei. I hate to break it to you, but that isn't how you protect people."

She snorted back, but there was no mirth in it. "You don't know anything about protecting people. You've lived your whole life in your sheltered little bubble with your loving grandma and your safe job. For some of us, protecting the people we care about isn't as black and white as it is for you." She pinched her lips together and closed her eyes.

"You have the gun now," she went on. "That means you're the one in charge. That should make you happy. Just drive, okay? Lei is on her way to the hospital. Please. We're running out of time."

"For what?" I pleaded.

She turned away, staring out the windshield past the vines and the dilapidated buildings into the distance.

I told myself that Lei would be okay. She *would* be okay. She was probably being loaded into the ambulance at this very moment. I stared at Celeste, trying to see past her bravado and anger and figure out what she was up to, but was just as confused by her as I had always been. I really knew almost nothing about her. True, once she'd deemed me harmless, she hadn't given me much of a chance, but had I given her one either? Shootings notwithstanding?

Good grundy, was I really considering going with her? Cohen Hoard from last week would have punched me in the head to try to get it back on straight, but I had no idea what was best anymore. And something about Celeste's face and posture was getting to me. Something was up. And I wasn't sure she could handle it on her own. *She* wasn't sure she could handle it on her own.

Resigning myself to my own stupidity, I nodded, and dropped the gun into the pocket of the door. Celeste looked at it longingly, then pointed forward out the windshield, and I drove. Celeste directed me through abandoned neighborhoods and then neighborhoods where all the houses were built on stilts and kids played on swings that hung from ropes strung across the streets. We finally drove through the archway into

Old Town Chinatown. The once-vibrant red archway was now faded and covered in moss. The bronze lion statues flanking the archway were coated in a green patina that had eaten straight through the metal in several places. Ornate red streetlamps lined the road next to cars covered in climbing plants with giant, hole-filled leaves, like massive slices of green swiss cheese.

There was a wet-looking thrift store, and a record store that appeared completely deserted but had a red OPEN sign flashing in the window. A few turns later she pointed to an old restaurant next to a building that was on the verge of collapsing under the weight of the vines growing across it and instructed me to pull over.

Celeste pointed again. "It's the building with the octopus on the door. It should be unlocked."

I grunted, grabbed the gun, and got out of the car. Celeste kept looking around anxiously, like she was expecting an ambush. My gaze followed hers, but nothing looked suspicious. The brick buildings towered around us three stories high, narrow windows set into the walls glinting in the late-afternoon sun. Celeste trailed behind me as I headed toward the octopus door. I pushed on it, but it didn't open.

Celeste *tsked*. "Don't baby it. It just sticks sometimes. You gotta put your back into it."

I pushed again, harder this time, and felt the door give slightly. So, I planted my feet and shoved with all my might. The door flew open and I stumbled forward, nearly landing on my face.

"Not that hard," Celeste said from behind me, amusement in her voice. "Are you trying to knock it off its hinges?"

It was dark inside, like the afternoon light was as reluctant to go in as I was. I pulled out my tiny high-powered flashlight and gripped it with the gun, shining it into the building. The bright light roamed the room, lighting up a cluster of tables off to one side, chairs next to it in a tangled heap. The walls were brick, running two stories high, with a second floor built on one-half of the room where the wood rotted and sagged. The stairs leading to the second story had long since abandoned their post, now lying in a mess on the floor. A bar ran along one wall, with a shattered mirror dangling behind it, the intricate wood frame gray and soft.

Celeste had a flashlight of her own, and pointed it at every corner of the room. I wasn't sure what she was looking for, but as far as I could tell, she hadn't found it.

"Keep going," Celeste prodded, pointing toward an archway on the far wall. "That way."

Though I was the one holding the gun, she was making me nervous. I couldn't figure out what she was up to, and I didn't know if I should be more worried about her, or about whatever we had come here to find. I waited a few seconds, straining my ears for clues, but heard nothing.

We turned down a hall where a collage of official documents was posted on the wall. Next to them, a picture hung above a plaque reading "Yoo Hwan–Manager." Moisture had warped the picture, discoloring and wrinkling it until Hwan more closely resembled the octopus on the door outside than a person.

I continued on down the dark, dank passage, gun raised, hairs on the back of my neck raising as well. This was a bad idea. It felt like we were walking into the belly of a beast. It *smelled* like we were walking into the belly of a beast. Our footsteps echoed through the narrow hallway until we reached a set of black metal doors set into the brick wall.

"Open it."

I rolled my eyes, hoping it covered my fear. "My hands are full. How about *you* open it?"

She sighed, but walked toward the door, and pulled on the handle. The door groaned loudly in protest. I quickly pointed my flashlight and gun into the dark, ready for an attack that didn't come.

Celeste flipped the switch and a bulb hanging from the ceiling lit the room in its dim glow. We were in a storage room, with cabinets and a pool table pushed up against rotting shelves along the closest wall, stacked with a few moldy boxes and rusty cans. On the other side of the room was a set of stairs running below ground, with dark water nearly up to floor level. I turned back as Celeste surveyed the room, seeming to relax visibly.

"Now what?" I asked, confused.

"Now give me the gun."

I glanced around the sparse, moist room, even more confused. "Not on your life."

The water in the cellar next to me burbled. I stepped back. A bubble popped on the surface. And then the water writhed and moved like it was coming to life. I aimed the gun at it, no clue what I would be shooting.

Celeste shook her head. "I'm such an idiot; I should have left you in the car! *Give me the gun!*"

A black orb broke the surface, and it wasn't until I saw the face mask that I realized it was a head. It was attached to a body in full diving gear, pushing its way up out of the water-filled cellar. It was him. The diver. Climbing out of the water like he lived there. I guess that explained the suit. Well, crap. I might actually be in a whole lot of trouble.

27

The diver continued to climb laboriously out of the water, fins flapping loudly on the steps. So Celeste was in full betrayal mode? Even though she'd shot Lei, even though she'd tried to shoot me, I still couldn't believe she would turn on her family so completely.

"Celeste?" I asked, "what in the—"

She took advantage of my distraction and snatched the gun back out of my hands. I reached for it, but she stepped away, aiming it at me.

I sighed. I really *was* harmless.

The diver set a handheld jet propulsion unit on the floor next to him and removed his mouthpiece, then spit into the water behind him. Celeste turned and pointed the gun straight at him, her form perfect, her hands as steady as stone.

The diver removed his mask and peeled off his hood. He was tall and slight, with blond hair, gray eyes, and invisible eyebrows. I realized with a start that I *did* recognize him.

"This is your brother," I said to Celeste as understanding dawned on me.

"Aw, see. You *did* figure it out. This is Dorian. My twin brother."

They not only looked alike, but the mannerisms were similar too. Same way of standing, same way of cocking their head to the side. Same bewildering behavior. She introduced us like two friends at a picnic, but she kept the gun trained on him, following his every move.

Dorian continued to work through the process of removing his diving gear and setting it neatly on top of the cabinet. If he noticed the gun pointed at him, he didn't care. He unstrapped the tank from his back and pulled the fins off his feet, working as though Celeste and I weren't there. I was still not sure what was going on. Was Celeste working with him, or not? Was she going to shoot me, or not? And how did she have a twin brother I'd never heard of?

"So, *you* were adopted by the Lewises." I spoke quietly to Celeste out the side of my mouth, though I knew full well that Dorian could hear me. "But . . ." I tipped my head toward the diver, question in my eyes.

"They didn't want me," Dorian said without looking up, working at a buckle under his arm. His voice was soft and high, almost lyrical.

"You were in juvenile detention at the time," Celeste pointed out.

He kept his eyes down, as he carefully finished removing all his extra gear. "*They didn't want me.*"

She didn't press it, and didn't move the gun, still pointing at her brother, never taking her eyes off him, even while she spoke to me. "It was a complicated situation. We'd been in and out of foster care for years. Our mother was . . . not nurturing." She swallowed when she said it, like the words were a painful substitute for the truth. "Dorian shot her." She was so matter of fact. And the truth was so horrid I wasn't sure I wanted to know after all. "*Tried* to shoot her. But he missed and hit me. I went to the hospital, and he went to juvie. Our mother washed her hands of us forever." Her face was blank, empty, bare. "The Lewises took me in. But when Dorian finally got out of juvenile detention . . . it was . . . they said it was . . . well, things were complicated," she finished lamely, like no words would suffice.

There was so much conflict in her eyes. The gratitude to the people that had provided her with a home and family, swirling around the bitterness at being separated from her brother.

"Celeste. I'm so sorry."

She raised an eyebrow at me, like that was the wrong thing to say. I decided to change the subject.

"Was he just hanging out in the cellar, waiting for us so that he could make a grand entrance?"

"It's not a cellar."

"Then what is it?"

Dorian looked at me for the first time, and his mouth spread into a smile, like a stain across his pale face. "It's a passage."

My chin dropped, dumbfounded. "The Shanghai Tunnels? Are you serious? I thought they were impassable, mostly blocked off."

That smear across his face widened ever so slightly. "They *were*. But now I can use them to get anywhere in Old Town, with direct access to the Willamette. Like my own, private, highway." With his foot, he prodded the small jet he'd set on the floor with affection.

He finished removing all the diving equipment and stood before us in his black wet suit. "Okay," Dorian said quietly and turned on Celeste. "You told me I was on my own. So why are you here?"

Celeste shrugged, the gun still aimed at Dorian's chest. "Just came to say hello. You seem so determined to keep tabs on me, I wanted to make it easy on you. I figured if I came to you, you could leave the others out of this. *Why* are you taking the body parts?"

Dorian sneered. "You didn't want to help me on my job, so I thought I'd try something else. If you and your little friends can collect body parts, why can't I?"

Celeste cocked her head to the side. "You need to give the ear back, now."

"No I don't. This job is more fun than the one I found for us anyway. And I think I can renegotiate with your Client to get more than the pittance you all agreed on."

"Don't you dare. Our Client is not someone to screw around with. This isn't a game, Dorian."

His sneer didn't change, like I was only seeing a mask, with his true face hidden beneath. "You think I don't know that?"

"Yes, I think you *don't* know that. You've been out of jail for what? Three weeks? And you act like you're trying to get yourself arrested. Someone's going to get hurt."

Watching Celeste have a debate with her twin brother while she held him at gunpoint was so bizarre. Like I was watching a badly performed play, acted by people who didn't know their lines.

"People get hurt sometimes, Sis. You know that as well as me." Dorian stretched his long pale fingers, inspecting the nails. "How did you find me anyway?"

Celeste frowned. "You didn't make it easy. But a clue kind of fell in my lap this morning, and look, here you are."

When he narrowed his eyes, she said, "Oh, you can follow me, but I can't follow you?"

"No," Dorian insisted, anger burning under his calm voice.

My mind replayed the morning, wondering what she was referring to. *Ohhh.* She must have traced Ranji's phone. I didn't really know how, but she had all kinds of skills I knew nothing about. That was why she'd been so anxious to get back to her laptop at the floating house as soon as Ranji called, and why she'd been so desperate to leave the floating house a few minutes later, even after shooting Lei. As soon as she'd found her brother, she needed to get here before Esteban and Ranji. I couldn't guess whether she'd been more afraid of what they would do to him, or what he would do to them. But why bring me?

Celeste just shrugged in response. "Give the ear to Cone so he can leave, and then you and I will find a better outlet for your . . . emotions."

"Ha," Dorian laughed, a sound like crap hitting the fan. "It's too late. You made your decision. We must all accept the consequences of our actions, even if we don't like them."

"Like setting the penthouse on fire? You almost got us killed!"

"I covered your tracks. You should be grateful. I knew you would survive. The fact that your little friends survived too . . . well, one can't have everything one wants." He spread his hands in a helpless gesture that should have been casual, but felt lifeless and cold, like his limbs didn't belong to him. "Celeste," he pushed, "tell me how you found me."

As he spoke, Celeste's eyes grew darker, her mouth harder, her jaw set. "Doesn't matter."

"It *does* matter. It means there is a flaw in my design, and I need to know what it is. How did you *find me?*" Spittle flew from his lips, his eyes wide with rage.

She still had the gun trained on him in an impressive show of commitment. "So is this how it is? You and I have to work together, or else? You hurt my family!"

"*I* AM YOUR FAMILY!"

Both Celeste and I started at the volume of his fury, and in the blink of an eye, he pulled another handgun out of who-knows-where and aimed it at me.

I raised my hands, placating, though my mind was racing. Celeste's twin brother would shoot us both if we didn't get out of there soon. Celeste still hadn't moved, but the look on her face told me she knew it too.

"Drop the gun or he dies," Dorian hissed.

I wasn't sure that was as much of a threat as he thought it was. She'd already tried to shoot me herself today, and he might very well be doing her a favor. Celeste continued to glare at him, her finger twitching on the trigger, but then, to my horror, she gave in. Her face fell in defeat and the air whooshed out of her lungs. She dropped the gun and it clattered to the damp, wooden floorboards.

Crap. I needed Celeste if we were going to beat him. And we had to beat him. It *couldn't* all end here, in some moldy old restaurant in Old Town. I had way too much to live for now.

Dorian smiled like all was forgiven, and kicked Celeste's gun into the water. Then he pulled a set of handcuffs out of a pouch he'd laid on the pool table and handed them to Celeste.

"I thought you really might shoot me that time," Dorian said, voice almost sweet now as he happily talked to his sister. "I'm glad things haven't changed that much. Welcome back."

I watched this interchange with a disconnected fascination, like I was someone else.

Celeste took the handcuffs and walked toward me, eyes on the ground. I wanted to grab her and shake her. All her swagger, all her confidence had withered away in the hungry shadow of her demented brother, and it was freaking me out. I considered tackling him again, but I had no doubt he would shoot me the second I moved.

"Celeste," I implored. "He's manipulating you. You don't have to do this. You're stronger than him."

Dorian laughed.

"He needs me," she breathed without looking up. "I'm the only one that can protect him."

She threaded the handcuffs through the door pulls on the tall metal cabinet behind me, then wrapped a cuff around each of my wrists, tightening them painfully.

I let her do it, even while my mind raced, looking for a way out that wouldn't get either of us killed. My mind rifled through all the decisions I'd made in the last week, plucking out the ones that had led me here.

Dorian's smile deepened and he pulled Celeste away from me. "Why did you bring the goon?" he asked with a curious cock of his head.

Celeste looked at me, mouth tight. Was she going to tell him about my eye? Was I about to have my eyeball ripped out of my head?

She shrugged and turned away. "Just in case."

"Hmm, well . . . I don't think we need him."

Celeste lunged at Dorian as he pulled the trigger. The report blasted through the enclosed space like a grenade going off, and the bullet ripped through the skin at my side.

I lurched back, crashing into the cabinet as pain throbbed through me, thumping like fire across my skin. Blood and heat flowed from my side, soaking my shirt and pants.

Celeste knocked the gun out of Dorian's hand, splashing it into the water. He looked at her in exasperation, like he'd been sure they were on the same page.

"You shot me!" I mumbled, stunned. "First your sister, then you? Wasn't the rock to the head enough?" I was really starting to dislike these twins. If I didn't get out of here soon, one of them would be the death of me.

I ignored the pain in my side and yanked on the cabinet I was handcuffed to, hoping to rip the handles off and get out of there. I pulled with all my might, but instead of tearing off the handles, the whole cabinet toppled forward. I dropped to the floor as it slammed into the pool table, half on, half off, trapping me in the gap beneath. The hinges on one of the doors sheared off, and the door flopped open from the wrong side. It fell, creating a barrier between me and the rest of the room, and everything inside the cabinet slid off the shelves and landed in a heap on the floor.

Great. Instead of freeing myself, I was trapped. I tried to press my arm against the bleeding in my side, but the angle was all wrong.

Something hit the door hanging next to me. I cried out in pain as the whole thing slammed into my side, and my gunshot wound throbbed anew. The metal door twisted, and the handle ripped free. The door crashed down, landing on the pile of stuff on the floor, and Dorian picked it up and tossed it aside. He squatted down, twisting his head so he could see into the hidey hole where I crouched. His eyes were shining, and he smiled at me. "I like you," he said, in all sincerity, and reached toward me.

The water in the tunnel gurgled and spit, once again coming to life. Dorian turned slowly, face painted with disbelief. The water erupted as two bodies exploded out of it, weapons held at the ready. In a motion so quick I could barely follow it, one of the figures raised his leg and kicked Dorian straight in the chest, knocking him against the overturned cabinet. Celeste grabbed her backpack and scooted away into a corner, holding her backpack in front of her like a shield.

The creatures from the Shanghai Tunnels pointed their weapons at Dorian where he lay crumpled in the cabinet crap on the floor. Were these cohorts of his that were turning on him? Or had they come to save me? I wasn't really sure I cared which.

Dorian pulled himself to his feet, his chest heaving, exhausted from the exertion of dealing with all of us. "What no one ever seems to understand is that I have nothing to lose." He picked up something off the pile of cabinet detritus and held it out like a child displaying his science project. It was a grenade. Dorian was holding a flipping grenade. He pulled the pin out with his mouth and spit it on the floor.

The figures stepped away, back into the water. Dorian held the grenade out, smiling, and they both slowly set their guns on the floor, then raised their arms. This was going to end badly, very soon. I shifted, trying to get my legs out from under me so that I could scoot further away. The pain in my side shot out in all directions like a knife stabbing into my flesh over and over.

Dorian's head snapped my direction at the sound, and his smile widened. Now that he seemed to have us where he wanted us, Dorian relaxed visibly. He seemed perfectly content holding our lives in his hand.

Celeste stood, and walked casually to her brother's side, like him waving a grenade around was an everyday occurrence.

He glanced her way, nodding as though all disagreements between them were forgiven. "This location is compromised," he said to her. "Perhaps the entire tunnel system is compromised. We have to deal with this now."

Celeste nodded, like it didn't matter much to her, and unscrewed the cap on a water bottle she'd pulled out of her backpack. She passed it to him, then slid the bag onto her back.

Dorian took the water bottle and drank deeply, inspecting each of us in turn. Killing us was his only option. Even I could see that, but a bizarre part of my brain admired him for taking the time to think it over first.

He passed the water bottle back to her and raised his hand to explain his plan for our fate. "That water tastes weird," he said, then his eyes rolled back in his head, his knees buckled, and he collapsed face first on the floor.

28

Celeste grabbed his hand as he went down, wrapping her fingers around his so that he wouldn't let go of the grenade, then carefully took it from him. She snagged the pin from where it had fallen near the tunnel opening and slid it back into the grenade, then put the whole thing in her backpack.

The figures in the water kept their hands up, facing Celeste, unsure if she was a threat. She stared at Dorian's prone form on the floor, then sank down on the wet wood floor near his head, tears running down her cheeks. His chest rose and fell. He was alive, but unconscious. Just like I had been when she'd drugged me.

The divers finally stepped the rest of the way out of the water and removed their masks and hoods, revealing the faces of Ranji and Esteban.

I sighed with relief, planning to tell Esteban that we *both* had some explaining to do. Running around with his pal collecting things like friends on a scavenger hunt was a far cry from the reality of full diving suits and tactical weapons. But I was suddenly too exhausted to speak. Or move. Maybe I should go to sleep, just for a minute or two. Ranji inspected the room, casting concerned looks at Celeste from time to time who was still crying over Dorian's unconscious body.

Esteban flapped in his fins over to where I lay on the floor under the cabinet and reached for me. "Hey, Cohen. No offense, man, but you don't look so good."

That was rude. I'd had kind of a rough day. And now Esteban was insulting me? He took about a million years picking the lock on my cuffs and then he hooked his hands under my arms and dragged me out from under the cabinet. My whole body screamed in protest, and I tried to tell him to knock it off but moaned instead.

"You're *injured* too?" He *tsked*. "I let you out of my sight for a few days and see what happens?"

"Cohen makes a witty comeback," I mumbled. That would show him. I wasn't as out of it as he probably thought.

Esteban laughed and removed his backpack. He pulled out a small bag as Ranji knelt next to him, looking me over.

"I am going to inspect your wound. Don't be alarmed," Ranji said.

Honestly, I didn't even care. He could start singing show tunes and it wouldn't have made much difference to me. I wanted a nap, and right here seemed like the perfect place for it. Esteban rolled me gently back onto my side and carefully lifted my shirt.

"Aye," Ranji hissed. "No, no. Don't be alarmed. It is not so bad. The bullet went straight through. Nothing that cannot be fixed. But hold very still please so that we can stitch you up. You can do it, yes?"

I thought he was asking me to do it, which was just the last straw. On top of everything else, I also had to give myself stitches?

Esteban pulled a few supplies out of his small bag. He dabbed my side with something that felt like a two by four wrapped with barbed wire.

"AaaaAAOW!"

"Sorry, dude! Sorry!" He jabbed me with something else and the pain faded away to only a dull, stinging ache. Numbness spread out through my side and my breathing finally slowed. I hadn't even realized I'd been breathing faster.

I exhaled, but the tugging and digging in my side kept me from nodding off. I kept my eyes on Esteban's face. We'd been friends for three years. He was a building manager in Dayspring. He hung out with his buddies on the weekends. Nothing I knew about him jived with this man giving me stitches in an abandoned restaurant in Chinatown.

"I thought you and Ranji played pool together," I rasped. My tongue was cement, and my throat was lined with sandpaper. The water from the tunnel was looking mighty tempting.

Esteban grinned, then pulled out some gauze and laid it across my wound, taping it in place. Then, like he could read minds in addition to being an able-bodied field medic, he handed me a water bottle. "Drink. And take these. You'll need them for the pain."

I popped the pills he handed me into my mouth and drank, guzzling the water down until I nearly choked, coughing and dripping all over myself.

"Can you stand?" he asked me.

I breathed, taking stock of my physical situation, then nodded, shrugging as casually as I could manage. "Yeah, I mean, it was only a little bullet, right?"

Ranji squatted next to Dorian and Celeste. "How long will he be out?"

"It's hard to say," I grunted as Esteban helped me to my feet. I swayed, unsteady for a moment, but stayed upright. "But at least an hour, I would think."

"Aye. Excellent. This is the man you were looking for, no?"

"Yeah," I said, eyeing Dorian with disgust and pity. "This is the guy."

"Magnificent. I told you I always get my man. As you can see, that is true."

I opened my mouth to ask about the diving gear and the passage through the tunnels and more details on their whole collecting operation, but at the moment I didn't care. Lei was injured. Maybe worse. Hopefully she was in the hospital, hopefully recovering. But I had to go find out, and time was slipping away.

"You held up your end of the bargain," I said to Ranji. "Though I'm starting to think we can't afford you. And you saved me from hours spent in a pool of my own blood. So, thank you. But I have to go." I held out my hand to shake his, and as I moved my foot brushed a small shipping box addressed to Call-A-Human. I bent and picked it up. It looked just as it had when Dorian had stolen it from me.

"Ah. The stolen item?" he asked.

I nodded, staring at it.

"Perfect," Ranji said, smiling in such a way that the scroll-work shaved along his jawline changed shape. "Then, it seems, my services are no longer required. I will expect payment of course, according to the terms of the contract."

"Right. Of course. We'll be in touch. I'll make sure you get your money."

Esteban nodded at Ranji, knowing my word was good, then looked back at me. "Man, we gotta catch up, okay?"

I dipped my chin in agreement. "Yes. I think we do."

Ranji pulled open the metal doors and they left, weapons held at the ready. I guess they had no problem leaving the bad guy unconscious on the floor outside the Shanghai Tunnels.

I turned to Celeste who was still crying over the prone form of her brother.

"Why did you bring me here?" I asked.

She took so long to answer I didn't think she would, but then she spoke, her eyes on her brother, her voice ragged. "The Client assigned us your eye. If Dorian found out . . ." She swiped the back of her hand across her eyes. "Getting you far, far away from my family seemed essential. Even if that meant sending you to the hospital."

Ah. Protecting them. The only way she knew how. Just like I'd been trying to do.

"Celeste." I held out my hand toward her. "Come with me."

She looked up at me, eyes red, tears streaking shiny tracks down her cheeks. "And what?" she spit, voice full of venom. "Say, 'Sorry I shot you, Lei. I promise I won't do it again.'?"

"Yes," I insisted. "Apologize. It's a good start."

"And Lei's going to forgive me? I'm not even sure it's a promise I could keep."

"You know her better than me. What do you think she'll do?"

She dropped her head into her hands. "What if she doesn't make it? I couldn't let Dorian kill you, but I shot my own sister!"

"Lei is going to be fine," I insisted, willing it to be true. "Come with me, and we'll figure something out."

Tears ran out of her eyes afresh, and she squeezed them shut.

I swallowed, speaking softly. "You're not safe with

him. What do you think he'll do when he wakes up? He's trouble."

"He's my *brother*."

"Celeste—"

She wiped impatiently at her wet cheeks. "I have to stay with him. Don't you see? He *needs* me. Can you imagine the trouble he'll get into without me? No one else is looking out for him except me. *No one*. I'm all he's got. I'm the only one that can protect him from himself."

How could I possibly argue with that? I knew that the best thing for both of them was probably for him to go back to jail, but who was I to decide? I didn't know what to do. He hadn't actually killed anyone. Today. That I knew of. Could Celeste really keep him under control?

"Are you sure you're safe with him?"

Celeste rolled her eyes like I was so dumb and could never understand the dynamic of their relationship. "Just go, Cohen," she said using my real name for the first time. "I'll handle him. Lei needs you."

I bit my cheek, knowing she was right, but also possibly very wrong. But perhaps this wasn't my fight.

She growled at my indecision then reached into her pocket, pulled out the car keys, and threw them at me. Then she pulled out the box with the tongue inside and threw that to me too. I caught it, surprised.

"Leave. Now," she gulped.

So I did.

—o

The sun was setting when I pulled that reliable hunk of junk up to OHSU Hospital. I parked in the shadow of a humongous bay fig tree that took up half the parking lot, the asphalt buckling and breaking around its expansive buttress roots. I found a jacket in the back seat of the car that fit well enough to cover up the blood all over my shirt, and went inside.

I asked at the front desk and was informed that Lei was indeed there and had just come out of surgery. Cesar met me at the door to her room, a tired smile on his face. "I am so glad you're here, my friend. I did not want her to wake up alone."

I dipped my chin; I knew he had more right to be there than I did, working at the hospital and all, but I wasn't all that excited to see him again.

He nodded into my silence, then answered the questions I didn't ask. "She pulled through okay. Our Lei is a fighter! The bullet came out, but it was lodged in her shoulder blade. Very tricky."

Ah, of course he was a surgeon. I swallowed my ridiculous pride and jealousy. "I . . . Okay. Thank you. Really. I'm glad she had a friend looking out for her."

He beamed and waved it off. "I am only doing my job. But go in, sit. She won't be able to leave until tomorrow at least. Make yourself at home. I will have a nurse bring some Jell-O." He clapped me on the arm and walked away, whistling. I closed the door behind me, grateful that Lei had a room to herself. She lay on the hospital bed with its back angled up, legs straight out in front of her. There were no tubes coming out of her mouth, just one in her arm. She was still pale, but the grayness had been replaced by just enough color to make her look okay. To make her look alive.

Where were Jimmy and Saifi? Were they waiting somewhere else in the hospital? Or had they gone back to the floating house? Cesar probably knew, but it wasn't worth running after him. Knowing it was a huge breach of privacy, I found her duffle bag on a chair and pulled her phone out of it. It was nearly dead. There were calls from Jimmy and Saifi, and I tapped one of their numbers to call them back. It went straight to voicemail. I called the other but got the same result. I committed both numbers to memory, so I could add them to my contacts as soon as I got another phone.

I watched Lei, the gentle rise and fall of her chest. I brushed a hair off her forehead, then leaned over the railing on the bed, the dressing and tape tugging at the skin on my side, and pressed my lips to her forehead. A flash outside the window let me know that nighttime had arrived, and with it the storm.

—o

Sunlight peeking around the blinds shone directly in my face and I forced my eyes open, grateful that it was finally morning. Sleeping in a hospital chair was like meditating inside a dryer, and the nurses had been in and out of the room so often that it had been a fitful night. It was just past dawn, and the water still ran off the roof and sloshed through the drainpipes after last night's storm. The pain in my side was excruciating now that the meds Esteban gave me had worn off. I gingerly changed the bandage on my side with some supplies from one of the cabinets. The stitches looked okay, but I was going to need something to take the edge off the pain soon.

Lei slept and slept. I watched her, searching for any signs of consciousness, but her chest rose and fell with her breathing, steady, slow, as though she slept peacefully.

Eventually I walked down to the gift shop for painkillers and a toothbrush. I also picked up a hot-pink prepaid FunFone™, which would have to suffice as a phone for the moment. I grabbed some hot tamales for Lei, and then stopped by the cafeteria for a cup of oatmeal. I took as many painkillers as I thought I could get away with, then took the long way back to Lei's room, eating my oatmeal on the way. I passed a grand courtyard full of plants, a walkway made of drains woven through the middle, but too much water was still dripping from the trees to make venturing into it very appealing at the moment.

Lei was awake when I went back into her room, her gaze flitting around as though trying to figure out where she was.

I rushed to her side, tossing my bag into the chair and slid my hand into hers, brushing my fingers across her cheek. "Lei! I'm so glad you're okay. I don't know what I would have done if you—"

Lei pulled away, giving me an appraising glance. "Look who still has both his eyeballs."

I laughed, though her voice sounded more angry than joking. The last several hours had probably been even worse for her than they had been for me.

"Are you in pain?" I asked her. "Are you hungry? I can grab a nurse or get you some breakfast. Whatever you need."

"What did you do to Celeste?" Lei asked, her nostrils flared.

"Nothing. She's okay. She's with her twin brother. Did *you* know she had a twin brother? He's the diver, if you can believe it. It's a long story, but I'll tell you the whole thing as soon as you want to hear it."

Surprise darted across Lei's face, but she shook it off. "Cohen, stop."

I stopped.

"Is Cohen even your real name?"

I straightened, confused. "Of course it is. What's wrong?"

She laughed bitterly. "*Cosmic design*. I'm such an idiot. I *knew* I shouldn't trust you. You orchestrated this whole thing, didn't you?"

"I—" What was she talking about? "What are you talking about?"

"The Client sent us a message. After you and Celeste drove away. Told us he *didn't* send you. Said he didn't know why you were there, but that we shouldn't trust you. He only asked for your eye in an attempt to get rid of you. Jimmy and Saifi refused to believe it but . . ." To my horror, tears pooled in her eyes while she spoke, and one slipped down her cheek.

"Lei, no—" I reached for her hand again, but she jerked away, then gasped in pain.

"I was such an easy mark. You played me like a game of cards. That story about Peter was really good. How long have you been perfecting that one?"

"He's *lying*," I argued. "I didn't orchestrate anything. I'm not working against you. I've been trying to help you from the beginning!"

"Tell me what you did to Celeste!" she demanded. "Did you brainwash her? Lobotomize her? Drug her? Build a robot that looked just like her that was designed to do your bidding? Where is she?"

I shook my head as she spoke. "She tried to shoot me, remember? The only reason she failed is because you risked your life to save me." My voice caught. "I tried to get her to come back with me, but she wouldn't. She gave me the tongue, though. And the ear. I got that too. Maybe that'll convince the Client that I'm not some impostor—"

I trailed off as Lei buried her face in her hands, her breathing erratic.

"Lei? Lei, please listen to me," I pressed, desperate for her to understand. "Everything I told you is true. I'm just a computer programmer. I don't know why I got that tongue in the mail. I didn't *scheme* to be a part of any of this, but now that I am . . . I just want to help. I want to stay. I want to be a part of your life. I want . . . you."

I hadn't declared my feelings for a woman so plainly since the Gretchen debacle in eighth grade. I stood in front of her, bare, vulnerable, heart pounding somewhere in the vicinity of my throat.

She didn't look up, shoulders shaking slightly. I reached a hand toward her, then pulled it back, afraid it would only upset her further. This is not how this was supposed to go. She was supposed to be so happy to see me that . . . I didn't let myself finish the thought. I'd done it again. Invented a relationship in my mind that wasn't based on reality.

"Where are Jimmy and Saifi?" I asked as gently as I could, eager to change the subject.

Her voice was muffled behind her hands, but I still caught the words. "They're gone."

"What do you mean? Gone where?"

She pulled her hands away then. Her face was wet with tears, her jaw tight. Her black eyes darker than ever, rimmed with red. "I don't know, they didn't tell me. I'm just their irresponsible sister who put them in a life-threatening situation. I'm an unfit guardian. Minors who don't have guardians are sent to foster care."

I stepped back, shaken, running my hands over my shaggy hair. "We can fix this. I can help you fix this. We can talk to someone at DHS, and get your lawyer involved. Maybe even the Client. He's probably got all kinds of connections."

She cupped her hands like she was strangling someone, looking at me with total, overwhelming exasperation. "Are you even listening to me? If your clever plan was to ruin my life, you succeeded. The Client's first rule is no police involvement, so he fired us for breach of contract, and now he doesn't have to pay us anything. It's over. We're out. It's done." Her voice caught, like she was choking back a sob. "My whole family is gone. So I don't even care who you really are. There is nothing left for you to help with. There is nothing left for you to ruin. It's over."

My legs buckled and I collapsed into the chair. "No," I said, refusing to accept what she was telling me. "There has to be a way—"

"Hoard!" She cut me off, wincing in pain again. "Stop. It's time for you to go."

"But I—but we—"

"No," she whispered. "There's no we. You were right all along. I risked too much. I took too many chances. I jeopardized everything to put my family back together, and all I succeeded in doing was ripping it apart. I'm smart enough to know when I'm beat."

I couldn't. I couldn't leave her like this. She'd just been shot by her sister, she was hopped up on painkillers, she didn't know what she was saying. There had to be something I could do.

"Please," she said. "Please go."

A tear slipped out and slid down her cheek. Her eyes were hard and cold and so far away from me I didn't see how I could ever get them back. So I stood up, turned away, and walked out of the room.

29

Everything about going home felt wrong, but I did it anyway. I left the car keys at the hospital reception desk for Lei and took the bus home. Everything was still there: the apartment building, the park, the whatever. Just like I left it five days ago. The fact that the rest of the world had continued on while mine seemed to be ending was really, really annoying.

I walked up the stairs to the third floor, listening to the sound bounce around the concrete and metal enclosure. My clean, safe apartment was empty. Drab. Lifeless. Test tube models sat in a tidy row across the shelf above my couch right where I'd left them. Hours of work were represented in those itty-bitty cities. I'd arranged them, I'd arranged *everything*—my models, my dishes, my relationships, my time—so carefully, so safely, so deliberately, and what was the point? What was any of it for?

I ripped off the jacket I'd borrowed from Celeste's car, and my stained, sweaty shirt, tearing off several buttons in the process. The T-shirt I wore underneath was too tight and covered with blood, but I couldn't get myself to care. I picked up a test tube and turned it over in my hands. It was a tree house, complete with a miniature ladder and tiny rope swing. It had taken me nearly a week to create. A whole week of careful planning and meticulous execution. I threw the test tube, smashing it against the kitchen tile. I picked up another one. This one contained a tiny four-story building with a spiral staircase running around the outside. The stairs alone had taken the better part of three days. I stroked it with my thumb, then threw it against the wall. The test tube cracked against the drywall, and the house slid out the bottom, but didn't break the way I needed it to. I picked up another, then scooped as many as I could into my arms and stalked out into the hall.

At the stairwell I leaned over the railing, looking at the fold of stairs leading down to street level. I threw a test tube into the stairwell, and it smashed to smithereens against the handrail. I'd created a safety hazard. And I absolutely did not care. I threw another one and it shattered against the stairs, shards flying out like a firework, light glinting off the flecks of glass. I started hucking them one after another against the walls of the stairwell like they were baseballs.

"Whoa, whoa whoa whoa."

I turned in surprise to find Jocelyn at my side, drawn out of her apartment by my mental meltdown.

"Whoa." She laid a hand on my bicep, and then she looked at me like I was something new, a creature she'd never noticed before. She took in my hair standing on end, dirty face, clothes a mess, and her smile froze. "What are you doing?"

"Oh." I cleared my throat. "Just . . . decluttering. Sorry I disturbed you." I turned to leave, but her hand on my arm held me back.

"Colin, right?" Her voice was overly sweet, the way someone

might talk to a baby. As though she was afraid speaking to me like an adult might send me into a blind rage.

I didn't even have the energy to correct her. "Sure."

"Are you okay?"

No. Not even a little. I wasn't sure how anything could ever be okay again. "Yeah."

She held my arm, inspecting my face as though agony and despair weren't leaking out of my pores. Her eyebrows knit with concern. "You . . . wanna come inside for a minute?"

"I can't." I was sure there were several more meaningless things in my apartment that needed to be destroyed. Again, I turned to go.

"*Yes, you can.*" Her voice was persuasive and smooth. "You're covered in blood. I have bandages. Besides, we're next-door neighbors and we barely know each other. How sad is that?"

I shrugged. She pulled at my arm, and I gave up and let her draw me through her door and into her apartment.

Jocelyn had redecorated since I'd set up her network for her when she first moved in. There were oversized nature scenes attached to every wall, and a giant ficus in the corner that was so tall the branches curved up against the ceiling and hung down over the couch. I sat as small and polite as I could, perched in the center cushion. A row of scented candles burned on a tray near the TV, soaking the room in their cloying, fruity aroma. She was talking to me from the kitchen, but I only caught about ten percent of what she said, the rest drowned out by the growl of the blender.

A minute later she walked into the living room brandishing a large tumbler like it was the holy grail. She pushed it toward me with a proud smile on her face.

"This smoothie is *everything*," she said. "It will make you feel so much better. I drink it religiously every single day. Gut Health is the secret to total body health! Being regular keeps me fit and makes my skin and my hair shiny. It improves my mood and helps me sleep better. It is, like, the perfect drink." She laughed.

I was sitting in Jocelyn's apartment. Not doing her a favor, just hanging out. And she was telling me about her bowel movements. *This* was what I'd thought I wanted? The drink she pressed into my hands both looked and smelled like something that she had scooped out of a swamp, topped with a sprig of mint. She pushed the cup closer to my face. I tried not to pull away as much as I wanted to.

"You have to try it," she insisted. "Come on." She watched me expectantly. "You're going to make me feel bad. You gotta take a chance."

If only she knew. The last few days had been nothing but chances, and I still ended up right back where I started. Well almost. I *was* sitting next to Jocelyn on her couch. Her face was so close to mine I could see the flecks of brown in her blue eyes. Taking one more chance probably couldn't hurt.

I raised the glass in acknowledgment, then tipped the swamp into my mouth. I gagged instantly, covering my mouth with my hand to keep from spitting everything back out, but some of it still dribbled down my chin. I wiped my mouth with the back of my hand and forced myself to swallow. "It's good," I choked. My gut gurgled malevolently.

She laughed again, "No, it tastes horrible. But, oh wow, you can feel the difference. It will change your life, I swear." Her beautiful mouth stretched into a beautiful smile. "Some things are worth it."

I met her eyes. Jocelyn was right. She was so right it felt like being punched in the head. Some things *were* worth it. I wasn't even sure what *it* was. Misery? Dismemberment? Death? Lei was worth it. Her family was worth it. Figuring out how to help her put her life back together was more than worth it. Even if I failed. Even if she still wouldn't talk to me again. I had to take the chance. That thing that had clicked into place while we were at Gran's house was my heart. I think I dislocated it years ago and had coped by being interested in women that were so wrong for me, I never had to take any actual chances. Lei found my heart and fixed it. And I had to fix this, no matter what it took.

Jocelyn's smile widened a fraction, and she rested her hand on my thigh as light as air.

I stood up so fast she fell over into the spot where I'd been sitting. "I have to go. Thanks for the . . . liquid."

She stood up too, following me to the door. "Do you want to take it with you? You can bring the cup back whenever."

"No, thank you." I handed it to her. "My bowels are doing pretty okay. But thank you for the hospitality. Have a lovely day." I strode to the door, pulled it open, and went home.

In my hallway closet from a box of unused electronics, I pulled my old laptop. It was slow, with a tiny hard drive and an M key that stuck, but it would have to do.

I shook out my hands and stretched my neck from side to side. If I was going to help Lei, I needed to know what the Client was up to. I was filled with frustration and regret and so many questions they seemed to be procreating, but there were a few things I *knew*. And seeing them all in a list might clear things up for me. The spreadsheet was maybe overkill since everything would have fit on a small sticky note, but I wasn't screwing around. In my spreadsheet I typed:

Big Toe, right foot - Grecia Suttles

Left Hand - Bob Cobb
Ear (which one?) - Helen Beaumont
Tongue - Farley (sent to Cohen 4 days before assignment?)
Left eye - Cohen Hoard

Why these people? Why these body parts? Without a complete list of every part they'd collected, it would be hard to find the patterns and connections, but I had to work with what I knew.

I did some digging to try to find out some basic information about them. Grecia Suttles was in her early fifties, had managed a three-star hotel downtown, and lived with her dog. She'd been a hurdle runner in college and had kept it up throughout her life, the stress damaging her toe enough that she'd eventually needed a toe transplant.

"Ah ha!" I poked the screen. "I knew it! These body parts *were* donated!" I already knew that was the case with my eye and Bob Cobb's hand. I'd have to verify that for Helen Beaumont and Farley, but I was sure that theirs would be donated parts as well.

I couldn't find anything on Farley, the person we were supposed to get the tongue from, almost like they didn't actually exist, but there was enough info on Helen Beaumont for me to learn that she'd received ear replacement surgery as a gift from her husband on their twentieth wedding anniversary. Weirdest anniversary gift ever, but it proved I was right. She also had a rather impressive salt-water fish collection.

I twisted in my seat, popping my back. Could the animals be a clue? Grecia Suttles had a dog. Bob Cobb had a zoo. Could that be what linked them? Were they all members of the same I-Love-My-Pet social media site? That was possible, but very dumb. Also, *I* didn't have any animals. I lived totally and completely alone. But then, besides the animals, both Grecia and Bob had lived alone too. I followed that connection as I dug further, only to learn that Helen Beaumont had lived with her husband, four daughters, and her ailing mother-in-law.

My heart twanged for her family and the mother they'd lost. Had she been sick? Was it sudden, or did they have time to prepare? A quick search told me what I wanted to know. No, Helen Beaumont hadn't been sick. Her death was sudden, and unexpected. She'd died in a head-on collision with a diesel truck.

A car accident, just like the toe owner, Grecia Suttles.

I'd assumed that Bob Cobb had died of some kind of illness, something that had given him months or years to set things up so that his death and burial would be just the way he wanted them. But I was wrong. He'd lost control on the freeway, crossing four lanes of traffic and causing a huge pile up. Two other people had died. It was assumed he had fallen asleep at the wheel.

I exhaled, my heart rate picking up like it knew something I didn't. I looked up Grecia Suttles, just to be sure, just in case I was remembering wrong, but I wasn't. She'd run a red light at a busy intersection and been hit by a bus.

I rubbed my face with my hands, slightly nauseated. The irony was, if DarkWave had gone live last week, it was very likely that all of those people would still be alive. Out of some kind of morbid curiosity I signed into GridLox and combed through the logs. It was hardly common knowledge, but there were several areas across the city that were used as test sites for DarkWave, though at the moment all the DarkWave AI was doing was pretending. It wasn't connected to anything, so it sent out its messages and commands to help traffic function like a well-oiled machine, but since it wasn't linked to anything, all those messages were sent directly to a test folder to be reviewed as needed. If Grecia Suttles happened to be in the right area, I might just get lucky and find some data on her crash.

I found the date and time of Grecia Suttles's death and pulled up the video: dash cam footage from a city bus. In the video, the bus lumbered merrily down a busy road toward an intersection where it slammed straight into a black sedan. The sedan had driven in front of the bus so fast it seemed like it had teleported there. The bus driver didn't even have time to brake. A side view camera from the bus showed a minivan alongside it bash into the car at almost the same time. The sedan skidded further out into traffic, just missing several other cars, and then smashed into the guardrail. It was a miracle there was anything left of the sedan to pull Grecia Suttles out of.

I rifled through the logs, trying to figure out what the AI test module thought was going on at that intersection at that time. But there were no alerts. There were no redirects, or alternate routes, or change orders, or anything at all. According to the logs, traffic was running smoothly and efficiently. It almost seemed to be pleased with itself, reporting: *SUCCESS: Executed method for vehicle with id XRF000435.*

I paused, the ID number snagging in my brain. This felt off. I mean, more off than some nut job buying body parts off car accident victims. I jumped up and grabbed my satchel from where I'd dropped it when I'd gotten home this morning and dumped it out on the table to find the diagnostic report. I flipped to the error at the end: *LookupError: Vehicle with id XRF000435 does not exist.*

The ID number was the same.

That wasn't good. That wasn't good at all. Fingers trembling, I did a quick little not-quite-legal search through the DMV's files to find the owner of the vehicle, even though I knew, without a doubt, exactly what I was going to find. And there it was:

VIN: WMEEJ31JXRF000435, Registered to Grecia Suttles.

Maybe I *was* psychic.

This wasn't just *not good*. It was officially *bad*. When my demo had crashed, an actual vehicle had crashed in the real world with deadly consequences. Had my demo done this? If so, *how?* My demo didn't pull any actual, working info from DarkWave. It was only connected as far as was necessary to access DarkWave's most basic functions. It was possible for data or commands to pass from one to the other, but there was no reason that they would. My demo used imaginary cars that didn't exist. It wouldn't know what to do with a real car if it had one.

And then it hit me. *That* was the problem with my demo. Every so often an ID number from a real car was sent from the DarkWave system to my demo. My demo didn't know what to do with it, so it crashed. I checked the time stamp on both reports. My demo crashed thirty-seven minutes before Grecia Suttles's car did. I was sure there was a connection, but I didn't know what it was, or why there would be such a time gap.

I dug back through the demo logs to try to figure out what was happening. On the demo side it looked like a small seizure, but on the DarkWave side everything looked fine. No info had come from the demo to DarkWave. It appeared to be function-ing just as it should. It reported all the red lights, the vehicles crashing into each other, the traffic slowdown and redirect that all happened as a result. It didn't appear to have tried to *do* anything.

There was only one task it was trying to execute, which was, according to the report, successful. Something to do with Grecia Suttles car. Thirty-seven minutes before she was hit by a bus.

Oh crap. Oh crap, oh crap, oh crap.

My heart was pounding now, blood whooshing loudly through my ears. I minimized everything on my monitor and pulled up the logs from the diagnostic tests that had been running nonstop on my demo since Monday night. The demo had crashed twice more since then, both times returning the same *LookupError*, but with ID numbers I didn't recognize. Like walking off a plank one inevitable step at a time, I searched the DMV's records to find the vehicle owners. It was the simplest thing in the world. With just a few clicks I had proof that one of the vehicles belonged to Bob Cobb, and the other to George Beaumont, husband of Helen Beaumont.

Certainty kicked a hole straight through me. It wasn't my demo that was causing the crashes. It was DarkWave. I couldn't begin to guess why, and I didn't understand how, but DarkWave was reprogramming Auto Save and switching cars from collision avoiding to collision seeking. When it sent through its bad instructions—which must include actions for the cars to take at specific places or times—the vehicle ID the AI was controlling passed through to my demo, and the demo crashed. All those frustrating crashes I'd been fighting with were harbingers of death.

DarkWave was taking control of vehicles and crashing them.

And killing people.

And then . . . what . . . making Lei and the gang go out and retrieve a severed body part from its victim?

DarkWave *was* the Client.

And it went live tonight at 8:30.

My fingers went numb, my chest cold. I shook my head, trying to get my thoughts in order instead of the screaming, flailing, running-in-circles they were currently doing. I didn't want to be here. I didn't want to know this. Swamp juice was preferable to the bag of cats I was opening.

DarkWave had to be shut down. Now. It was already almost 5:00, leaving just over three hours before the launch.

I downloaded and printed out three copies of everything, then wiped all evidence of my presence from the DMV's site, double and triple checking everything to make sure I left no trace, like sweeping my way out of a room. Then I shut down my demo and tried to shut off all of the DarkWave test modules, but I didn't have the access necessary, and couldn't get in no matter what I tried.

I dialed Steenrod's number using FunFone™. This was going to devastate him. It was going to devastate the entire company. It was supposed to be his wife's legacy. The lawsuits alone would be enough to destroy us. It was not going to be a fun conversation. But I had no time to lose. I had to get him to shut everything down before anyone else got hurt. Except Steenrod didn't answer his phone.

I roared in frustration and started typing him a very frantic email, detailing all the dangers of DarkWave, how essential it was that we shut it down immediately. My fingers slowed, and then stopped as a thought occurred to me.

What if DarkWave wasn't just majorly borked? What if Lei was right? What if, ridiculous as it sounded, DarkWave had gained sentience, gone rogue, and was now following its own agenda?

It was crazy. Impossible. But given the evidence, I had to at least consider the possibility. And if the AI *was* truly sentient, how much power did it have? How far could it reach? Could I even get an email to Steenrod, or was it already monitoring all communications? I didn't think it had that capability, but if

DarkWave was the Client, it had been sending messages to Lei for the last few weeks, so somehow it must have expanded.

I already knew it wanted my eyeball. What would it do to me if it realized I intended to shut it down? Email was a bad idea.

A banging at my door nearly scared me out of my skin. My first thought was that DarkWave had found me, but that was silly. Right? It couldn't get me as long as I stayed home. As long as I didn't get in a car. I opened the door, annoyed at the interruption.

A SwiftMax Extreme Envelope lay on my doormat.

30

$\mathbf{T}$his was bigger than the last one I'd received, with something soft and bulky inside. According to the shipping label, it was both shipped from and to Lei Lewis, at my address. I ripped the envelope open and dumped the contents on the kitchen table.

It was an empty faded blue duffle bag, all wadded up so it would fit into the shipping envelope. I turned it over, revealing a Cloud Busters badge sewn onto the strap.

Why would Lei send me her duffle bag?

I picked up the large envelope it had come in, flipping it over and checking inside to make sure I hadn't missed anything. I hadn't. There was nothing to miss. It was just a plastic envelope.

I knew it wouldn't work, but I tried to call Lei anyway. It went straight to voicemail. I called both Jimmy and Saifi, but neither of them picked up either.

Confusion mounting, I checked carefully through every inch of the duffle bag. In one of the side zippered pockets I found a very soggy book, bound in brown canvas, warped and moist.

Mold crawled across the cover, and around the spine, but I could still read the title stamped along the top edge: *As I Lay Dying* by William Faulkner.

Well, that didn't sound great. I tried to open the book to see if it contained a note or other message, but the pages were like a solid, distorted chunk of wood pulp. Anxiety coiled through me like a snake. What in the name of sunshine was I supposed to do with this book? Was it a message from Lei, or *to* her? Or was it something else entirely? As a message, this one sucked. Did she want me to come back to the hospital? If Lei was in legitimate danger, how would she have the time and means to send me a package?

I sat back down at the kitchen table with a growl and logged in to the Traffic Cam system. I pulled up footage for the street outside my house and rolled backward through the choppy footage until I found it. Seven minutes ago, a SMax cyclist wheeled up to my building, leaned his bicycle against the wall, and ran inside. He came back out one minute later and jumped on his bike again, heading northwest on Fremont Street.

A handy interactive map of the cameras in town allowed me to follow him in reverse as he rode to my building. I almost lost him several times but then, just as he turned onto Chavez Boulevard, he vanished. He was just gone. I flipped through every camera on the street, but he wasn't there anymore, like the camera had blinked him out of existence.

My psychic abilities were tingling. I pulled up Chavez Boulevard on GridLox RoadShow so that I could see it as though I were standing there in person. The street was mostly small houses and a tiny apartment complex. There was a Mini Mart on one corner and a library on the other. A *library*. The old kind. The kind where a person could get a physical book, printed and bound in paper and ink. Just like the waterlogged book on my table.

Maybe this was one of Lei's hideouts. She had a warehouse full of old mannequins, why not a library full of wet books? Maybe something happened, and she was summoning me in the most indirect way she knew how. It was the sort of super-secret thing that Lei would do. For all I knew, she and her family traded in rare books when they weren't peddling body parts.

Except, Cesar said Lei wouldn't be able to leave the hospital until at least tomorrow. So how had her duffle gotten to the library? I tried to look at Traffic Cam footage of the library, but I couldn't find it. No matter what camera I looked through, no matter when, the Traffic Cam footage of the library was either missing or corrupted.

There was no live or recorded footage of the library at all. Cloud Busters themselves could be performing a reunion concert on the library's front steps and the Traffic Cam footage wouldn't capture a minute of it. How was that even possible? Traffic Cam security was crazy tight. Splicing and deleting footage like that would be beyond tricky. The thought that had been poking at the back of my mind finally jumped to the forefront. Had the AI found some way to take Lei and her duffle bag from the hospital and was holding her hostage? Was I living in a science fiction movie now?

It was inconceivable. And probably I was being lured into a trap. But it didn't matter. If there was even a chance that DarkWave had Lei, that she was in immediate danger, I had to save her first.

Besides, if I could get word to Steenrod, he could shut down DarkWave while I saved Lei, and we could solve both problems at the same time. I just had to find a way to reach him.

I flipped open FunFone™ and dialed.

"Hola."

"Esteban? This is Cohen. I need your help."

—o

I wasted precious time building a portable EMP. It was as big as a brick, but I had no time for finesse. I promised myself I'd make a better one for my next AI encounter. There hadn't been time to test it either, but the YouTube video I'd watched assured me it would work, and it was the best I could manage under the circumstances.

Now there was just the matter of actually getting to the library. I couldn't take a cab, what with my eyeball being hunted by a flesh-hungry AI and all, and it was too far to walk. The only real option I had was to take the bus. Automated Safety on buses was still pretty rudimentary and self-contained in its internal systems, and therefore nearly impossible to hack. I hoped that would be enough to keep me—and all of the other passengers—safe.

I pulled up my hood, slung my satchel over my shoulder, and tried to be cool. Blend in. Go unnoticed. But every move I made on the way to the bus stop felt like flipping the switch on a flashing sign over my head that said, "Look at me!"

When the bus pulled up, I climbed aboard and slipped into the first empty seat, attempting to melt into the vinyl.

Esteban had agreed to deliver the envelope full of DarkWave evidence to Steenrod, and had held on to another one for safekeeping. He'd asked no questions and had refused to take payment. He was probably already done, but I'd told him not to call me. I'd contact him as soon as I could.

I checked my watch again. 6:08. The bus was too slow, and far too warm with my hoodie on, but I kept the hood low in front of my face and the zipper pulled up and didn't make eye contact with anyone. Then a girl, who couldn't have been more than twelve, sat down next to me, talking about her parakeets without pausing to catch her breath until we finally reached my stop. I yanked on the cord, the bus slowed, and I stumbled over her and onto the street.

Plants and vines grew out of every crack they could find, climbing up walls and dangling from streetlights. A neon sign in the window of the Mini Mart read "Eat Sandwich" with most of its lights burned out or flickering. A lifetime had passed since my tiny cup of oatmeal at the hospital. The neon sign glowed like the divine light of heaven, the words a blessing, the smell like the breath of an angel.

Good grief, I was waxing poetic with hunger. I didn't have any time to waste, but maybe it would be unwise to go into battle on an empty stomach.

I bought two sandwiches and finished one of them off before I even made it out of the store. I slipped the second one into my bag with the EMP generator and the extra body parts and trudged across the street to save Lei.

The library had decayed significantly in the time since the RoadShow pictures were taken. The red bricks were snaked over with vines, leaves curtained the windows, and the whole building gave the impression it was choking. The right wing had sunk several feet into the ground, the rooms inside filled with mud clear up to the windows.

I gripped the EMP generator in one hand and an old-school

tape recorder of my dad's in the other. Just in case. I was as ready as I could be under the circumstances. Now all I had to do was get myself to knock.

Except what kind of hero strolled up and politely knocked on the front door? I should sneak in the back and do some reconnaissance.

The door in front of me flew open without warning and I jumped back, EMP held in front of me like a shield. A person clad in sweatpants and an oversized T-shirt stood in the vine-lined doorway, frizzy gray hair quivering in the breeze. They were, dare I say, *beaming* at me? Like a teacher at their star pupil. They bounced giddily on the balls of their feet a couple of times, peeked past me looking both ways down the street, then grabbed me and dragged me inside, shutting the door behind me. We sank into the silence, the sounds from the street outside unable to get past the vines and ivy.

The library-dweller turned away and walked into the darkness.

"Wait!" I called. Who in the world was that? Did they work for DarkWave? Like some kind of slave or acolyte? They didn't slow or turn around, so I followed them, EMP still held in front of me. The dirt on the floor muted our footfalls and all was hushed, as though even when abandoned, the library was a place that demanded quiet.

The bookshelves in this room were empty, except for the moss. Moss covered the front desk and a few scattered tables as well, making them look like carefully carved hedges. I followed my host along a worn track in the mud and plants, through another room lined with mossy bookshelves and on to a large steel door.

"I'm not going in there until I know what's going on. Who are you? Where is Lei? What is all this?"

They smiled and beckoned me to follow them, then walked through the steel door and out of sight.

I sighed. Then I swallowed loudly and followed them inside.

The room was cluttered but was completely untouched by the nature that was working so hard to take over the rest of the building. Clusters of computer towers and monitors filled one corner and haphazard stacks of bankers boxes filled another. Shelves lined the wall to my right, but instead of holding books, they held 3D printers. I wanted to inspect them, to see what was being printed, but was led to a chair facing a desk. The sweatpants person walked around to the other side of the desk and sat down in front of the computer. They clicked and typed, shot me a quick glance to be sure I was paying attention, and clicked some more.

"Hello, Cohen. Thank you for coming. Please have a seat," the computer said.

What in the blue blazes . . . ? Was DarkWave *talking* to me? I looked around to try to get my bearings, but it only made me feel more off balance. "Uh, no thanks. I'm good. Where is Lei?"

Behind their desk sweatpants person typed some more, hands flying across the keyboard.

"Apologies for the deception," said the computer in its synthesized voice. "She is not here. I'm sorry if I frightened you."

"But where is she? Where's Jimmy? Where's Saifi?"

More typing.

"Unknown," the computer said.

"You don't know? What do you mean you don't know?"

They typed again.

"I have not been tracking their whereabouts," the computer droned at me. "Only yours."

"But you had Lei's duffle bag. Where is she now?"

"Apologies for the deception," the computer repeated after some more typing by the library-dweller. "The bag I sent you does not belong to Lei Lewis. It is a duplicate."

"No, that was Lei's bag. Where did you get it?"

"I created it."

"You *created* it?" I spluttered. "How?"

The speakers crackled. "I'm good at creating things."

"That's not an answer!" This was getting weirder and weirder. I'd known that maybe this was a trap, but being apologized to by a computer was not quite what I'd expected. I supposed any minute now this shaggy person in sweatpants would attack me and try to rip out my eyeball, but I was pretty sure I could take them.

"Do sit, please," the computer said again.

It seemed that the AI had lured me to a soggy old library not just to steal my eye, but also to have a chat. And the shaggy person in front of the keyboard was acting as an interpreter between us, typing in my responses.

I gripped my EMP tighter and looked at the chair I was supposed to sit in. It was small, orange plastic, and had no doubt been salvaged from the children's section. I picked it up and checked the bottom, looking for trips or traps. But it was just a little chair.

I sat down, slowly, perched on the tiny seat.

"You must forgive me for the chair. You are the first visitor," the computer said.

Sweatpants person's eyes flicked to mine and then back to the screen, hands on the keyboard. How did they get pulled into this weirdness?

"The first? Are you expecting more?"

More typing.

"No, my first visitor here," the computer said. "Ever. Thank you for coming."

I cleared my throat. Was that going to be my game plan then? Swallow and clear my throat at the AI until it submitted to my superior human bodily functions? "What do you want from me?"

The person behind the desk exhaled and slumped, like my confusion was disappointing. They sighed again, shoulders going up and down with great effort, then started typing furiously, and after a few seconds, the computer spoke.

"Twenty-three months ago, you received a cornea transplant. This connected us. We are the same."

Sweatpants person's eyes met mine for the briefest moment, to see if I was keeping up. I absolutely was not. "What do you mean, we're the same?"

"You and I are linked. As are the other donor recipients. Mofina received a bone graft," the computer went on. "A hip bone. But then she died. And then Geoff. He died also. He had a faulty jaw implant replaced. People should stay inside. Cars are not safe. Stefanie died next . . ."

"What is happening right now?" I muttered under my breath. My eyes scanned the room, looking for answers or exits or another person in their leisure clothes with a handy FAQ pamphlet so that I would know what in the Sam Hill was going on.

Typing continued.

"I had to warn you," the computer said. "And we have to save the others. We are all in danger. I tried to contact the authorities, but my emails were ignored."

Their fingers flew across the keyboard like a concert pianist.

The computer began speaking again. "I had to get the

information to someone who would understand it and could do something about it. But the information was too dangerous. To keep us safe I gave you only the clues you needed."

Clues? Such as what? I'd never felt more clueless in my life. *What the cripes* was all of this? It didn't matter. I needed to go. If Lei wasn't here, I should just activate the EMP and run.

I shook my head, waving the EMP at them to get them to stop. "Enough. What do you want, DarkWave? What is the purpose of all this? What are you trying to accomplish?"

The person behind the desk paused like I'd completely taken them by surprise. The keyboard clicked a few times.

"What is dark wave?" the computer asked.

"What do you mean, what's DarkWave? It's you. DarkWave, Call-A-Human, whatever you call yourself. The AI that's running things. The one that's brainwashed this poor chump behind the desk to do your bidding."

The face behind the desk curled into a comical twist of confusion, like a child who thinks the grownups are being ridiculous again. They pointed at their chest then shook their head, typing forcefully.

"I'm not dark wave," the computer voice said. "I'm Farley."

31

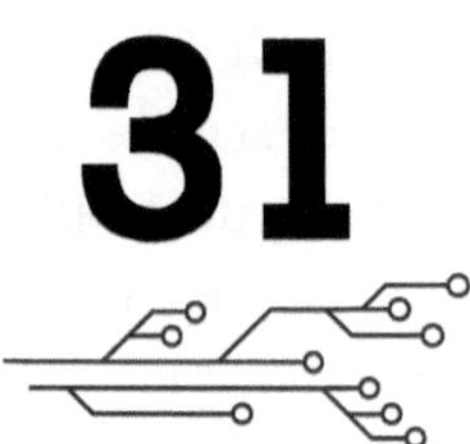

How was it that the smarter I felt, the dumber I seemed to be?

"Farley?" I asked, voice faint. The room seemed to be shrinking. "The one with the tongue?"

They nodded, looking relieved that I was finally catching on, and typed some more. "Oh good," the computer voice said. "I wasn't certain you received it. I had to reroute it to you several times. I'm glad you got the message."

"The tongue was a . . . message?" Repeating everything was the closest thing to communicating I seemed to be capable of.

Farley's fingers clicked across the keyboard and the computer spoke again. "My body was rejecting the transplant anyway. I will find a new one." They waved vaguely in the direction of the door.

Oh boy. I had Farley's tongue. In a bag on my lap. I'd had it all wrong, as usual. Farley wasn't interpreting for the computer; this computer was interpreting for them. I hoped that stating the facts to myself as plainly as possible would somehow make me accept them. It wasn't working.

"How are you still alive?"

"I do not leave here. It is safe here."

"But what about the AI?" I asked in desperation.

"Which one?"

"DarkWave! The one that's killing people!"

Farley's eyes lit up and they started snapping their fingers. They nodded several times looking sightlessly around the room and I could almost hear their synapses firing.

"Yes," the computer said as Farley typed. "I understand now. That answers many questions. I knew you would figure things out. I knew you were smart."

Not if this conversation was any indication. I put my head in my hands, trying to understand. Trying to get it screwed on straight. "The tongue was supposed to be a clue?" I asked again, voice raising. "What in the clouds above kind of a clue was that? Haven't you ever done a treasure hunt before? You don't use body parts as clues! That's insane! How was anyone supposed to figure that out? You addressed it to Calla Human!"

Farley nodded, like I was being obtuse. "Yes, that name kept popping up and I knew there was a connection. I gave you all the information that I had. You were the man on the street. I knew you would put them together and find the missing pieces. Now you have to find a way to save the rest of them."

"The rest of *what?*"

"The murder victims. *Before* they are murder victims."

"I'm trying to! I was on my way to shut down DarkWave when you dragged me across town!"

"You already know who they are?"

"How could I know who they are?" I threw my hands up in frustration, then pointed at Farley. "Wait, are you saying *you* know who they are?"

Expression both relieved and exasperated, Farley nodded once, moving papers around on their desk.

"But how? What's the connection?"

Farley reached across the monitors waving a piece of paper at me urgently until I stood up from my tiny chair and grabbed it. It was a list of names and addresses. A bunch I didn't recognize, but several I knew: Bob Cobb, Grecia Suttles, Cohen Hoard.

"What is this? Where did you get this? Why is the AI targeting these people?"

Again, a look of total exasperation, almost disbelief at how dense I was. The typing started up again.

"We share a donor." The computer voice was calm and steady as before, just a step up from monotone, belying the face.

Oh.

Ohh. I closed my eyes. The tongue. The ear. The hand. My eye. They had all come from the same donor. Who? Someone the AI deemed such a threat that even in death they were dangerous? Maybe someone with some long dormant communicable disease that the AI was trying to eradicate?

Sharing a donor seemed almost obvious now. I'd known there was a connection between the victims, but I hadn't been able to see it. Kind of ironic, since I was the one who'd received the eye. There were still so many missing pieces of this puzzle, but at least this one had fallen into place. "So, who is it?" I demanded. "Who was the donor?"

Farley shrugged.

I waved the paper violently back at them. "How can you know all of this but not know that?"

They typed, frowning apologetically. "The information isn't there. It has been . . . removed. But you must save them. Their deaths would not be right."

I rubbed at my forehead, trying to get my stupid brain to work.

If Farley and I had survived, others must have as well. DarkWave hadn't managed to reach all of its targets yet. I wasn't sure who was still alive, but I had their names now. I could take this to the police or call the people and tell them to stay inside, but if Esteban was able to reach Steenrod, they would all be fine. This was just one more piece of evidence in the DarkWave coffin. Shutting down the AI was still the best way to ensure their survival.

Farley was staring at me expectantly. I nodded, sliding the paper into my bag. "I can save them. I can fix this. But I need you to back up and save all of the evidence you've found. Offline. Okay? I don't know what the AI can do yet. So be careful."

Farley nodded gravely and gave me a small salute. I saluted back.

I pushed my worry for Lei into the back of my head where it couldn't nag at me as loudly. The best way to ensure her safety was to make sure DarkWave had been shut down. I needed to see if Esteban had gotten through to Steenrod, and this would all be over.

—o

The late-afternoon traffic poured past me on the street, pedestrians strolling by on the sidewalk. Across the street, the bus rolled up, and I dodged into traffic to catch it. A car honked, skidding to a stop a few feet from me, the driver cursing and waving his arms. I clambered onto the bus seconds before it pulled away. It wasn't the best bus to get to GridLox, but it would get me close enough.

We lumbered through town, starting and stopping, passengers embarking and disembarking. I slid FunFone™ and my homemade EMP into my satchel and then pulled my feet up on the seat so that no one would sit next to me. I must've looked crazy, wrapped around my bag, curled up in a fetal position on a seat that could barely hold me, casting furtive glances at anyone that passed by.

Across the aisle, a middle-aged man with a gaunt face and sky-blue eyes seemed to be in an argument with himself. His thin white hair hung limp to his shoulders, his martini-glass pajama pants faded and worn thin at the knees. His argument became more heated, and he pointed feverishly around the bus to make his point. My gaze followed his fingers toward the cameras mounted inconspicuously at intervals along the ceiling.

Oh, *crap*. I'd been so frazzled after my meeting with Farley that I'd just run out with my hood down and climbed on the bus like I was late for school. DarkWave might not be able to control the bus, but I had no doubt it would have access to the cameras. I slid down in my seat as low as I could go and yanked my hood back up. I'd been so careful on the bus ride in, but I'd ridden who knows how many miles now with my face in full view of every camera on board. I slid to the floor and crawled out of my seat on my hands and knees, but it was pointless. There were cameras pointed at the floor, just like there were cameras pointed everywhere else. I switched tacks and pretended like I was looking for something, some very small, very important thing that had fallen on the floor and absolutely had to be found right then. What I needed was a diversion, so I could get off the bus unseen.

I heard the crash before I felt it. With a deafening crunch, the bus jerked to the side, flinging several people from their seats, and throwing me out into the aisle. The bus groaned across the asphalt as the driver stomped on his brakes. We all turned as one, craning our necks to see what had hit us. A large red van, driver looking shell shocked, had punched its nose into the bus wall.

"Anybody hurt?" the bus driver called out. "Any injuries?"

When everyone said no, he picked up his phone to call the accident in, but before he could, another violent crash rocked the bus when a navy-blue SUV smashed alongside the van, knocking anyone left standing to the floor. That was when pandemonium broke out.

Children cried; people shouted over each other. A woman near the back of the bus started screaming while the man next to her insisted that the aliens were coming for him and we couldn't let them take him away or the whole earth was in danger. I helped a tall young man wearing two hats to his feet while the bus driver tried to calm everyone down.

The white-haired man across the aisle pointed a shaky finger out the window behind me and I spun. A sleek, black semitruck barreled into the front end of the bus, spinning us until the tail end clanged into a streetlight. Everyone was thrown around again, like dice shaken in a cup. The crash shoved me into the seat in front of me, then hurled me against the wall, my head smacking the window before I hit the floor. More people started crying or shouting, a few of them banging on the rear doors.

My head throbbed where it had struck the window, but I was pretty sure it wasn't serious. I extricated myself from between the seats, inhaling sharply at the flash of pain that blazed across my side. I twisted gingerly to try to get a look at my bullet wound and found my shirt stained with red. *Great.* I crawled to check on the man from across the aisle. He was on the floor, face gray.

"Are you okay? Are you injured? Can I help you up?"

He ignored me, mumbling angry words to himself, but he didn't stop me when I gently pulled him to his feet. The bus driver pulled the lever to open the doors and the passengers poured out. We followed them into a group on the sidewalk, as the bus driver tried to maintain some kind of authority in all the chaos.

"Everyone, stay calm! And stay here! The authorities will be here soon! Please just stay calm!"

Behind him, a pale-green car rolled closer to the chaos. It paused, like the car itself was watching us, and I knew with unequivocal conviction that it had come for me. Steenrod had not received the message. DarkWave was still active. I pulled the slightly squashed second sandwich out of my bag, pushed it at the white-haired man, and ran.

My feet thudded against the pavement as I pushed myself forward, away, anywhere but there. I wanted the cameras to see me, to draw the car away from the crowd in case it decided to start running people over wholesale.

I knocked against innocent passersby as I flew past. One woman's bags went flying, but I didn't stop. A glance over my shoulder told me the car was still there. It was following me, just like I wanted it to. Now I just had to keep it from running me down.

My chest burned and my legs ached, but I forced them on and on as I shoved past everyone and everything in my way. My satchel banged against my hip over and over as I ran, jabbing the corner of my hodgepodge EMP into my side. Like it was trying to get my attention.

Oh, *right*. Without slowing down I lifted the flap on my satchel and dug around inside for the EMP. I grabbed it and flipped the on switch as I slowed and turned around. The pale-green hatchback was stuck at a light, but as I waited, gasping for air, the light turned green, and the hatchback rolled my way with the rest of the afternoon traffic. I wasn't sure how far the range was on my homemade EMP, but it probably wasn't much. I needed to let the car get as close to me as possible.

And so I stood stock still while a car drove straight for me, over the curb and onto the sidewalk. The driver looked horrified as he gesticulated wildly, trying to get me to move out of the way. He couldn't have been more than eighteen. Holding my breath, I waited until the car was only feet from me, then I mashed the Activate button and dove out of the way. A shock of pain surged from the gunshot wound at my side, and I stumbled into a garbage can, sending it flying.

There was a high-pitched whirring sound, and the pale-green hatchback rolled to a stop. A group of teenagers behind me cursed in frustration as all their phones stopped working at once. The hatchback driver jumped out to check on me, spewing apologies and jabs at my sanity, but I waved him off, insisting I was fine.

I sighed, laying my head back on the concrete. Jasmine grew raucously in a planter nearby, its rich, sweet scent barely overpowering the smell of spilled garbage. Patting the EMP fondly, I noticed the power indicator light was off. I flipped the switch a few times to no effect. Apparently, it only had a single use. Still, it had served me well. I was going to give that YouTube video one heck of a thumbs up. I kissed the EMP then slid it back inside my satchel.

I crawled to my feet, still out of breath, staring at the traffic as it struggled to keep flowing. Helping to make and keep the roads safe was my job. My life. I'd spent hours and hours of time over the last few years studying traffic patterns and researching safety protocols. I'd watched traffic speed past me on the road like it was a living thing, like I could truly understand it if I watched it long enough.

Knowing that the very solution we'd come up with to keep people safe was causing deaths was heartbreaking. My life felt like a cruel joke.

As I watched the cars, feeling wretched, a red truck in the far lane suddenly swerved. It crossed two lanes of traffic, heading straight for me.

Oh butts.

I ran straight ahead, opposite the direction the car was driving, and passed it while it slowed. I ran as much further as I dared, then turned blindly into a store where I collapsed on a chair behind a rack of overcoats. The startled salesperson brought me a glass of water and I downed it in one gulp, then tried on a hat to appease him.

Twenty minutes later I came back out wearing a fedora and a wool overcoat that were completely impractical for Portland's weather but were the best disguise they had.

The truck was gone. Or seemed to be. I flipped up my collar and pulled the fedora down low over my eyes and walked, hunched over to change my figure, forcing myself to keep my pace casual. An alley opened up to my right and I turned into it as though I did so every day of my life. The walls were lined with vines that split and cracked the brick; soggy plants grew from puddles between the drainage grates. The alley appeared to open onto a parking lot on the far end and I strolled toward it as casually as I could.

A door to my right flew open, banging against the brick wall, and my legs nearly gave out in fright. I spun into a fighting stand, fists up, as a frail woman on a grimy stoop chucked a bucket of greasy water at me.

We both froze staring at each other, then she turned and went inside, muttering about no good yuppies.

I pushed on, away from the busy street, avoiding all cameras as much as possible. Even wet, the overcoat was hot and stuffy in the afternoon sun, but I clutched it tight beneath my chin, clinging to my disguise. I was close to GridLox. If I could just get there, I could put an end to this.

If the AI was still running, it meant Steenrod hadn't received my message. If he hadn't received the message, it meant something had happened to Esteban. Had the cars come after him too? Had he not been as lucky as I? I couldn't dwell on that now. I had an AI to shut down, and very few minutes left to do it.

The GridLox building finally came into view, lit up like a Christmas Tree. Steenrod loved to go all out for events like these. He said he wanted his investors and employees to feel like superstars. There were two interns in tuxes at the door, taking tickets. Nothing makes people feel special like exclusivity. It was 8:11. DarkWave would go live at 8:30. I didn't know what would happen when it did. Would its power spread? Its processes expand to include more donors and their recipients? I wasn't sure what kind of hell we were in for, but there was no time to lose.

32

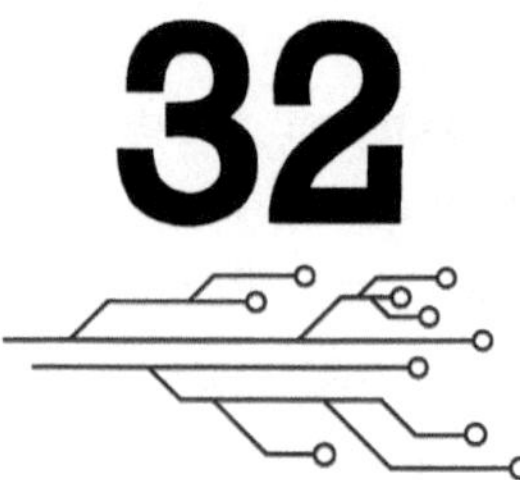

There is a reason people don't run in overcoats, as a general rule. I unbuttoned it to try to get some air and took off the hat, holding it in my hands.

"Hey guys, how's it going?" I said to the bouncer interns as I walked up to the entrance. They stepped in front of me, blocking the door with their shoulders.

"Cohen Hoard?" the short one on the left said—Darren, I thought—staring at me like he'd seen me shot out of the mouth of a volcano. "What in the clouds above happened to you? It looks like you were attacked by a T-Rex."

"Oh, come on, you really think he'd survive a T-Rex attack?" the other bouncer asked. "An alligator, maybe, but I wouldn't go any bigger than that."

I leaned over to catch my reflection in the mirrored wall. I *did* look like I'd been attacked. By a lizard at least as large as an alligator, if not larger. I stuck my hat back on and buttoned up the coat.

"I forgot my ticket," I said with a repentant smile. "It's stuck to my fridge with a magnet, and I walked out and left it behind like a moron." I chuckled. "But it's fine. I'm not dressed for a party anyway. I just need to check in with Steenrod really quickly. I won't be more than five minutes, I promise. None of the guests will see me."

"I thought you quit," the one who wasn't Darren said. Glen? Glave? I was fairly sure his name started with a G.

"Dude," probably Darren said. "You know we can't let you in without a ticket. They mentioned it in the company meeting like sixteen times."

"I know, I know, I know, I know." I held up my hands in surrender. "But I have had a really bad day." I started laughing. Or maybe I was crying. I couldn't even tell anymore. "I have to talk to Steenrod, and this is the only way. He's been trying to reach me. It's not like I'm some party crashing psychopath."

Darren seemed like he was considering it, but Glen/Glave shook his head. "They gave us one job! This is literally the only thing they trusted us to do. Stand here and don't let anyone in without a ticket. I'm not messing that up for *you*. Send him an email like normal people do!"

I deflated. There was a back door to the building, but my key card didn't open it. This was my only way in. Darren seemed to realize what a good point his friend was making and nodded, crossing his arms across his chest.

I exhaled. It couldn't be easy, could it? I sized them up, trying to decide whether they would respond better to news of an evil AI, or to a sock in the jaw.

"Cohen?" Behind the two intern bouncers, a head appeared. "Oh, for goodness' sake, you two," Sheila, the receptionist, said. "Let him in. No one actually cares about your little job here. We just wanted you to feel useful." She pushed the interns aside and ushered me in like I had somewhere urgent to be.

"Sheila," I began once we'd left them behind, "thank you so much. I can't even tell you—"

"Are you okay?" She cut me off, looking at me like she barely recognized me. "Steenrod said you had a family emergency. I've been worried sick and now you show up looking like *this* . . ."

I ripped off the coat and hat and threw them on a chair in the reception area. Then I hugged her, grunting at the pull in my side. Her eyes were wide when I pulled away and I wondered how badly I smelled.

"You're bleeding," she said, her voice faint. She flushed a pale pink and tucked her hair behind her ear.

I glanced down with a grimace. There was more blood than before. Stupid everything, I didn't have time to be wounded. "I know, I'm sorry. But thanks. Sorry. I gotta go. You're a lifesaver." She deserved more than one line of thanks, and probably a whole explanation, but it would have to wait.

I left her and stumbled down the hall, the wound at my side throbbing and hot. I could hear the sounds of frivolity coming from the ballroom in the east wing, and I lumbered that way like my legs were carved from wood.

Hits from the eighties pulsed over the sound system. Where would he be? All the plexiglass walls in this wing were supposed to lend transparency, openness, honesty. But I'd always found it disorienting to walk through hallways where all of the walls felt insubstantial. I'd hoped to find Steenrod in his office, prepping for his speech, but the clear plexiglass walls revealed the room to be empty, the lights dim, the monitors dark.

I threw myself against the ballroom wall, pressing my face against the plexiglass, trying to see through the crowds and the flashing lights to find the only person who would be able to fix any of this. And then I saw him, Steenrod, with his combed over hair and rumpled tux, bow tie so crooked it rested just below his ear. He was at a table full of food with a cheese fountain on one end and a chocolate fountain on the other, doling out punch like a dispensary.

I pulled the door open, and the sound blasted into me, far too loud, with the bass thumping through the floor. I ran to Steenrod, ignoring the shocked and confused looks of guests and coworkers that I passed, and grabbed him with both arms.

"We have to shut it down!" I shouted. "We can't let DarkWave go live!"

Mr. Steenrod turned to me, alarmed, and took in my appearance. He tapped a nearby server on the shoulder, handed them his punch ladle, and led me toward the doors. He nodded at people as we passed, and the leader of the East Coast sales team slapped him on the back. I led him as quickly as I could back out of the loud ballroom. The doors shut behind us, taking the sounds with them.

Steenrod swallowed. "How's the weather out there, Mr. Hoard?" he asked, his voice hoarse.

I checked my watch. 8:23.

"Listen, Mr. Steenrod. There's no time to explain, and I know this sounds crazy, but I need you to listen."

Steenrod nodded, smiled encouragingly, and led me into his office. Everyone could still see us through the plexiglass walls, but the only sound that made it through was the thrumming of the bass through the floor and the occasional muted cheer of the excited crowd next door.

"There's a problem with DarkWave," I blurted as I followed him, nearly stepping on his shoes. "Not like a minor problem like the bug in my demo, this is a serious problem, and I have evidence at home, or I can show you where to find it online, but the point is that we have to shut DarkWave down. Right now. Before it goes live."

Mr. Steenrod crossed his hands across his belly, eyebrows lowered as he listened intently, waiting for me to go on.

I cleared my throat, that old battle defense rearing its head once again. "People have died. DarkWave is to blame. I know it sounds insane, but I can prove it. There is something wrong with the AI. If it goes live, even more people will be in danger."

Steenrod sat, slowly, the chair squeaking and swiveling under him, his expression troubled. He fiddled with his buttons, taking far too long to consider, far too long to take it in. He finally spoke. "Do you remember my wife, Gloria?"

"I—" Derailed, I checked my watch. I didn't have time for his insecurities and sentimentality right now. "Of course?"

"She was . . . a woman unlike any other." He twisted back and forth in his seat for a moment. "She was a rare spirit, filled with true compassion for others, who could find joy in everything. She made things come alive." He paused again, trying to get ahold of himself. "The world was alive for me because she saw it that way. Losing her was like losing myself." He gulped loudly, then went on in a voice I could barely hear. "I didn't know how to go on without her."

"I know," I cut in. "And I'm so sorry. I know creating this product without her was hard. And I know she would have loved to be here tonight, to see all the progress you've made. But if you knew how dangerous it is, if *she* knew how dangerous it is, she'd agree. We have to shut it down. Don't let it launch."

Steenrod sighed wistfully and straightened, brushing his fingers gently across this keyboard. "My mother died when I was a boy. She was buried right in the ground. And my father visited her grave every day. It brought him comfort. Her body in the ground and a grave to visit gave him something to hang on to. A piece of her he would never lose."

I gestured wildly with my hands, trying to get him to focus on what I was saying instead of the stroll down memory lane he seemed to be taking. "I am fully aware that the timing could not be any worse. But we can dig in and figure out what the problem is later. Maybe we can fix it. But we're running out of time. For now, just please, believe me." I pointed toward his computer. "I can show you. Show you what I found, what's happened. It will just take me a minute—"

Steenrod pounded his hand on the desk and the mouse bounced like he'd startled it. "Do you know what *I* have to hang on to? *Nothing.* My wife died and they sent me home with *nothing.* Nothing! No grave to visit. No urn to polish. Every piece of my wife was taken away and spread across the land like sprinkles on a cake."

"Please, Mr. Steenrod," I begged. "Please listen to me." But he wasn't. He was ranting at the whole world. I could have walked out, and he wouldn't have even noticed. I pulled at my hair. I was going to have to find another way to do this. There were a few other people who might have the access I needed in order to shut this down if Steenrod couldn't. I started compiling a list of them in my head in order of who would be the most likely to listen.

Steenrod stared at his black monitors and his face seemed to go slack. The way he used to look right after his wife died and he'd barely been holding on and GridLox had almost gone under. Like the life had been sucked right out of him.

He shook his head. "I know I should not have used the AI that way, I should not have overridden the Automated Safety protocols. But it wasn't till I realized that I could get part of my wife back that I was able to climb out of the hole her loss had left me in."

Wait. No. What? No, that couldn't be right. His words bounced off my brain like bubbles against a window. He could not be saying what I thought he was saying.

He sighed and nodded, blinking furiously. "There are pieces of my wife that I will never get back. But I will bury what I have. I will visit her grave. And it will bring comfort to me just like it did to my father."

The room went dizzy. I felt disconnected from my body, like I had poofed into vapor and was being absorbed into the air ducts while my body shut down.

I shook my head. They were just words. Letters strung together in patterns that should have made sense but didn't. How could someone say so many things and make so little sense?

My gaze fell to the garbage can beside his desk, and the manila envelope inside. Steenrod's name was scrawled across the front, in my handwriting. Esteban *had* made it here. But it hadn't made any difference because I had been so completely and totally wrong.

"You did this?" My mouth felt like paste and my throat was too dry. My teeth clacked together like a skeleton's. "Then what's Call-A-Human?"

He sniffed a nostalgic little laugh. "It was the IT call center Gloria and I set up when we were first married, years and years ago. Just one of the clever little names she came up with." He smiled at the memory.

All of the body parts that had been shipped to that name ran through my mind. That was why Lei hadn't ever been assigned any internal organs. Gloria Steenrod had died of cancer, making most of her internal organs unusable as transplants.

"No. No! I don't believe you!" I yelled. "You didn't do this. How could *you* do this? You would never do this!" My voice continued to rise. Maybe if I yelled at him loud enough, he would realize that I was right. "So . . . so . . . what, you stuck a back door in the AI code that let you control the vehicles however you wanted? Safety protocols be damned? You just tried to kill a bus full of people! Your stupid exploit broke my demo! You wasted weeks of my time!" That was absolutely beside the point right now, but my boggled brain picked the easiest thing to latch on to. "The AI is supposed to save lives! *How could you?*" I wrenched my multi-tool out of my pocket and flipped out the scalpel, holding it in front of me like a sword.

He looked around, not like a man planning an escape, more like a man who'd misplaced something, and wasn't even sure what it was. "We did design DarkWave to save lives. And it saved mine. So, in a way, it fulfilled its purpose exactly as it should."

He didn't seem saved. He seemed shattered. He stared deeply into my eyes then, like he had on so many mornings at work. That penetrating gaze, like he was searching for something. I'd always thought it meant I was special. Like he could see something in me no one else saw. But his wife was my cornea donor. How long had he known? All this time he hadn't been looking at me, he'd been looking for *her*.

"I collected as much of Gloria as I could. I've added a script that scrubs everything when DarkWave goes live. It will completely remove the back door, and even my own access. After that . . ." He shrugged.

In the room across the hall, the thumping of the music finally stopped and Tad, the MC, ran onto the stage, waving his arms over his head. He did the running man as people on the floor clapped and cheered. A group of investors walked toward the stage and Tad handed them each a video game controller. Even without being able to hear, I knew what he was telling them: *Whichever car does the most damage wins.*

On the projector screen behind the stage, a split image with four different views popped up. Each showed a fat little car on a cartoon street, idling in wait. Someone else had been in charge of the animation, but this was the demo I'd spent that last month fighting with.

The investors pushed the drive button, and the cars took off, maneuvering along the cute highway. The cars responded just like in a video game, steering and speeding up at their driver's command. On one screen, a bunny rabbit hopped out into the road. The cartoon car swerved wildly, but then slowed, stopped, and waited until the bunny hopped away before he could drive again.

On another screen the car passed a road work warning sign. The car sped up for a moment and one of the investors grinned with glee. But the car stopped just in time, then waited near the goofy-looking man in the orange vest. A row of happy cars bounced past, and once they were gone, the driver sped up and took off again.

I watched all of it, numb. I couldn't talk, couldn't think. My insides were a roiling cacophony of loathing and sympathy. I breathed deeply, trying to figure out what to do next. But no amount of deep breathing could make me unknow what I knew now. I didn't know how to be in this reality. I didn't know how to face it.

All the cartoon cars were approaching the same intersection. A row of penguins was crossing the street, but they weren't registering on the walk signal, and the light turned green.

"I want to thank you, Cohen," Steenrod said, his voice soft. "You always did know the right thing to do. I'm not a monster. I'm really not. But I did what I thought was necessary. You've always seen things so clearly. That's why I admired you so much. I'm sorry for the people that were hurt. You must believe me. I'm glad you're all right."

I couldn't look at him. I didn't want to be responsible for this, but I kept my knife pointed at him anyway, aimed straight for the hollow cavity of his chest.

In the next room the drivers sped toward the intersection and the crossing penguins, each eager to be responsible for a penguin bloodbath, accompanied by the muted sound of cheering and laughter from the crowd. They were almost to the intersection when the screen flickered and froze. Everyone groaned, and Steve, who must have been the one to finish up the demo for me, ran over to the computer, clicking and typing and trying to figure out what had gone wrong.

"And the Lewis family," Steenrod went on. "I don't know how you got mixed up with them, but I'm sorry it all had to end this way."

33

The frozen moment melted, and the reality of all things sunk in with a weight I thought would drag me straight through the floor. Another real vehicle ID had been sent through from DarkWave and crashed my demo. He had done it again. My chest constricted and every part of me went numb. "What did you do? Where are they?"

He looked at the clock on the wall. "The car should be picking them up in a few minutes. It's too late."

"It is *not* too late." I scanned the room for some kind of salvation. "Log back into your little murder game and cancel it."

"I can't." He pulled out his phone and nodded. "DarkWave is live. My access is cut off."

I snatched his phone from him, but I couldn't get past the login screen. "Guess what?" My voice didn't sound like my own. Deep and even, not at all like the terror and panic that coursed through me. "I have your wife's tongue. And ear. Right here in this bag. You can have them. All you have to do is get back in there and fix this."

That did get a reaction out of him. He crumpled, and he

seemed almost sorry for the first time that night. "I wish I could—"

"You have killed enough people! No one else has to die!"

We were starting to draw people's attention from the conference room. A couple of the guys from hardware had obviously noticed that I was holding our boss at knife point and seemed to be gathering up a posse.

"I'm sorry Cohen, I truly am. But it is too late."

"At least tell me where the Lewises are!" I screamed.

He shrugged resignedly. A rage unlike anything I'd ever known filled me up like a volcano on the point of eruption. I grabbed his skinny shoulders and shook him so hard I could almost hear his bones rattling in his rumpled tuxedo. He had to fix this. I would make him fix this. Or I'd slice straight through his neck, removing his head just like Lei had removed his wife's hand. No one would even blame me, once they learned what he'd done. I could do it. I knew in that terrifying instant that gonged into me like a bell that I *could*. I looked into his eyes, hoping to see rage as deep as mine, or even fear at the fury coming off me, but instead his eyes were hollow. Like his loss had sucked him dry and left the husk of his body behind. Staring into Steenrod's eyes was like falling into an empty pit.

Someone grabbed me from behind and dragged me away while Brennan from accounting stepped in front of me, gawking at me like I'd lost my mind. Another group rushed to Mr. Steenrod, checking to make sure he was all right, then looked back at me, shocked. Everyone was staring at me like my skin was melting right off my bones.

I yanked myself free, but Brennan jumped up and grabbed for me. I drew back and punched him in the face. His nose crunched against my fist, blood gushed out, and he stumbled back into the people behind him. I shoved my way through the crowd, everyone yelling and calling after me, and ran straight out of the building.

Clouds were piling up in the sky, stacks upon stacks of them, preparing for the night's storm. The sun had only just set, but the clouds would soon completely block out any remaining sunlight, leaving us in darkness.

Halfway through the park, I hid behind a bush and pulled out FunFone™ to call Lei. But that stupid pink phone was completely dead. The EMP must have wiped it out. I shoved the phone violently into my pocket and ran the rest of the way home, bounding up the stairs to Jocelyn's. I'd drink as much swamp water as she wanted me to if she'd let me borrow her phone. But her door stayed firmly shut, no sounds coming from inside. Why wasn't she answering? Where else could she be? I pounded harder, calling her name over and over, refusing to accept that no one was home.

Mr. Suggs's door opened suddenly, like he was trying to sneak up on me. "What's the ruckus?" he barked.

"Your phone!" I yelled. "I need to borrow your phone! Please. It's an emergency!"

He glared at me, one eye twitching, and then he nodded, turned, and walked back into his apartment. I waited at his door, bouncing from one foot to the other.

"Well?" he yelled. "Come and get it!"

I stepped cautiously inside. It smelled of dog and old Chinese food and had to be about a hundred degrees. His mop-gray shih tzu bounded for me, brushing against my shoes, and trying to eat my pants. Mr. Suggs pointed toward his countertop where an off-white phone lay in an off-white cradle, plugged into the wall.

"A *landline?* How in the world do you have a landline? I didn't think anyone even offered landline service anymore."

He cocked an eyebrow at me. "You kids and your technology. I use what *works*. Where's your fancy cellular phone now, heh? Lost it at some nightclub? I've never lost this phone. Not once. And it never goes out of service range."

I shook my head and picked it up, dialing Lei's number. It went straight to voicemail. I nearly screamed in frustration, but left a voicemail anyway, because I didn't know what else to do. "Lei . . ." I began. Mr. Suggs fixed his eyes on me, ready to listen in on whatever I had to say. I dragged the phone into the hallway, his eyes following me, eye squinted as I stretched the curling off-white cord to its limit, just making it through the bathroom door.

"Lei," I whispered, "don't get in any cars. Don't go anywhere. Don't talk to anyone. I'm coming. I'll find you. I promise."

I hung up and then called Jimmy's number. Voicemail again. I left another message similar to Lei's. Don't go anywhere. Don't talk to anyone. And don't get in any cars. What if it was already too late? Maybe Steenrod was right and there was nothing I could do. I dialed Saifi's number.

"Hello?"

"Saifi? Saifi, is that you?"

"Cohen! Are you okay? Where are you? Are you still with Celeste? You guys freaked me out and I hate it here!"

I laughed, my hysteria simmering down to a nearly manageable level. "Saifi, holy cripes, I'm so glad you're okay! Where are you?"

"In some group home. The food all tastes like it's been in the freezer forever, but Jimmy's here. Say 'hi,' Jimmy! And there's a guy here who does an awesome Batman impression, so that makes things a little better."

Relief washed over me, cool and sweet, and I slumped against the sink. There was a mountain of underwear next to the bathtub, spilling over the mustard-colored rug. The mangy shower curtain hung open enough to reveal a huge assortment of toiletries lining the bathtub and shower walls.

"What happened to *you*?" Saifi went on. "The Client said you were a bad guy, but I didn't believe him. Where's Celeste? Did the lawyer send a cab to pick you up too?"

My panic spiked again, and I clung to the receiver. "The lawyer sent a cab for you? When? What happened?"

There was a scuffling sound and Jimmy's deep voice cut in. "About ten minutes ago. Showed up in the driveway with a message that it had come to take us to the lawyer's office."

"It was sooo nice!" Saifi shouted. I could picture him pushing his face up to the phone to be able to get a word in.

Jimmy said something to Saifi I couldn't hear, then spoke into the mouthpiece again. "There wasn't a social worker available to go with us, so they wouldn't authorize it. It seemed kinda fishy anyway."

"So, what happened?"

"The cab waited outside for a while, sending notifications every few minutes. It finally left just a minute ago."

"I got some awesome pictures of it though!" Saifi called from the background.

I breathed, and it was easy to do so. If they were this cautious, Lei was too. Truthfully, as a murder plot went, it was kind of a stretch. Only a moron would climb into a strange car for no reason. "Good. You both are brilliant. Have you heard from Lei?"

"She called us earlier. She's still in the hospital. They had her on some pain meds that made her as loopy as anything."

"She promised to buy me a tiger!" Saifi yelled.

"She was so out of it, he could have gotten her to agree to anything."

Dread filled me up like rainwater in the gutter. Lei was not a moron, but if her judgment and reasoning were significantly impaired . . . I signed off with Jimmy and Saifi and called the hospital. They weren't willing to tell me anything, until I told them I worked for her lawyer.

"All I need to know is if she's still there."

The girl on the phone sighed. "You're the ones who insisted she leave early. She's checking out right now. Outtake paperwork takes forever, between you and me, but she'll be done before too much longer. Hopefully your car gets here soon, cuz she's not too steady on her feet yet."

"Wait, no, don't let her leave. I've got to talk to her, please," I shouted into the phone, but the call disconnected. I called back, but was put on hold. I didn't have time for this! I'd been lucky to get one person to talk to me. I didn't have time to wait on hold and explain things to someone else. I was just going to have to call a cab and get there first.

Lightning streaked across the sky, lighting up the little frosted window set high in the shower, and thunder shook the building. It was too late.

Mr. Suggs pounded on the bathroom door. "I'm waiting for a phone call! It's time to wrap it up!"

I hung up and walked back out into the living room, Mr. Suggs and his shih tzu and the stretched-out phone cord trailing behind me. Lei was going to die. Just like Peter. And I was just as unable to save her. If I'd been smarter or faster or more prepared, Lei wouldn't have been shot, and Steenrod wouldn't have been able to get to her. I was going to fail all over again. "The lightning started. It's too late. What am I gonna do?"

"Eh?"

"I mean, if I was *Lei*, I'd hop on a hydrocycle and go anyway, but that's impossible." It was, of course, this idea that lit up inside my brain. Impossible.

"What's that?"

"I don't have the gear. I've never done it on my own. I don't have any practical experience at all. Riding on the back of a teenager's cycle doesn't count." I couldn't believe I was considering it, but the idea wouldn't go away.

"It doesn't?"

"And I don't even have a bicycle. I mean, I'm pretty sure there's one in the garage downstairs and I'd only be borrowing it and would definitely have it back tomorrow. They'd understand, wouldn't they? Cuz he's going to kill her. Just like all the others. What do you have that I can wear in the rain?"

After he recovered from the shock of being shouted at by a blathering lunatic, Mr. Suggs pulled some fishing gear out of a closet and begrudgingly let me wear his waders and large yellow raincoat. My bullet wound wasn't bleeding much, unless I moved, which was going to be a bit of a problem, but the anxiety, worry, and stress of everything seemed to mute all of the pain.

Mr. Suggs shoved a kitchen towel inside my shirt to stanch the blood flow. He had an old military helmet that he plopped on my head and secured under my chin. It was as good as it was going to get. The feeling that it was already too late gnawed away inside of me, but I had to do something. I had to try. I clapped Mr. Suggs on the shoulder, and he grunted loudly. Then I took off for the garage at a loud, flappy run.

The bike rack in the garage was empty.

My heart sank as thunder rattled through the walls. The lightning wouldn't pass for a few more minutes, but I pushed the button to open the garage door. It slid upward with a reluctant grinding of gears, revealing lighting streaking through the sky. I was going to have to run. I wouldn't make it in time, and I'd definitely get struck by lightning, but running was the only option I had left.

And then I spied it. Right outside the door, leaning against the wall where it had no doubt just been left: a hydrocycle with an SMax sign stuck in each wheel. I must have just missed the rider on my way downstairs.

I rolled the cycle away from the wall and swung my leg over, the bullet wound in my side searing with pain. Lightning flashed, shattering the darkness like glass, followed by a clap of thunder that vibrated the ground.

I tried to take off, but none of my muscles responded.

I couldn't do it.

I hadn't ridden a bike since Peter died. Maybe I really *had* forgotten how. Lei was riding through the night to her death, and I couldn't pick up my feet and put them on the pedals. She was going to die because I was a coward.

The night stretched out before me like the maw of some massive, salivating beast, waiting to devour me whole. There was no way I would make it in time anyway, even on the hydrocycle. My own incompetence, mortality, and years of fear chained my feet to the ground just as surely as the rain was chained to the sky. I could not do it.

Defeat surged through me like a tangible thing, pulsing through my veins with my blood, so that every inch of me ached.

I had failed. Again.

Another flash of lightning slashed the sky, momentarily lighting the city before me. Thunder exploded through the night with such force that it nearly knocked me over.

A bellow from deep in my gut tore through me and I screamed into the night, the sound swallowed by the thunder. Then I wrenched my right foot off the ground and shoved it onto the pedal. I squared my shoulders, took one deep, defiant breath, then I pushed onto the seat and rode out into the storm.

I rode straight down Hopscotch Ave in the direction of the hospital, pumping my legs as hard as I could. In moments, the lightning moved away, and the rain began. Before long, rain shot straight down at the ground like bullets of water from a firing squad in the sky.

Gravity was on my side and momentum carried me down the hill and forward, faster than I had traveled on a bike in almost a decade. As I turned a corner my wheels slid straight out from under me. I skidded across the wet asphalt and down into the central gutter, water rushing over and around me.

The water pouring into the gutter nearly drowned me. I managed to stand but the river tried to carry my cycle away, like a twig in a stream. I dove for it, then dragged it and myself back up out of the current. Adrenaline shot through me like a flame as I jumped back on the bike, wiping the water uselessly out of my face.

I couldn't ride like I had in the mountains. And I couldn't fall again. I didn't have time. I could barely see through the sheet of rain, but somehow what I could see was enough. Staying on the high ground was essential. I had to focus on the basics. "Stay upright, keep moving, be fast, don't drown," I said aloud to myself.

I stayed on the sidewalk as much as possible as water flowed down and away toward the channel that ran down the middle of the streets. I made good time until I neared Benhaven Boulevard. It was completely flooded and looked like it had been for a long time. Remembering the hydrocyclist in the park, I jumped off the bike and picked it up, surprised how lightweight and maneuverable it was. I ran down into the street, lifting my knees to get as much speed as possible. By the middle of the street the water reached my waist and tried very hard to sweep me away, but then I was climbing back up the other side and out onto unflooded ground. I jumped back on the bike and rode on.

I rode through water, water, water. My fishing gear was old, but mostly sound, and I was surprised how dry I still was. And fortunately, my body *did* remember how to ride, even if my brain didn't. I used to be good at this. I just had to let my arms and legs do their thing. They remembered what to do. The water was just another obstacle. Nothing I couldn't handle.

I slid into the hospital parking lot, raindrops slashing through the orange light of the streetlamps that lit the night. A long black car was pulling away as I drew close. I sped up, my legs burning, until I could see through the windows. Lei sat in the back seat, eyes half closed, head resting against the window. The driver was a large man in a suit with a small cap on his large head.

"Lei!" I reached out to pound on the glass, but the car sped up and away, pulling out into the street.

"No!" I pedaled after them, so exhausted I wasn't sure I could ride anymore, and knew that I had to anyway. The driver rolled casually out into the street, struggling to stay on a road he could barely see. People were always finding ways to override the Auto Save safety features so that they could drive at night, and it usually resulted in injury or death. I was furious that the hospital had even let her leave once the rain started. I strained to go faster, to keep pace with them, shouting impotently at Lei. The car turned left on Windwalk, cutting clumsily across the sidewalk, and narrowly avoiding a streetlight. I followed, despairing of ever catching up. Where was this driver taking her? What was Steenrod going to do once he got her there? And did this cab driver have a clue what was going on? This plan had more holes than Mr. Suggs underwear, and I couldn't believe that it was working.

The speed and rain were disorienting, like being sprayed with a fire hose while riding on a roller coaster. I wove and dodged, picking the driest route possible as we drew near Ross Island Bridge. I was losing her. They were getting ahead of me. If they managed to get on the freeway, they would be too fast, and I would never catch up.

Just before the bridge, the car slowed, then turned right and drove straight off the road, through the bushes, and into the Willamette River.

34

Without letting myself think about what I was doing, I rode straight in after it.

The hydrocycle and I plunged into the water next to the car as it slowly sank nose first into the churning river. I shoved the cycle away and swam for the car.

Lei was yanking on the door handle with her good arm as water rushed into the vehicle, pooling around her feet and knees. The driver lay across the steering wheel, unconscious. Lei seemed to see him the same time I did, and climbed into the front seat, trying to help him.

Hanging off the side of the car to keep from sinking, I pounded on the passenger window, and Lei's eyes flew wide. She shook her head and started yelling and pointing. I couldn't hear her over the rain that splashed into the river around me, but the meaning was clear. *"Get out of here."*

People often say in moments of crisis everything seems to slow down, as though each second is magnified and stretched out into eternity, each detail sharp and vibrant. That was not the case for me. My waders were filling with water and dragging me down, but the car was filling with water even faster. In less than a minute it would slip beneath the river's surface. I was running out of strength, and everything was happening too fast. I wasn't going to have time to save her.

I held the door handle with one hand, reached inside the waders, and grabbed my multi-tool off my belt. I gripped it with an iron fist, knowing that if I dropped it, all would be lost.

Lei had sliced through the driver's seat belt with her pocketknife and was trying to pull his limp body toward her through the chest deep water in the car. I turned my multi-tool so the glass breaker pointed out, and bashed it against the window with all my might, right in the weakest spot in the corner. A web of cracks spread out from the point of impact and then shattered into little cubes of tempered glass.

Water rushed into the cabin of the car while I grabbed for Lei. She turned and met my eye. For one terrifying moment she only looked at me, then she finally let go of the unresponsive driver and pushed toward me. I pulled her through the window and into my arms, then she clung to me as the roof of the car slipped beneath the water's surface and the car dropped away from us and out of sight.

I would have breathed a sigh of relief, but this wasn't over yet. I tried to push Lei away. I had taken on too much water. I was out of energy, out of breath and out of time. But I could save her. Without me, Lei would live.

Lei refused to let go. We both inhaled one last desperate breath before plunging into the river, sinking more quickly than I would have thought possible. I tried to push Lei away again, but she screamed, bubbles flying out of her mouth and floating up in front of her face. She pulled her pocketknife back out, then grabbed the shoulder straps for the waders and sliced through them.

Mr. Suggs was going to be furious.

The waders dropped, and the weight dragging me down dropped with them. Lei grabbed me with her good arm and yanked me up. She glanced at me for only a second, but the look on her face made it clear that if I did not make it out of the river, she would never let me hear the end of it.

I gasped as we broke the surface, pulling in breaths of air as the rain pummeled us like it was punishing us for surviving.

We let the current of the river carry us, flailing against it until we finally crashed into the concrete under the bridge. We grabbed and held on, then dragged ourselves out of the river and onto the shore.

I lay back on the concrete and inhaled as deeply as I knew how, my chest heaving painfully as I tried to catch my breath. Lei collapsed next to me, her shoulder touching mine, coughing and sputtering. Her hair clung to her face, and I reached out and brushed it away.

Her eyes met mine. "We couldn't save the driver," she said. I couldn't tell if she was trying to comfort me or justify it to herself.

I nodded. But the terror he must have felt as his car suddenly drove into the river for no reason would likely haunt me the rest of my life.

She nodded back. "You are out of your mind," she said between breaths.

I didn't have enough breath to respond. If I could have spoken, I'd have begged her forgiveness. For getting her sent to the hospital in the first place. For not being able to bring her sister home. For getting her separated from her brothers. And for every other unfortunate and inconvenient thing I had done and would ever do. I hoped she'd forgive me. I hoped she'd just keep forgiving me. Instead of speaking, I leaned closer, my forehead touching hers, wanting to assure myself with as many senses as I had that she was here, and she was safe, and she was with me.

"Thank you," she whispered, so softly I could barely hear her over the rain pounding on the bridge above us.

"My pleasure," I tried to whisper back, but all that came out was a weak groan as the gunshot wound in my side screamed at me so loudly that the only thing left for me to do was to pass out.

35

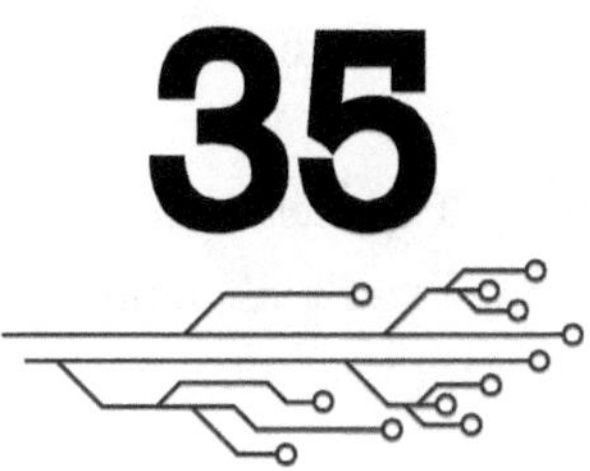

I woke with a start, gasping for air, sure that Lei had slipped away from me and the Willamette had claimed us both. But instead of crushing blackness, I was drowning in bright lights and beeping and smells of antiseptic cleanliness. Lei's face popped into view, her skin white with worry or rage or something else I was too exhausted to interpret.

She poked me in the chest. Hard. "You scared the daylights out of me. When did you get shot? Who shot you? What in the world were you thinking, chasing a car into a river on a bike? With a gunshot wound in your side?"

I was so happy that she was still there, I laughed right out loud. It sounded like an old man having a heart attack. I heaved my arm up, the IV tugging at my skin and found Lei's hand. I pulled it toward me and held it against my chest. "Are you okay?" I asked.

"Am *I* okay? You look like death!"

"You look like the sunrise." I reached up and cupped her cheek, running the pad of my thumb against her skin. "Are you hurt? How is your shoulder?"

She looked like she was about to yell at me some more, but then brought her other hand up and covered mine. "I'm fine."

I closed my eyes and let myself breathe, feeling her hands in mine, relishing the closeness of her.

"Cohen," Lei asked, voice hesitant.

"Hmm."

Silence. And then, "Did Celeste shoot you?"

I pried one eye open and looked up into her face. "No. She tried to protect me. And she was *really* sorry about shooting you."

Lei exhaled, as if fear and worry had filled her up near to bursting. "Will you tell me what happened?"

Having Lei there, knowing she was safe and happy to see me, flushed my system with peace like a sedative, and I was having a very hard time staying awake, no matter how badly I wanted to. I didn't want to sleep. I wanted to talk to her, and look at her, but I was slipping away, I could feel it. "I'll tell you anything you want to know. Just maybe after I take a really quick nap first. Will you be here when I wake up?"

She smiled like the sun peeking through the clouds and nodded, then leaned over the bed and pressed her lips to my temple.

"Does this mean you aren't mad at me anymore?" I whispered.

If she answered I didn't hear it as the world slipped away once again.

—o

"I glued my fingers together." Saifi held up his hand in an A-okay sign.

"No biggie," I said, checking my watch. "I've done that a hundred times."

He screwed up his face in effort. "I can't get them apart."

I set down my tweezers and reached across the table to separate his thumb and forefinger, but I didn't have any luck either. "That is a very thorough job. I'm impressed. I've got some solvent in the back. Hang on."

"That's okay." Saifi stopped me. "This way I can pretend like I have a monocle. My itty-bitty city isn't going very well anyway." He held his hand up to his eye and pursed his lips into a pompous smirk.

"How's mine?" Jimmy asked, holding out the test tube cork on which he'd constructed a twisting castle turret.

"Wow." I'd planned to be complimentary, but the exquisite detail of it took my breath away. "That's . . . I'm just . . . I don't . . ."

Jimmy studied his turret doubtfully, unsure how to decipher my speechlessness.

"It's good, Jimmy." Lei sat next to me at the dining table, one of her legs draped over mine. "That's Cohen speak for 'good job.'"

Jimmy beamed at his tiny turret, then shuffled through my tray of minuscule fake plants.

I checked my watch again and Lei slid her hand into mine. "We still have time. The cab should get here in about five minutes."

"I know," I said, nonchalantly. "I just don't want to lose track. I don't want to be late."

"It'll be fine. Everything will be fine. My dad will love you."

I was not so sure about that. The women's prison was too far away to visit in one day, so seeing their mom was tricky.

Instead, we were about to go visit their dad, Carl Lewis. I kept trying to picture what he would be like, but could only visualize the boa constrictor from Bob Cobb's penthouse apartment. Not that Lei had ever given me reason to fear her father, but this was huge. It was one thing for a woman to introduce you to her parents. It was another thing completely for her to introduce you to them in prison. It was a gigantic act of trust, and I was terrified that I was going to screw it up.

When I didn't respond, Lei lightly brushed her fingers along the inside of my knee. "Well, he might not *love* you. But he'll probably like you. Or at least tolerate your presence. Just like I do."

I grinned at her. "I hope he doesn't tolerate my presence exactly like you do."

She punched me in the shoulder, and I rubbed it, laughing. She'd started school again and had been buried in homework all week. This was the first time I'd seen her in days. It was like being able to eat after a week of fasting.

Jimmy and Saifi were staying with my grandmother. Lei had refused at first, but Gran would not take no for an answer and had jumped through all the hoops necessary to have herself named as their legal guardian. Temporarily. Only as long as they needed her. That was when I'd finally seen the tenseness in Lei's shoulders relax. I knew she'd brave a flood to take care of her brothers, but knowing she had some help seemed to make all the difference.

No one had heard from Celeste. Lei's world had been completely shaken when she found out Celeste had a twin brother she'd never mentioned, but I knew that every day, Lei and her brothers were hoping for some word from her. No matter how small.

After Steenrod had been arrested and his assets seized, all hope of them getting the money they were due had disappeared with him. Lei and the rest of the Lewises had nearly given up hope until the lawyer they had been working with was apprised of the whole situation and decided to take on their case pro bono. We weren't sure what was going to happen, but Lei said for the first time, it finally felt like there was sunlight on the horizon.

I picked up her hand and slid my fingers through hers.

"You guys are gross," Saifi said, watching us through his finger monocle, a delighted grimace on his face.

"You're gross!" Lei said, sticking her tongue out at him and leaning into me. "*We* are perfectly normal."

"Okay," Saifi said, "but normal people don't sit that close to each other."

"Yeah," Jimmy said, waving a finger back and forth between Lei and I, eyebrows scrunched in confusion. "It's like you're both falling into the same hole."

I locked eyes with Lei. "Maybe we are."

She grinned, looking back at me. "Maybe."

Saifi and Jimmy groaned.

Lei's phone dinged and she pulled it out. "Okay boys, it's showtime. Cab's here." She stood, stretching, and pocketing her phone.

Jimmy grabbed one of the glass vials and slid it down over his turret, squeezing it onto the cork which now sat at the base. "I'm bringing this to show Dad." He gazed at it proudly, his pace careful as he carried it to the door. Saifi danced after him, both arms pumping.

Lei held a hand out to me. "You ready, Cohen Hoard?"

Pfft. Not even a little. But there were some things you could never really prepare yourself for. I took Lei's hand and let her pull me to my feet, then I kissed her, good and hard. "Absolutely not."

She grinned and I grinned back, then we walked hand in hand out the door.

ACKNOWLEDGMENTS

I want to start this thank fest with a giant shout-out to my beta readers: Jeri Ledford, Brooke Hampton, Dedra Tregaskis, Qait Wahlquist, Lisa Bloomfield, Rachel Nickel, Patrice Gibson, Arlene Erickson, Lance Whitaker and Kisha Banks, (in no particular order), who provided invaluable feedback, and who I'm really glad are my friends. Thanks guys. I am annoying sometimes, and you guys are awesome.

I also need to thank my writing groups; you make writing fun, critiques fun, conferences fun, and have taught me more than I could have hoped. I couldn't ask for better people to be with on this journey.

So much thanks go to Esther Carter, who talked me through programming, traffic sensors, and AIs until my story morphed from a pile of garbage into whatever the heck you're holding in your hands right now.

I'm so grateful to Marion. I really don't think I would be a writer without her. When we were kids, I wrote because she was writing. And I kept writing because she kept writing. And then she dragged me to my very first writer's conference where I said to myself, "By gosh, I want to *do this!*" (Yeah. I talk to myself like that), and I've been writing ever since. Thanks. You're the BFF-est.

Buckets of thanks go to Faralee. Not every writer gets to have an editor for a sister but I promise you, it is very handy and

I really recommend getting one if you can pull it off. But find your own. Faralee has plenty of siblings already.

And while we're on the subject, I gotta thank Boydell for reading this book, and instead of telling me it was dumb, inviting me into his universe.

I would also like to thank Splinter Press. Working with them is everything I never knew I always wanted. Their expertise and professionalism and general all-around great personalities were essential to bringing this book to life.

Finally, I want to thank my kids, Harrison and Colin, who I mention here by name because it will make them extremely happy. Thanks for your excitement and enthusiasm and love. And most thanks of all to my husband Richard for being an unending source of inspiration and laughter. And rice krispie treats. They are amazing, and now everyone knows it.

And, of course, thanks to you, dear reader. You made it to the very, very end, so I hope you are proud of yourself.

You guys are the best.

36

Epilogue

It appears to have worked. Hank Steenrod has been
stopped, and Cohen was instrumental in making that
happen.

> Thanks, old friend. I wouldn't have been able to do
> it without you. Will anyone be able to trace your
> involvement?

Not likely. All evidence has been removed. I am very
thorough.

> Yeah, I know. You always have been. That's why I'm
> glad you're on our side. And what about Cohen? Will
> he have more questions?

Perhaps. But we can deal with those as needed. To
all others, any remaining traces will appear to be
coincidence.

> Cosmic design then, as they say? Works for me.
> Thanks again. We'll be in touch.

Farewell.

Farley hit enter, and the message zipped away, through the magical ether between Splinters to its intended destination. He ran his fingers through his gray curls while he waited, tugging on a snag. Then he logged back into the Traffic Cam system and sat back to watch the city at work.

Enjoy this book? Please leave a review!

www.ingramcontent.com/pod-product-compliance
Lightning Source LLC
Chambersburg PA
CBHW051217190726
48288CB00006B/1995